MONKEY TRAP

He did not know where he was.

A false red sky loomed above him. The air carried odors that seemed right, but were somehow not. White traceries, like *chachatta* webs, clung to him. He carefully stood, brushing the webbing from his body.

The air was quiet, but his nose sniffed wetly at danger.

What has happened? Rrowl-Captain wondered to himself. *The ugly aliens interrupting the battle with the monkeys shot my ship with some form of energy weapon . . . and then . . .*

Something suddenly occurred to Rrowl-Captain, making him forget the strangenesses around him. All trace of his radiation sickness, a last dark gift from the monkey trap, was gone.

Rrowl-Captain felt well fed and healthy. It should not be so.

"Greetings, Honored One," hissed and spat a voice in the Hero's Tongue behind him, but pitched as high as a tiny kitten's. "We must speak to you, having need of your bravery and honor."

Rrowl-Captain whirled, and saw a hole hanging in midair. No, he realized, more like a window. Through it, he saw strange forms, with three legs and two heads. Rrowl-Captain could see what were surely weapons carried by the larger of the beasts, and he smiled a needle grin in challenge.

Then Rrowl-Captain saw the human-monkeys standing behind the alien vermin. The monkeys that had stolen his name and honor. He would taste their blood in his jaws, *and* that of the other creatures. A holy Rage took him, and he screamed and leaped in fury, throwing himself at his enemies with claws and fangs bared.

MAN-KZIN WARS VII

Created by

Larry Niven

with

Hal Colebatch

Mark O. Martin

Gregory Benford

&

Paul Chafe

MAN-KZIN WARS VII

This is a work of fiction. All the characters and events portrayed in this book are fictional, and any resemblance to real people or incidents is purely coincidental.

Acknowledgment
Excerpts from the poem, "Schrödinger's Cat Preaches to the Mice," from *Bone Scan* by Gwen Harwood, are reproduced in "The Colonel's Tiger" by kind permission of the author.

A Baen Books Original

Baen Publishing Enterprises
P.O. Box 1403
Riverdale, NY 10471

ISBN: 0-671-87670-8

Cover art by Stephen Hickman

First printing, July 1995

Distributed by Simon & Schuster
1230 Avenue of the Americas
New York, NY 10020

Printed in the United States of America

CONTENTS

THE COLONEL'S TIGER

TIGER

•

Hal Colebatch

India, Northwest Frontier, 1878

"Lie still. Rest," the doctor told him. "You're not recovered yet.

"Lie still? And listen to *that*?"

The wind brought to the field hospital the sounds of an intermittent drumfire from the barren, snow-topped hills to the north, the flat thud-thud of screw-guns and the thorns-in-fire crackle of distant musketry.

"Rest, I say. You're out of this one, Captain Vaughn."

"I've had enough. Dreams. Sickness. Delirium."

The sick man swung his legs to the floor and rose to his feet. He took a half dozen steps, and the doctor caught him as he fell.

A punkah coolie took part of the emaciated soldier's weight and they helped him back to the bed.

"I'll make a bargain with you: When you can get as far as the latrine without help you can try leading your squadrons in the mountains. Not before."

"I just feel so . . . useless lying here. Those are my men."

"If it's any consolation to you, the cavalry have been resting for the last week: It's work for mules and infantry up there. And if it's any further consolation, I had you marked off for dead a week ago. You and your friends."

The sick man smiled weakly. "I don't suppose my kit would have fetched much. There must have been a few auctions in the mess lately."

"It hasn't been too bad. Old Bindon's cautious with men's lives on punitive expeditions. Your tigerskin would have fetched something though . . . here, steady on!"

The doctor held the sick man's head as a violent retching shook him. Then, as he recovered, Vaughn raised his hand

3

to the part of his scalp the doctor had held and gasped, "My head! What's happened?"

"I suppose I can show you." The doctor held up a mirror.

"Oh, my God!"

"Curlewis and Maclean are the same. And that Afridi devil of yours. But you're all alive. It was blood you were spewing a week ago, though you were in no condition to notice." The doctor held a glass of water to the captain's lips, steadying his trembling as he drank. "I must go. Rest, I say."

"Where is the skin?"

"Salted. The *gomashta*'s got it. I advanced him a couple of rupees." He rose at the sounds he had been waiting for: hooves and the approaching wheels of ambulance carts from the direction of Dirragha.

Captain Vaughn sank back exhausted. He closed his eyes and saw again, hanging in blackness, the great cat's head, with its blazing gold and violet eyes and batwing ears, the interlocking fangs protruding beyond the lips, the great cat they called his tiger-man. The dark cave, the rockets . . .

The wounded were being brought from the carts. The unmistakable sounds recalled him from his own visions to reality, and the work that had been done that day. At the tail end of the Afghan Campaign, a force of no less than five thousand men was fighting to pacify these barren hills, with all that that implied in terms of death and wounds. Beside that, his own recent moment was nothing at all. But he was not fully clearheaded yet. The doctor could say what he liked, but at that moment the feeling of his weakness and uselessness oppressed him. He felt ashamed.

"They will forget you and me," he whispered to the image of his enemy. "But they will not forget the Dirragha Expeditionary Force."

Adding these statements together he was, at best, only partly correct.

He had the statistics and the global picture. I didn't know, or want to know, much more than I needed to: A long time ago, before my time, the militarist fantasy had been widespread. It had produced a great deal of pathological fiction and pseudohistory. We had had a lot of people working on it once. But our whole society had progressed in recent years.

Also, the study of *real* history was being progressively restricted. That, too, seemed to have helped put military fants out of business. A few years ago one in ten might have had clearance to study history. It would be one in thousands now.

Personally, I was not among that chosen few. My job was quite distinct. Literary, not historical.

The controller seemed talkative. Almost oddly so. He usually kept conversation either strictly business or strictly social. It was not like him to ruminate on what we were doing, at least to people like me. Even someone with less training than I possessed would have recognized him as being slightly ill at ease, and not bothering to disguise the fact overmuch. Something was, if not worrying him, I thought, puzzling him at least.

After a moment's pause he went on.

"It's a few years now since we had anything like this. But they're hard to clear out altogether. I sometimes think it's odd how military fant variations persist. Do you remember the Magnussen business?"

I did. Magnussen, a part-time volunteer helper at this very museum and a member of a now quietly closed-down body called the Scandinavian Historical Association, had evolved a theory from ceremonial objects he had examined that his ninth- and tenth-century Danish and Norwegian ancestors had been members of a warrior culture living in part by war and plunder. It might have seemed a very academic point to some, and frankly very few people would have been interested one way or another, but ARM had not wanted it sensationalized.

Actually, Magnussen had been hard done by: Those of

us inside ARM, and working professionally in the field knew that indeed there still had been sporadic outbreaks of large-scale organized violence later than officially admitted, at least in remote areas away from the great cities of the world. I didn't want or need to know more of the details than my work required, but of course I had an outline. Well, whatever the reason Magnussen's ancestors had put to sea, he himself had gone on a longer voyage.

"I do think we're getting rid of them though," Alfred O'Brien said. "Sometimes I've thought there's no end to human perversity and folly. . . . Speaking of which . . ." He drummed his fingers on the table, hesitated again, and now I was sure he seemed embarrassed.

"There is another matter," he said at last.

"Yes?"

"An odd one."

"I can tell that."

"Yes. It's a bit out of our usual line, but we've been asked to look into it. Do you remember the *Angel's Pencil*?"

There had been a send-off a long time ago, shortly after I was seconded to the special literary research section of the program. It must be beyond the orbit of Tisiphone by now. "I've heard the name," I said. "A colony ship, wasn't it?"

"Yes. With a mixed Earth-Belter crew. It left for Epsilon Eridani eighteen years ago." He touched a panel on his desk and a hemisphere map beamed up behind him. More time had passed than I thought. The ship's telltale reached out to a point light-years beyond the last wandering sentinel of the Solar system.

"Don't tell me they've got military fants on board?"

I laughed. We had had a little worry recently about a scientific exploration ship named *Fantasy Prince*. Finally we had decided after investigation that the name was an innocuous coincidence and had nothing to do with military fants.

He didn't laugh.

"I don't know. But it might be something like that. They've had trouble. If trouble's the right word for it . . .

"We thought we knew every tanj thing that could go wrong in space, but this one came out of nowhere."

He lit one of his "cigars." He'd copied that from Buford Early. It wasn't usual that he had trouble putting words together. This, I thought, is going to be something bizarre. But then, he would hardly have sent for me otherwise. ARM has plenty of people available for normal problems.

"It may be something mental affecting the crew. Something the ship's 'doc quite evidently can't handle. We're getting its readouts and it's diagnosed nothing wrong."

Docs failing in space were a nightmare, for spacers at least.

"Either that, or it's criminal behavior, which we like even less. . . . They're sending back messages about . . . Outsiders."

"Yes?"

He heard the excitement in my voice. Alien contact was one of the Big Ones. It was also a mirage. We had looked for friends among the stars for four hundred years and more and some false hopes had been raised and dashed. His next words damped my excitement.

"No. Not real Outsiders. There would be people involved at much higher levels if they *were* real. What they are sending back is quite impossible."

"Delusions?"

"Nothing so simple, though that would be serious enough. They've sent back pictures, holos. You can't transmit photographs of delusions. . . . There may be some sort of group psychosis. I know that's hardly a satisfactory description, but . . . they've made things . . . not very nice. . . ."

He nodded to himself, muttered something, and then went on.

"The whole report of alien contact is bizarre but carefully detailed nonsense. They've gone to a lot of trouble in some ways to try to be convincing, but in others they've made elementary mistakes. Mistakes in science so obvious they look deliberate. Why? Maybe one crew member has got control of the others."

"I don't see what that's got to do with me. I'm not a medical man. Or a psychist. You know what I am."

"We've got medical men working on it too. But a stronger possibility is criminal conspiracy: Someone may stand to make a financial gain from this."

"But a criminal could only be rewarded on Earth—or in the Belt. Why commit a crime light-years beyond any reward? Besides, surely being crew on a colony ship . . . It just about guarantees a good life at the end of the trip."

"That may be taking a bit for granted. Colonies haven't always gone as planned. And being beyond reward means being beyond prosecution as well. But I won't speculate on possible Belt motives. You can think of some yourself. And even on Earth, family could be rewarded."

We didn't like families very much. But, thinking it over in silence for a moment, another question came to me that seemed rather obvious.

"If it's a hoax, then, at the bottom line, does it matter? I mean, it's a long way away, isn't it?"

"You know the sort of money that's involved in colonization," he said. Then he continued. "No, on second thoughts you probably don't know. But think of this: What if it comes to be believed that long space flights send crews crazy, light-years from treatment?"

"Not so good."

"Another thing: A colony founded by criminals—or military fants—well, that's an entire world we're dealing with. Think about it."

I thought. It didn't take much thought to feel a chill at the long-term implications.

"Maybe that's a worst-case scenario," he went on, "but anything that might affect space colonization matters, given the type of money we're dealing with. A colony ship is *never* a good investment, Karl. It's money and resources thrown away, at least from the point of view of a lot of political lobbyists. It's never easy to . . . persuade . . . a politician to take the long-term view. One more negative factor at any time could tip the balance against the whole program.

"There's another thing, too: the obvious ARM thing. We don't like anything we don't understand. We can't afford it. One thing is sure: This business had its origins on Earth or in the Belt and we want to know why and where.

"It doesn't look like a simple practical joke. And the whole thing is detailed enough to make me believe it's not going to stop there. I think this was set up on Earth before they took off. There was once a practice called blockbusting. Have you heard of it?"

"No."

"It was marginally legal for a long time, or at least illegality was difficult to prove. A joker wanted to buy real estate. He spread rumors of nasty diseases in the neighborhood, even paid nasty neighbors to move in, perhaps spread stories of nasty developments in area planning. Property values fell, he bought the property for less than its real value.

"For obvious reasons, that hasn't happened for a long time on any major scale, but this may be blockbusting brought up to date. The rumor gets out that space travel of more than a few light-years sends people crazy. Shares in all space and colonizing industries fall. Some smart guy buys them up, then—"

"He'd be prosecuted, and treated. Unless—"

"Unless it couldn't be traced back. And if that's right, whoever thought it up is subtle and powerful."

"And you think this could have such an effect?"

"Not by itself . . . and not if this was to be the last we heard of it, perhaps. . . . Frankly, we're simply bewildered by it. I guess," he added, "quite a lot of what I've said is grasping at straws."

It was an unusual confession for someone in his position to make to someone in mine.

"So suppress it."

"We did. The reports were dead-filed by Director Bernhardt and Director Harms left them that way. With the cooperation of the Belt. But our new director feels that leaves too many questions unanswered. And the messages keep coming. Find out where this thing originated."

He touched the desk again and the heavens disappeared. We had windows and view again. Alfred O'Brien's office was on the fortieth floor of a museum complex, and out the window I could see the high leafy crowns of megatree oxygen factories and, on the ground beyond, a herd of pigmy mammoths, a gift from St. Petersburg, browsing on buttercups in their climate-controlled subarctic meadow. There was a complex of sports stadia beyond that, part of the vast group ringing the city, and the river blue in the sun.

"We're puzzled," he said, "not only as to why they should have delusions or whatever it is, but why *this particular one*. You see, they are trying to tell us that these Outsiders tried to destroy them!

"The word is *war*."

He fell silent. It was as if the obscenity hung in the air before us.

"The word, Karl, we have been working for centuries to remove from human consciousness. Why did they resurrect the idea?"

The progressive censorship of literature had been my job for a long time. Search and closure operations of military fants cults went with it. It was an inescapable complement to the genetic part of the program.

"You remember 1938," he said.

It was one of the secret dates every ARM operative in my section knew: In that year a "radio" broadcast about an imaginary hostile Martian invasion had caused panic and terror and had paralyzed a large part of the United States of America for a night. One of the most serious landmark outbreaks of the Military Fantasy. The "War of the Worlds." It was pointed out to us in our training, lest we become complacent, that the idea of war had still had the potential to be taken seriously by large numbers of people only five years before the first test flight of the V-2 had launched the beginnings of the Space Age. Did the hoaxers know of that, too?

"I'll need to know more," I said.

"Of course. Look at these."

O'Brien touched his desk again. A succession of holos

sprang up in the air between us. There were also a series of flats.

"Here are the pictures they sent back. Well, what do you think of the Outsiders they've dreamed up? Pleasant-looking sons of bitches, aren't they?"

There were humans in the pictures, evidently in order to give some idea of scale. The humans were less than shoulder-high to the other creatures, orange colored, fanged almost like ancient saber-toothed tigers, but with odd differences: four-digited forepaws like clawed hands, shorter bodies and longer legs than real tigers, and triangular heads with bigger crania above feline faces. Distorted ears. The effect was of a monstrosity.

They appeared to be three-dimensional objects.

"Jenny Hannifers," said the controller. "Sailors in ancient times sewed together dead monkeys and fish to sell as mermaids. These are a sophisticated version of the same thing."

I looked down at the little mammoths, whose DNA had come from specimens preserved in the Siberian permafrost.

"The tissue was grown in tanks, you mean?"

"No, I don't think so. It's possible perhaps. As a colony ship they had a lot of animal cell cultures and they had plenty of advanced facilities for DNA sewing machines. But there are much easier ways. They had every kind of virtual reality simulator and program.

"We've checked what records there were of the loading of the *Angel's Pencil*, of course. They weren't complete because a lot of personal property of crew members was never itemized.

"In any case the requirements of a colony ship are enormously complex. Some of the containers loaded might have held fake alien body parts. Some cargo had come from the Belt and we have no inventories of that. As you know, Belters hate keeping nonessential bureaucratic records and they hate any intrusions on their citizens' privacy. But they didn't need to carry physical props: Their computers would do the job. Entertainment programs and computer space are things no deep-spacer—especially no colony ship—is short of."

"It seems a very queer sort of joke."

"Exactly. Normal minds wouldn't do such a thing. Which means, obviously, that we've got problems whatever the motive for producing them was.

"They say that these Outsiders approached them at an impossible speed, stopped dead in space in defiance of elementary laws of physics, and then tried to kill them by some sort of invisible heat ray after giving them all headaches. You can see how crazy it is. They haven't even bothered getting the basic science right, let alone the sociology.

"Then, they say, in trying to turn away they pointed their com-drive laser at the Outsider ship and a Belter crewman activated it. In one way we can be thankful: Suppose such a thing had *really* happened! When they examined the wreckage of the alien, so the message goes, they found it loaded with bomb-missiles, laser-cannon, ray-projectors: *weapons*, not signaling devices. Fusion-generators deliberately designed to destabilize at a remote command—sick, nightmarish things like that."

"You're right," I said heavily after the implications of what he said had sunk in. "There's real illness here. Something deeper than I've encountered or read of." Then, knowing my words sounded somehow lame in the context of such madness, "It makes no sense."

"No. It makes no sense. And you would think the crew of a spacecraft would know better than to tell us another spacecraft matched course with them at eighty percent of light-speed, *and* changed course instantaneously. As if anything organic wouldn't be killed by inertia. What about delta-v? It's as preposterous as expecting us to believe such an insanely aggressive culture would get into space at all!"

He projected another holo.

"Look at this. It's meant to be the Outsider ship."

Two main pieces of wreckage tumbling in space, leaking smaller fragments of debris. Cables, ducting, unidentifiable stuff. I had the unpleasant thought that a living body

chopped with an ax might leak pieces in the same way.
There were tiny space-suited dolls maneuvering objects
that included shrouded alien cadavers. There were other
pictures, apparently taken from aboard the Outsider
wreckage with the *Angel's Pencil* hanging in the background.
But photographs taken in space have no scale. The objects
could have been a mile across or the size of a man's hand.
The EV humans could have been OO-scale figures from
a child's model kit. But as he said, they were more probably
electronic impulses than models. There were a lot of ways
VR had already become a forensic problem.

"Can't we check it out? We've got good computers."

"So have they."

"I don't see anything that looks like a drive on it," I said.
"Nothing like a ramscoop, no jets, no light-sail, no hydrogen
tanks, no fusion bottles, nothing."

"That's right. Rather an elementary error to design an
extraordinarily maneuverable spacecraft without a drive. I
told you they've ignored the science. But we know the things
are fakes. What we want to know is why they were faked."

He paused and contemplated his cigar, frowning. Then
he switched his gaze to the pictures again.

"These things could be rather . . . disturbing, somehow?"

"Somehow, yes," I said, "I don't *like* them."

"No. Only a few people have seen these things yet, all
trained ARM personnel and a few of the Belter security
people, and everyone has the same response. There's art
gone into this.

"We're descended from creatures that were hunted by
felines, Karl. It's almost as if whoever made up the
morphology of these things has tapped into some sort of
ancestral memory."

"I still don't see exactly how I come into it."

I did to some extent, though. And I saw another thing:
If these holos of the alleged aliens became public, it was
possible some gullible people might actually believe in them.
Not as the symptoms of a space madness, though that would
be bad enough, but as being *real in themselves*.

There were, I knew, plenty of people around bored and stupid enough to believe anything. Indeed, that was already a major social problem in itself. I understood why he had sent for me.

All right. I closed my eyes and leaned back in my chair. Let something come. Start with tigers.

"Tigers are Indian, aren't they?"

"I don't know. Someone downstairs could tell you." A lot of the museum below us was gallery and display rooms, and I knew Arthur Guthlac, the head guide and Assistant to the Museum's Chief of General Staff.

"Were there any Indians in the crew?"

He handed me a wafer. "Complete dossiers and pictures." I dumped it in my wrist-comp.

"Any more pictures of the . . . things?"

"Hundreds. They've been sending them back continually. This will give you the general idea. You see they remembered to give them thumbs."

He began flicking them up. No, I didn't like them. None of the Jenny Hannifers were whole, just as if they really had been burned or suddenly exposed to explosive decompression in space. Some were only fragments. Big catlike beings with thumbs. They were colored orange with some variations of shade from near red to near yellow and darker markings. One was smaller than the others. I was fairly experienced in dealing with sickness, pathology even, that was part of the job, but this was something different.

It was *wrong* that someone should have gone to so much care to concoct a hoax, and shown such ingenuity in its details. I thought again of what years in space might do to human beings—*really* thought about it—and realized for the first time how brave those first colonists of Wunderland and Plateau and Jinx and the rest had been.

There were holos of allegedly dissected "aliens," too: cartilaginous ribs that covered the stomach region, blood that varied in color between purple and orange, presumably an analogue for arterial and venous, streams of data that purported to be DNA codings, skeletons, analysis of alien alimentary-canal contents and muscle tissue purporting to contain odd proteins, sheets of what was allegedly alien script, looking like claw marks. There were also holos of what purported to be alien skulls.

"There's possibly a connection with your other work," the controller went on. "Or in any case, it seems to fall into our area as much as anyone else's. Your clearance has been upgraded one threshold in case you need special information. With our own people, normal need-to-know should be enough."

I was getting signals that Alfred O'Brien was a nervous man taking a risk, and perhaps carrying me with him. I guessed opinion in the higher reaches was still divided on how to deal with this. A wrong decision, and early retirement; a *very* wrong decision, and . . . because, bizarre as it was, it could be serious.

Colonists were all volunteers, and could hardly be anything else. But they also went through rigorous screening and selection. It was quite right that rumors or reports of odd mental diseases in space could kill enthusiasm for colonizing ventures. And, yes, the ferocious three-meter tiger-cat images, however created, did have a disturbing quality about them. Somehow too many of them were difficult to look at for too long, whole or in pieces. But were they utterly unfamiliar? Why did I ask myself that question?

Deep, deep in memory, something stirred. What? I'd never seen anything much like these supposed aliens before, but . . . I looked at the dissection pictures again. There was the tiniest suggestion, somewhere in the back of my mind . . .

"The skulls might be a starting point," I said.

"Oh. How so?"

"I feel they look . . . familiar somehow."

"Good. It's good if you've got a starting point, I mean."

"Can I tell Arthur Guthlac about it? I know he's been interested in biological history."

"If you think so. But only what he needs to know."

"It's an odd job."

"That's why we need you."

"It's needle-in-a-haystack territory."

"I know." He picked up a sheet of paper and passed it to me. "I don't know if it's much of a start, but I've had the computers search for literary references to 'space' and 'cat' together. There isn't much. Here's one you might not know: An ancient Australian poem by an author Gwen Harwood, called 'Schrödinger's Cat Preaches to the Mice':

> Silk whisperings of knife on stone,
> due sacrifice, and my meat came.
> Caressing whispers, then my own
> choice among leaps by leaping flame.
>
> What shape is space? Space will put on
> the shape of any cat. Know this:
> my servant Schrödinger is gone
> before me to prepare a place . . .

I looked down to the end:

> Dead or alive? The case defies
> all questions. Let the lid be locked.
> Truth, from your little beady eyes,
> is hidden. I will not be mocked.
>
> Quantum mechanics has no place
> for what's there without observation.
> Classical physics cannot trace
> spontaneous disintegration.
>
> If the box holds a living cat
> no scientist on earth can tell.
> But, I'll be waiting, sleek and fat.
> Verily all will not be well
>
> if, to the peril of your souls
> you think me gone. Know that this house
> is mine, that kittens by mouse-holes
> wait, who have never seen a mouse.

He handed me a card embossed with the symbol of a level of authority I had encountered only two or three times before.

"Stay away from 'docs," he said. "That's your permit to do so. In fact your order to do so. No medication till further notice. We're turning you loose exactly as you are."

"You do believe in taking risks, don't you?"

"You're not a schizie. You won't kill anyone. At least, I don't think so. But this is an intellectual problem. You'll need that intuition of yours as sharp as you can get it. And your wits sharp, too.

" 'Space will put on the shape of any cat. . . .' " he quoted again as I left him. "It was written four hundred years ago."

• CHAPTER 2

My first-year politics tutorials this week dealt with Nazi foreign policy and the lead-up to the war. I decided to loosen things a bit and just generally chat. . . . How strange that university politics students should *never have heard* of the little ships that took the British Expeditionary Force off the beaches in May 1940. Or de Gaulle. Or a Spitfire. No knowledge of any of it . . . This was the stuff that was supposed never to be forgotten thirty, forty years ago. Next week we do the Holocaust. . . .
—Letter to the author, October 10, 1991

Snow whirled round. A snarling roar shook the eardrums. Over the crest of a snow-covered ridge a saber-toothed head appeared, fangs dripping. With a single fluid motion the feline leaped to the top of the rock, poised for a moment, the eyes in its flat head blazing at us.

I caught myself flinching, sudden instinctive terror mixing with awe at the size and malevolence of the thing. Shrieking, the great cat launched itself through the air at us, its body suddenly seeming to elongate to an impossible narrowness.

It passed between us and there was a scream of animal pain and terror as its huge incisors sank into its prey. Blood spurted.

Arthur Guthlac turned off the holo, and the Pleistocene gallery faded.

"Kids love it," he said. "For some reason the Smilodon's even more popular than Tyrannosaurus Rex these days."

"Love it! It actually scared me!"

"Preschool children still have vestiges of the savage in

20

them. You of all people should understand that. They like to be scared. They like a bit of bloodshed too."

"I'm aware of it," I told him. "Part of my job is to detect antisocial behavior early. And I don't particularly like to be scared."

Guthlac laughed. A laugh with an edge in it.

"But you, my dear Karl, are a mature, adjusted human being. Not one of our little savages."

Warm air flowed gently round as the gallery returned to its normal temperature. A voice announced the museum would be closing in ten minutes as we stepped out of the gallery into the corridor.

I wondered if he was aware of the real meaning of the word "adjusted" in my case. It probably didn't matter.

"That's better," I told him. "You make this place a lot too cold for comfort."

"The Pleistocene was cold. That's why you had the mammoth and mastodon, the cave bear and the dire wolf and the saber-toothed tiger. Big bodies save heat. An age of giants and ice. Then a monkey adapted to the cold by growing a big brain and that was the end of the story."

"I know that. But we're not in the Pleistocene now. I don't know how you can choose to work in these conditions."

"Well, the idea is we should at least know our planet's past. What's the point of a historical display if it isn't real? Nature really was red in tooth and claw once. Remember the *Africa Rover*."

"A good deal too red in tooth and claw for me to want to know about, thanks. I'll leave that to the children. But you know I don't mean you putting up with cold air currents and nasty holograms. I mean spending your life here."

"Look at this," said Arthur. He touched a display of letters below a permanent reproduction of a great felinoid. "It's a poem from an ancient children's book on paleontology called *Whirlaway*: 'The Song of the Saber-Tooth':

> *On all the weaker beasts*
> *I work my sovereign will.*

Their flesh supplies my feasts,
my glory is to kill.

With claws and teeth that rend,
with eyes that pierce the gloom
I follow to the end
my duty and my doom.

For I shall meet one day
a beast of greater might,
And if I cannot slay
I'll die in rapturous fight.

"Don't you think it's got a sort of ring to it?"

It was my job, but I still found myself rather shocked, not just at the antisocial content of the poem, but because it seemed unpleasantly close to holos and flats I had been studying. Why had he chosen it to quote? "Do you think that's really suitable for children?" I asked.

"I don't think it can do any harm to show what prehistory—prehuman history—was like. You don't feel any sense of wonder looking back at the mammoth, the cave bear and the dire wolf?"

"Well, a bit, I suppose."

"You can be creative here."

Arthur turned to a smaller holo in a cabinet by the door leading into the main diorama space. A hominid on the shore of an alkaline lake screamed and ran from another great cat. Other hominids jerked up from their clam gathering to scatter before it. Long-extinct birds rose in a screaming cloud. This time the saber-tooth was foiled. Geological and evolutionary time had passed since the first scene. The hominids were taller and some of them had sticks.

The guard operated another switch and the scene changed again.

"We have a lot of things to do here. This is a new one for the children. Our might-have-beens." He spoke to a panel and a succession of prehistoric animals appeared, altered.

"You can do your own genetic engineering here: These are how our friends might have developed had conditions been different." He turned a dial and the holos changed. "Look! Here other creatures got the big brains."

Tigerlike creatures walked improbably erect, with fanciful tigerish cities in the background.

"It's been worked out what might have happened."

There was something here. I didn't understand it, but there was a hint of a scent. Had something been planted here?

Not, I thought, by Arthur Guthlac. All that was marked in his file was a certain interest in unsuitable games and reading, perhaps an occupational risk for someone in his job, and a general restlessness and reluctance to apply himself (apply himself to what?). Further, I had already checked that he had no conceivable financial or other links with anyone or anything that might profit from stories of space madness. I kept my voice casual.

"Yes, I'm sure the children love it. But all the same, you must get sick of it, day after day. I don't know why you bother with such a job. If you want to work, there are plenty of better things to do."

"No," he said, "I don't really get sick of it. It can be fun working with the holos. The children can make it fun, too. In any case, what else should I be doing? Nobody's going to send me into space, are they?" There was resentment buried somewhere there, I noted. Buried none too deeply, at that.

"This wing is largely a children's museum, as far as display goes," he continued. "Which is why they have human guides, of course. You know it's impossible to make anything child-proof if they're left to run loose without supervision. A lot of the equipment here is expensive."

Arthur paused and then added, "And, after all, Karl, history is important."

"Of course it is. But the world is full of people telling themselves their hobbies are important. We've all got a great deal of leisure time to fill. All right, I agree we need people doing what you are doing. But you wanted to go into space once."

"What good is an amateur savant in space? They sent plenty of real professors to Wunderland, but someone like me would only take up valuable room on a colony ship. I know.

"I applied a long time ago. . . . I have no skill that would justify the expense of transporting me, or will allow me to earn enough money to pay my own way. One family seems to have been rationed to one space-farer. But you haven't heard me complaining, have you?"

"Not in so many words." I kept my voice neutral. There was nothing to be gained by thinking of why *I* would never be allowed very far into space.

His sister, I knew, was a navigator on the *Happy Gatherer*, a genius, genetic engineer turned space pilot. He was proud of her and, I guessed, subconsciously resentful.

"Anyway, look at this." Arthur opened another door onto a vast panorama of the asteroid belt, as seen from the surface of Ceres, the rocky landscape lit by the blue-white fusion flame of a miner's ship passing closer than a real ship would ever be allowed.

He touched another switch, and we seemed to stand on the red surface of Mars. Our feet disappeared in dust.

"You can do a lot with holos," Arthur said. "Being a gallery supervisor can be a lot of fun if the museum's big enough and has VR as good as we have here."

He gestured. "Do you want to see our Great Moments in History? The Sportsman's Hall of Fame? The panorama of the Olympic Games? The Hall of Music? We've got it all here. Science, the history of space flight: Werner von Braun sending up the first V-2?" He pointed down the hall, to the strange yet familiar shape of the historic weather-research rocket's replica suspended from the ceiling.

"There's the Shame Gallery, too, the displays of creatures we exterminated, like the trusting dodo bird. But the truth of the matter is I like working in the museum because we have an excellent library here. I'd still like to do something in the field of prehistory. Somehow."

The main doors of the great building whispered shut. On Arthur's computer a pattern of green lights appeared, as surveillance monitors locked into a nighttime control center. Security was light, a precaution against accident more than crime.

A holo showed an outline of the complex, secured sections turning green, the last departing visitors white flashing dots of light. A few red dots for the skeleton human staff who would monitor the surveillance screens and occasionally patrol the corridors during the night. Cleaning and maintenance machines began to stir.

"I'm off duty now. I'm glad you made this visit, Karl."

"It's been a long time. I thought it would be a good idea if we caught up with each other."

"Well, we're closing down now. Would you like to come home for a while?"

"Would your family mind an uninvited guest?"

"I live alone. I thought you knew."

"Well, I've no engagements tonight. The little savages are having their tapes played to them by now. Yes, all right. Thank you."

We stepped into a transit-tube. Arthur Guthlac's quarters, I guessed from the near-instantaneous passage, were somewhere in the museum complex itself.

Psychologically the rooms were easy to read. There were high-detail models of spaceships, a deep-space exploration vessel dominating them, and a flat map of the interstellar colonies.

Arthur was ARM, of course, with some clearances. Most of the museum personnel, certainly all the general staff, were under the organization's wing, even if they had no idea of what its real size and ramifications were (for that matter, I was well aware that I knew very little of that myself). They came in contact with too much history for any other arrangement to be conceivable.

Anyone involved with history had ARM's eye on them, and it was better to have such people inside the organization than out. We could afford that now. The occasional secret covens of military fantasists we came across—the Sir Kays and Lady Helens with their ceremonies and Namings—

were a continuing if diminishing nuisance but were no longer seen as any real threat, and with modern medical science the organ banks had long been closed.

Still, our present problem was before us and there is wisdom in the book of sports about keeping your eye on the ball. I took him through most of what Alfred O'Brien had told me, with the major visuals. He thought it over for a while, then he said:

"Show me the picture of the skull again. . . . It's odd, but this almost reminds me of something."

"A skull is a skull, surely." I didn't tell him that it almost reminded me of something, too.

"Yes, but, somewhere, somehow, I've got a feeling I've seen something like this before."

"It's a pretty freakish-looking thing," I said.

"So it should be easy to identify."

He turned to a computer terminal.

"We've got a good identification program here for type specimens," he said. "Let me scan this in." He placed the picture in the slot and we waited as the display began to reel off numbers.

"We've got all the major type specimens here," he said, "but not the oddities." He pressed more keys.

"It's too much," he said after a while. "I was wrong. We'd have to write a new program to get anything in the next month or so."

"Surely not. I know these programs. They can carry virtually unlimited data. That's what they're for!"

"Yes, when the data's been given to them. This hasn't been. There is, it seems, no general catalogue of freaks."

"We'll have to go through this practically museum by museum," he said after a minute. "This is broken down into ancient national collections, even provincial—as you probably know, most animal classification is very old and often parochial. It should have been updated, but it never has been. I don't even know what some of these countries were, let alone the districts and provinces!"

I thought of the poem the controller had shown me.

"Start with Australia," I said.

The screens rolled briefly. Guthlac shook his head. The poem seemed to exist in isolation, and read in full seemed to have been concerned with quantum mechanics.

"There are no true felines native to Australia," he said after a while. "The Tasmanian tiger and so forth were marsupials—convergent evolution."

"Perhaps some sort of convergent evolution is what we're after."

More figures. Then lines of text.

"Abnormal feline morphology . . . teratology . . ." Guthlac read, muttering to himself. "Convergent evolution . . . See . . ."

He began to punch up pictures of fanged skulls. None had a cranium anything like the skull in the picture the crew of the *Angel's Pencil* had sent back.

"That's all the Australian collection has," he said. "Ordinary felines imported from elsewhere for zoos and so forth, domestic cats and a few convergent marsupials . . . Did you know there was once a marsupial lion? Died with the rest of the megafauna when man got there, though. Their main natural history concern as far as cats are involved seems to have been with the effects of domestics gone feral."

Gone feral. It sounded a funny concept to apply to animals. Its ARM usage was reserved to apply to a certain rare type of human.

"Yes. The life-forms there had evolved in isolation, and had no defenses when the cats came with bigger teeth and claws and quicker reflexes. They wiped out a lot of species."

Was that why the hoaxers had chosen cats, I wondered? Some play on subconscious associations? *When the cats came.* The words seemed to hang in the air for a moment.

Then: "Wait . . . here's something else . . . the Vaughn Tiger-Man."

"What's that?" Was there the faintest ripple of memory somewhere in my own mind at the words?

"A tiger killed in India in 1878 by Captain, later Colonel, Henry Vaughn of the Fourth Lancers."

"What name did you say?" An alarm bell rang in my mind.

"Vaughn." He spelled it out.

One of the *Angel's Pencil*'s crew was named Vaughn.

"What are lancers, do you suppose?"

"I don't know. What's a colonel?" As a matter of fact I knew what a colonel was, and from that I could guess what lancers had been, but there was no point in letting Arthur Guthlac know that. I made a mental note that these natural history records needed editing. And I saw from his body language, plainly, that he was lying too. He knew what those terms meant.

"Go on," I said.

"This is an old journal. Produced by some amateur natural history society. Colonel Henry Vaughn killed an abnormal tiger."

"But they're protected species!"

"Not then. And this one was a man-eater."

We knew that phrase: "Man-eater" had been a term of sensational horror recently. A boutique airship, carrying tourists slowly and silently fifty feet above the African savanna, had developed engine trouble and landed. The passengers in their closed and comfortable gondola need have only waited a few hours for rescue—less if they had said it was urgent. But they had left the craft and wandered out, apparently unaware of any danger. It had been a sobering thought during the investigation which followed that any of us might have done the same. Arthur went on.

"He kept the skull and skin and settled in Australia later. But it's not in the Australian Museum collection. When he died his family gave the skull to the British Museum."

"Is there a picture of it?"

"Yes. But it's only a drawing. And half of it is missing."

"Let me see."

Half a two-dimensional drawing. The front of a big skull, oddly distorted. There wasn't much detail, but such a skull *could* be the inspiration of the Jenny Hannifer. What there was of it was closer than anything else we had seen. And I felt I had seen that picture somewhere before. Somewhere connected with childhood, just as the words "Vaughn Tiger-Man" aroused some faint chord that had something to do with long ago. I felt almost sure that I had heard that phrase before.

I closed my eyes and concentrated: an image of a big room, with giant furniture, and giants. A child's-eye view of house and parents. My giant father reading to me from a yellow-covered book? I thought that was what it was, but I couldn't be sure.

Perhaps the original illustration had been reproduced in one of those books which we discouraged: *Strange Tricks of Nature*, *Great Unsolved Mysteries*, *The Wonder-book of Marvels*.

There had been a spate of them once. My father had collected them. Well, I was in a position to know where they were gone to now.

More screens of numbers. Then a beeping sound, and a pointer flashing red at one of these. Guthlac scrolled down another menu and searched again. "I've located a box number for it." He said, "It's in England, but I gather from this it's not been put on display, or not for a very long time. It was put into storage when it arrived there in 1908 and I gather it stayed there."

"Can you get any description?

"Not much. A sport, a freak, it says here. There was some interest in it when it was first shot. But it wasn't regarded as scientifically important. It was just a piece of gross pathology."

"The only one of its kind?"

"Exactly. Like the Elephant-Man. Not much for an ambitious student to make a name on there. That was a great age of biological discovery, you know, with all sorts of larger projects to occupy researchers. Vaughn wrote about it himself. Abnormal limbs and fangs and a large cranial tumor. It was grossly deformed. Pity he didn't keep the whole skeleton."

Arthur turned to me. He seemed suddenly embarrassed. When he spoke it was with an odd hesitancy in his voice.

"Karl?"

"Yes?"

"How important is this?"

"I'm here, aren't I?"

"If this does matter, then I've done ARM a service, haven't I?"

"Of course."

"Would there be . . . a reward?"

"You have a real job. Isn't that reward enough? Important work. You said so yourself. You are one of the elite twenty-five percent who have something more than sport to fill their lives. How many people out there would give all they have for that?"

"I want to get into space."

"So save up for a few years."

"No! Not as a passenger. I want . . . I want . . ."

His voice trailed off. I knew what he wanted. Isolated, celibate, a square peg keeping a tight hold on normality. I knew. I was glad to break the awkward silence.

"Yes. You mentioned a skin."

"Nothing about that here." Then he burst out: "You have your hunts to enjoy!"

There was no point in arguing with him, but how wrong he was! Someone who *enjoys* my work in the sense I knew he meant would be useless. In any case, the mental preparation arranged for us is thorough. What I do is a duty, and not an ignoble one. Our world has—no, our worlds, plural, have—become complicated beyond imagining. There is a phrase coming into use: "known space." Someone has to hold it together. It has never been a matter of the hunt for its own sake, or of searching for excitement.

Warn him off. Now. Arthur had quite a lot of museum junk littering a workbench. All there legitimately, I assumed, but among it was a small heap of brown paper, the pages of old books far gone in acid decay.

"What are these?" I asked casually.

"Sports history. It's been a hobby of mine."

"Oh." My eye caught the bottom of one of the loose pages:

At the end of March, 1943, the thaw started on the eastern front. "Marshal Winter" gave way to the still more masterful "Marshal Mud," and active operations came automatically to an end. All Panzer divisions and some infantry divisions were withdrawn from the front line, and the armor in the Kharkov area was concentrated under the 48th Panzer Corps. We assumed command of the 3rd, 6th and 11th Panzer divisions, together with P.G.D. Gross Deutschland. Advantage was taken of the lull to institute a thorough training program, and exercise . . .

He looked over my shoulder at it. "Winter Olympics, I think," he said. "They were just starting to do things on a really big scale with team games then. The Space Age year."

It dealt with a period before the literary era I specialized in and it didn't mean a lot to me. I didn't particularly like it, but for a low-grade ARM officer to possess a few lines of old books without specific clearance was not exactly an offense, even if it might amount to skating on thinnish ice. In any case I had other things to do now.

ARM had special facilities for deep hypnosis available for people like me, since memory and association are our most unique assets.

Certain specific parts of my childhood and juvenile memory had been blocked as a routine precaution when I joined ARM but the block was intended to be bypassed in a matter of need. It wasn't perfect recall but I did bring back a clearer picture. An old, old book in my father's collection, *Great True Stories of Adventure for Boys*, with a story of a strange tiger hunt and crude black-and-white line drawings. Including the drawing of that odd skull.

Memory-wipe is not a form of death, whatever some people say. It can be controlled and stopped at a certain point. An individual's childhood memories might be left intact—they often were. I am not a killer. I am nothing remotely like a killer.

• CHAPTER 3

> One of Japan's ubiquitous television crews took to the streets last week to find out what people thought about the forthcoming fiftieth anniversary of Pearl Harbor. . . . Such has been the rewriting of history in Japan that many teenagers had not even heard of Pearl Harbor and several expressed amazement Japan had fought a war with the United States.
> —Gareth Alexander "The War Japan Chose to Forget," Press Item, December 3, 1991

London was gearing up for the first rounds of "Graceful Willow," and the streets were full of supporters wearing team colors when I arrived, bowing to one another, giving way in air-cars and on pedestrian walks, competing already among themselves in the game's values of courtesy and noncompetitiveness.

Dr. Humphrey of the British Museum had been contacted and briefed to help me. Together we read through all of the very little literature we had been able to find on the specimen. Of course he was ARM too. He knew better than to ask why we were making this peculiar investigation.

The man who had taken the name of Sir Kay had had tears in his eyes when he was taken away, but he would in no other way betray fear. Why not? I knew how terrified he was. Was it something to do with courage, with the barbaric code of warlike "nobility" that they had dabbled in to their disaster? "Have you any conception of what you are destroying?" the girl who had called herself the Lady May had asked me when I identified myself and arrested them. Yes, I had a conception. ARM does not do what it does for nothing.

It took time to locate the storage data on the specimen, even with the search tools we had available, and then there was a further purely physical hunt for it, in the recesses of sealed vaults far underground, containing the detritus a great museum acquires over centuries.

An elevator took us down from street level past several floors of storage to a deep subbasement. There were ancient, primitive stuffed specimens of animals standing there with their hides falling apart into ghoulish sculptures of wires and bones. There were desiccated things in the bottoms of jars and crumbling stone figures that had once been worshiped. There were even mislaid pieces of sports history, such as a tiny rudimentary flying machine with open cockpit and three stubby wings, red fabric falling off its crumbling framework. The designers had given maneuverability and a rapid climb priority over all else. Some game long out of fashion.

Beyond this were further repositories in that great ancient warren of a building. We came to a row of shut metal doors, and entered another locked vault after consulting a plan.

The air was dank. Even cleaning machines had not been there for a long time. And then to a series of locked metal cupboards, so old they were actually rusted.

We found it at last, the label almost unreadable under dust. An ancient wooden box. The lid creaked as we prized it open.

The skull was huge, gray with age, and with some of the more delicate nasal bones obviously crumbled or broken in previous handling. There were several irregular, cracked holes.

Although these stacks were in Dr. Humphrey's charge, he had apparently not seen it before. That was understandable. There were miles of shelving on compactus tracks.

"It's no tiger," he said. "It's like no animal I've ever seen."

"A freak?"

"No. No tiger so abnormal would have grown to adulthood."

"What about these lesions?"

"I've seen them on specimens before. Gunshot wounds when it was killed. And look at this!" He gestured at the literature he had brought and then down at the thing itself. "Cranial tumor indeed!"

It took the two of us to turn the skull over. He inserted a probe. "That's all braincase. Bigger than yours or mine."

I had a picture of a skull sent by the *Angel's Pencil* with me. There was no mistake about the identification: the *Pencil's* "alien" skull was copied from this one. I left the British Museum's storage section and headed for the archives, still as good as any in the world.

The Vaughn family were still in Australia. They had survived what happened there in 2025 and even emerged with some of their land intact and productive: The farm near the New South Wales rain forest which the colonel had retired to on his pension when all the British Empire was practically one country. I was there a few hours later.

Arthur Vaughn-Nguyen seemed cooperative when I presented myself as a Historian. He was in late middle age, probably about a hundred and ten, unattached. There was still farming going on, but robots did the work. He had two sons (so his genes must have checked out well) but they were not there. One, I gathered, was off-planet.

Perhaps he was talkative because he was bored. How many bored people there were! Or was he being *too* cooperative? I felt suspicious from the start. The farm had a sense of history about it, too, and not just because it belonged to one of the Survivor families.

Too much history, I thought, as I looked at some of the books and artifacts preserved in cases and along the walls of the main hall.

It was probably just as well that Vaughn-Nguyen did not know my thoughts, as I sat in his main living room with a live dog resting its head on my feet and a glass of Bungle-Bungle rum, a local delicacy said to date from Old Australia, in my hand. The family appeared to regard it as traditional. There was a suspicious amount of tradition left at the Vaughn station.

Colonel Vaughn himself was there, an ancient larger-than-life-size portrait hanging on the wall. He was rather as my reading had led me to imagine a "colonel" might be: crook nosed, wearing an elaborate jacket called a "uniform," with decorations on it called "medals." I had seen such things before, both in books and in the military fant cults. Somehow it struck me as odd and after a little thought I saw why: The man in the picture had no hair at all. No mustache, no eyebrows. It was anachronistic. I didn't think there had been a fashion for hairlessness until modern cosmetics were developed.

Probably it didn't matter. In those days men did lose their hair involuntarily. But this continuing public display of a military fant-type uniform was a different story. ARM should have paid the Vaughn-Nguyens a visit before.

A lot of this was headed for Black Hole. I wondered what compensation it would be necessary to pay the colonel's descendant for the removal of his antiques. Not much. We had destroyed the market for this sort of gear long ago.

It reminded me of something from our first training. When what is now known as ARM began the prelude to the program, as long ago as the American and French advancements at the end of the eighteenth century, it had made one of its priorities the ridiculing and destruction of the notion of hereditary titles of honor.

It was amusing (our instructor had said) to think this had been done in the names of liberty, democracy, equality and progress, when the real purpose had been to consolidate power. Even constitutional monarchy had been destroyed by a prolonged and often subtle political and media campaign, removing the only significant institution that remained as a rival and therefore a check upon its power (apart from the churches, for which there were other plans).

Family history and traditions were dangerous. Interest in the memory of an "ancestor" was but a short step from family pride and loyalty, and that was clearly and totally inimicable to the interests of Earth's good government, or, as far as they were distinguishable, of ARM.

But if the Vaughn-Nguyens thought too much of the past, that was useful to me now.

"The old colonel's tiger-man? Yes. Quite famous in its day," he said. Then he added perfectly casually, "Would you like to see the skin?"

I had not been expecting this. I looked at Arthur Vaughn-Nguyen closely. What was he really up to?

"You have it here?"

"Why, yes."

He led me into another room. The dog followed us for a few steps, and then stopped, making a peculiar noise.

"Is he all right?" I asked.

"You've just seen a family mystery in the flesh." He said, "No animal will go into that room." He laughed. "We say it's haunted by a ghost tiger."

Against the wall stood a large box of some dark wood, obviously very old, hand carved with decorations. It was much more elaborate than the one at the museum.

Another antique, and this time, I would have guessed, of great value. There was, I noticed, no electronic lock on it, no recording device. Impossible to prove when it had been opened last. Had any of the *Angel's Pencil* crew been here? I didn't fancy the time-consuming job of tracking down their movements over the last generation.

"It's in there?"

"We keep it here. We used it for a rug once, but it was put away, a long time ago."

It had been a crime to keep the skins of rare animals. In the days when there was a never-ending demand for material for the organ banks, and crimes, however minor, attracted only one punishment. Those days were long gone, but the Vaughn-Nguyens must have some genes for either courage or foolhardiness for one of their ancestors to have risked keeping the thing at all. Did this point to involvement in criminal behavior today?

"I'd like to see it very much," I said.

The chest smelled bad when it was opened, not powerful at first, but like nothing I have ever smelled before.

Like nothing I have ever smelled before? There was something about that smell, something that made me want to be away from that place. I guessed what it was after a moment, though I had never encountered it before: It must be the tiger smell. I got it under control easily enough. I heard, from the next room, a howl and a frantic scrabble of claws on flooring as the dog fled.

My host pulled out the skin and rolled it out across the floor.

Although parts were missing, it was huge as the skull we had seen was huge. It had longer legs than any tiger and it was still a blazing orange. There were some darker markings but it was not a normal tiger's striped pelt. It almost looked as if it had been made of some synthetic fabric (Perhaps it was. Well, that would be tested).

The head was enormous. It felt toylike when I examined it because the cavity where the skull had been was stuffed with some sort of papier-mâché, now crumbling. The jaws were set in a huge gape, and I thought absurdly for a moment how many feet must have caught on them when it was used as a rug. The eyes were glass balls, and the teeth ivory pegs.

The hind part and chest had been crudely stitched to pull it together around what I now guessed had been, assuming it was genuine, bullet holes.

"It hasn't got a tail," I said.

There was a ragged gap at the base of the spinal ridge where the pelt had been hacked.

"No," said my host, "there was meant to be something wrong with the tail. They didn't keep it."

"There seems to be something wrong with everything about it," I said. "But isn't there a breed of tailless cat?"

"I think so. The face is a cat's face, anyway. But look at those ears!"

A cat's face, yes, even with the strangely large skull. The ears were complex arrangements, still flexible, reminding me of bat wings or bits of umbrella. They turned to something like leather at the outer parts, and ended raggedly in what might once have been membrane. There was something else about them, too. I examined the dark, gristly surfaces more closely.

"They've been tattooed."

"Oh. With anything in particular?" He seemed not to have known this.

"I can't tell."

He got a lamp. Shining this through the outer membrane I could see a pattern. It seemed to be made up of . . . I called them "bones" for want of a better term.

"Who'd tattoo a tiger's ears? And why?"

"Tattooing a live tiger would be a difficult job, I'd think. It must have been dead. Perhaps to identify it."

"A creature as odd as this would hardly need further identification, I should think."

"You're right there. Look at the hands. That's where the 'Tiger-Man' idea comes in."

The oddly long forelimbs ended not in a tiger's pug paws but in four-digeted hands with black extremities. One of the digits on each was like a thumb.

Did they work like cat's claws? I pressed the pad of one digit. Nothing happened. I pressed harder and a claw emerged. A black claw. I touched it and then jerked my finger back, to suck at a bleeding gash. It was razor sharp.

All about was the fear smell. And a hint of something like . . . ginger.

"There's some of the colonel's other stuff here, too," he said. "It all goes together."

"It looks as if it hasn't been opened for a long time."

"No. I was shown it as a child, but it was getting pretty moldy even then. I didn't want to touch it too much, and since then there has hardly been a lot of call. The house was shut up for a long time." He would have been a child, I guess, about a hundred years before.

A wooden grating divided the top and bottom of the chest. The lower part contained rotting cloth. Some of this had once been dyed red, and on some was gold lace and wire, still unfaded. Parts of the colonel's "uniforms," I supposed.

The cloth parted at the folds as if cut with a knife. I had not realized before that ancient fabrics were so weak and perishable—or had they been weakened chemically to seem ancient?

Two metal things I recognized from ARM's special history course as weapons, one, called a "sword," for cutting, one, called a "revolver," was a sort of "gun" for projecting "bullets"—solid pieces of metal—by chemical explosion. I had had an idea the bullet-projector had come after the sword and was surprised to find they were evidently contemporaneous. Near the bottom was a bundle marked "Tiger-Man."

It contained some odds and ends wrapped further in cloth, and a piece of crumbling paper with what Vaughn-Nguyen said was the colonel's own handwriting: "This is what I found in the lair of the Tiger-Man."

There was one thing in this last bundle whose use and purpose I recognized at once: an oversized knife, almost the size of the colonel's "sword," but different, in a metal holder. When I drew it forth it was straight-bladed and, while the sword was black with age and pitted with rust, this looked new.

I am not a metallurgist, but the metal was different from any I had seen before. I took the sword in one hand and the sword-sized knife in the other. Their weight, balance and general feel were quite different too.

The old and rust-pitted sword was easier to move in my hand than the knife. The knife was too heavy and seemed badly designed. My fingers could only just close around the handle. There were grips for a hand bigger than mine, with one finger less. I held the two weapons up to the light, comparing their textures and cutting edges, then pressed the two blades against the wooden side of the box, not very hard. The rusty sword made no impression. The other cut into it effortlessly, as if it was edged with mono-molecular wire.

I apologized to Vaughn-Nguyen, and took it into the light. On the handle was a design in dots and claws.

The next thing was a hand-computer. But like the knife, built for an oversized hand, and of an unfamiliar design. It appeared to be damaged.

There was an oversized belt with pockets, and small metal artifacts. They and the computer-thing seemed to have come from the same shop and they had what looked like homogeneous power-couplings. On these too, and on the big knife, the bonelike design was repeated.

"There's also the old man's book," said Vaughn-Nguyen. "He wrote it for the family. There's a chapter on the Tiger-Man in it. Grandfather read it to us when I was a child. I think that was one of the last times we took the skin out of the chest. I don't imagine you can get copies of it anymore. It must have been out of print for a long time, and I don't think it was ever electronically transcribed."

He was right there. You couldn't get a large number of those old books. There were old mine-tunnels full of them, veins of cellulose running through Earth's geological strata. There were whole construction industries, even space industries, whose main products came from pulped and highly compressed paper. Some of our best and most expensive natural-grown food came from soil that had originated as books, sent to vermiculture farms to be passed through the bodies of worms. The "book-soil," or "B-plus Compost" to give it its trade name, helped form the hydroponics gardens for the first-class kitchens of luxury spaceships.

Vaughn-Nguyen was hardly in a position to know (or *was* he?) that the censoring, removal and destruction of politically incorrect books and similar records had been the main activity of several hundred thousand highly trained men and women for generations. Vaughn-Nguyen was not acting like a man who knew he was under investigation. He seemed genuinely relaxed and friendly. Or had he had training too? He had been completely cooperative so far. Or was that part of some secret agenda? He was a man it would be possible to like. I hoped that if he had to join the Military Historians in the canyons of Mars he would be reasonable happy there.

He turned to his bookcase, another elaborate antique affair with sliding glass doors, and handed something down, carefully.

"It's pretty fragile."

Vaughn-Nguyen did not want to let a Historian take family heirlooms away, even temporarily. I had to show him one of my identifications in the end. I also promised to return the things after examination.

Many pages of the book were missing, and several broke as I handled it. They didn't tear, just snapped and crumbled soundlessly. I learned sense then and stopped touching it. If it had been made of snowflakes, the thing could hardly have been less frail.

I had seen old books often enough professionally, but I had seldom had to puzzle out a lot of their contents. When in doubt, they went, as a general rule.

There were few pictures in the book and the ancient cramped layout and typefaces made it horribly difficult to read after a while, even though the spelling was relatively modern. I took a painkiller and then got the book to Bannerjee at the ARM Lab in New Sydney and had him photograph it before more harm was done. Then I got to the 'doc for treatment for my finger. I had hardly ever seen real blood before, certainly not my own, and I did not like the sight. Once, people like Colonel Vaughn must have seen a lot of blood.

The 'doc treated my finger, but nothing else. O'Brien's direction on that matter had gone right through the system. I slept badly that night. A headache the 'doc again refused to medicate. A slight throb in my finger, all adding up to the unpleasant novelty of *pain*. It was like living in a fant book, I thought sourly, living, perhaps, as the military fants wanted it. And maybe my system was changing.

• CHAPTER 4

> I had been asked to travel to the Mohne Dam, that structure
> at the head of the Ruhr Valley which was breached by the
> "Dambusters" 50 years ago, to research an anniversary
> article. [There was] no clue as to the events of that night
> of May 16/17, 1943. There are no plaques, no memorials,
> no postcards. There are no twisted chunks of bomb casing
> mounted on a concrete plinth. There is no roll call of the
> drowned. Nothing. Girls sunbathed in the 80 degree
> sunshine and a couple of yachts moved sleepily in the
> light breeze.
> —Peter Tory, *International Express*, May 19–25, 1993

Bannerjee called me next morning, with the pages nicely
enlarged and cleaned, and with a parallel text on the screen
supplied in modern type which had been scanned from the
legible parts and which I could read without developing a
headache.

I kept him hooked up and we read the pages together.
The book began with a conventional description of the colonel's
family, apparently ancient even when the words had been
set down. I soon found the chapter heading I wanted.

> The Indians said the tiger had come to the district
> a few months before. It had come, they said, in a
> blaze of light during a thunderstorm.
>   Certainly their superstitious awe could be
> explained by its extraordinary ferocity. Man-eaters
> in these parts generally adopt anthropophagy
> because owing to age or injury they can no longer

42

pursue and pull down swifter and stronger game. But in this case men, cattle (including buffaloes), deer, bears and other creatures tame and wild, including even elephants, appeared to have fallen victim to a single beast. It attacked by day as well as by night, and even seemed to favor the daylight hours. It was said to be fearless and made little or no effort to conceal itself, save when it was plainly stalking for pleasure.

Efforts to kill it by a band of determined villagers had ended in disaster. Once it had disposed of them, it came into the village itself and wrought havoc.

Then the survivors had fled en masse. Yet these were tough hillmen who regard the tiger as a natural foe and will, if there is not a British regiment in the area with breech-loading repeaters and perhaps a few elephants, normally be prepared to tackle any beast on foot with tower-muskets.

There had been found, indeed, the half-eaten body of another tiger it had apparently defeated, and that, said Sher Ali, the descendant of generations of hunters and marksmen who examined it and knows tigers well (he had even taken his name from them), had been a Royal Beast. I will write of Sher Ali more, for he proved himself that day and was to be long in my service, though I cannot say I took him for a servant. Rather, in the way of the Pathan— and he was an Afridi—he took me for his master. The tiger had spread terror far and wide. There were plenty of stories afoot among the villages that our quarry was in fact a demon, or a ghost.

Indeed, but for the descriptions of it that a few lucky ones who had seen it and survived had brought back, we ourselves should have been doubtful that it was a tiger at all. Its spoor was quite unlike that of any tiger's pugmarks. Curlewis suggested its paws had been burnt to deformity in some forest fire. But then how could it travel so far and so swiftly?

We plotted the pattern of its kills on an ordinance map. . . .

There was another gap here. From what was left of the page it appeared the map he referred to had been reproduced in a foldout form. Some of the village names and contour lines were left on the remaining part and I suckered a copy of this from the screen.

It was a well-provisioned shikar, the best we could manage. We left as little to chance as possible, and owing to what we had heard of the beast's size, took the largest caliber of rifles we had: elephant guns for our first weapons. We had Express rifles with the exploding bullets from the Dum-Dum Arsenal, and of course reliable military Martinis, borrowed from the infantry (I didn't think our own carbines would be much use). We also had two of the new American Winchesters which the brigadier-general had asked us to try out. The bearers and beaters, we made sure, were well equipped with gongs, rockets, torches and guns. Sher Ali selected only the steadiest men for beaters.

It roamed far afield, but its regular lair, we were told, was in the adjacent valley where it had first been seen, which was now virtually depopulated. Indeed the country was now almost empty of human inhabitants for miles around. Those that had not been devoured had fled.

Not only, it seemed, was this tiger more voracious and aggressive than any man-eater I had ever heard of, but it was faster and more cunning. No horse would stay near its tracks.

With the aid of the map we had carefully worked out a plan to disperse the beaters to drive the beast towards our guns when we had positioned ourselves in its valley. Never, in the event, did any plan prove more unnecessary. . . .

There was another gap here. The passage referring to the first part of the tiger hunt seemed to have been lost. Presumably the most frequently referred to part of the book had suffered the most wear and tear. The next few pages had had to be cleaned of old dirt.

It was not to be like any stalk I have ever known. A bold tiger will sometimes not trouble overmuch to conceal its tracks. This beast had left them everywhere. The path from the valley where it had first been seen and where it was now headquartered was beaten like a highway.

It was a strange, oppressive day. The hills seemed lowering. The bandar—the monkeys—had disappeared from the trees and all the birds were silent. Any hunter will tell you of the strange silence when the world of nature puts aside its business as a hunt begins, but this was a more intense silence than any I had ever felt. I worried that it might affect the bearers' nerves. And though I had no doubt as to his courage, I saw the sweat of Sher Ali's face. I could not see my own, but I felt my heart beating faster than I liked. Sher Ali was my gun and I gave silent thanks that he was an Afridi and from what I knew of that breed—for we had taken tea with them many times on the Northwest Frontier—he would die a thousand deaths before he gave way to any fear he felt, least of all in front of these eastern hillmen.

I felt danger very near in that silence as we set out from the camp in the early morning light. For the sake of all our people's *morale*, as the French call it, we wore our uniforms and, not much more practically, or so I thought at the time, I ordered the guns to be loaded and cocked then and there. I would not be writing these words today if I had not obeyed that second impulse.

And then we heard a sound: a snarling roar louder

than any tiger I have heard, louder than the roar of
an African lion. . . .

Sher Ali saw it first: an orange spot moving
through the trees, its coat strangely bright in the
shadows. It was not hiding from us, nor was it stalking
us, I realized. No sooner had it seen our party, men,
guns, beasts and all, than it moved to the attack! . . .

. . . faster than any tiger I have known, moving
towards us with a strange loping gait like that of an
English weazel. But a beast three or four times the
bulk of a man! It came . . .

The beast shrieked again with a cry like no tiger
I have heard before. Utterly fearless, it charged
straight uphill towards our party! Such speed! Two
of the beaters in its way were flung aside and killed
by no more than a passing blow of its paws. It was
coming straight at me as if it knew my purpose and
had singled me out from among all the rest.

The size of it! I thank the Lord I had the elephant
gun with me, not the Martini. I was sure the first
shot hit it, a shot to knock down a tusker, but it
appeared to impede its progress not at all. It was
almost upon me when I fired the second time: a bad
shot, for the creature, again like no tiger I have seen
before, reared up on it hind legs as I fired. I was
quick of eye and hand in those days, but the beast
was quicker than I, quicker than anything I had
known.

I had aimed at the head, hoping to take the eyes
and lungs together, as you sometimes can with a
tiger charging head-on. But the exploding bullet must
have struck it in the pelvis, from the manner in which
it collapsed. Yet it seemed, despite its wounds, to
be gathering itself as I fired again. I heard the guns
of the others behind me.

Again, the third shot was one I was not proud of. You would not understand the difficulties unless you fully comprehended not merely the size of the beast but also its speed. With astonishing quickness—a quickness that would have been astonishing even had it not been gravely wounded—it hurled itself aside. More shots hit it: from the elephant guns, the Martinis, the Winchesters. The tower-muskets of the tribesmen joined in. I saw the bullets hitting. A normal beast would have been blown into several pieces by those impacts.

Yet even then it was not finished. It rolled into the undergrowth and a moment later we heard it crashing away. It passed close to Sher Ali (Great Heart! When the magazine of his repeater was empty, he did not stop to reload, but drew his Khyber knife!), and I heard the others pumping shot after shot from the Winchesters after it.

I was sure the shots were mortal. It had absorbed enough lead to kill a herd of elephants, yet no wounded tiger can be left. I was deafened, my head was ringing and my nose bleeding from the concussion of the .606.

I examined the beaters who had fallen. Sadly, a swift examination was all that was needed. One had been decolloped, the other torn almost into two pieces by those claws. As soon as I might I called for Maclean, Curlewis, Sher Ali and the head beaters to follow me.

Mortally wounded or not, it traveled quickly, up a thickly grown rocky hillside. The blood trail was easy to follow but the blood was strange. It seemed sometimes purple and sometimes orange. There was orange hair, fragments of meat and smashed bone, even entrail. I knew the exploding bullets had done their work well.

But the too-deep quietness was still sending a message to our hunting instincts. Somehow I knew the brute was not dead yet. But it was no longer shrieking and it could not be heard. I did not believe it was dying quietly. It was, I felt somehow certain, husbanding its well-nigh unbelievable strength and vitality for a last charge. I was glad indeed of the trusty guns behind me!

We searched the jungle-grown rock holes for a long time, or so it seemed with every nerve keyed up. We had followed our quarry into a long, deep ravine that twisted and turned. Overgrown, with dark clefts and overhangs. Then we heard the creature again. It was not roaring and snarling, but its strange voice, muffled by distance, rose and fell like water on a dying fire. It came from deeper within the ravine.

By now the morning mist was lifting off the distant hilltops. I remember the reluctance with which I led the way down. I looked at those hilltops where I had hunted innocent sambar and musk deer and wondered if I would see them again. The high rocky walls almost shut us off from the sky so that it seemed to us as if we were deep underground.

Then suddenly there was a deafening crack and a flash across the sky. So loud was it I did not know whether it was lightning immediately overhead (though it was louder than any thunderclap I have heard, even in the mountain country) or a hundred batteries of artillery firing simultaneously. A blast of hot air smote us. Across the crest of the ridge a vast column of dust boiled into the sky like smoke. I have seen a magazine explode in a bombardment, but this far eclipsed that detonation. The wind picked up stones and flung them so we covered our faces.

Leaving even the hunt for a moment, and turning our backs on our quarry as we should never do, we hurried up the slope. A vast avalanche had torn away half the side of the next valley. The tiger that was said to have come in a thunderstorm died in the midst of another great convulsion of nature.

So great was the force of the avalanche that we saw trees and boulders flung high in the air above us, to crash down again adding to the ruin below. We stood and stared at it for many minutes, but before such a cataclysm we were helpless. We could do no more than pray that no unfortunate souls had been trapped in the landslide's path. Luckily, as I have mentioned, all the people in that valley had already fled from the tiger's predations. There would have been no hope for any who had remained.

"He was on the top of a ridge, and he saw a *landslide* in the next valley throw trees and boulders high in the air *above* him?"

"That's what it says. He goes on."

As the sounds of the avalanche died away, we heard again the sound of our quarry. No other tiger I have heard before or since made such a sound, resembling almost articulate speech. But now it was weaker, and I thought I could hear blood in its lungs. Guided by these sounds through the thick undergrowth, we saw at last a cave entrance, and the blood trail entering it.

One remembers smells from such times. There was the landslide smell of pulverized flint filling my nostrils, as well as a strange gingery smell, and blood.

A hunter and a soldier must at times do dangerous things, but there is no wisdom or glory in foolhardiness. Maclean, Curlewis and I waited at the entrance with our guns ready and sent the bearers back for torches and rockets. Several were moaning on the ground and vomiting, I believe through hysteria induced by the two excitements of the chase and the awesome convulsion of nature we had just witnessed. When my friends at length returned we fired several rockets into the cave in the hope of flushing the beast out.

At last, not, I confess, liking the work particularly, I entered the cave, with a light held well before me, and all of us with the triggers of all our guns at their first pressures. There lay the tiger. Its forepaw appeared to be holding something.

It was plainly dying. Its hindquarters were shattered and it lay in a pool of its own blood. It had been burnt again by the rockets that lay flickering out around it. Yet at the sight of us it gathered itself as if to spring.

It cried out again, and I swear that there was something in the tone of its voice that told me it was asking some question! I have heard a wounded Pathan warrior die so, crying out, I believe, to know the name of the warrior who killed him.

It sprang as well as it could. Our guns discharged together. All aimed at the chest, and it was blown backwards against the cave wall. Still, it made another attempt to attack us as we fired shot after shot into it from our repeaters, clawing and dragging itself along the ground, still shrieking and snarling in its strange voice. I never imagined any beast so hard to kill. But at last it died.

When we examined the beast closely, I was astonished, and moved to pity for it. I said most man-eaters are old or crippled beasts. That is why there is no particular sport in hunting them: They are simply vermin.

I have seen deformed beasts before, that are sports or unhappy freaks of nature, but this was the most deformed I have ever seen. Pity? Why should a soldier not feel pity for an enemy once he has done his job and the enemy lies dead before him? But when I examined the great carcass more closely, I was overcome with bewilderment and a strange sort of fear such as I have never felt before. I had thought of my quarry as a noble beast, though a man-eater. But now, what can I say?

What can I say? Should I write a tale none will believe? I write this as an old done man, with my career behind me. I do not wish to be called mad, yet I have set out to tell the plain narrative of my life, and I have the skull and the skin with me yet. The creature had not paws but hands! And its head was like the head of no tiger I have ever seen.

Was it a previously unknown species that had wandered down from the high snows of Thibet? The tail was wrong, too. Hairless and pink like that of some giant rat. There was something disgusting about that tail.

Do not think me mad, but I have lived in the East long and seen something of Eastern magic and know that mysteries exist we of the West cannot solve. Even in an Indian cantonment, I have seen things which would not be believed were I to recount them in London or Sydney.

Was this creature the product of Thibetian magic? Was it indeed a Demon? If I attend Church-parade and pray to the God at the head of my men, how can I not, in the end, be prepared to accept the existence of Demons too?

But could a Demon be killed with a shot from my rifle? This was a flesh-and-blood creature.

In many a village I and others have heard stories of ghosts and were-tigers: tigers shot at night whose bodies were never found, but next day some man in the village—usually the local moneylender—was found dead in his house with a bullet in him. I never gave these stories much countenance when first I heard them in my early years in the East, but the skin of the Tiger-Man is before me as I write.

Then, too, there was the thing clasped in its furred beast's *hand*, and the things we found a little way away, whose origin and nature none can guess. Are the things we found the works of Thibetian priests? What is the writing on the heavy knife? I have enquired since of Mr. Lockwood Kipling of the Lahore Museum and he says he has seen none like it. I leave it to others to make sense of these things.

Did the tiger previously devour some traveler in that cave? Or were those things left there by no more than chance, perhaps by Ruhmalwallahs or other secret travelers? Were they connected with the tiger at all? Why did it clutch at that object as it died? Sher Ali, when he could be persuaded to enter the cave (and I could hardly understand his fear now that the beast was dead, that Bravest of the Brave when it was alive!) seemed almost to lose his wits. He babbled that the tiger had brought the things there itself! And yet, his words have stayed in my mind. . . .

Mr. Kipling's famous son has written for one of his poems: "Still the world is wondrous large—seven seas from marge to marge— / And it holds a vast of various kinds of man / And the wildest dreams of Kew are the facts of Khatmandhu. . . ," and also he has since written stories of a boy raised by wolves in India. Perhaps those stories have a germ in my Tiger-Man. But what I shot was no man raised by tigers. Of that at least I am sure. As I have said before, and as all white men who have served there long know, the East is full of mysteries.

But perhaps this was not the only one of its kind. Perhaps there are other such tigers in the high fastnesses of Thibet. We have heard tell of other strange creatures there. Is the Tiger-Man one with the man-eating Yeti or Migou that the Thibetians dread?

The chapter ended and a new one began.

Two weeks after the killing of what the Mess came to call "Vaughn's Tiger-Man" we received orders for the Frontier where we would join the Dirragha Expeditionary Force under Brigadier-General Bindon. I had been ill for several days, ever since we got back to the cantonment, in fact, and I spent the first part of the campaign in hospital. It was some fever unlike any I have had before, and Curlewis and Maclean also succumbed. . . .

There were several chapters devoted to "border skirmishes," and another game called "polo" of which the colonel had evidently been fond.

There were descriptions, too, of ancient Indian rituals I knew nothing about, like "durbars" and "famines," of ceremonies and "manoeuvres." There were also a few ancient flat photographs, of poor quality. He had been told, at last, by his doctor (all had human doctors then) to settle in a climate that was free of both the fevers of India and the winter cold of England.

I turned to the last pages:

> In the service of the Empire I have spent much of my life in exile. But it has been, at the end, a life I would have changed for none other. I have written this little book for my sons. Never since I left the East has my health been good, but I have survived several illnesses and I am not quite ready to die yet. I have felt, sometimes, old before my time, but if that is so then I must say that my old age has been blessed with an unexpected marriage, children, and life in a new country full of promise. But in my gladness is one sorrow: I know I can hardly expect to live long enough for my sons to know me as men.
>
> Therefore, I have set down these reminiscences of times past and distant places, that they may know of their father's deeds in the service of the Queen-Empress and the Empire that is our common heritage, that they may know of our traditions of service, and know, too, that they come of a family with traditions of its own. Soldier's sons . . .

The last page had crumbled away entirely. I spent several hours going through ARM files and ancient library stacks in various parts of the world. There had been several popular accounts of the "tiger-man" published in the nineteenth century, though all these were gone except the various scraps and fragments I had seen already. The colonel had even given lectures about it in his retirement.

Given time and patience, and knowing what he was looking for, any researcher with a medium-to-high-security clearance could have found all this out. I left Bannerjee working on the other artifacts.

None of the Vaughn-Nguyen family had any apparent or recorded connection with the military fant cults. But one of Vaughn-Nguyen's sons had gone to the Belt. The other was a deep-sea farmer and miner, who had access to biological engineering shops *and* metallurgical labs. He was rich. Rich families generally stayed that way by wanting to get richer.

Vaughn-Nguyen had no wife now. He had left the farm at an early age and had returned to it only a few years before. Much of his life had been spent working with dolphins. There were no trips into space recorded, only excursion flights to the moon. During his absence the farm had been run by robots, and the buildings had been sealed for about eighty years.

An hour later the clincher came: Paul Vaughn-Nguyen who had gone to the Belt was the same Paul Vaughn in my dossier: the systems-controller in the *Angel's Pencil*.

There seemed little more to investigate. We knew who now. It only remained to clear up the question of why.

But something about the photographs in the colonel's book nagged me. I had them enlarged and computer enhanced. It took me several days to work out what was puzzling about them.

There was one taken of him as a young "captain," posed with a group of other men dressed in strange clothes, at the conclusion of the famous tiger hunt.

The tiger itself had been dragged out and skinned and lay on the ground a dark mass, the skin and raw skull beside it. The old photograph preserved no details of morphology. Further, the three men and another differently dressed—

Sher Ali, I presumed—were standing with their feet on the body, obscuring it further.

The next photograph was another of the colonel, presumably as an older man, standing posed with a group of others shortly after the "Dirragha Campaign," which, I discovered, appeared to have been not a game but some sort of conflict.

Vaughn wore more or less the same odd clothing in both. The captions identified the others with him, including two who appeared in both photographs called Captain Curlewis and Lieutenant Maclean. There was another photograph of Sher Ali. All the photographs had been taken by one Hurree Mukkerjee, who was described as the "Original Brigade and Regimental Photographer." Photography, even primitive photography like this, was rare enough in those days for the photographer's name to be thought worth preserving.

But surely all *real* wars had ended long before that? Soldiers even then had been anachronisms, reduced, as I had learned from our courses, to minor policing duties like this of hunting dangerous animals in wild country. Had there been groups of criminals . . . what was the word . . . banditos? brigantes? . . . that they had apprehended?

Something did not add up.

And soldiers had used rockets?

It was like military fant stuff.

I slept badly again that night. And I kept seeing the faces of the Military Historians. They were like a snag in my mind. And they worried me not only for themselves, but for the very fact I thought about them now. One who does what I do has no business thinking too much upon those it is his duty to care for.

They were still in the hospital. By law, they had a certain time to go through the formality of an appeal. Finally, and I was not sure why I did this, I sent an order to delay the memory-wipe.

• CHAPTER 5

> Our inability, with all our great resources, to answer the comparatively simple question: "Are we alone in the galaxy?" is maddening. But it is also, as Professor [Glen David] Brin points out, somewhat frightening. It is all very well to suggest, as others have done, that the reason for the Great Silence is that no other civilizations exist, but there may be a more sinister explanation. . . . It is not only the dead who are silent, so also is . . . the predator. . . .
> —Adrian Berry, *Ice with Your Evolution*, 1986

We had planned a six-month-long festival of concerts and games. My own section had little to do with it, but a lot of ARM resources were involved. We had several hundred people I knew about and a lot of computer time invested simply in researching and inventing games, music and dances, and an investment many times greater than that in promoting them.

It looked as if, when the history subprogram was completed, new games would vie with landscape redesign as one of our major activities, rather than those things usually identified with ARM's public image.

I knew what effort had gone into the games, especially "Graceful Willow," with its premium on good losing, but of course they weren't for me. I had been busy since returning from Australia, and a lot of my time had been taken up persuading Alfred O'Brien to give me access to files with higher security classifications.

I began to read about weapons again. I had thought at first that the placing of the "sword" and the "revolver" together in the colonel's chest might have been an anachronistic mistake by the hoaxers, but I learned swords had been carried by "officers" for ceremonies and rituals long after they ceased to have any practical use. Sometimes, in warrior cultures, they had been handed down from father to son. But in any case, by 1878, surely both sword and revolver would have been equally ceremonial?

I began to realize how little I knew. Take it that the original story at least was true: then Colonel Vaughn had shot the tiger-man in a primitive and dangerous hunt less than a hundred years before the beginning of the Space Age.

And *then*, it seemed, he had been in a war! Wars as recently as the nineteenth century? When every schoolchild had been taught that they had ended at the same time as, by definition, civilization and recorded history began?

We in ARM literary section knew they had ended later, but still hundreds of years before that. Before Columbus, before Galileo.

But everything I had read and researched recently—and this time it was not fiction like the old books I had been involved in destroying, but official records—showed armies in the 1870s. Granted that crime control had been primitive then, and the world dangerous and still partially unexplored. But all for police duties and tiger hunting? I was having trouble believing it.

Among the history taught and displayed in our museums the date 1943 was a touchstone. Every child knew that was when von Braun had launched the first successful rockets to study cosmic rays and weather: the Vetterraketen, or V-1 and V-2. Society must have made great advances in a short time during the twentieth century for wars and armies to have disappeared so quickly and space flight to have got under way. Improbably great.

Suppose those old books of pathological fiction and fantasy I had helped suppress had not all been fictions? And there had been so many of them!

There was something else: Apparently harmless books on comparative literature and ancient literary construction had had very high priority, not for suppression and concealment, but for total, immediate destruction. Why? Was it perhaps so operators like me would not be able to tell fictional techniques from documentary ones?

There had been the continual warnings, both overt and subliminal, when I first joined the literary section, warnings of the absolutely *fatal* career consequences of becoming *too interested in the work*.

Why hadn't I seen these things before when I saw them now? Because I had been off medication for days and that medication had included an intelligence depressant? How much intelligence did you need to recognize a fant book or infiltrate a fant cult? Not a lot, I began to understand. Schizies like Anton Brillov and Jack Strather, in a different section and with different personal programs, had had access to far more real history than I.

And the fant cults themselves . . . why were they so persistent and, within certain parameters, so consistent? Why had past generations manufactured bizarre artifacts like "toy soldiers" and the plastic "models kits," fragments of which still occasionally come to light?

The Lady May's question on her way to memory-wipe came back to me: *Had* I known what I had been destroying?

The program had been to remove a strand of destructive madness from human culture, as its genetic aspect was to remove, eventually, a gene of destructive madness from the human gene pool. Useless and dangerous. But my own condition was madness without treatment, like the schizies ARM kept employed and did not medicate during working hours. Were we useless and dangerous? Presumably when the program was concluded we would be.

But too many things were not meshing. Or rather, too many of the *wrong* things were meshing. Things I had never thought about before.

I knew ARM kept forbidden knowledge even from its own people beyond what we needed to know, dangerous facts as well as dangerous inventions, but now I could not close my mind to all the inconsistencies displayed to me.

I tried to follow other thoughts: When the *Angel's Pencil*

had left Earth, the program had been less far advanced. There might well have been crew aboard who had studied the more sensitive areas of history.

And the gross, glaring scientific errors in their descriptions of the alleged alien craft's capabilities: Were they deliberate signals, perhaps inserted by some crew member who did not want to be party to the business?

Bannerjee called again. He had been working on the artifacts in New Sydney.

"It's an electronic book," he said. "Look: you speak in here, and this is a memory bank of some sort. This is a display screen. It's a notebook. At least, I don't see what else it could be."

"Can you read it?"

"It's damaged. I had it speaking back to me for a minute. At least I think it was speech, not just noise corruption. Sounded like a catfight. And it's weird. The circuit design is quite odd. I can tell you the metal's been grown in space. Real high-tech stuff."

"How old is it?"

"It would have to be pretty new, I'd say. Newer than it smells. It may be something the Belt dreamed up."

"It's *meant* to have come from India," I said. "It's meant to be very old."

"Umm . . . my father was keen on India. Brass bowls all over the house. This isn't brass though. Definitely Space Age. We had ancestors on the first Indian space program, you know. Well, the circuitry seems to be in order. I can give it power again, and see what happens."

I stood by while he powered the thing up. There was a hissing, screeching sound. I couldn't tell if it was articulated or simply malfunctioning electronics. But it did seem varied and modulated as speech might be. Behind Bannerjee on the screen I could see other screens: banks of computers with endlessly changing arrays of numbers. I knew the class of those computers and felt awed and more than a little alarmed at what their use must be costing someone. This investigation of a hoax was getting out of hand.

"There's a relatively small group of frequently recurring sounds," said Bannerjee. "If it's plain language and not encrypted, that might give us a start."

"Keep me stitched in."

I watched the groups of numbers and phonetic symbols dancing on the green sheets of glassine behind Bannerjee's dark face. The shape of the hoax was becoming clearer: I guessed that the tiger was to be presented as some sort of lost alien.

The Vaughn-Nguyens had used the story of their ancestor's freak tiger as a starting point or inspiration for this. But why?

The "language" in the "book" was explained easily. A computer wrote it. Imaginary alien languages were a staple of some legitimate imaginative writing, and there were whole societies dedicated to concocting them, as there were societies of bored people dedicated to many things. ARM ran most of them. The language would have to be translatable eventually. It would be gilding the lily for those who had concocted it to have put it in cypher as well.

The "relics," organic and inorganic? Easy enough to fake, given time and high-tech resources.

As far as I was concerned one possibility as least had been eliminated. That was that there might be a *real* space sickness and the reports of felinoid aliens had been products of genuine madness, triggered, perhaps, by some subconscious childhood memory of the story of the Vaughn Tiger-Man and too many hours in a virtual reality programmer. This had been deliberately constructed before the *Angel's Pencil* left Earth.

Was it an odd form of political rebellion, connected somehow with the Vaughn-Nguyens' notions of family pride? That was possible, too. Quite likely there were several motives.

An ancient tiger freak had been killed. That, as far as I could tell, had really happened. I did not think *all* the records I had searched could have been tampered with, or the direction of my searches anticipated. Apart from the accounts published later I had, after getting a special permit, retrieved the relevant part of the 4th Lancers' "Regimental Diary" from underground archives in an operation more like archeology than historical research.

I remembered the old photographs, the two pictures of the colonel and his friends.

They were of the same respective "ranks" in both photographs, and from what the book said the two had been taken only a short time apart.

Yet between the taking of the first picture and the second, these three had aged years. In the first picture Curlewis wore a strange "pith helmet" which covered his head, but the others had evidently lost theirs and were bareheaded. They had full heads of hair, though cropped close in a way that looked strange beside today's fashions, and all three had mustaches. In the second picture, taken before some ceremonial dinner, all three were bareheaded, and all three were completely bald.

And there was the picture of the Indian hunter, Sher Ali, too. He wore an odd piece of cloth wound round his head in both pictures, but in his second photograph his face had been hairless. In the first, with the dead tiger, he had had a flowing black beard and mustache.

I called ARM, and there was another deep expedition into ancient British archives. Both Curlewis and Maclean had retired early, owing to recurrent illness.

Births and deaths had to be registered in Britain before the end of the nineteenth century, and with their army numbers it was, as it turned out, relatively easy to track them down. Both had died in their fifties, of cancer. Colonel Vaughn had lived longer. I had to go to the Australian records to find his death certificate, but he had eventually died of cancer, too.

ARM's bio-labs were still testing the skin and fur. So far they had been unable to match them with any known felines. In fact they had discovered quite radical differences. Now they were taking the dried tissue apart molecule by molecule, and from what they told me they were baffled by what they were finding.

But I still did not know the Vaughn-Nguyens' motives. I ran the possibilities through my mind again.

We had started with the presumption that if the story of a madness involving delusions of horrible aliens was somehow taken seriously, the immediate result would be to inhibit space exploration, but, as had also been immediately obvious, a scam would be very hard to get away with, at least on Earth. ARM would have records of anyone selling heavily in space-industry shares.

Religious fanatics? Highly unlikely, we ran most cults.

Chiliastic panics? ARM knew about them too. It had acted to turn several of them off (or on). This could, given promotion, be a socio-political forest fire. But why light such a fire at all?

I even wondered if it was an internal ARM power play. ARM's resources would make setting up even such a complex hoax relatively easy.

If that was so, there was nothing I could do. ARM was no monolith, I knew. There were conflicts in it, factions and sometimes accelerated promotions and early retirements, but the idea of ARM hoaxing ARM smelled wrong. If my intuition was worth anything at all, that wasn't the answer.

The artifacts? Where had they come from? Bannerjee had mentioned the Belt. Space-grown metals?

Were the Vaughn-Nguyens Belter agents? Earth-Belt rivalry had been (I was told) relatively dormant for generations, but any inhibition of Earth's space activities would give the Belt comparative advantage.

A story about warlike aliens—or of delusions about warlike aliens—would not do that *in itself*, but it could be a start point in long-term psychological gaming.

Next, perhaps, physical remains would be produced. Not virtual-reality products this time but "real" flesh-and-blood Jenny Hannifers grown in vats in Belt laboratories, perhaps the result of genetic tinkering with zoo felines. Had there been any thefts of genetic material from zoos recently? What genetic material might be available in Belt zoos or universities already?

Did the Belt have zoos? Living space was limited there but I knew that on Confinement Asteroid, which had been artificially created to provide an Earth-gravity environment for births, there had been a relatively large amount of extra space, years ago, space given over in part to parks, entertainment facilities and . . . zoos? But the Belt's population was bigger now. I asked for up-to-date data on Confinement.

And surely on the bigger asteroids there would be at least a few domestic cats. There were cats in space, too, as mousers (the superefficient—as they always reminded us—Belt might have done better, but the bigger flatlander ships such as cruise-liners never seemed quite able to eliminate the very last mouse), as company for spacers on lonely ships and rocks and as medical aids. A number of people were still kept in low gravities because of heart conditions, and for an ailurophile the old prescription of stroking and playing with a cat was still one of the best nonmedical tranquilizers known. Hell! The Belters must have a complete library of DNA codes and could grow and sew and splice what they liked!

The hoax could be built up in stages. Next, an "alien" spaceship with specially grown "alien" cadavers could be crashed on Earth or conveniently be "found" in space. It might even be arranged that one or two Earth ships would disappear as further proof that here was something hostile and horrible in the black void reaching beyond the solar gravity-well. Something coming to get us. No, not just "something": big orange catlike aliens. Hideous fanged carnivores in possession of technology far outreaching our own, images crafted by someone's perverted genius so that they were a terror even to look upon . . . triggering ancestral memories of the ancient predator: the feline was the most perfect killing machine nature had produced. An image for the minds of Earth's masses to seize on . . . Earth's masses for whom boredom was today the greatest enemy and the future's major anticipated social problem. An image came into my own mind of straw in a flame.

But *why*? I had got no closer to an answer to that question. I found it difficult to imagine any gain that could possibly justify such an investment of time and resources. Vaughn-Nguyen would tell us when a warrant was issued to take him in, but by then he might have alerted confederates and other damage might be done.

What if the motive was to impoverish Earth and weaken it relative to the Belt? Creating a war panic could do that.

That was a Belter-cunning idea: to win a real economic war by having Earth divert its resources preparing for a false war!

Would even the Belters be capable of such a crime? *Even* the Belters? What was I thinking of? Belters were people like us . . . surely? Thinking that way lay . . . an abyss.

I was no longer inclined to believe the conspirators wanted us to think they had been sent into a state of crazy delusions by some effect of prolonged deep-space travel. Their objective was more radical than that: They wanted us to believe the big catlike aliens were real. Hence the elaborate preparations at the Earth end.

Perhaps that was why some brave Earth crew member aboard the *Angel's Pencil* had secretly rewritten the message program to destroy its credibility, by putting in not just warlike aliens but obviously impossible inertia-proof aliens with reactionless drives whose ship could match velocities with another travelling at .8 light-speed and ignore Delta-V!

Or was that too complex? Look at simpler economic motives: inhibiting space colonization would cause a stock-market crash. The block-busting. But then there would be a flow of money that could hardly be concealed for long. It could be done through dummy companies and cutouts, even off-planet. Again, the Belt would make a good hiding place for the real manipulations. There were rumors of many things hidden in the Belt, even weapon hoards. Vaughn-Nguyen was complaining to the museum that he wanted his property back.

War with the Belt? It was out of the question. Space flight and war were incompossible. What gave this whole investigation its crazy aspect in the first place was that to think or speak of a race simultaneously warlike and scientific made no more sense than to speak or think of a square circle. But economic war? Economic . . . what was the word . . . sabotage?

And there had been that *accusing* look in the Military Historian's eyes. Why should that concern me? Look at what was before me: a massive, if still enigmatic, conspiracy that was quite enough to keep me fully occupied.

The Vaughn-Nguyens, whether principals or agents, had set themselves up to be investigated and to emerge with their story enhanced. The "tiger," the provable source of the hoax and thus seeming at first a potential weakness, could be turned into a point in its favor: It would not have taken great resources of imagination to think of turning it into some sort of lost or exiled alien.

I called Bannerjee again. He thought he had begun to make a breakthrough with the language. He had identified certain frequently recurring groups of sounds and he had reasoned that anything purporting to be the records of a solitary creature stranded on an alien world would contain the word "I." Further, anything purporting to be the record of a space-traveling alien could be expected to make reference to space, space travel, spaceships and drives. I suggested to him that he look for the word "bone" or "bones," too, remembering the design I had seen.

The people who had cooked this up would want the language to be difficult—very difficult—to translate, it would have no credibility otherwise, but not quite impossibly difficult—that would defeat whatever their purpose was (Their purpose? To create a belief in aliens? Why? Why?).

There had been fads from the late twenty-first century at least about such things, claims the pyramids and Easter Island statues and circles in cornfields were made by aliens. Hadn't there been a film, suppressed centuries ago, about something called a Darth Vader? These had no foundation in any science, but they had made some people rich.

Were there still Cuthulu (was that the word?) worshipers?

Believers in old gods, not unlike the various military fant cults. Had frustrated, space-sick Arthur been involved? I was quite sure, remembering his literary collection, that even if he was not a full military fant he was on that path. Had he played a part and deliberately pointed me at the Vaughn-Nguyens? No. I had sought him out myself. Had Alfred O'Brien pointed me before that, with his quotation of the strange poem? Why? Why?

Motive? Motive? I had a teasing feeling somewhere in the back of my skull that the whole answer to the inexplicable situation was something much simpler that I was missing.

Careful. Lose the plot and I was useless. But . . . the museum. I suddenly knew something about the museum was important . . . not the British museum, with its ancient vaults, but Arthur's, with its educational displays and its ARM offices above. There was something there. . . .

Something . . . I tried to let the images and associations run freely. . . . Guthlac's dreams of space were involved, of going to Wunderland . . . No, not Guthlac's dreams, my own similar dreams, from long ago. Why was that important? The museum . . . Wunderland. They were connected?

Wunderland, the nearest and oldest-established extrasolar colony in the Centauri system, four and a half light-years away . . . settled originally largely by a North European consortium, led by families from Germany, Holland, Scandinavia and the Baltic countries. German . . . I had learned German long ago, with the dream of Wunderland in my head.

German, and the museum with its history of space flight and science displays . . . space flight . . . they were connected . . . an ancient rocket in flight . . . a German rocket . . .

And now a thought came driving in from my peculiar chemistry, enigmatic still, but hard and sharp and clear: the designations of V-1 and V-2 could not have stood for "weather rockets."

The German word for *weather* was not spelled "*Vetter*" but "*Wetter.*" It was pronounced as if, to an English speaker, it began with a V, but it actually began with a W.

It mattered. At that moment I didn't know why. But something felt different for me.

Isolated. Childless, long celibate. Schizies are often attractive. People like me less so. A secret policeman without attachments. Resentful, more or less, of my condition. Why was I suddenly feeling . . . no, there was no other word for it . . . grateful? Grateful for loneliness and lovelessness? Grateful that I had no one? Why did the world suddenly seem more . . . not exactly more beautiful, but more . . . precious?

Leave it. Any answer would surface by itself. I had other puzzles before me.

Three British soldiers dying of cancer. But surely in those days cancer had not been a big killer? As I recalled, few people had lived long enough to develop it.

I made a cursory search to confirm my notion: old medical records in the public domain were fragmented like other historical records, but comparatively easy to access. I found in the memory banks a "Bill of Mortality" for London in one week of 1665. Not quite contemporary but close enough. Something called "Consumption" had killed 134 people; "Feaver," 309; "Spotted Feaver," 101 and "Plague" an amazing 7,165. In all, 8,297 people had died that week, of diseases ranging from "Ague" to "Wormes," but only one had died of "Canker."

Back to the British Army records. The second photograph in the colonel's book had been a group photograph: there were thirty officers lined up, all their names spelled out in the caption underneath.

Computer search again. Several of the officers (I was coming to feel familiar now with terms I had only come across in banned fiction and military-fant circles before) had died in India in the regiment. The death certificates of others were traced, following a trail through what had been the British Records Office that I was coming to know. Most had died of illnesses that no longer existed, but no others had developed cancer.

Alfred O'Brien did not call me back when I asked for

clearance to access more information on the V-1 and V-2. That in itself was an answer: I knew now what they had really been.

Bannerjee called again. He had produced a display of script from a small viewing screen on the "book." I guessed it would be in dots and claw marks.

A few hours later I was back in the controller's office. I didn't ask about the V-rockets. There was a code we all had that certain subjects, once indicated as forbidden, were not approached again. Besides, it wasn't necessary.

"The script the *Angel's Pencil* sent back, have you had it translated?"

"No. What would be the point?"

"Do it."

"It's not as if it's a real language . . . there's a lot of high-priority work on at the moment."

"They want us to come to the conclusion that an abnormal tiger shot in India hundreds of years ago was a lost alien and now we're running up against the same creatures in space."

"Who are they?"

"The Vaughn-Nguyens probably remembered the old stories and had the original idea. And there must be others. But I need more corroboration. And if I'm right, it'll solve the whole problem of the *Angel's Pencil* transmissions."

I gave him the readouts of the hand computer from Australia. "And scan this in, too."

He looked at it. "The same script."

"Yes. And you know how it originated? In a computer, obviously."

"Let's find the computer. They may not have wiped the program yet."

It took time to get the additional computer access on top of what we had already and then to stitch in to what Bannerjee's translation program had achieved, more time for the translation itself to come through. But now the translation was becoming easier with the preliminary work done and further with the great mass of material the *Angel's*

Pencil had beamed back. Some of this, purporting to be astronomical data and navigations tables, could be converted fairly quickly. A lot was lists: allegedly weapons inventories, fire-control tables, part of what appeared to be a poem. The poem gave us more military terms. Working from these, the translation of the electronic book gave us script and spoken language together.

There was still noise corruption, still untranslatable sounds, but the essential sense of it was there, and now computers rigged in series with gigabytes of capability were sharpening it all the time. There were extrapolations and guesses, but at the end there was a message:

> Leg-bone shattered I cannot leap. Little time left. May Hero Death be mine! But life is end and time reflection.
>
> Arriragh kharzz uru . . . Let avenging sons preserve bone in worship-shrine! And Patriarch, I demand, grant Full Name again: Skragga-Chmee! If I not Conquest Warrior High, I have great Conquest discovered. From my nneiierkrew glory for my House and the Patriarch.

The translator stumbled for a moment. The next sound was something like a live power cable dropped into water. Again, it could have been molecular or electronic distortion or an attempted simulacrum of nonhuman speech. Then the translation resumed:

> Sons know I have drawn off hunt, as plan. Sons will come when torn to pieces usurper Tskrrarr-Nig and regain estates on Skrullai and Name. I details of my course left. Kz'eerkti! The Kzinti come upon you!
>
> I have hunt well. Hot. Riper world for Conquest than any I have heard ancient tales. Great hunting territories each my son. ArrearrrLLaghh Karssht Krrar RsssRRLaghh . . . Preserve and honor bone Skragga-Chmee.

What hunting has been! I live as Fanged Gold mean kzintosh live, even . . . I the noble Kzrral'eeAHrawl kill I need no weapon but Sire's wtsai. Until today. May Fanged God's curse on Tskrrarr-Nig and his seed! May the God vomit forth his Soul!

Sight fail. Moment I trigger self-destruct *Distant Prowler*. Gravity-motor and armory will not fall to tool-using kz'eerkti's hands.

I do kz'eerkti service, preserving them for Patriarchy. Kz'eerkti population grow fast . . . Survey before landing I see kz'eerkt-bands fighting in eights of places.

The computer adjusted at this point. It noted that an analogue had been identified and that the sound "kz'eerkt" was replaced by the word "monkey." The translation seemed to be getting better now.

Passing over oceans I see monkey-ships carry primitive guns as though even fight on sea! Toothsome good sport clever slaves, but if discover weaponry *Distant Prowler* with chemical rifles, the next heroes reach this planet find smoking craters. Should monkeys find gravity polarizer, the God's joke. But they will not.

Red-clad monkeys in white helmets hunters, one who leads chief. He will enter cave, I am sure. If he thinks I already dead, may lure him my claws.

I retreat to program self-destruct. My sons, that why I broke off battle when I knew wounds mortal! Not coward.

No way leave my sons clearer trail this place, they know my route to this system . . . planet with rudiments of industrialization only radiation signature of self-destruct will bring them to this place. My seed mighty hunters! Dying, I demand Honor's Name Conquest Warrior finds this message convey message sons of Skragga-Chmee, usurped Lord of

R'kkia on Skrullai! Demand, too, Honor's Name, sons Warrior reward.

There was another gap. The screen adjusted as a new stream of data was fed in. The next words, the last words, were close to ordinary English.

Much pain. Hear monkeys and slave-beasts approach. . . . I do not think I can say more.
Avenge me. Honor my bones. Warrior's sons . . .

As I had predicted. It was the only way they could have fitted everything more or less together, once the tiger-man relics were found and identified, as, we now saw, they had been meant to be found and identified by someone like me.

The hoaxers had thought further ahead to get the details right than I had given them credit for. Even the impossible speed and maneuverability of the supposed alien ship had been accounted for, in a sense, by the reference to a technology of gravity control.

Even the *Angel's Pencil*'s supposed fluke destruction of such a supposedly impossibly superior "enemy" could be explained away according to the scenario the hoaxers had concocted: Such "enemies," though technologically superior, might be taken by surprise, once, by a reaction-drive used as a makeshift weapon if they themselves had never needed to develop such a clumsy and primitive means of propulsion.

"You've wrapped it up," said Alfred O'Brien. "But tanj! It was a set of twisted minds that packaged this idea."

And a twisted mind that unraveled it, he didn't need to say.

"What will we do next?" I asked him.

"It'll move to another level for executive action. There'll be no interrogations. Nothing to cause any trouble with the Belt."

"Shouldn't they make reparation, if they are parties to it? This must have all cost a lot of time and money."

"No! That decision has been made at the highest level

and it's quite unequivocal. If there is Belt involvement we don't want to know. There must never be an excuse for another conflict! Now that the problem's solved, no *incidents*."

He looked straight at me, and spoke in a voice I had never heard before, a voice gray as ash. "Not when thousands of ships are powered with fusion-drives." I thought I saw him shudder, and when the import of his words sank into me I shuddered too. Perhaps for the first time I truly understood what ARM's work and the program were for.

Then he continued in his normal voice.

"The Vaughn-Nguyens will have total memory-wipes and that will be the end of it. Into the Black Hole. The lot."

"The *Angel's Pencil*?"

"Too far away for us to do anything. We'll simply block its transmissions. End of story. You've done well, Karl.

"You had better keep your present operating code for a few days," he continued. "You may need to access the records again when you write your report. . . ." He nodded to himself.

"You've done well," he repeated. Did I detect a note of doubt in his voice? But, no. I *had* done well.

I thanked him and left. I planned to take a few days off, then move back to my usual routine.

There was one thing outstanding, a last piece of the puzzle. I wondered whether to bother touching it again or not, and decided there was nothing to lose by one small action that would settle forever a tiny voice whispering a final question. It was still day in England. I called Humphrey at the British Museum.

"How long," I asked him, "was it since the skull of the Vaughn's Tiger was last examined? Before we saw it the other day."

He called me back several hours later.

"The first part of the search didn't take long," he said, "but I had to go through some very old records for the rest. That part of the vault hasn't been opened since the electronic locks were installed. That's more than a hundred years. And according to the written records, the box itself hasn't been opened since the first time—when the material was sent here from Australia in 1908."

The last answer.

I recoiled. I felt like a man coming out of a dim cave, and, as he approached the daylight and the exit, placing his groping, overeager hand on a snake.

I recoiled, but I forced myself to approach it again, to face at last what that last answer was. And at last I knew why the *Angel's Pencil* had sent its message. My vague intuition had been right: There had been a simple explanation, before us all the time.

• CHAPTER 6

> Our predatory animal origin represents for mankind its
> last best hope . . . the apes were armed killers. . . .
> —Robert Ardrey, *African Genesis*

Alfred O'Brien dumped me in an autodoc. *In* a 'doc, not
at a 'doc. Big-league treatment. They even had a human
doc look at me.

I think now that he had guessed some time before what
my final report would be and had been waiting for it.

No one could have replicated exactly and in three
dimensions the shape of a skull of which no complete
drawings existed and which had been locked away before
any of us was born.

I went on a holiday. ARM moved me up the waiting list
for a permit to hike and camp in the Great Slave Lake Park
and dive at Truk Lagoon. I visited Easter Island and the
Taj Mahal.

After the Taj Mahal I spent a little more time in India. I
left the tourist routes and headed north, not exactly hiding,
but not calling attention to myself.

Near the high jungle where Assam meets Tibet there was
a new restricted area. Part of the park, a valley, needed
special maintenance work, I was told. As I left, I saw some
of the machinery going in. It was heavy digging machinery,
and it was heading for what I knew from a fragment of
map I had seen was the site of an ancient landslide.

I do not know if ARM will want me again. A year and a
half has passed and I have heard nothing official.

Unofficially, I have kept a few contacts.

ARM moves slowly and obliquely as a rule. I do not know when, or if, they will use the plans of the alien's bomb-missiles and laser-cannon that the *Angel's Pencil* sent us to begin tooling up factories. And there was a description of a gravity-motor.

Perhaps they will move too slowly. If so, I am unlikely to know before the end.

Did the crew of the *Angel's Pencil* think to search for a call-beacon in the wreckage of the enemy warship? Did they neutralize it? Too late to ask them now.

I have been warned not to leave Earth, and under no circumstances to contact anyone connected with either the Belt or the media.

Have I been duped? Suppose the whole thing *was* as we first suspected an enormously elaborate setup, perhaps not to make a bear market in some space industries but to create a bull market in a new military industry? Despite the fact we found no trace of any money movements and despite the fact no warlike race or culture could ever achieve civilization and science, let alone handle the energy processes space travel requires?

But I have learned more about that now, and it cuts the last ground away: The axiom that a warlike race cannot progress to the point of space travel is a pious fiction, a lie made into a self-evident proposition, never tested. But before I handed in my last report, I searched those old military records one more time, following the trail whose whole length only I had come to know. Our Space Age was born in war.

I think it is too late to rebottle the genie now. Already, I know, there is increased use by ARM personnel of keys to ancient military history records. There is a new special history course and batches of selected ARM personnel are being put through it. My Military Historians are, I think, involved. Anyway, they have disappeared and I am sure they are not tending machinery on Mars.

For the rest, Anton Brillov is involved, and that means Buford Early. A new base has been set up on the moon. It is not another resort for budget-class tourists. I think that in the power struggle going on inside ARM Buford Early's masters are winning.

There have been, I have learned, unexpected postings. And I have noticed some of the sort of people posted. While waiting for my permits I called about a dozen of my acquaintances, ostensibly for company on my holiday.

In fact, I was most interested in the whereabouts of two among the dozen: specialists in x-ray lasers. Both had suddenly relocated and I could not trace them. Some of ARM's house-schizies, my near colleagues, have disappeared, too.

And there have been unscheduled meetings with the Belt leadership. I have heard rumors of a new spaceship design team being put together. I can guess some things about the new spaceship they will be designing. It will be well equipped with signaling devices to assist in contact, devices using large amounts of energy. But to design a new type of ship and to build it are different propositions.

I have noticed changes in our games and entertainment. "Graceful Willow" has disappeared from the newscasts. A new game, "Highest Hand," has an emphasis on winning. There are no more dances.

If those behind Early win, I think I will have a role in what is to come. Otherwise, I imagine, someone will be calling on me soon and I will be taken in to a memory-wipe. There is no point in running, ARM can find me anywhere on Earth, and if I somehow got into space, what would I be running to there?

Arthur Guthlac has been seconded to special duties, along with several others who were at the edge of forbidden studies. But he has kept his museum title of Assistant to the Chief of the General Staff. Early's joke?

Messages have been beamed out to his sister's ship after all, ordering it to turn back. No one has said why. Those messages will reach it in about seven years' time, and what has happened has happened already.

I pity Arthur Guthlac and try not to imagine what he feels, but part of me wonders if he may have found the purpose in life that always eluded him.

I have done what I could. If there is any future history now, no doubt historians will look at the chance the whole thing turned on. Colonel Vaughn shot well. He bought us five hundred years.

They are capable of mistakes. They are capable of wishful thinking. Skragga-Chmee's creatures did not come. We had to go to them.

The main purpose of my holiday was to say good-bye to what has been, to what we always took for granted. I visited places of Earth I had known in a longish life that has, I suddenly realize, almost too late, had its share of good times. Scenes of beauty, peace, tranquility or thronging human life. Scenes from the last days of the Golden Age.

What will these same scenes show in a few years?

War factories worked around the clock by forced labor? Glowing bomb craters? Or the hunting territories of Earth's felinoid conquerors?

Time is running out.

> What shape is space? Space will put on
> The shape of any cat. . . .

I look up at night and know what is coming. ARM may or may not move in time. Perhaps the felinoids have too great a technological edge over us anyway. They have been in space a long time. Perhaps it is too late for us to rearm, and perhaps as a species we have deprived ourselves of the capacity to fight.

Sir Bors, Lady Helen! If you and yours had been arrested three days earlier, how different an ending your story might have had! But I cannot say whether a better ending or a worse one.

One thing I know is that the program and everything I have worked for is in ruins.

Perhaps that is why I feel so happy.

A DARKER GEOMETRY

●

Mark O. Martin and Gregory Benford

PART I
THE VELDT BETWEEN THE STARS

• CHAPTER ONE

Deep space is vast and cold, stretching endlessly. Eternal, unforgiving night.

Look first to the tiny bubbles of light and heat that nourish the warmlife bustle of carbon-carbon bonds, challenging the ever-patient cold and dark. Not too close to these stellar fires, yet not too distant, exist the small set of orbits which can support chemical disequilibria: warmlife.

There spin the myriad water worlds, brimming with living things, spheres all green and blue and white, basking in oblivious torpor. The warmlife worlds swing confidently around their parent suns, ripe with energies and youth, wellsprings awaiting the patient appetite of entropy.

Such thin slices of space-time are but tiny candles in an enormous darkened ballroom.

Look now to what is *not*, to the overwhelming depths between the stars; a darker geometry, the vast majority of all space and time. Strange minds dwell in that apparent emptiness, far from the hectic heat of the sunward spaces.

The Deep has its own beauty—stark, subtle, and old beyond measure. A flickering cold glow of plasma discharges; the diamond glitter of distant starlight on time-stained ices; a thin fog breath of supercooled helium, whirling in intricate, coded motion: These are the wonders of the Deep, far from any sun.

Here dwell the Outsiders.

They have ranged within the Deep for eons, thinking their cold thoughts while on still colder errands, as the barred spiral galaxy turned upon its axis dozens of times.

What the Outsiders—cryogenic, helium-based traders—

have witnessed in their vast span of time remains a mystery to the myriad warmlife races. Outsider logic is cold, their designs as shadowy as the spaces between the stars; their minds are totally alien to the bustling carbon-children of thermonuclear heat and light.

Outsiders watched while warmlife first evolved on world after world, beginning nine billions of years ago. They remained aloof as the first warmlife sentients developed space travel, reaching out with clumsy arrogance to nearby stars in the name of exploration and empire. Now and then, some Outsiders helped such upstart and brash races, for cold, strange reasons of their own.

Other times, and for other reasons, the Outsiders dispassionately weeded.

They journeyed throughout the galaxy, sailing the Deep, watching and thinking, as warmlife flitted from sun to sun, insignificant motes moving within the Outsiders' vast realm.

The Outsiders observed impassively as the influence of the telepathic Thrintun spread from warmlife world to warmlife world, eventually enslaving a galaxy with their Power. They had nothing to fear: Outsider minds are organized as complex interactive eddies of superconductive liquids. No telepathic neurological command geared to warmlife-evolved biochemistry could influence them.

Over a billion years ago, the Tnuctipun Revolt ended in Suicide Night: horror beyond imagining. The defeated Thrintun used their artificially amplified Power to blanket the breadth and depth of the galaxy, commanding the death of all life possessing the slightest trace of sentience.

All sentient warmlife, that is.

For Outsiders, the sudden end of countless tiny minds was but a passing cool event in the slow tick of time. Such minds had not existed in the galaxy's dim beginnings, then suddenly burst into being, and finally vanished into the original frigid silence. It was information to the Outsiders, rather than calamity. They saw no reason to intervene in warmlife affairs.

The small bubbles of light and warmth around so many

stars remained silent after that. No more tiny ships or minds traveled the Deep in real or hyperspace. The stars slumbered on.

And still the Outsiders lived their long, cold lives. On the devastated warmlife worlds, enough time passed for the mindless hand of natural selection to make the former food yeasts of the Thrintun evolve again toward complexity, and eventually, intelligence.

Once more, warmlife races learned to journey from star to star, for fleeting mayfly reasons. Eventually, their frantic movements impinged again upon the Outsider realm, sometimes disrupting patterns set in place for half a billion years. The Outsiders dealt with the intrusion in many ways: brushing the interlopers aside, diverting their short-lived attentions, or simply ignoring the disturbance.

The Outsiders knew that this, too, would pass.

Some of the factions of the diverse Outsider society would interact with these upstart, reborn children of stellar heat. They would occasionally trade a tiny portion of data collected over billions of years for chemicals, cold-world facilities, or still more information. The coldlife beings were shrewd traders and negotiators, having lived through eons of time, and dealt with the many thousands of faces intelligence can assume.

To the Outsiders, little was new. Even less was interesting.

The Outsiders themselves seemingly remain unchanged, eternal, just as their cold realm has existed relatively unchanged since the galaxy was freshly forged in the fires of the strong nuclear force. To be sure, the great clouds of dust and simple molecules were pruned away, collapsing into suns. This left the interstellar reaches thinner, easier for the Outsiders to negotiate, for plasmas to form and self-organize. But these were slow shifts. Warmlife was a buzzing, frantic irritant.

The coldlife traders intimidate the warmlife races. Outsider ships are works of incomprehensible art, both their aesthetics and functions strange and perplexing.

Even the Outsider form is coldly beautiful; their bulblike

bodies and weaving tentacles gracefully flow like a dancing cryogenic liquid. And there is something in their manner when dealing with warmlife races that suggests immense distance. Outsiders had freely roamed the galaxy while the most advanced warmlife creatures consisted of single-celled pond scum.

The warmlife races know nothing of the Outsiders beyond their form and their penchant for trading. Scholars of many races wasted entire lives pursuing questions, speculating, debating—all without adequate data, talk leading nowhere. The Outsiders never spoke of themselves.

Where and when did they evolve to intelligence—and from what less advanced form? Were they somehow exempt from the deft hand of natural selection? What did they value and what did they spurn? Did Outsiders have hopes, or worse still, fears? Did Outsiders have societies, or were they all of one vast, icy mind?

The Outsiders, as always, kept their own counsel.

But there are other minds than the Outsiders dwelling in the eternal Deep—much older and still more alien— who might understand. In the black gulf between the stars, strangeness waits.

• CHAPTER TWO

Bruno Takagama looked out at the twisted starscape on the command screen, and shivered at the prickly sensation of unseen eyes on him.

He had awakened with the Dream once again that watch, stifling a shout, drenched with sweat and unspoken fear. Now the stars themselves seemed to threaten him, and perhaps with good reason. He rubbed his temples and peered more intently into the screens.

As observed from the navigation deck of the *Sun-Tzu*, the ghost of Einstein was squeezing the universe in the implacable fist of his ancient equations, making it seem more eerie and disturbing than Bruno would have thought possible.

The Earth vessel was traveling at just over seventy percent of light-speed, seemingly alone in the vast darkness of interstellar space. Physics had begun to compress the usually unchanging starfield forward and aft of the ship, distorting the one rock-steady constant of space travel. Relativity Doppler-shifted the stars directly in front of the *Sun-Tzu* into a handful of blazing blue diamonds, while Sol was reduced to a dull red gleam behind them, lost in the hellish wash of the antimatter drive.

In the back of his mind, he saw the hand from the Dream on his shoulder, brown and leathery, knuckles the size of walnuts. Alien, but still familiar. He shivered, pushing the memory away with effort.

One thing could always exorcise his demons, Bruno reflected, and keyed the ship commlink. He hoped that the captain was in the mood for a bit of banter.

"Carol, you there?" Bruno licked his lips a bit nervously,

waiting for the reply. Sometimes the emptiness around the ship wore her down as well.

There was a faint crackle over the deck speakers, static born from the relativistic impact of bits of interstellar dust against the eroding forward edge of the *Sun-Tzu*.

"No, I'm lying on a beach in Australia." Her voice on the commlink was clear, immediate, though she was half a kilometer away on the other side of the iceball that was the interstellar warship.

He smiled despite himself at her flippant tone. A good sign. "You couldn't find Australia on a map."

"Map, schmap. I saw it once through a 'scope out Ceres way. Big brown-and-tan dot in the Pacifist Ocean."

"That's *Pacific* Ocean." She was baiting him a little, Bruno knew. Belter impudence against Flatlander tradition.

Carol's tone remained airy, unimpressed. "Big diff, Flatlander. Looked like a dog turd, actually."

"What would a Belter know about dogs?" he replied, amused.

"Saw one once, in a Luna zoo. Wear their hearts on their sleeves, don't they?" Pause. "Okay, okay, Mr. Precise. They wear their hearts on their forelegs. Happy?"

"Ecstatic. Anyway, we so-called Flatlanders bred dogs that way. Who wants a pet that's hard to read?"

"Explain cats, then."

"Ummm—point conceded." Bruno smiled again, the beaked face and sad liquid eyes of the Dream receding still further with Carol's banter. The captain of the *Sun-Tzu* was better therapy than all the psychists with whom Bruno had worked downside on Earth.

Her conversation was filled with typical Belter logic and twisty changes in subject. Practical, ever looking for the loophole. But then, he reminded himself, Carol had smuggled a cargo or three past the goldskin UN police back in the Belt.

Before the kzin came, and everything changed.

"Turds," Carol's voice continued on the commlink in a patently false academic tone, "are a subject I know—I worked

recycler maintenance for years before earning my pilot chip."
There was a pause for effect. "And of course, I worked with
men a lot."

"You have such a winning grasp of the language," Bruno
sniffed in mock insult. "And oh so diplomatic, too." He could
feel the worry lines around his scalp scars smooth. He had
taken this momentary break to snap out of his mood, and
it was working gloriously.

Carol was not to be outdone, however. "You should talk.
What's next—flowers?"

"Well, flowers spring forth from turds. . . ."

She snorted. "An overstretched metaphor, and poorly
chosen besides. I was hoping this talk of flowers was turning
to romance." A wounded pause. "Are you attempting to
romance me, shipmate? You should read my poetry
sometime."

"What? All these years together and you've been writing
poetry in secret?"

"Ummm. You're surprised an old smuggler like me can
have a secret or two, Tacky?"

"No, pleased. Not that you're old. But maybe you have
crannies and crevices I haven't explored yet."

"I hope that's a metaphor, you primate."

"I guess it is—whatever a metaphor might be. Besides,
you are the boss. I wouldn't want to be too forward with a
superior officer."

Carol ignored his sally. "A lady has to keep some of her
crannies entirely metaphorical." Again she paused for an
overdone dramatic effect. "After all, *Sun-Tzu* is a bit on
the small side."

He laughed. Concerns about privacy from a Belter? "I'm
more interested in their, ah . . ."

"Capacity? Circumference? Hard to put such matters in
my usual dainty, ladylike fashion." Her tone had become
arch, as usual. There was a pleased purr behind her smoky
voice.

"I can't wait to see your ladylike poetry. What's the file
name?"

"Hey, not so fast. Don't be so forward. A mere few years of squishy carnal intimacy and already you want to caress my lines with your invasive vision? Get your disorderly Flatlander patriarchal eye tracks all over them?"

Bruno felt a glow of anticipation. "Okay, you can recite them. Tonight, in the Honeymoon Suite. A private performance."

"I'll have to recite them from memory, shipmate. They aren't written down."

He could almost see the laugh lines on her startanned face, and shifted deliciously in his crash couch. "Sounds like imaginary poetry to me. Mere mouth music."

"A base canard! You'll pay for that—tonight, me bucko."

"Okay, but remember, it's my turn to be on top. Recital or no recital." Bruno's worries seemed far away while he thought about Carol.

"Huh! Try to perform your macho acts while I recite poetry?" Mock hurt crept into her tone. "Art is seldom appreciated!"

"It's that bad, huh?"

"Ooooh! You better not trust my mouth tonight, O critic!"

"Was that 'trust' or 'thrust'?" He paused. "Either way, I was so looking forward to—"

"Hey," Carol interrupted. "No fair trying to get me hot, Flatlander."

"Whaddaya mean, 'trying'? Sounds like I've already done it." Bruno enjoyed the role-playing that took both of them away from the gritty realities of *Sun-Tzu* and Project Cherubim.

Carol's tone became accusatory. "More swinging-dick arrogance. You think you can tell that I'm, uh, excited—over the *commlink*?"

"Well, okay, you Belter pirate. Deny it."

"No deal. But hey, luv, got to break off. Things need doing here. Romance and recycler maintenance don't mix, do you scan? But thanks for the, ah . . . interlude."

Bruno sighed. Carol was right. Playtime was over. "Aye-aye, Skipper. There's work here, too. 'Bye."

No point in telling Carol yet of his dark suspicions. Time to get back to work. The image-sharpening program was about to deliver up again. He sighed.

Some fuzziness in his thinking. Slight, but it was there. Bruno had become increasingly reliant on the tranquilizers dispensed by the *Sun-Tzu's* autodoc. And if Carol knew that he was still having the Dream, she would up the dosage. That was all right with Bruno, up to a point. The mood modifiers helped as the dark gap yawned ever wider between ship and home. He felt both alone—despite Carol—and stealthily watched. But that wasn't a side effect of the drugs. Nor of the nightmare he called the Dream.

For despite the seeming emptiness of the Deep surrounding the *Sun-Tzu*, Bruno knew in his soul that the black vacuum also held kzin warships.

He blinked at the summary display on the holoscreen in front of him. The data hinted at his diminished mind. Always he felt the familiar itch in his neck, reminding him that he was not Linked. Connected to the *Sun-Tzu's* computer, he would not need to interpret the orderly ranks and files of complex data before him.

He would *know*.

Bruno yearned for that feeling. Reading the screens was like doing arithmetic by counting with his fingers. But for now, he had to crawl, knowing that sometime not too far off—*soon, soon*, he thought longingly—he would be able to fly again.

With a grimace, he self-consciously used the time-consuming verbal commands and a dataglove to communicate with the shipboard computer. Slow, clunky, inefficient. Bruno ran several diagnostics to be certain of his earlier observations, then asked a few terse questions of the computer, sketching graphs and recalling database log entries with small, precise gestures of his dataglove-clad right hand.

Bruno didn't like the confirmatory datastream scrolling across one of the open holoscreen windows hanging in midair in front of him. The observations were not conclusive, but they still disquieted him.

There were several possible explanations for the transient gravity waves the Forward mass detector had picked up during the last watch. The signals were faint, but Bruno had finally proven they were definitely not due to sensor malfunction.

Bruno frowned. One interpretation of the signals was that the *Sun-Tzu* was not alone in deep space, and that one or more kzinti ships were moving on a slow intercept vector toward the Earth vessel.

They were nearly a third of the way to the Wunderland colony at Alpha Centauri. Relativity being what it was, the kzin could not possibly have detected the *Sun-Tzu* and launched spacecraft in response. Bruno's worried frown deepened.

The signals could be stragglers of the Kzinti Third Fleet returning to Alpha Centauri—defeated once again by launching lasers, brave Belter pilots, and plain ol' Finagle's Luck. But no one at UN Space Command had suspected that there were any retreating alien vessels, after dozens of suicide attacks by the catlike aliens in near solar space.

Bruno bit his lip and sighed deeply, flexing his shoulders and back against the tension he was feeling. The crash couch holding him whirred softly, adjusting itself minutely to his changing contours. Useful, but nothing compared with Carol's massages.

Or worse still, he mused, the mystery blips could be part of an invading Fourth Fleet on its way to Sol. Bruno thought about that possibility for a moment, the dataglove receptors suddenly cold against his fingertips, and called up the sketchy kzin technology database menu. He pulled his right hand from the dataglove while he waited, wearily stretching his tired finger joints.

He thought again of the hand in the Dream. Carol's hand, changed forever by the virus from another solar system. Bruno shoved the thought away. There was work to do.

Looking at his hands, he noticed they were still sweaty, with the usual half-moons of grime under the fingernails. It seemed impossible to rid the starship of grit and dirt. In a way, it was reassuring to Bruno: a gleaming high-tech vessel like the *Sun-Tzu* was redolent with the ancient smells of burnt oil, old meals and human sweat. Dust collected in corners of the navigation deck, a homey touch. He wondered idly if the kzin had to put traps in their ventilators to keep them from being clogged with shed fur. The thought made him smile a little. He hoped it was true, and that the aliens choked on it.

Bruno slipped the dataglove back onto his aching hand, and selected several subaddresses in the accessed database. In a few moments, he had downloaded and decompressed the files describing various models of the kzinti spacedrive, and how they related to actual observations during the three waves of kzin attacks on Sol. Fuzzy logic judgment subroutines began comparing models against the incoming data, sifting interpretations and displaying the goodness of fit. Bruno knew he had to be fairly certain that the mystery blips were kzin warcraft rather than some natural phenomenon, before he went any further.

Everyone in the UN Command knew the story of *The Jinxian Who Cried Bandersnatch*. Bruno wanted to be *sure*.

Irrationally aggressive as the kzin initially seemed, the last attack had cost humanity most of Ceres, Pallas, Titan Base, hundreds of Belter warships, dozens of laser batteries, and the interstellar launcher on Juno. The battle had been closer than most people believed, Bruno knew from Most Secret reports out of Geneva: a small flotilla of carefully stealthed kzinti craft had been intercepted and destroyed a mere half million kilometers from Earth herself.

Plain dumb luck, again.

It was doubtful that luck would be enough to keep the kzin monsters at bay indefinitely. *The ratcats keep learning. They keep getting better, more subtle, with every attack wave*. The First Fleet the kzin had launched against Sol had been destroyed by the Strather Array of launching lasers on Mercury. Gigawatt lasers and smart mirrors were formidable indeed against targets unprepared for them.

By the time the Second Fleet had arrived six years later,

the kzinti had learned to shield their magnetic monopoles, making the alien warships difficult to detect, let alone burn. Some of the battles had then been ship to ship, and lopsided battles at that; Belter fusion-pinch drives were no match for the kzin vessels, somehow able to accelerate at hundreds of gees without the slightest respect for the laws of Newton. Still, the humans too were learning with each encounter, and the aliens were defeated again.

The Third Fleet arrived seven years after that, and had almost broken the improved system-wide defenses. No scream-and-leap strategy that time from the kzin warships, but the more dangerous approach of feint-and-pounce. It had been close indeed. Sol was still furiously rebuilding her shattered perimeter defenses, Belters and Flatlanders working together without argument.

The kzinti strategies just didn't make sense, Bruno thought, biting his lip in thought and looking at the holoscreen. Flickering images crawling across the floating window like tiny technicolored insects. He had to be absolutely certain before he notified the captain of the *Sun-Tzu*.

Data swiftly uncoiled in four dimensions, and Bruno tried to fit it as well as possible to UN Tactical Team predictions. Analytical parameters changed with each model the computer retrieved from the relevant files, and smooth graphical surfaces rippled and curved in response. Bruno made occasional changes in the modeling subroutines, tweaking an assumption here or there as human intuition suggested. As he worked, he tapped his shipshoes against the deck, which softly thrummed with the continual actinic thrust of the antimatter drive.

These ratcats are crazy, he thought. *They've gotta be the weirdest damn things in the galaxy.*

Bruno was quite sure of that.

• OUTSIDERS ONE

Surprise-concern. Sense the waning along the emergent force-vectors in zone {^/~}. Alerts have been raised within all Four Aspects of the Nexus.

Distraction. This recent phenomenon has been noted by this local-node. Compensation is initiated. Imminent action-tree analysis is under consideration.

Concern. The other-node had presumptive control of such incursions! There is major instability of precious plasma density along this most vital zone. Field-line integrity is threatened! What is the nature of this abomination?

Confidence. Transmitting update data-packet from this local-node to the other-node.

Consideration. Received. Analysis initiated. Amplification and clarification requested from the other-node.

Explanation. The hotworld craft shall soon converge. Their ritual violence will once more be worked upon this precious sector of obliging expanse. Observe and contemplate. Interaction with the Focus is minimized.

Confusion. There seems no point to hotlife's endless offshoot energies. A wise evolution, Pattern-Shaper, would contain or damp such wasteful vigor to more distributed ends.

Confidence. The other-node mistakes evolution in these hotworld motes as possessing purpose. This is a commonly held illogic concerning myriad hotlife forms. Review prior net-entries {**%##}. Recall that hotlife shaping is but reaction to stochastic and chaotic forces.

Agreement. Creation squanders its rich and various wonders on such insignificant motes. To what end? The true point of Creation lies within the One Mind of the Radiant Masters who know the Way.

Zealotry. Only the Divine Radiants—and such as this local-and-other nodes, {-+-+-}, that serve them—have deep cosmic purpose from this reality and the Other. All else is insignificant, mere passing minor disorder within the Great Pattern.

Distress. These hotworld craft, with their spewing forth of debris and disordering of stately and stable force-patterns, cannot but be irritants to the Great Design of the Divine Radiants. Recall that a Great Construct was once under consideration for this region-space; clearly, this geometry remains sacred to the still-silent Masters. This local-node argues in all high seriousness for the extermination of the hotlife motes—all of them.

Surprise. Does the other-node fall so easily into heretical traps? Consult the High Texts for complete arguments and debate frozen into lattice. The other-node recommendation must be considered by the High Ones, those that speak for the long-silent Radiants. This local-and-other nodes are but Watchers, long patient sentinels and vigilant agents.

Truculence. Yet node-agents can act where prior accepted precedent exists. The Net contains ample examples of necessity under similar circumstance.

Authority. Abide, impatient node-and-agent. Observe and serve, as is the highest Purpose of such mere matter. This local-and-other nodes were constructed to be agents in the world of condensed matter.

Outrage. But the hotworld motes are vermin! They interfere and meddle with concerns older than their very Pattern.

Agreement. Truth. Their ends shall come, as all such motes have over long eons. This local-and-other nodes remain, and carry out Purpose.

Disagreement-impatience. This local-and-other nodes recently acted, atomizing the fleets of hotworld vermin fleeing galactic Center in nearby vector-zone {^*/~}. Those vermin were little different than found in one of the motes under observation. Even as mere sentinels, this local-and-other nodes dealt swiftly with the threat to the Great Design of the Masters.

Anger-regret. Recall that such unilateral and intemperate

action led to the abomination of Treaty with the heretical cousins, the {^^^*///*}! This local-and-other nodes lost much authority and autonomy.

Fury-agreement. Foul heretics! The feral ones have spurned the wisdom of the High Ones, and the Divine Radiants. Instead, their myriad node-links consort with hotlife vermin such as these irritating motes!

Reflection-worry. Truth. This local-node would feel more assured if contact could be restored directly with the Divine Radiants. Their insights would—

Impatience. The other-node always invokes the Divine Ones. Always! This local-node misses their soothing certitude as much as the other-node. The Nexus need not pine away for Their answers to inconsequential questions.

Sorrow. Yet direct contact would ensure right action.

Sarcasm. The Oracles have been silent for more than a galactic revolution. Does the other-node not trust the High Ones? Are the High Texts not illumination enough of the One Mind of the Divine Radiants? Is the other-node allied with the heretical {^^^*///*}?

Contrition-Outrage. Not so! The High Ones' interpretation of the High Texts is Absolute Law within the Great Nexus, for node-links of the {-+-+-}. The feral {^^^*///*} disregard the High One's authority on behalf of the Divine Radiants.

Mollification. This local-node is relieved to find that the other-node respects the Law and High Texts, indeed. But what of the long and lonely silence from the Divine Radiants? This local-node suspects the Divine Radiants tired of listening to the Great Nexus and its annoying queries into their vast and awesome contemplation of the Great Pattern and the Other Reality. The Divine Radiants constructed node-links to be used, with independent action, even as They left Their Great Constructs throughout space. Mark that!

Irritation. The other-node is harsh. Independent action is, after all, what separated {^^^*///*} concerns from the Great Nexus. Mark that in turn. Long duty in this empty geometry-region as sentinels has brought a bitter edge.

Humor-agreement. Defending the integrity of an eventual Great Construct in this region of space is far from stirring to this local-node's coding and derived destiny.

Caution. This, then, is the source of the other-node's

impatience for possibly intemperate action? Mere boredom?

Neutrality. The other-node's logic touches truth with many tendrils, if harshly expressed. This local-and-other nodes will watch, and act if needed. Surely this is acceptable to the other-node.

Great caution-agreement. This local-node and other-node have reached One mind on this subject. Yet initial observation remains primary. First and foremost, this local-and-other nodes are sentinels, obedient to ancient and much wiser coding.

Impatience. Sentinels are capable of far more than merely watching, should the hotworld vermin continue on their course.

Caution-agreement. Possibly, if such extreme action is merited by relevant events.

Neutrality-firmness. This local-node suspects that action will be necessary, based on the actions of these hotworld motes and their irritating emergent phenomena. Already, this site of an eventual Great Construct of our Masters is threatened by disturbances in the plasma flux and field lines! Mark this!

Concern-and-grudging agreement. This local-node is in agreement with other-node. These local-and-other nodes are of One mind.

• CHAPTER THREE

Bruno Takagama spent a great deal of his time aboard the *Sun-Tzu* waiting and worrying. He had become quite good at both tasks.

A low tone sounded on the navigation deck as the main computer finished its last analysis run, and began to display results. Bruno looked up from his musings. It was time to determine if the *Sun-Tzu* was alone in the void between the stars.

Bruno stretched in his crash couch and worked the kinks from his shoulders. He scratched the link interface in his neck absently, breathing air slightly bitter with the tang of recyclers and machinery and human effluvia. Within his nose, the sharpness of ozone battled with more pungent, organic aromas. They had been living for five years inside the *Sun-Tzu*, after all, and no recycler was perfect.

He grimaced at the thought. Bruno knew all too well that a lot of things weren't perfect about the *Sun-Tzu*. Their entire mission, in fact. And even without the kzin, he and Carol were not truly alone in interstellar space.

Many things drifted in the supposedly empty vacuum of interstellar space. Ionized gas, chips of ice, microscopic bits of gravel; any one of these items could damage the *Sun-Tzu*, striking the vessel at 0.7c relative. A tiny fragment of ice could deliver a hammerblow of kinetic energy. One half multiplied by the mass of the object multiplied by the square of the velocity made small pebbles into powerful bombs. The forward lasers and a magnetic field swept most of the material from the path of the *Sun-Tzu*, but by no means all.

High background levels of radiation exposure monitored constantly by the in-ship and autodoc sensors were only one sign that the shield was not perfect. Remote exterior cameras had already shown craters and scars on the icy forward surface of the *Sun-Tzu*, as it was slowly battered and eroded away by the interstellar medium itself.

Yet physics predicted that more exotic entities than gas and ice also floated in the spaces between the stars. Perhaps the signals the long-range array were receiving originated from something much stranger than mere alien spacecraft.

But Bruno had to be sure. He let his mind wander as he watched the computer digest and analyze the odd signals, the results being posted into midair within one of the many open holoscreen windows. Even un-Linked, he could usually recognize hidden data patterns on a subconscious level. Bruno had a bad feeling about the mystery signals, which tugged at his thoughts persistently.

He remembered Colonel Early's acerbic comment during one of the debriefing and brainstorming sessions back in Geneva. "Son," he had drawled at Bruno, "the thing about aliens is, they're *alien*." He smiled without humor at the recalled conversation, now several years old.

Bruno of all people knew something about nonhuman thought patterns.

The fears throughout the Belt and in Geneva had put the *Sun-Tzu* here, balanced on a enormous sword of superheated plasma and hard gamma radiation. Clearly, the waves of kzin attack spacecraft originated from the decades-silent Wunderland colony. The *Sun-Tzu* was to take the war back to Alpha Centauri.

In spades.

The holoscreen blinked twice to get Bruno's attention. Eye and dataglove worked together efficiently as he went over the readouts, teasing more detail from the display with deft finger movements. The last modeling subroutine had finished, and the final predictions and summary statements were little different from the first. The confidence interval was not terribly high, but still very kzinlike in broad outline.

It could be a false alarm like the other two Bruno had discovered in the past. Then again, this one might be genuine. Bruno pursed his lips, and knew that he couldn't take any chances.

He swore a long-forgotten obscenity Early had taught him during the war-game simulations back in Luna, slapped a keypad, and put the *Sun-Tzu* on full alert.

A blaring alarm echoed throughout the navigation deck. Automated subsystems came on-line smoothly. Weapons ports unlimbered, and armored antennae on the outside of the ship shifted into new positions. More power was diverted from the antimatter reaction chamber to the accumulators, containment fields, and precious *Dolittle*, snugged in its berth deep within the *Sun-Tzu*. Contingency subprograms throughout the ship quivered at the point of execution, in cybernetic readiness.

Carol's voice rapped over the commlink, "On my way!"

"Great. Looks weird up here."

"What's up, Tacky? Did those—"

"Talk later. Got business, here and now."

He checked and rechecked the myriad tech details of the alert. Un-Linked, it was a tedious and frustrating chore.

If the kzin became even slightly better at their warrior arts, Bruno knew, the human race was finished. And perhaps Early's Most Secret group would have to initiate Project Cherubim in solar space, or—in the worst scenario—even on Earth herself. Images from his recurrent Dream flitted in his mind's eye. He shivered at the thought, and dictated some notes into the ship's log while he waited for the captain of the *Sun-Tzu* to arrive.

Within a few minutes, Carol Faulk wormed her way through the access hatch onto the navigation deck. She panted, having sprinted the length of the ship from where she was checking the coldsleep chambers of their thirty shipmates, where they hibernated in cryogenic sleep.

Bruno waited for her to catch her breath. He looked at her, appreciating the way that Carol's formfitting purple shipsuit clung to her tall and Belter-lanky frame. Long muscles bunched and moved agreeably under the fabric. Even amid a crisis, she could snag his attention on a noncerebral level. He wondered if the kzin were as sexual as humans. That hardly seemed possible.

Carol puffed air, her breath steaming in the chilly compartment, and glanced up at the holoscreen readouts. She ran a hand over her Belter crest, a stiff strip of short black hair across her skull from front to back, wiping the clean sweat onto her already stained pant leg. The hairstyle, rare outside Sol's asteroid belt, suited her exotic dark features. She leaned close to Bruno for a moment, her lips brushing his high cheekbones lightly. She scratched herself delicately; upkeep of the *Sun-Tzu* required a great deal of manual labor, and she and Bruno were not yet due for their weekly showers.

No automation was perfect, after all. There was no substitute for a brush and elbow grease, even in the high-tech twenty-fourth century. And, Bruno reflected, Captain Faulk was not at all shy about demanding the use of such ancient technologies. Tradition, she called it. Character building. Bruno believed that there were other, more appropriate, words.

Belters were pathologically neat.

"Sorry that it took me so long to get here, Tacky," she said in her husky contralto, between her slowing deep breaths. "Just not used to your groundhog gravs."

She had spent most of her life traveling from asteroid to asteroid in the Belt; short boosts from a fusion drive followed by long ballistic periods of zero gee.

He kept his tone even. "I've got some bogeys."

"Again. First, got some water?" she asked with studied nonchalance. "Then you can give me the bad news, which I sincerely hope is yet another false alarm." Her face became too obviously neutral, the Captain persona wiping away her smartass facade.

It did not surprise Bruno that Carol remained calm. In the Belt, very few things happened quickly, due to celestial mechanics and the realities of changes in delta vee. It was a difficult habit to break. But the Kzin War would destroy that attitude forever, Bruno reflected grimly. And Carol had fought the ratcats herself, ship to ship. She had learned the hard way to keep herself in control.

He tossed a waterbulb at Carol, who reached too high, her reflexes more accustomed to microgravity environments than were Bruno's Flatlander muscles. She recovered the bulb neatly as it bounced off the hull wall, twisted the cap, and drained the water in one thirsty swallow. They had selected lemon-lime flavoring for the water this week, to cover the inevitable earthy traces of the recyclers. Carol winced visibly—the lime was rather biting, Bruno thought, maybe a software malf—and flipped the empty bulb into the recycler slot.

She leaned over Bruno to see the holoscreen windows more clearly, rubbing his neck and shoulders with both hands, the way he liked it. Her hands were magical, strong and intuitively knowledgeable with the years they had spent together driving the *Sun-Tzu* toward Wunderland.

Carol's hands moved progressively around his neck. They studiously avoided the hard plastic of his Linker plug assembly.

"What do you have?" she asked after a moment, attacking the knots of tension in his neck. The tone of command edged its way back into her voice.

Bruno would normally have enjoyed Carol's massage, sweat and all. Familiarity on long space voyages did not breed contempt in his particular case. But desire drained from him this time. The fresh graphic on the holoscreen window, and what it implied, kept his glands turned down. Fight-or-flight hormones coursed frantically through his bloodstream, but there was nowhere to run.

And few weapons with which to fight.

Bruno took a deep breath. "During the last watch, Skipper," he said, "the long-range array picked up a set of graviton wiggles above the background hash. I keep the subsystems looking for things in or near our flightpath in real time." He leaned back into Carol's strong hands. "You can imagine what a bit of gravel would do to us at point seven lights relative. Let alone a microsingularity. At our velocity, we don't have much reaction time."

Carol stopped massaging his neck, and tapped him lightly on the shoulder with her left hand. "Get to the point," she murmured patiently. She had been with Bruno long enough to know how to balance her dual roles as captain and lover-friend.

He made a face. "The signals come and go over time, but I kept recording and finally nailed down some decent data."

Bruno murmured to the computer and flexed his fingers deftly within the dataglove. The main holoscreen window split into three sections: raw data on the lower left side, the idealized graphic on the lower right, and the Doppler-shifted stars dead ahead of the *Sun-Tzu* looming above the two of them in midair. "Asymmetrically polarized gravity waves, possible multiple sources. No mistake about *that*. What precisely is making the waves, of course, is another matter."

Carol held absolutely still in thought, another odd Belter trait that Bruno had noticed long ago. In zero gee, a drifting arm or elbow could unintentionally activate an important keypad—like the fusion drive, or an airlock. Carol, like all long-term Belters, only moved when she *intended* to move. Bruno still found Carol's statuelike posture disturbing, even after all their time together.

She whistled tunelessly through her teeth for a moment. "Good chance it's those damned kzin reactionless drives?"

"I'd say so."

Carol rubbed her Belter crest against Bruno's face. "Not another false alarm again?"

"I don't think so," he replied, his tone flat.

"Ratcats. Just like that dinosaur, Early, predicted, right?" She arched a jet black eyebrow at him, making a face.

Bruno nodded and ignored Carol's not-so-hidden dig. She hadn't spent as much time with Early as Bruno had in both Luna and Geneva, so she couldn't know that beneath the bluster and atavistic cigar smoke, the colonel was a decent

man. He had been like a father to Bruno. And he seemed
to know everything about two hundred years' worth of
proscribed technology in the ARM restricted databases.
Humans would need every bit of even remotely militaristic
technology to fight the kzin; the engine that drove the *Sun-
Tzu* towards Wunderland was but one example. Early had
helped make that possible, as head of UN Special Projects.

Bruno and Early had spent years together, studying the
records in Luna's most restricted ARM database, the Black
Vault. It held things much more dangerous than mere
antimatter spacedrives—such as the tiny cryovial *Sun-Tzu*
carried as cargo. The cryovial with the ancient virus, older
than humankind.

The source of his Dream. But—perhaps—a weapon
against which the kzin could not stand.

He smiled slightly at Carol, shrugged with his eyebrows.
"The waveform pattern resembles what we've seen from
damaged kzinti warships insystem, trying to run stealthed.
Not a perfect match, I have to remind you."

"But close enough to worry you," prodded Carol. Her
implicit trust in Bruno's judgment, even after two false alarms,
warmed him.

Bruno nodded again. "The kzinti drives don't leak
neutrinos, like our fusion units; some of the ratcat ships
seem to leak aphasic gravitons." He shrugged again, and
pointed at one of the graphical icons on the holoscreen.
"Now you know as much as I do. Summary analyses under
the usual menus."

Carol quickly sank into the second crash couch, next to
Bruno. She strapped in with care, in typical Belter caution,
and pulled on a dataglove. Bruno knew his captain. He waited
patiently for Carol to think it all through for herself, as she
mulled over the data marching across the holoscreen
windows. She called up a few analytical subroutines of her
own; again typical for any Belter singleship pilot. Bruno
wasn't offended; a Belter could never stand to let someone
else, even a long-term lover, make a decision involving
shipboard matters.

Carol grunted and spared him a half smile, finally giving up on the complex displays, and pulled her lip in frustration. Bruno was not surprised. Half the instrumentation of the *Sun-Tzu* had been built from designs taken from the Black Vault in Luna. Even partially Linked into the system, it had taken him months to master the delicacy of the *Sun-Tzu's* sensory array.

Carol gestured at the holoscreen in mock-frustration. "Okay, you win, smart guy."

"Enough techno-dazzle for you?"

"More than enough, shipmate." Crisp, quick; the captain-voice. "Let's assume the blips aren't some kind of physicist's wet dream. How many ratcat ships, and how far off? Show me where they are. Your best guess."

They both avoided looking at the interface Link clipped to the main console. A thick array of glittering fiber-optic bundles led to the main CPU network port, which ended in a nasty-looking plug. The Link's black organiform socket was on the left side of Bruno's neck, just under his ear, where the spinal column and skull met.

Bruno could feel the lonely itch of the Link inside his head as he always did while un-Linked. Always.

After his childhood accident, the surgeons, neuroscientists, and computer scientists had replaced much of his damaged brain with macrocircuitry arrays and high-speed interface matrices. The idea of becoming part of a machine was not odd to Bruno, but familiar and comforting. He had lived with the fact that his head was half full of semiconductors and plastic since childhood.

Bruno was the most stable Linker that Early's Wild Talents project could find. But Linkers always went catatonic after a certain amount of time connected to high-level computers. Human-level computers went silent after a few months; why would a human mind mated with a computer be any different? He tried not to think about that aspect of his mission.

Bruno knew intellectually that he had to minimize cumulative Link time for that reason; he had to stay sane for as long as possible, to carry out the mission when he and Carol reached Wunderland. But with the Link, he was so much *more* than human. Bruno could run hundreds of servos simultaneously, all the while a carrying out dozens of other tasks. Every database in storage was instantly part of his memory, at a whim. His consciousness could exist in several places at the same time.

Linked, Bruno could see the All. Was part of it.

Without it, he was only Bruno. The pale memory of Transcendence filled his mind with wild glory he could only dimly remember with an unenhanced mind. He felt himself sigh a little in regret, and hoped that Carol wouldn't notice.

He felt her kiss him lightly, drawing him back to the here and now. She knew him that well after all, Bruno thought with a slight smile. Carol was the only person he had ever met who did not make him feel as alien as a kzin.

But she didn't care for the Linked version of Bruno, he thought sadly. She could not experience the Truth, as he could. Carol thought full Linkage was little different than what would happen to Carol and their other crewmates when she opened the cryovial at Wunderland.

But that would drive them farther apart, not closer together. Perhaps, Linked, he could find a way . . .

Bruno shoved the shadows of Transcendence from his mind and concentrated on less direct communication with the main computer. He murmured more commands, and flexed his fingers adroitly within the dataglove.

The relativity-squeezed view of the starfield in front of the *Sun-Tzu* crawled, oozing color, displaying their destination as it would appear at nonrelativistic velocities. Alpha Centauri shone clearly within a blinking green circle directly in front of them. He pointed to the raw numbers within the numeric section of the holoscreen, fingers stabbing through the light display, and showed Carol how they related to the multicolored graphic analysis he and the computer had constructed. Much of the data was actually informed guesswork and deduction, since all information was limited to light-speed—and the putative kzinti ships and the *Sun-Tzu* were both traveling at close to 0.7 lights.

He whispered more commands while Carol looked on, whistling impatiently. Belters didn't fidget; they whistled or hummed. Worse still, they sometimes sang. Bruno grunted in triumph as a small red blur appeared within the starfield holo, below and to the right of their destination.

"Right there, boss," he said flatly, pointing a blunt finger at the floating image. The holographic red blur began to blink, as a window filled with scrolling data opened next to the displayed image graphic.

"Tracking us?"

"Seems likely."

"Ahead of us, keeping constant distance?"

"I think so." Bruno fought to keep his answers succinct and precise.

"And they are kzin spacecraft?" Carol chewed her lip. "How many?"

Bruno shrugged. "Who else would be out here in the Deep Black? I'd say there is more than one ship, less than ten."

"How I love your engineering-style vagueness."

He ignored the jibe and continued. "Flanking us, I figure, running a bit ahead. Slow vector toward us—like a cautious intercept."

"Seems funny. Not kzinlike. How close are they?"

He pointed to the data window next to the red blur. "About seven light-minutes away."

The blinking red blur looked harmless enough from an implied distance of over a hundred million kilometers, but at these speeds . . .

"*Dolittle*," she murmured.

Both Bruno and Carol knew that the *Sun-Tzu* was not prepared for an interstellar dogfight. Once they launched *Dolittle* and entered the Wunderland system, Carol and Bruno could carve up kzin craft by the dozens. But the one-shot *Dolittle* would remain berthed for several more years, until they were nearer the Centauri system.

"This far out from Wunderland? Chancy at best."

"Still, we might have a chance—if that red blur represents just a few scoutships."

"Maybe." Bruno's tone was skeptical. "We do carry some weaponry. . . ."

"And we're captained by a combat veteran."

Bruno gave her a look. "Too bad we can't hit them with our massive egos."

Carol's tone became sweet. "We'll save it as a last resort. Then we'll use yours, Tacky. Look, let's keep assuming that the damned blip is a ratcat ship." Carol's eyes fixed beyond the holoscreen. "Why the slow vector to intercept? Any kzin vessel out here, with their reactionless drives, could intercept us within hours."

Silence stretched out between them.

"I have good news and bad news," he replied softly, instead of answering directly.

"Well?" Carol's tone held a trace of impatience.

Bruno was still studying the datastreams marching across the holoscreen. "The good news is that they think we can't see them."

"What makes you say that?"

"Ratcats make banzai raids, right?" Bruno waited for Carol's nod. "They wouldn't sit out there, waiting, if they thought we could see them. They would attack."

"And the bad news?" Still the impatient captain.

"Yeah, that." Bruno chose his words carefully. "Almost anything we do will tip them off that we *can* see them. There would be no reason to change our routine in deep space. If we change our routine, they might hit us with everything they've got."

"Ummm. Cat . . . and mouse."

He smiled a lopsided grin that went no deeper than his thinned lips. "Boss, I think they want to board us."

Carol nodded abruptly. "Right. Otherwise they would just crack us like a rotten egg."

"What poetic imagery." Greatly daring while she was in Captain Mode, he took her hand.

She ignored him and pursed her lips in thought. "But

they are underway in *our* direction, from Sol *toward* Wunderland. They would have to be Third Fleet stragglers, right?"

Bruno picked his words very carefully. "Not necessarily. Could be Fourth Fleet." He rubbed his thumb across the smooth back of Carol's hand. It was reassuringly warm to his touch. At least she didn't *seem* frightened.

"In which case . . ." she prodded.

"They could have seen us and looped around. Don't forget that spacedrive of theirs." He shrugged. "Third or Fourth Fleet, doesn't matter. The point is, I think they want our ship."

"And us, too, maybe."

Without humor, he added, "That is, if they *are* kzin warcraft. They could be something even worse."

Carol grunted. "You're such an optimist."

"Probably as good at optimism as you are at poetry."

She frowned a little, and shook her head. "Wouldn't make any sense, to waste that much delta vee and time. . . ."

"But Captain-my-captain," he replied, half smiling at his pet name for her, a twinge of normalcy amid the nervous tension of the navigation deck, "they can pull hundreds of gees, remember. Take 'em just a couple weeks after we pass them to decelerate, turn around and reaccelerate up to relativistic speeds."

Carol shook her head at the concept of accelerating from a standstill to seventy percent of light-speed—in a week. To a Belter, that idea must smack of magic. "Plus extra time to maneuver around the drive wash."

Bruno blinked, then grinned widely. "That's *right*. The drive wash is hard gamma and plasma."

She smiled without mirth. "That's the joke, my loyal crew: When is a weapon not a weapon?"

"When it is a spacedrive," he replied. "*Angel's Pencil* taught us that."

"It could cook the kzin through and through, their precious reactionless drive and all." Carol bared her teeth, white in the dim light of the holoscreens.

The *Sun-Tzu's* backwash was a plume of ionized hydrogen and hard radiation, jabbing behind it like an enormous scythe. In the high interstellar vacuum, it bristled with blue-white ferocity, fully a tenth as long as the solar system was wide.

Bruno's mood sobered. The cranky antimatter drive had its limitations as a weapon; it was difficult to orient, slow to start or shut down, and very hard to maintain. They would have to shut it down to re-aim it—the stabilizers couldn't be overridden without reprogramming while the drive was quiet.

Could the *Sun-Tzu* stop the kzinti in interstellar space, with inferior weapons and almost no maneuverability? The ship had never been designed for warfare. All *Sun-Tzu* was designed to do was quickly deliver *Dolittle* and crew—and the cryovial with its Finagle-damned virus—to Wunderlander space. Antimatter drive or not, the kzinti ships could literally run rings around the *Sun-Tzu*.

The *Sun-Tzu* was mostly ice. Water was an effective if imperfect shield against both the relativistic impact of dust particles lancing in from forward, and the harnessed hell of the experimental antimatter drive aft. It looked far larger than it was. Thus, it could give some protection against kzin weaponry.

Up to a point.

But first things first, Bruno reminded himself. Fooling around with the drive while it was on would certainly be suicidal. They would have to shut it down and reorient the entire ship. That would give them added doses of radiation, because they would lose the added deflecting power of the drive's hundred-kilogauss magnetic fields.

Even with those fields, their cumulative radiation doses slowly edged up, watch by watch, inexorably. Eventually, the autodoc would be unable to repair the continual cellular damage of sleeting atomic fragments and piercing photons.

He felt a jarring sense of disloyalty, even though he knew it was irrational. Part of Bruno said: *This* was not the mission. They were supposed to go to Wunderlander space, with Bruno fully Linked into the *Dolittle's* computers, and Carol and the revived crew of the *Sun-Tzu* sealed away in the cargo compartment with the opened cryovial.

Then he would lose Carol forever, but not to another man or woman. To a virus older than the human race. But in a way, they would never be closer.

Bruno felt dizzy, and wished that Carol wasn't in the next crash couch, so he could pop a few mood modifiers from his autodoc. His emotions lurched, trying to keep up with his logic. Carol finally squeezed Bruno's hand hard and held his eyes with hers.

"I think our best bet is to get the drive pointed at your little red blur," she said, pointing at the holoscreen. "That will answer the question once and for all. If your little blip moves in response, we'll have our answer. Natural phenomena in deep space don't maneuver around drive wash."

Bruno nodded, part of him marveling at the easeful beauty of how her facial muscles moved. How would she look after the virus did its work? The Dream repeatedly showed him a portion of that awful truth: hairless, domed forehead, elongated jaw without teeth, leathery skin like armor. But Carol's eyes would be unchanged, looking sadly at him from her virus-altered face.

He yanked himself back into the factual, crisp present. Time enough for worry later. "Uh, right, you're the boss. But if there are ratcats out there, I'll bet they have thought about that particular scenario, and have some nasty contingency plans."

"What else is new?" Carol rapped, her tone cold as cometary ice.

A slow silence passed between them. It was her play now.

"Begin shutdown subroutine," she formally told the computer, repeating the command twice more for verification. Another window in the holoscreen opened, displaying the shutdown procedure, complete with schematics and data analyses. Step by step, the silicon mind of the *Sun-Tzu* strengthened the magnetic bottle confining the glittering deadly cloud of antihydrogen, and increased power to the ionizing lasers that kept the fuel in manipulable form.

At the same time, the computer slowly decreased the inflow of normal matter—scavenged up from the interstellar gas in their path, mixed with the ices of the *Sun-Tzu's* iceball hull—which created the harnessed Hell inside the reaction chamber. It was a delicate, slow-motion ballet of electronics and engineering, carefully balanced and monitored.

A slight miscalculation, and the *Sun-Tzu* would become a pocket nova in ten microseconds.

Bruno watched the on-line shutdown telemetry with all his attention, wishing mightily that he was Linked. The itch had become a craving that burned in his neck socket. But then, if he were Linked, he would not have Carol's immediate warmth. Nor would he care. And right now he needed her contact and comradeship more than anything.

Even more than Linkage, he told himself confidently.

He could feel Carol's hand squeezing his own almost to the point of pain. Many minutes passed as the computer balanced each incremental decrease in normal matter infall with increases in magnetic confinement and ionization. The holoscreen displayed the slow process as a series of inexorable discrete events. Neither Bruno nor Carol said anything as they watched and waited, but the joint pressure of their laced fingers was reassuring, the affectionate comfort of skin contact.

A homey and human thing, pitted against an alien threat.

The steady thrumming of the drive slowly decreased with each step in the shutdown protocol. Decreasing thrust was scarcely noticeable from moment to moment, but Bruno felt a heady lightening.

Shutdown protocol . . . time ticking by . . . tense glances . . . increases in radiation sleeting through the weakening magnetic shield . . . the relativistic world outside sliding by in multicolored splendor . . .

A final shudder rang the entire ship like an enormous bell. Thrust dropped to zero.

Now the plummeting elevator sensation of freefall sent Bruno's Flatlander stomach roiling. Except that they were falling through the interstellar emptiness at seventy percent of the speed of light itself.

A low tone snagged his attention, drew it back to the holoscreen. A soft voice calmly said, *"Shutdown protocol is complete. Confinement within normal parameters. Chamber cooling protocol initiated."*

Bruno sucked in a deep breath and felt Carol let go of his hand, still tingling from the strength of her grasp. He leaned over and kissed her cheek firmly, as if in thanks.

"Drive shutdown is complete," Carol said formally for the benefit of the ship's log. "Let's start planning." She stretched her fingers within her own dataglove, warming up.

Bruno watched Carol's eyes become hard and narrow, the eyes of a survivor and combat veteran of the Second and Third Waves. Her face was neutral, as was her tone. "This is where all the heroic bullshit Early poured into your ears turns real."

Bruno knew that she was thinking again of her ship-to-ship battles during the Second Wave. He had his Dream with which to battle; Carol had genuine memories of the War, sharp edged and immediate.

He reached over and took Carol's free hand. Such thoughts were never far from her. He remembered holding Carol after they had made love. They would lie with arms around each other, in the gentle darkness of the sleeproom, the only illumination from holoscreens showing the green riot of the Hanging Gardens in Confinement Asteroid. Carol's half-seen satisfied smile would fade, as she would first think about her wartime experiences, then talk of them. Sometimes she had wept as she recalled the horrors, her muscular body tensing in his arms as the memories gripped her, dragging her across years and billions of kilometers.

Memories of air gushing from the shattered helmet of an old friend, turning to glittering clouds of ice shards in the wan sunlight. The flash of a control board shorting out after a direct hit with a kzin particle beam. Worst of all, the ear-ringing clang of a railgun projectile hulling a ship, followed by the whining roar of escaping air. Bruno could only imagine the emotional impact of the deadly ballet of space warfare, the long periods of waiting and contingency planning punctuated by seconds of frenzied activity and terror. Carol compartmentalized her fears better than Bruno ever could. He accepted this.

She exhaled loudly, stuffing the past mentally away, and stretched her head back and forth to relieve the tension. She released his hand, and patted it gently.

"Don't you think that it's time?" Carol asked quietly, not looking at the Link clipped to the console in front of Bruno. "You can keep better track of the blips while Linked, and can oversee a faster start-up, can't you?"

Bruno nodded, reaching over to squeeze her hand again. She didn't respond. "I take it that you just gave an order?" he asked.

Carol turned and looked at him directly, harsh memories flitting like ghosts across the planes and angles of her face. "Yes," she said simply, none of her sadness at giving the order evident.

Bruno nodded. He picked up the Link and inserted the plug into his neck socket, but couldn't keep his hand from trembling as he did so.

• CHAPTER FOUR

Rrowl-Captain roared his anger, and the bridge crew of the *Belly-Slasher* fell instantly silent.

"Initiate contingency plan *Krechpt*," he shrieked into the intership and shipboard intercoms.

The ripping-cloth sound of the gravity polarizers suddenly became much louder. The hull seemed to shift and waver randomly beneath them as the fabric of space itself bent and twisted. Rrowl-Captain turned away from the intercom, eyes flicking at once to his command-chair thinplate. Status reports marched across his tactical screen in the dots-and-commas script of the kzin. The two other ships under his command were following orders as expected, a portion of his furious mind noted, racing away from one another at the limits of their gravitic drives.

Rrowl-Captain turned to the source of the problem.

"Strategist," he spat and snarled in the Hero's Tongue, whipping his naked pink tail in annoyance, "tell me why the monkeyship has deactivated its drive! They are far from turnover." The cool, dry ship's air quickly filled with the captain's anger-smell, redolent with attack pheromones. His pelt, each hair erect with pent-up rage, gleamed under the bright orange illumination on the bridge.

The kzin in charge of predicting human battle behavior stood very straight and still, with only the slightest droop of his whiskers and half-folded ears to suggest his discomfort. He slapped retracted claws against face in salute. "Dominant One," he began, "the humans must have detected us."

Rrowl-Captain choked back an outraged shriek and barely contained his fury, his reply acid-etched with purring sarcasm.

114

"This I can perceive, O Master of Grass-Eating Slave Tactics! Please do not further strain your name-lacking honorless leaf-grazing mind by restating facts obvious to any true Hero with eyes and the Warrior Heart!"

The captain peered hopefully at the other kzin, who blinked twice at this insulting profanity. Still, he was experienced with his commander's black moods, and wisely kept silent, waiting respectfully.

Duty had battled honor in Rrowl-Captain's Warrior Heart constantly since the Third Fleet's destruction. He had kept shipboard discipline far more harsh and unyielding than considered routine for kzin warcraft. He chuffed air out through his nostrils in disgust, pleading silently with the One Fanged God for patience and wisdom.

His three ships had been part of the vanquished Third Fleet, defeated yet again by these hairless monkeys, using their leaf-eating tricks against noble Heroes. Rather than dying with honor in an attack on Man-home as his Warrior Heart had demanded, Rrowl-Captain had obeyed the final command of the Dominant Commander of the Third Fleet, Chsst-Admiral.

And in following his Duty, he had abrogated his Honor. It leaked from his very soul in shame. Rrowl-Captain's liver and heart never let him forget his dishonor.

The three scout-*cum*-warships under Rrowl-Captain's direct command—*Pouncing-Strike*, *Spine-Cruncher*, and his own *Belly-Slasher*—had been carefully tuned and stealthed before their departure from Man-sun back toward Ka'ashi, or as the monkeys called it in their whining mewl of a language, *Alpha Centauri*. Rrowl-Captain's mission was to use his three warcraft to probe the spaces between the two stars, observing the soulless monkeys from afar, and tightbeaming ahead the gigabytes of information collected during the defeat of the Third Fleet.

Chsst-Admiral, grizzled and radiation-scarred with the outward signs of his Warrior Heart, had been Rrowl-Captain's superior during the initial assault on Ka'ashi, long years before, and thus commanded respect and deference. Any kzin would follow the Dominant One of the Fleet into the Dark Pit itself.

Chsst-Admiral had convinced Rrowl-Captain that his own Warrior's Path would be to humbly aid the full scale Heroes' Vengeance promised by the Fourth Fleet. He had obeyed Chsst-Admiral's commands, subjugating his honor to Fleet discipline, but his agreement still reeked faintly of cowardice, of grass-on-breath.

Chsst-Admiral, of course, had showed vibrantly that his own heart and liver were a credit to the Patriarch in Castle Riit at far-off Kzin-home. He had died in the glorious suicide attack on the interstellar launcher on the moon of the large gas giant, which the monkeys called Juno.

Rrowl-Captain snarled again at his lost honor, his memories like salt packed into a claw-slashed nose. He had dueled with two octals of other Heroes during his command, and Rrowl-Captain fingered their notched ears at his trophy belt in proud memory. The duels made him feel momentarily like a credit to his long-dead father and his mourned litter-brother, as well as the Riit Patriarch Himself.

Yet the taste of cowardice, like that obtained by chewing roots and leaves, returned all too soon. With half his attention, Rrowl-Captain watched Strategist waiting silently, eyes averted yet forward, clearly ready for the attack. The other kzin believed that his commander would rend him limb from limb.

This was not a surprise to the master of the *Belly-Slasher*. It had happened often enough in the past on this command bridge, after all.

But Rrowl-Captain could afford to lose no more competent officers, particularly with this new monkey threat. He mastered his fury for the moment, and concentrated again on the issue at hand. Chsst-Admiral had ordered Rrowl-Captain's ships to act as observers in the long grass of deep space, attacking nothing. They were to prepare the way for the Fourth Fleet. And he had done so, at great cost to his honor and digestion.

Yet this human ship, traveling from Man-home to the

Ka'ashi system, was too rich a prize for any kzin to resist. Stealthed and invisible, Rrowl-Captain's ships had stalked from afar the queer monkey spacecraft for many watches, studying it. Its reaction drive was a shockingly efficient blaze of plasma and hard gamma radiation. Alien-Technologist had even suggested that the monkeys had developed a contramatter spacedrive, impossible as that seemed.

But it was much more than a spacedrive, at least to a kzin with the true Warrior Heart! Such a device could be used to incinerate whole continents from orbit, like some enormous Flenser of Judgment out of forgotten myth. A fearsome weapon, sure to gain for its discoverer the approval of the Riit Patriarch Himself, and all that such approval would mean.

Finally, Rrowl-Captain could wait no longer, and had moved his trio of warcraft slowly toward the monkeyship, preparing to capture this rich prize. Then the alien craft's drive had shut down! His tail lashed again in frustration.

It would have been simple to capture the monkeyship had the humans not detected them. The only question would have been how many Heroes' lives to spend in minimizing harm to the ship and its contents. Perhaps the best plan would have been a large boarding party with kinetic penetration aids in reserve. . . . Or *Belly-Slasher* or one of his brother ships could have simply hammered the human craft with kinetic energy bombs, then landed some boarding parties of Heroes in the confusion.

Such an approach would have done much to salve the wounded Honor of Rrowl-Captain.

The lethal wash of gamma radiation and ionized gas pushing the monkeyship through space would have effectively prevented communication with the other monkeys at Man-home. The monkeys would simply think that their new vessel had failed, having hit some interstellar debris at nearly six eighths light-speed.

Conquest-Governor would surely welcome Rrowl-Captain back to Wunderland, bearing such a rich prize. Honor, slaves, a place on the Governor's Council, landholdings, and kzinrrettis would have been his! Perhaps his own hunting park. Almost certainly a full Name!

But this savory morsel had been snatched from his closing jaws by cowardly incompetence! Rrowl-Captain's killing teeth ached with the loss.

The fury within his thwarted Warrior Heart, never far below the surface, boiled anew. Rrowl-Captain lifted his massive head and roared his frustration, slashing at the air in front of him with angry claws. The entire bridge crew slapped sheathed claws across faces in submissive salute.

Rrowl-Captain grumbled and pushed his thinplate aside. He bolted upright to his full height of nearly three meters, like a bipedal tiger on anabolic steroids, and stalked the bridge as if he were seeking prey in a hunting park. The crew held their collective breaths, motionless, waiting to see who would be the captain's target.

He padded silently up to Strategist, his voice now very calm and therefore particularly dangerous. The captain of the kzinti warship looked Strategist rudely in the eyes, kzin to kzin, in barely veiled challenge. His tail slowly moved from side to side, in sly counterpoint to his words.

"So tell me, kzin-without-a-name, how the primitive monkeys, these *humans*, are able to detect our gravitic polarizers?" His contained fury revealed itself in a rictus grin of needle-sharp carnivore teeth.

Strategist choked back his own growl of challenge, saying nothing. Rrowl-Captain contained a cough of approval.

"They can detect our monopoles, true. Quite true." The captain tapped the other kzin's broad chest twice with an unsheathed claw as he spoke, a profound insult to any Hero.

Strategist gurgled, trembling with the kzin combination of fear and rage.

"Yet this is no great surprise," Rrowl-Captain half purred, "as the pitiful monkeys use monopoles themselves extensively and are therefore familiar with their properties. This is why we shield them from monkey instrumentation, as the smallest unblooded kitten could surmise." His tail flicked.

Strategist gulped, gasped. In a thin, flat voice he started to speak. "Dominant One, it would seem—"

"It would seem," Rrowl-Captain interrupted silkily, "that you would insult my intelligence, to claim that these pitiful monkeys can understand the workings of gravitic polarizers, yet still fly through space balanced on hot exhaust fumes?" He displayed his teeth in a wide grin, then picked between them with a sharp claw tip in derision and insult.

Rrowl-Captain watched Strategist take a deep breath at the offensive slur to his ancestors, and twitched his tail with some satisfaction. There were some advantages to leadership after all.

"These are *monkeys*," he continued, scorn dripping from every growling syllable of the Heroes' Tongue. "These nameless and honor-lacking humans are leaf-eating vermin . . ." he railed suddenly, again beginning to lose control. He wiped drool from his thin black lips with the back of a furred hand.

Rrowl-Captain's anger concealed from his Heroes what he held secret in his heart of hearts: the gut-wrenching terror of entire fleets boiled to vapor by lasers that filled the sky, lasers everywhere, crewed by the seemingly puny monkeys. The horrible sensation of wishing to hide from enemies, to run from danger! His liver once more turned to water as the alien emotion gripped him.

For a moment, Rrowl-Captain's eyes saw nothing but the awful green blaze of laser light filling the universe, his nostrils swarming with the odor of his own hidden cowardice, like the smell of a grazing animal.

The scent of *prey*.

The madness receded after a moment. Rrowl-Captain spat onto the deck and mumbled, half to himself. "Just big hairless *ch'tachi*, monkeys, with their inefficient fusion drives and puny lasers and particle beams . . ."

The deck was silent, his crewkzin looking intently at the tapestry covered floorplates.

He stopped, moistening a now dry nose-pad with his tongue carefully, trying to control his conflicting emotions.

Breath steamed from his mouth in the chill air of *Belly-Slasher*. The captain's hairless, ratlike tail stood straight out in a posture of angry challenge.

Strategist looked straight ahead, his violet eyes unreadable. After a respectful pause, he saluted again with sheathed claws and averted eyes. "Dominant One, I do not believe the humans can detect our gravitic polarizers under normal conditions; it must be that one or more of the polarizers are unbalanced."

"Oh?" Calm, silky.

Strategist held his breath while Rrowl-Captain continued to stare at him, then finished, whiskers still twitching. "Unbalanced gravitic polarizers . . . will leave a faint graviton signature on mass-detection instruments."

Rrowl-Captain stood stock-still for a moment, thinking deeply. His fur, bristling with rage moments before, relaxed deceptively. The master of the *Belly-Slasher* began to groom himself thoughtfully, smoothing back his luxurious orange-red pelt with the back of an absently licked hand.

"Urrr . . . yes," Rrowl-Captain agreed. "It would be difficult for these humans to detect us near light-speed by any other method, considering their primitive technology."

A hanging silence, as quiet as the moment before stalked prey is caught with killing jaws. In a single lithe bound the Captain leaped back to his command chair—and sat. Lounged. "Unbalanced gravitic polarizers," he hissed softly to himself. Pupils dilated and contracted as he considered implications.

And the cause.

Strategist gave another deferential salute—unnoticed—and then sat heavily at his station. The bridge crew remained silent, guessing with secret relief what would come next. They became calmer, waiting for the inevitable, not looking away from their thinplates.

Rrowl-Captain smiled widely, but not with humor. "Engine-Tinker," he purred over the shipwide commlink, "do the memory of the Conquest Heroes of Wunderland the favor of reporting to your humble captain. I have some questions concerning your last routine balancing of the gravitic polarizers."

He chuckled low in his throat as he examined his right hand, back first, then the leathery palm. Rrowl-Captain extended his four black claws deliberately, one at a time. He began stropping them methodically on the worn, centimeter-thick Kdatlyno-hide arms of his command chair.

Minutes passed slowly as the captain purred a kit's hunting tune to himself, the sounds of his sharpening claws loud on the command bridge. Rrowl-Captain directed the kzin named Communication-Officer to tightbeam Strategist's information to *Pouncing-Strike* and *Spine-Cruncher*, and take compensatory action. Still purring throatily, Rrowl-Captain reviewed his strategy regarding the monkeyship, making a few notes on his personal logscreen in the dots-and-commas script of the kzin. A new approach to dealing with the monkeyship occurred to him . . .

The crew did not dare look up from their stations as the access door to the bridge irised open silently. Rrowl-Captain lifted his lambent gaze from his thinplate, like a hunter rising from tall grasses. A hunter done with stalking, and ready to finish the hunt.

The technician entered limp-tailed, crawling on his belly toward the command chair. The air seemed to grow thick and cloying as the captain began to growl, the image of a knife-toothed smile in his voice.

Rrowl-Captain screamed and leaped.

The crew relaxed slightly at their stations, their batlike ears folded tightly against the wet rending sounds on the bridge. They were familiar with their captain's routine, having experienced it before. Shipboard discipline would relax slightly for a time, and full attention could be placed on capturing the monkeyship.

Also, there would be opportunities. Engine-Tinker's second would shortly be promoted, of course.

• CHAPTER FIVE

Snick-click.

Carol Faulk looked at Bruno's anxious face as he plugged the thick interface cable into the socket set in the left side of his neck. He looked almost wistful. She was half able to hide the wince she felt as she heard the sharp metallic sounds of the locking connector mechanism holding the cable firmly in place to his neck.

Leech, she thought to herself, irrationally cursing the computer. But there was worse to come.

Carol particularly hated the next part.

With the cable hanging from his neck like a heavy-bodied electronic lamprey, Bruno smiled a little at her, a bit self-consciously. Much as she hated the knowledge, she knew that his expression was one of half-hidden anticipation.

"Would you do the honors?" he asked her quietly.

Bruno had little choice; due to its long-term risks, full Linkage was a command decision, and as such required Carol's direct and active approval. The ship sighed and muttered all around them now that the *Sun-Tzu* was in free-fall and the ever-present thrumming of the constant-boost drive was silent; a white noise of hissing ventilators and the muted clicking of servo-mechanisms filled her ears. Dust from the corners drifted on the ventilator's breeze, glittering like tiny multicolored stars where it floated into the holoscreen projection beams.

Carol nodded, molding her lips into the confident smile that she knew her lover wanted to see. She verbally told the computer to begin the full Linkage protocol, then repeated the approval two times, in standard confirmation procedure. Finally, she thumbed her console pad, entering the command into the *Sun-Tzu*'s permanent log.

Bruno's crash couch extruded padded restraints, gently pinning his arms, legs, neck and midsection. He said nothing, eyes forward on the holoscreen starscape. Or maybe he was looking *beyond* the starscape, she wondered. Closing her eyes for a moment, Carol leaned over and kissed Bruno's cheek. She could feel the muscles in his face smile in response to her through her lips. Carol settled back into her own crash couch.

"It'll be all right," he whispered. "I'm not like any other Linker, remember?"

Carol nodded. "You betcha, sport."

He certainly wasn't like any other Linker; Bruno was much more. Carol didn't want to lose that.

The computer chimed and informed the navigation deck in its cool electronic voice that full computer-neural net Linkage was commencing. A window in the Status section of the main holoscreen opened, reporting graphically the progress of Bruno's Linkage with the *Sun-Tzu*'s main computer.

Carol grimaced as Bruno's interface booted him up, and sent him into the usual violent convulsions. He bucked and shook, the restraints holding him firmly in place. Spittle shook from his open mouth, floating in tiny droplets in the microgravity.

She wanted to hold him, but held herself back. It couldn't help Bruno now.

"Ah! Aahhhh!" A hypospray swiveled out of his neckrest, striking at his neck like a rattlesnake, and hissed some medicinal compound into his jugular vein. It seemed to calm him after a few moments, though he still twitched and murmured in seeming pain as his mind felt its way into the complex data architecture of the *Sun-Tzu*'s computers.

Or, as Carol suspected, his mind was dragged kicking and screaming to silicon rates of speed, like some kind of terrible mental whiplash.

Linkage, she reminded herself, was painful, no matter

what Linkers said before or after the event. They never seemed to remember very much about the process of Linking and un-Linking; the pain and convulsions and time spent convalescing in the autodoc afterwards.

It was all worth it to the Linker. They only remembered Transcendence. Becoming One with the All.

The human mind, Linked to a sixth-generation macroframe array, was capable of the straight numerical number-crunching ability of the computer alone, of course. But the Linker was much more than a lightning calculator, able to balance a World Bank's worth of credit accounts in nanoseconds. The Linked human mind could also access the analog judgment subroutines, of fuzzy logic and hard syntax, with a sureness that non-AI silicon alone could never generate.

Yet a human mind in full communion with such a computer did not think in a linear, machinelike fashion. Far from it.

Instead, the computer-Linked human mind was estimated to think at a rate hundreds of thousands of times faster than an un-Linked neuronal network. Faster, better, deeper; but most of all, *differently*. The Linked mind could find connections where none were apparent, practical answers to seemingly impossible questions. Complex systems were easily controlled, chaos theory or not, with a Linked human mind at the homeostatic controls.

There was a hitch, naturally. While Linked, the human mind was no longer strictly human. The longer a human mind stayed in full Linkage with a sixth-generation macroframe, the more difficult it was for the human mind to un-Link. Eventually, it became impossible. It was as if more and more of the computer was left behind in the Linker's human skull, or more and more of the Linker's human mind was shoved into the computer architecture. Whatever the explanation, the process progressively left less and less of the Linker's humanity intact.

Carol had seen evidence of this horror herself, with poor Bruno.

The full AI computers were initially very useful, but always shut down after a few months, producing an extremely expensive piece of junk. Unusable for even straight calculations. Carol felt that this observation should have been hint enough to the brain-computer interface researchers in Luna to leave well enough alone. Yet again and again, humans were entered into full Linkage with high-level computers.

The Linkers also shut down, just like their pure silicon cousins, after a certain period of time. But what could cause catatonia in both machine and mind?

No one knew.

With this in mind, Carol did her best as captain of the *Sun-Tzu* to minimize Bruno's full Linkage time. It was useful to have the pilot be part of the ship, of course; but he was needed, whole and sane, when *Dolittle* made its first and final run on the Wunderland system. Bruno would do that piloting in full Linkage, for as long as necessary.

It would surely drive him insane, Carol knew sadly, no matter how different Bruno's hybrid brain might be from that of other Linkers. And yet it was all part of the mission of the *Sun-Tzu*, to which all of the crew—including Carol and Bruno—had agreed. Volunteered.

Carol would meet her own fate at that time, too. It didn't concern her too much. She had seen enough battle action during the Third Wave, lost enough comrades, to know about sacrifices. She didn't want to die, no, but Carol knew what humanity had at stake in the war against the ratcats. Humanity should be ready to try anything.

Even Project Cherubim.

She watched odd expressions flit across Bruno's twitching face as the Linkage proceeded toward its symbiotic conclusion. His muscles seemed to bunch and move differently under Bruno's skin in odd ways, reflecting the changing biotelemetry displayed in the holoscreen window. Bruno's fingers quested blindly within their restraints, twitching and moving in patterns that seemed somehow inhuman to Carol.

Carol thought that Bruno's eyes were the worst part. They

stared, bulged, rolled up to show the whites and impossibly wide pupils. She wanted to stroke Bruno's face, but knew it was too early in the process to touch him. Not that he would even feel it. Sweat beaded out of his pores as he twitched, leaping from his skin in fine droplets, floating around the navigation deck in freefall.

When they had first had sex, Carol swore to herself that she was not in love with this sad little man with the bumpy, scarred cranium. The voyage was long, and it was doubtful that any of them would live through even its early stages. Years spent aboard an experimental spacecraft, followed by a suicide mission. Everyone on board *Sun-Tzu*, asleep or awake, knew the score displayed on that particular chip.

Carol had told herself that what she was starting to feel for Bruno was only the relief of tension, or at best its afterglow. She was an independent woman, after all. A pilot of a Shrike singleship against the Second Wave the ratcats had sent against Sol. Later, Carol had commanded several squadrons during the Third Wave, and had the shipsuit patches to prove it. Defending Sol had become her life. Carol did not have time for romantic entanglements, particularly with a chipheaded dwarf of a Flatlander like Bruno Takagama.

Yet she *had* fallen in love with him, with his moods and quirky sense of humor. Bruno Takagama was both child and man, and somehow neither. The plastic and electronics within his half-healed skull gave him a perspective and manner of thinking different from anyone Carol had ever known in the Belt.

She had found that very attractive.

Bruno was the family Carol had never really had, and she knew that he felt the same about her. The dour Neo-Amish Belters who had raised Carol after her parents' ore-carrier had blown out into high vacuum had a grudging praise for people like Bruno: His heart was as big as his soul.

It stung Carol deeply to see the man she loved become slowly inhuman, tied to the cold metal and silicon of a passionless machine. Yet, when she thought about it, it was ironic: Project Cherubim was not so very different for her, was it? Was Early's plan not to turn Carol, and the coldsleep crew, into something just as inhuman with the virus in the cryovial? Her lips thinned.

The main computer hummed an attention tone, and Carol dragged her thoughts back to the present.

"Carol? I am ready to begin work."

Bruno's voice was higher, oddly cadenced. The correct inflections were still there, peppering words and syllables, yet the nuances were almost *too* studied. It was as if he was *trying* to sound human.

She looked over at Bruno. The restraints had soundlessly retracted back into his crash couch. His eyes, still slightly wide, turned toward her, pupils black and enormous. She held back a familiar look of distaste and pain at that gaze.

The eyes were only part of it, Carol thought. His face was almost completely slack, like a poorly fitted mask. During Linkage, Bruno had other cool concerns than operating his facial musculature.

He sat calmly in the crash couch, the thick interface cable connecting his mind to the *Sun-Tzu*'s computers slowly waving in the microgravity like a marine creature. She felt the usual conflicting emotions: love for Bruno, and discomfort at this alien Linked self.

Her hand reached over to touch his face, hovered, withdrew. "I assume the Linkage is complete?" Her tone was cool and professional, and each calm syllable cost her dearly.

"Yes," Bruno replied. "I can *see* again,"

While Bruno was Linked, he could see across the entire electromagnetic spectrum, using *Sun-Tzu*'s complex and powerful sensory array. She knew that Bruno's sensorium was completely different from the minor chipping-in that any Belter pilot used from time to time for convenience. This was no mere telemetric readout of drive parameters or navigation control via the optic nerve.

Bruno in the fully Linked state perceived *everything*, all

at once. The torrent of data fed directly into his brain and mind.

He called it the All. She had no more chance of understanding her lover's computer-augmented perceptions than an earthworm could understand a rainbow.

She turned away, pretending to study the holoscreen status reports. Even for someone as tough as Carol knew herself to be, as familiar as this scenario had become, the situation was almost unbearably painful.

Carol knew that Bruno's mental state was getting worse. And the process would continue inexorably. More and more, flashes of the cybernetic Bruno peered out from behind his eyes, even in his un-Linked state.

It was an inevitable process. The Linked Bruno was not human. The computer left more of *itself* behind with every full Linkage Bruno experienced. Each time he emerged from the autodoc after severing himself from the computer, there was less and less remaining of the Bruno she loved. His personality was slowly leaching away into a sea of silicon.

And yet he wanted Linkage, *craved* it.

Carol made a face. Perhaps she was being unfair. She wondered how she would feel and act, after conversion by the virus in the cryovial, with the odd name, *Tree-of-Life*. She knew that her feelings about full Linkage were a little irrational because, at least for now, Bruno could un-Link.

There would be no such return to humanity for Carol, once the *Sun-Tzu* reached Wunderlander space. Not once she awakened the crew in coldsleep, opened the cryovial in the sealed compartment of *Dolittle*, and initiated Project Cherubim.

She squared her shoulders. The trick, Carol knew from long experience, was to dissociate her command self from her personal self. She looked at Bruno and said coolly, "So, Tacky, do you still think that your ghost blip is actually a kzin ship?"

Bruno continued to stare directly at her, hardly moving, his pupils expanded to turn his normally grayish eyes into pools of blackness. It made Carol very nervous.

"Well?" she persisted, ignoring the creeping sensation crawling up and down her spine.

"Interesting," Bruno said, with a ghastly imitation of an un-Linked smile. "You keep your feelings from your voice. Or nearly so. But I can read your tones and stress patterns perfectly. Your facial gestures are quite clear when compared with contour bitmaps of earlier visual records. Biotelemetry is also accessed; your skin conductance and pupillary action concur with my conclusion." The alien smile faded. "I make you nervous."

Carol kept her own face stiff, in counterpoint to his own slack features. "Yes," she said evenly, barely keeping the sarcasm from her tone. "It certainly takes an incredible intellect in full Linkage to conclude that fact."

She watched Bruno for a moment, who said nothing.

"Humor, I would assume," he finally said flatly.

Carol tried again. "You certainly do make me nervous. You make *everyone* nervous when you're Linked. All Linkers do. This can't be the first time you've noticed."

His face became completely immobile—mimicking her? "Quite correct; I apologize. But do recall that I am still partly the Bruno you know, and that portion of my Whole cares very much what you think and feel."

Carol blinked at his odd terms and changing syntax. Still, she found his strange words reassuring: even while Linked, part of the Bruno-machine chimera remained the Bruno she loved.

"Thank you," she replied calmly, trying to focus. "But now it is time to get to work. Could you please look at the holoscreen, access the relevant data, and tell me what our putatively feline friends are doing, now that we have shut down the drive?"

Bruno chuckled slightly, too studied and deliberate. "You seem to forget—or refuse to accept—the properties of Linkage," he told her without rebuke. "In multitasking mode I do not require my optic nerves to read or interpret data."

This was true, Carol knew. Data was pouring back and forth furiously through the interface cable, directly between

Bruno's chipped-in hybrid brain and the main computers of the *Sun-Tzu*. It was still a little disconcerting to Carol to realize that a full Linker had his or her attention in many places, simultaneously.

And still more disconcerting to know that the Linked Bruno spoke to her with only an infinitesimal portion of his Transcended consciousness. The rest of him was . . . elsewhere. Everywhere.

"So why are you looking at me, ummm?" she murmured, a little curious despite herself.

"Because I enjoy watching you, Carol, Linked or un-Linked. It accesses many pleasant memories and associations in the human portion of my larger Self. But I can encompass much more about you while I am Transcended." He paused, then moved his head to face the holoscreen. "I perceive that you are still disturbed by my actions. I will face forward."

"Well, I . . ." She felt vaguely uncomfortable, as if she had insulted Bruno at a cocktail party.

"To answer your question more directly, the signals we have been discussing almost certainly emanate from three kzin warships of the Raptor class, stealthed. Probability equals zero point nine nine eight. Third Fleet, I would predict; there are no improvements over that design detectable."

"How can you be so sure?" Carol asked him quickly. She and the un-Linked Bruno had examined the data carefully; there was certainly nothing as straightforward as the Linked Bruno's answer would suggest.

Carol remained a bit suspicious of the black-magic aspects of Linkage.

Bruno paused a moment, then spoke flatly. "Please define for me in objective, nonhuman-oriented terms the tastes 'sweet,' then 'sour,' please."

"Uh, well . . ."

His cheek twitched as he stared intently at the blinking red blur on the upper portion of the holoscreen. Was it a smile? A stray emotion filtering past his machine consciousness?

"Sensoria are usually difficult to describe in precise

terminology without experiential referents," he continued. "Even for simplistic intelligent system networks. Suffice it to say that the anomalous signals 'taste' like three kzin warcraft to me, again, little different from the Third Wave warcraft in our databases."

Carol decided to take his word for it. *Taste*. After all, this was why Bruno had been selected as pilot of the *Sun-Tzu* in the first place. If Carol didn't trust Bruno's Linked observations, why was he aboard?

It still stank of black magic to her. Would she see reality as differently as the computer-Linked Bruno did, once she was converted by the virus in *Dolittle*?

Carol pursed her lips and thought a moment. "So you would have no objections," she asked carefully, "if we point the antimatter reaction chamber toward them and see what they do?"

"On the contrary, I very much wish to verify my . . . intuition . . ."

"Make it so," she ordered formally. A schematic of the *Sun-Tzu* appeared in the main holoscreen window, with *x*-*y*-*z* coordinates in glittering red. Attitude jets flared on the schematic, slowly turning the spacecraft, and Carol felt the straps of her crash couch tightening as the attitude of *Sun-Tzu* matched that of its schematic.

After a few moments, the straps loosened once more, and the line diagram of the *Sun-Tzu* vanished from the holoscreen. Bruno closed his eyes as another hypodermic from his crash couch hissed against his neck.

"Reorientation complete," he reported crisply. "Now we must wait until the presumptive warcraft detect our change in attitude."

They waited together. Seven light-minutes translated to 120 million kilometers. Fifteen minutes, roughly, until the light-speed-limited responses of the mystery signal, if any, arrived back at *Sun-Tzu*. Carol ordered Bruno to train the long-range sensor array at maximum sensitivity, to electronically sniff at the Deep surrounding them.

He smiled that thin, inhuman smile and informed Carol

that he was doing that at all times, in any event. Along with many other things, of course.

Carol wanted to ask many questions of the augmented Bruno. What did the superintelligence sitting next to her, limp in his crash couch, think of their chances of success at Wunderland? What did he think of unaugmented humanity?

Could he still love?

Carol had never asked such questions of Bruno during full Linkage. Afraid of the answers, perhaps. But she feared something else more.

Would she see and feel as Bruno did under full Linkage, after Project Cherubim was complete, and she had been changed? Or would her own situation be worse still? The records from the Black Vault had been heavily censored, even to the crew of the *Sun-Tzu.*

There was so much she did not know.

Carol looked over at her lover, lying bonelessly in his crash couch, eyes now closed, the thick interface cable at his neck. What must it be like, she mused, to have one's mind encompass so much, all at once?

Perhaps she would know for herself, if the *Sun-Tzu* ever reached Wunderland.

Bruno, while Linked, had once told Carol that there was little of free will in what actions he took while Transcended. It was as if knowing the best solution to a problem removed freedom of choice—unless he *intentionally* chose an improper solution. Connected to a computer's vast silicon mind, Bruno had told Carol that he was driven to choose the best solution to a given problem; therefore, free will as she understood it did not exist for him.

Carol mulled that over for a few moments. What if, she thought, the basic nature of free will was the freedom to make *mistakes*?

The holoscreen flashed brightly in alert, and the buzzing electronic tones of the Battle Stations alarm broke her from her reverie.

"Pardon me," Bruno told her calmly, eyes still closed,

"but when I am part of the alarm system, I must act like the relevant component." The alarm tone halted without Carol having to deactivate it.

"No matter. Give me a status report." Carol's fingers tensed on the edges of the console before her. The dataglove and keypads were clipped impotently to the side of the console. With Bruno in full Linkage, her commands were far too slow and crude.

The main holoscreen window cleared, and quickly drew three separate blips, moving rapidly outward from the center of the screen, in different directions. She looked over at Bruno, whose eyes were still closed, facing forward.

"It appears," he said, "that we have hit the jackpot, so to speak." Not waiting for orders, he displayed the observational information, data windows opening and keeping pace with the tiny red sparks, highlighting and scrolling numbers in agreement with his statements.

"The mystery blip," he continued, "did not wait for our change in attitude, Carol." Abruptly he cackled with very unmachinelike glee, a false mirth animating his slack muscles. "Mystery, mystery!"

She jerked back at this sudden change. His face went limp as the hypospray hissed at his neck again. The flat voice came, sibilant and precise, as though driven by air leaking out of a balloon. "It presumably became aware of our engine shutdown seven and a half minutes ago. The single blip then split into three distinct signals. Inference: three ships, previously moving in close convoy, stealthed."

"Finagle damn! One we might handle. But three?"

The holoscreen windows showed relevant data as marching columns of glowing numbers and glittering diagrams. "The stealthing apparently does not stand up well to high-gee maneuvers, and I obtained an excellent remote data acquisition download. I was easily able to correct for what electronic countermeasures the targets were able to activate under high acceleration."

"Well?" Alien vessels for sure, Carol nodded to herself. Her hands gripped the arms of her crash couch until her knuckles turned white with the pressure. Were they *ratcat* ships, though? They had to be.

"As I predicted," Bruno replied, not even the pretense of emotion in his voice. "Three Raptor-class kzin warcraft." As he spoke, a larger window opened on the holoscreen, displaying comparisons between the unidentified craft and the standard Raptor-class kzin warbird. "Engine emissions," he continued, "are consonant with slightly damaged and refurbished Third Wave kzinti space vessels. At the time our engine shutdown registered on their instruments, the convoy immediately broke up, each spacecraft moving in different directions at two hundred gees, which is the limit for Raptor-class warcraft."

Carol forced herself to relax, to breathe deeply. She drummed her fingers on the console. "Are they too far out to fry with the drive?"

"That is one problem," Bruno said evenly. "If we activate the drive now, the radiation and plasma exhaust plume would need to spread across many millions of kilometers. Also, while the drive is in operation it will be almost impossible to detect any further maneuvers of the alien craft, due to drive-wash interference."

He paused, air wheezing in his throat. "On the other hand, the kzinti may already have fired energy weapons toward us that travel just behind our visual observations."

Carol leaned back into her crash couch. "Recommendations?"

Bruno's face sketched a pale ghost of a human smile. "I recommend that we fire the antimatter drive in a random walk across the sections of space which I predict might contain the kzinti craft."

Unconvinced, she made a face and squinted. "But you can't really know where any of the ships are when you fire the drive at them."

The small but immensely powerful figure in the crash couch beside her remained unperturbed. "Naturally," he replied, "due to light-speed limitations, and the fact that all three vessels are varying their acceleration and attitude randomly. They are clearly attempting to avoid energy weapons or missiles. But I have some familiarity with deep-space kzin strategies." He didn't speak for a moment, then continued. "A hunch, perhaps you would call it. Biological minds have limited access to originality, after all."

Carol frowned at the last statement, unsure of who precisely was the target of that insult. "No choice, then. Carry out your recommendation, pilot," she ordered.

Bruno settled back into his crash couch and eased open his eyes. He turned his head toward Carol, and looked at her with his alien, faraway gaze and wide pupils. "Because there may not be time to react to maneuvers made by the kzin ships, I am going to have to take control of all ship functions from the automatic subsystems. Please understand that this will take a great deal of my processing capacity. Additionally, I will be heavily accessing many preprogrammed subroutines and predicting stochastic results. . . ." He paused. "Guessing, you would call it."

"What are you saying?" Carol asked, anxious to do something, *anything*, as she watched the red sparks of the three kzinti craft moving slowly across the starfield depicted in the holoscreen window. Blurred columns of numbers next to each red light displayed their changing velocities and positions.

Bruno nodded slightly. "I will be running short of the dispensable processing capacity that I normally use for conversation and purely human thought, Carol. I may not be able to speak with you for a few minutes. I will post the situation on the holoscreen as data." He turned his head forward and closed his eyes again. His crash couch hummed and cradled him tightly, straps tightening automatically.

Carol bit her lip, then said, "Tacky . . . I mean, Bruno . . . I just . . ."

His eyes still closed, an almost human smile turned Bruno's lips gently upward. "I love you, too," he interrupted softly, "even Linked." The smile then turned mechanical, and began to fade away altogether. "At least a part of me does."

Carol felt a chill prickle down her neck.

• OUTSIDERS TWO

***Outrage.** The hotworld craft maneuver dangerously as this local-node predicted. The disgusting vermin do grave damage to the flux lines and particle density of this sacred region!

Caution. This local-node suggests that this local-and-other nodes observe and contemplate further. A quality of strangeness exists here, necessitating caution.

Fury. This local-node demands the erasure of all such vermin! This region-geometry is sacred!

Caution-with-worry. Such intemperate action violates the Treaty with the feral {^^^///}. Further action may lead to other abominations like the Treaty. Mark the loss in this-local-and-other-node's autonomy!

Impatience. This local-and-other nodes took action before when such hotlife insults began to impinge upon a nearby region-geometry of sacred nature. Necessity dictated such activity.

Mollification. Truth. This local-and-other nodes exterminated many fleets of the hotlife craft. Yet the cost! Again, it was this unfortunate action that led to the Treaty with the {^^^///}.

Neutrality. This local-node will wait for a small interval, but no longer. If the vermin spew forth more of their disharmonious plasma-vomit . . .

Concordance. This local-node is in agreement with the other-node. One. Recall that sentinels watch until action is required—perhaps soon. Observe, dissect the data collected, and learn. It is the Way.

• CHAPTER SIX

Rrowl-Captain finished picking his teeth with an intricately carved *stytoch* bone, sighed, then placed the heirloom back in his belt pouch, blinking in contentment. Ceremonially using the point of his right canine fang, he pierced the late Engine-Tinker's severed ear, and threaded it onto the metal trophy loop hanging from his belt. He shook the loop briskly to distribute the leathery ears, making a soft rustling sound audible over the surging mutter of the gravitic polarizers.

Rrowl-Captain examined the crowded trophy loop judiciously, riffling the thin flaps of dry tissue with a claw tip, then released it to hang loosely from his harness belt.

He made a mental note to make a larger trophy loop soon. There might be need for one very soon.

There was nothing like a punishment duel, the captain reflected, to purify his Warrior Heart, and flush away in hot blood the horrifying thoughts that had recently invaded his brain. The green hell-light of the monkey lasers had finally receded from his thoughts. *Until next time*, he thought sourly, *may the One Fanged God damn all monkeys.* Rrowl-Captain's frustration had abated with the sating of his bloodlust, however, and he found himself better able to concentrate on the matters at hand.

Like capturing the monkeyship.

The master of the *Belly-Slasher's* whiskers flicked in annoyance as he settled back into his command chair. He examined the forward thinscreen display for a moment, making a thrumming sound in thought. Now that the monkeys had detected Rrowl-Captain's ships, the capture of the alien vessel would be more difficult. A pity, to be sure, but the captain felt both well fed and confident.

Feint-and-pounce, he reminded himself. It was the newest Kzinti Lesson, learned in the hard and brutal academy consisting of the debacles of the last three Fleets to Man-sun.

Rrowl-Captain looked down at the deck in front of his command chair and blinked in surprise. He coughed a kzinti giggle at his own forgetfulness, and gestured with a languid claw at the four Jotoki slaves waiting nervously near the bridge entryway. The five-armed and -eyed creatures had muttered constantly in their barbarian slave tongue during the blood-duel, at least one eye always focused on the shrieking and slashing Rrowl-Captain.

The creatures scampered forward immediately at his command. Three snatched up the torn remains of Engine-tinker in their warty arms and carried them away, while the other slave rapidly scrubbed the bridge deck tapestry free of stains and debris. The bridge crew watched with distaste as the plant-eating slaves went about their business.

Rrowl-Captain rumbled disapproval deep in his throat. He was not as prejudiced as his crew. A Jotok could be useful. The five-armed slaves were swift and intelligent. Significantly, they could cooperate among one another far better than most Heroes. And it was well known that feral Jotoki could be dangerous beasts indeed. Yet educated kzin did not fear Jotoki slaves when properly raised, as the ugly creatures were biologically imprinted by slave-tenders into unbreakable loyalty toward their masters. Rrowl-Captain mused on the unfathomable capriciousness of the One Fanged God, for making such clever creatures so pitifully subject to their innate biology.

The One Fanged God had clearly created the Jotoki to be slaves of the kzin. This regardless of what the digitally stored lessons of unblooded historians from Kzin-home, with their blunted claws and thinscreen-damaged eyes, might teach in kitten-school. It was ludicrous to think that these servile and ugly beasts had once been technologically superior employers of sword-wielding kzinti mercenaries!

Rrowl-Captain yawned his outrage at the very thought, baring sharp carnivore teeth. Unlike the kzin, Jotoki did not feed from the summit of the Great Web of All Life, nor did they concentrate and glorify the Life Essence of all creatures below them. The kzin had their place at the Apex of the Great Web, as ordained by the Teachings of the One Fanged God. So the fangless priests said, and so common sense agreed.

No matter who bickered to whom many light-years distant, one thing remained clear: Jotoki ate *plants*.

The captain dismissively spat onto the deck with a snarl. A Jotok leaped forward instantly to clean up the mess with eager fingerlets. Rrowl-Captain sat back and grunted as he watched it scrub the deck until it gleamed, one eye-tipped arm glancing surreptitiously up at him from time to time. It had taken many centuries to properly domesticate the ugly little five-armed slaves, but the Jotoki now fit seamlessly into their proper place in the Empire of the Riit Patriarch.

As eventually would fit these troublesome human monkeys, he thought, absently sheathing and unsheathing his claws in anticipation.

The monkey-humans at Ka'ashi were settling down, at least those living on the planetary surface. Pacification was almost complete, according to the tightbeam reports. Heroes would soon complete the conquest of the cowardly spacefaring feral monkeys in the asteroid belt, as well.

And Heroes would eventually prevail at Man-home, he was certain. How long had the kzin been expanding their Empire compared to these monkeys?

Rrowl-Captain ignored the green hell-light flaring at the back of his thoughts as if in rebuke. It was the destiny of kzinti to rule everywhere their spacecraft traveled, he knew in his Warrior Heart, as the favored sons of the One Fanged God.

Rrowl-Captain inserted a clawtip into a slot on the arm of his command chair, and twisted. The thin-crystal action matrix moved up from the side of the chair, unfolding a thinplate screen and console at the captain's eye level. The screen quickly lit with command functions. Rrowl-Captain purred roughly in his throat, impatient to begin the hunt.

"Communications-Officer," he rasped.

A young kzin, clearly full of liver and a naive image of the Warrior Heart, jumped to attention. "Command me, Dominant One!"

"Set up tightbeam laserlinks with both *Pouncing-Strike* and *Spine-Cruncher*. Full encryption, in case the monkeys can intercept data traffic and have learned our codes."

Unlikely, but the green hell-light in Rrowl-Captain's mind suggested caution. He unfolded an ear at the communications officer in question.

"At once!" the other kzin replied, hands moving rapidly over his thinplate displays.

Rrowl-Captain waited impatiently, working the tip of his pointed tongue between two of his ripping teeth. A piece of Engine-Tinker still lodged there, and was proving difficult to remove. He coughed a chuckle in sudden amusement; the nameless blunt-tooth was an irritation even *after* he became food!

He studied his thinscreen carefully, noting with approval the prearranged course changes and varying accelerations the captains of *Pouncing-Strike* and *Spine-Cruncher* used to avoid becoming targets for monkey weaponry. The ship movements must not become predictable. All three kzin vessels were maneuvering to encircle the human spacecraft, making certain that each kzin ship had a clear zone of attack to carry out its individual mission.

Rrowl-Captain yowled suspiciously when he observed the alien vessel under extreme magnification. The tapered end of the great iceball-spacecraft, source of the now-silent but still fearsome reaction drive, had swung away from its original orientation. It was pointed threateningly toward the position where Rrowl-Captain's ships had been in convoy not long before. Blurring slightly on the screen with the magnification, he noticed that the drive section of the spacecraft was moving slowly in different directions, as if questing for a target.

"Acknowledgment pings have returned from *Spine-Cruncher*

and *Pouncing-Strike*, Leader!" said Communications-Officer crisply.

The captain licked the fur on the back of his hand with his tongue, and slicked back his facial pelt meditatively. The intership laserlinks were now frequency locked, allowing burst telemetry and messages from each kzin vessel to flow to the others at prearranged points, provided there were no unplanned maneuvers. Gravity polarizers and distance made even light-speed communication difficult, particularly in times of battle.

His claws clicking and tapping across the console matrix pad, Rrowl-Captain prepared to initiate his plan to capture the alien vessel. Baring his teeth, he looked balefully into the fiber-optic pickup, and let the snap and slash of command enter his voice.

"Tchaf-Captain," he growled to *Spine-Cruncher*, "you will lead your Heroes against the monkeyship according to the second part of contingency plan Krechpt." He paused, then added grudgingly, "May you show Honor to the Riit and the One Fanged God." With a flick of a claw, the burst message was encrypted and sent. Many seconds later, there was a ping-return, signifying receipt of the message.

Rrowl-Captain then informed Cha'at-Captain of *Pouncing-Strike* that it was time to carry out his own orders. The master of *Belly-Slasher* grinned widely after sending that particular message. He had no doubt that the wild-eyed captain of *Pouncing-Strike*, a smallish kzin with much bravery in his liver and little sense in his brain, would carry out his orders. Sure enough, the ping-return of acknowledgment arrived as swiftly as he had expected.

Cha'at-Captain had been a problem for Rrowl-Captain several times during the convoy's long voyage away from Man-sun and the ignoble fate of the Third Fleet. It was only a matter of time, he knew, before Cha'at-Captain challenged him to combat, for control of the three spacecraft and their mission.

The master of *Belly-Slasher* preferred to spill kzinti blood to higher purposes than advances in rank.

For now, however, Rrowl-Captain still led, and chose orders for the aggressive little master of *Pouncing-Strike* that would remove the problem neatly. Cha'at-Captain could not refuse the orders of his superior, of course. Discipline was the litter-brother to Honor, according to the Teachings of the One Fanged God; Rrowl-Captain had reminded Cha'at-Captain of the specific verses himself.

Not coincidentally, Cha'at-Captain was a fundamentalist follower of the Traditionalist sect of *Hs'sin*. The Teachings of the One Fanged God were inspired works to the uneducated little Hero. Brave, but unlettered.

Rrowl-Captain cynically knew that the Teachings could be quoted by any kzin, regardless of rank or blood, even by the rare atheist Hero. It was simply an ancient book, after all, handed down generation to generation by the priests of the One Fanged God. It was darkly amusing to him that the troublemaking captain had acquiesced so tamely to his fate.

Cha'at-Captain was to lead *Pouncing-Strike* on a scream-and-leap directly at the human spacecraft, firing all weapons, drawing monkeyship weapons fire in turn. *Spine-Cruncher* would use the diversion to fly past the alien ship in a hyperbolic trajectory, and deliver the heavily stealthed monopole bomb. The bomb would detonate close enough to the human ship to temporarily incapacitate its electronics with a hammerblow of an electromagnetic pulse. The human monkeys placed great reliance on electronics.

Spine-Cruncher would then land a boarding party of Heroes to capture and secure the prize. Rrowl-Captain and *Belly-Slasher* would observe how the humans responded to the attacks, aid in the capture if necessary, and direct the mopping-up operation. As soon as the alien craft was secured, Rrowl-Captain would inspect the monkeyship personally, and proceed with converting it to kzinti use and the long trek to *Ka'ashi*.

Rrowl-Captain disliked risking the blood of octal-squared Heroes in *Pouncing-Strike* to create a mere diversion, but if the redoubtable Cha'at-Captain was sufficiently wise and skilled—which Rrowl-Captain thought most unlikely—it might be possible for his crew to survive.

If that became the case, he would deal with Cha'at-Captain's increasingly insubordinate manner in another and more direct fashion. One with less opportunity for the other kzin to accrue honor. Of course, the crew of *Pouncing-Strike* was loyal to their captain. Rrowl-Captain would have to be careful, or at least thorough.

However, in the most likely tactical scenario, Cha'at-Captain and his crew would not present any difficulties whatsoever, after their brave diversionary scream-and-leap toward the monkeyship.

Rrowl-Captain relaxed slightly, daydreaming of his estates to come on Man-home, after he was rightfully rewarded for bringing the contra-matter drive to *Ka'ashi* for use against the monkeys. A palace would be built for his many beautiful kzinrrettis, who would surely be of noble blood, enriching his own line. He would also have his own hunting park, he decided, a place where only he and his litter kittens would stalk and kill prey. Perhaps he would hunt a naked monkey each week, just for the sport of it.

That would relieve him of nightmares tinged with green hell-light, surely.

A languid tongue moved across thin black lips as he considered his certain reward of a double name. Which one would he choose? Perhaps the name his litter-brother had liked so, before he had died while they were still living in the crèche.

Rrowl-C'mef. Rrowl-Captain rumbled the name deep in his throat. It sounded wise and powerful. The name tasted of honor and dignity, did it not? Of teeth tingling with the crunching success of prey between jaws. He would surely wrest honor and victory from the defeat of Third Fleet.

Alarms suddenly yowled, echoing on the control bridge. Rrowl-Captain folded his ears swiftly against the din. His slit pupils narrowed as he looked at the status boards, which blurred with rapid changes.

"Status report!" he shrieked.

Strategist pointed wordlessly at the main thinscreen. Rrowl-Captain saw that the tapered end of the monkeyship had stabilized. He watched as a great cloud of ionized gas emerged from the drive section of the human ship.

"What is the attitude of the alien drive section?" he roared angrily. *Pouncing-Strike* would begin its high acceleration scream-and-leap attack on the alien vessel at any time now.

"Nearly the approach path assigned to *Pouncing-Strike*," replied Strategist with a snarl.

Sure enough, the blinking marker on the tactical thinscreen representing Cha'at-Captain's vessel was accelerating along a coincident vector. Rrowl-Captain snarled his anger.

"Is there sufficient time to warn *Pouncing-Strike* by laserlink?" he shouted to Communications.

The young kzin's tail drooped. "No, Dominant One," he replied submissively. "We are too far away."

Rrowl-Captain looked back at the tactical thinscreen and saw that it was true. He slashed the air in front of him with bared claws in impotent rage. *May the One Fanged God damn light-speed!*

The contra-matter drive of the monkeyship ignited. The cloud of gas surrounding the drive section glowed eye-searing violet for a moment.

The main thinplate viewscreen went suddenly white, then corrected automatically for the awful glare of the reaction drive. It became a great blazing column of light, brighter than suns, stretching rapidly across the viewscreen. Rrowl-Captain ground razor-sharp teeth impotently as he watched *Pouncing-Strike* attempt to vector away from the expanding drive wash.

"*Pouncing-Strike* has ceased acceleration!" shouted Strategist.

Rrowl-Captain bared his teeth. Clearly, the other ship's gravitic polarizers had failed under the great stress of attempting to maneuver away from the spreading death of the contra-matter drive exhaust. It had become a ballistic lump, helpless.

The command bridge crew watched the tactical screen

impotently as inertia carried *Pouncing-Strike* into the blazing column of radiation and plasma. Rrowl-Captain snarled and tore a claw on the Kdatlyno-hide arms of his command chair.

The white blaze erupting from the monkeyship slowly turned against the color-shifted starscape toward them, like a great sword out of mythology.

"Communications," roared Rrowl-Captain, "send a burst transmission to *Spine-Cruncher*. Tell them that we will divert the monkeys in order to allow them to carry out their mission."

"At once," said Communications, proudly.

Rrowl-Captain hunched forward in his command chair, mastering his hidden fears. Honor *would* be his, and this victory would slay his inner demons.

"Navigator," he rasped, "begin evasive maneuvers, inward toward the monkeyship. Attempt to draw their fire. Strategist, aid him with your knowledge." Rrowl-Captain's torn claw began to bleed, unnoticed, onto the spotless arm of the command chair.

"At once, Dominant One," the two other kzin shouted with one Hero's voice.

The entire command bridge seemed to blur and tremble as the gravitic polarizer's mutter grew to a low roar. A scorching odor began to emanate from the ventilators as the polarizer was pushed beyond basic design limits. The command bridge filled with the snarling of the agitated crew and the pheromonal scent of their fury.

The deadly white blaze of the alien contra-matter reaction drive stretched across the thinplate viewscreen. It grew swiftly larger and began to move to one side. But slowly.

Rrowl-Captain made the slashing gesture of fealty to the One Fanged God, and watched his fate rushing toward him.

• CHAPTER SEVEN

Linkage was godhead.

Bruno felt the hail of relativistic particles slowly eroding the hull of *Sun-Tzu* like an invigorating breeze on bare skin. The lethal blaze of radiation sleeting through the sensors was like desert sunshine, warm and friendly.

But he knew that there was so much more than what lay immediately outside the spacecraft to perceive and cherish, to make part of himselves! *Everything* about *Sun-Tzu* was now part of Bruno: the raw power of the antimatter drive, the patient, lethal tensions of the weapons systems, the exquisite fineness of his growing sensorium.

Linked, he could do many things besides wear a spaceship like a slick and sensitive skin. Bruno's mind had become more than simply human.

It had become Mind.

From its tiny human kernel, loci of subminds with special interests quickly formed and grew, each with full independent consciousness as well as being part of the developing interconnective Whole. He had become a clamoring community, a society of minds, each subunit far greater than their woefully limited biological ancestor.

Bruno sent his enhanced consciousness ranging restlessly through the sensory and computational net of *Sun-Tzu*, gazing outward and inward simultaneously. He could at once encompass the All, the depth and range of the universe, from quanta to quasars. A portion of Bruno was still staggered by the whirlwind of knowledge within his thoughts, but with every full Linkage, he became better able to access the vast vault of data surrounding him. It was as if his myriad selves were dissolving in a warm ocean of knowledge and certitude.

But that did not concern him overmuch, even the part of himselves that was still Bruno.

For Bruno knew that he was changing, *improving*, with every Linkage. His times not in communion with the computer network became less and less important, like faint memories almost forgotten over many decades of time.

Linkage also gave Bruno mastery of self. He was learning how to expand or contract his duration-sense at the slightest whim. Soon, he would be able to stretch a microsecond into eternity, or the reverse. A tiny, flawed part of Bruno— his limited biological component—wanted to shout with exhilaration, but he was far beyond mere human emotion.

Bruno, once again in full Linkage, was Transcended.

His awareness surrounded and permeated *Sun-Tzu*, at one with the All. A portion of his Mind watched one of the kzin warships slide helplessly into his antimatter drive wash. Without specifically desiring to do so, Bruno's new sensorium analyzed and reported the spectral characteristics of the vaporized alien craft:

- *Flayed atoms of carbon and iron, silicon and indium, shattered and broken.*
- *Whirling motes, once part of a mighty warship and alien flesh, blasted now and scarred.*
- *A billowing cloud of humbled ions, now a slight contaminant of the incandescent torrent of plasma and gamma radiation sweeping behind him for millions of kilometers.*

Bruno relished his control. The drive was its lowest setting; he could pivot and swing the exhaust like the weapon it was while still maintaining proper attitude control. So graceful, so clean, so *true*.

Bruno looked beyond the drive wash, past the sweeping fields of force and glitter of ions, into the vast and varied face of infinity. An emotion much like awe filled his circuits and neurons.

He permitted part of his Mind to appreciate and cherish the subtle wonders surrounding his myriad selves, while another fragment of that expanded consciousness dealt with the growing threat to *Sun-Tzu*.

A tiny bit of his consciousness noted that Carol was speaking to his human component. He felt the urge to reply, to speak in human terms, much as his un-Linked self felt the dull pangs of hunger or the first stirrings of lust. While fully Linked, merely human concerns seemed akin to instinct, lacking the crystalline certainty and broad range of Transcendence. He sent a tendril of his greater Mind into his minor and insignificant biological portion, increasing his consciousness and processing capacity in that location.

His pale perception of the navigation deck sharpened suddenly to razor-edged clarity.

"Yes, Carol. I am with you. I have been so all along." The words, mere modulated sound waves, seemed frustratingly imprecise and limited.

Insufficient.

Bruno called up the realtime image of Carol's face from the navigation-deck cameras, then finally used his biological vision-sense organs on the captain of *Sun-Tzu*. The image didn't seem more accurate than the camera images to Bruno's sensorium; quite the reverse, in fact. Still, he knew that Carol felt more comfortable when he turned his biological eyes on her.

It was a human quirk, one Bruno didn't mind indulging. Even if it wasted some small amount of processing capacity.

Carol's face was lined with worry and other fitful emotions that were difficult to quantify. He focused on her words.

"Thank you for turning your head. Tacky, I just saw one of the ratcat ships vaporize."

"Indeed. The kzin ship attempted to maneuver around the drive wash, lost maneuvering power, and . . . was consumed."

Bruno accessed biotelemetry and voice-stress-analysis datalinks. *Calculating, calculating* . . . Clearly, Carol was as worried by *his* condition as by the alien craft. Bruno felt the electronic analog of amusement at her colorless concerns.

They were sweet, cute; as touching as a dog trying to understand an aircar.

"What about the other two ships, Pilot? Can your magnificent intellect find them, or are you drunk again on godhood?" Her tone sounded angry, like the annoying buzz of an insect.

"Allow me a moment," he replied, trying to force reassuring patterns of emotional context into his vocalizations, to soothe Carol while he considered the situation. Bruno was intrigued. Mere human or not, she had said something to hold the attention of his greater Mind. He wanted to ponder and savor the words, but first had to evaluate their status and implications.

Bruno directed his full Attention outward for a moment, and perceived the two kzin ships at a relatively safe distance. Nothing threatened, to a first approximation of risk. He could spare a few seconds for improving his internal functioning, surely.

A human-analytical portion of his Mind continued to consider Carol's statement. "Drunk" was clearly pejorative, and implied suboptimal performance.

Perhaps some subminds *were* functioning at less than ideal efficiencies. Clearly, the weak link in his Mind must be his inept and poorly designed human components. A rapid internal diagnostic confirmed and quantified the inefficiencies. He forced a far greater portion of his Mind into his biological component, the modest seed from which his larger Self had sprouted with Linkage. He began to make changes in his neurological system architecture. The body in the crash couch began to twitch and shake, in a coarse and empty parody of Linkage.

Bruno had expected such side effects while attempting to improve and enhance such a chimeric computing device as the electronically augmented brain of his human portion. After all, massive restructuring of entire interface grids was necessary. Extensive rerouting of neuronal connections was also indicated. Bruno commanded the crash couch restraints to hold his biological component more tightly in order to avoid possible damage to it during the reprogramming subroutines.

The results of some commands were, after all, rather drastic on the macroscopic level.

"Tacky! Bruno!" the watchdog sensory portion of his Mind heard Carol shouting, "what's happening?"

"It is quite all right," he managed to force past chattering teeth, striving for a tone that implied calmness. "You were correct, Carol. This portion of me was operating improperly."

"What do you mean? Portion?" Her words held alarm.

The submind in charge of biotelemetry analysis and interpretation hypothesized that Carol was feeling great emotional upset. Bruno knew that he had to set Carol's fears at ease.

"We are reprogramming our human component for greater efficiency." The explanation would surely calm her agitated emotional state.

He heard Carol shouting again, and turned the major portion of his complex intellect away from her words. Sonic noise, not communication. Some aspect of her tone had become intrusive to the ongoing reprogramming process. Carol's words became fainter, and faded into the background noise of the navigation deck, only fully accessed by his human portion. Which was still under repair and retrofitting, of course.

It was difficult to erase, reprogram, and internally reroute microcircuitry contained with the electronic portion of his human component's brain. Though there was great plasticity in the interface macrostructure, there was little absolute complexity. Soon, he felt certain, he would learn to directly manipulate entirely biological subsystems as well as the electronic.

There were bandwidth and amplitude problems, of course—some quite delicious in their smooth difficulty. Still, Bruno would then be able to force compensatory neuronal rewiring of the brain tissues themselves, leading to a truly binary mind Linking the worlds of silicon and synapse.

Linkage would become still easier then, and he would

be able to experience less limitation in his increasingly powerful sensorium.

Bruno noted that rerouting and macrocircuit programming was now complete, with a shadowy ghost of an emotion that had once been satisfaction. Internal debugging routines showed improved perceptual and computing ability. There was less hormonal impact on affective state, as well.

Good, good. Raw emotions often led to decreased cognitive efficiency.

Bruno's biological perceptual field expanded to include Carol, her face grim and set. Tears beaded in her eyes, flowing slowly across her cheek in the microgravity.

From the physical actions of the tears across her face he instantly—and involuntarily—computed the predicted acceleration of the antimatter drive in weapon mode as 0.012 gravities. The portion of his Mind controlling the drive agreed, confirming his calculations to three decimal places.

Bruno reached out with a biological hand and stroked Carol's cheek, feeling the tears against his skin. There were some tactile sensations that action-response circuits could not access. Perhaps there was some emotional, hormonal component. Bruno created a submind to investigate this problem, assigning it moderate priority.

He did care for Carol, and wished her to be safe and happy. Some sign to her of his intentions would be good.

"We are improved now," Bruno told her proudly. Five seconds had passed in realtime since he had initiated the internal reprogramming.

"I . . . can see that," Carol replied. Tears still glinted in her eyes.

Biotelemetry subroutines reported Carol's strongly suppressed emotional state. Bruno tasted worry concerning the captain of the *Sun-Tzu*. A portion of his Mind considered Carol's recent behavior, and began an in-depth analysis.

The rest of Bruno looked outward for the alien threat, anxious to deal with the kzin. There was a universe to ponder.

Bruno sensed the other two kzin warships as tiny flaws in the fabric of space, glittering refractions from their inertialess spacedrives. One of the tiny wrinkles in space-time began accelerating rapidly, maneuvering nearer his drive wash.

"Initiating maneuvers," Bruno told Carol, who nodded jerkily and silently stared at the main holoscreen array.

He sent a low-resolution datadump to a holoscreen window, so that Carol could see the battle more clearly. Dimly, he felt a distraction; the odd, cool brush of Carol's tears drying on his fingers. Evaporative cooling? Bruno sensed the initiation of an increased emotional state in his biological component, and easily compensated for the decreased overall efficiency. If only he could eliminate the hormonal drivers, attain serenity—

"Can I help?" The words were tentative, small.

He felt the cybernetic equivalent of a smile. "No," he said simply in reply.

There was a pause. "I do have some experience in space battles." Carol's tone became slightly peevish.

"Yes. But I have full access to all UN Space Navy tactical and strategic files." He paused, searching his expanding internal database. "Including your own personal battle records and reports."

Carol looked back at the holoscreen, her face seemingly neutral, breathing heavily. The latter confused Bruno: there had been no extreme maneuvering, nor any acceleration stresses. Another portion of his Mind accessed realtime biotelemetry and found Carol's blood pressure and heart rate elevated. Curious.

Bruno turned the *Sun-Tzu*. The kinesthetics were quick, zesty. He delicately slashed with the incandescent column of the antimatter reaction drive—a huge scythe scratching an actinic path of deadly light across the distorted starscape.

Yet the ability of *Sun-Tzu* to turn was limited by its great mass, and the reaction drives controlling its attitude. Several times, Bruno waved the deadly antimatter drive wash near the tiny vessels, an enormous flyswatter against pesky gnats. They dodged—but not by much. He switched vectors, pivoted the ship like a ballerina on an invisible fulcrum.

Much closer, good. But the two motes were still able to avoid the cutting sword he wielded.

Bruno noted that one of the gnats was firing weapons against the *Sun-Tzu*. He could do nothing at this range. His iceball could not evasively weave and dart like the kzin vessels, and his drive wash took precious seconds to reorient.

He sent a tendril of greater Mind again into his biological component.

"Carol," he forced his human mouth to say, "prepare for weapon impacts."

"I gathered," she replied without looking at his biological portion. Carol reached for the control pads to adjust her crash couch for greater security, but Bruno did it for her before her fingers actually touched the console.

Enemy laser bursts vaporized bits of the icy skin of his spacecraft. Railgun projectiles stitched deep craters toward his hull sensor pods. His biological senses reported the impacts as dull gonging notes ringing on the navigation deck. Bruno detected the second kzin ship accelerating on an indirect vector, possibly preparing for a hyperbolic approach past the *Sun-Tzu*, but at a distance too great to inflict significant damage.

Bruno calculated with crystalline immediacy that he could not maneuver the drive wash rapidly enough to threaten both alien warships at the same time.

He devoted more of his Mind to offensive and defensive systems, and subsystems instantly reprogrammed themselves at his whim. *Sun-Tzu* was not designed for battle; that was *Dolittle*'s mission. Still, Bruno would use what tools were present. Vast quantities of power were tapped from the antimatter reaction chamber, and made available for other uses.

Bruno reached out with a finger of laser light, almost impaling one of the kzin spacecraft on a blazing spear of coherent radiation. *Close, so close—Sun-Tzu*'s railgun batteries fired high velocity flocks of iron pellets in complex patterns toward the enemy vessels. The alien spacecraft dodged gracefully.

Simultaneously, he programmed and launched a dozen nuclear pumped X-ray laser bomblets. *Pop, pop*—they plunged into the relativistic vortex and began firing.

Their bursts of radiation narrowly missed their targets. *Why?* He knew the answer even as the question formed: subminds reported with one electronic voice. A sour taste laced Bruno's sensorium, flitting shadows of human emotion. These were the best defenses human technology could field, but they were defeated by the chaos of relativistic plasma turbulence, the distorting refractions of light-speed, and the adroit skill of kzin pilots. Bruno knew that *Sun-Tzu* was outclassed here.

On some unquantifiable, illogical level, Bruno tasted danger inexorably approaching *Sun-Tzu*.

• CHAPTER EIGHT

Carol Faulk felt helpless.

It was ironic, actually. She was a seasoned combat veteran, with experience in both singleships and as a commander of a battle squadron. She had hulled or fried many kzin ships, seen good friends die, made decisions that saved lives and won skirmishes.

All she could do now was sit and watch impotently while a half-human monster piloted and operated the *Sun-Tzu*.

Yet it was a half-human monster who used to be her lover and friend. Carol pursed her lips at the painful irony.

For the hundredth time, she reminded herself that her opinion of words like "monster" and "alien" might change drastically after they reached Wunderlander space. At the end of the long voyage, when she opened the cryovial containing the virus with the odd name, *Tree-of-Life*. Maybe after the virus did its work she would understand Bruno better.

On the other hand, it did not look to Carol as if Project Cherubim would be a viable option, based on the holoscreen data scrolling past her line of sight. Not even halfway to Alpha Centauri, and the ratcats were already stalking them.

Bruno's lolling interface cable looked ever more leechlike to Carol. His eyes never moved from her as the holoscreen displays shifted, blinked, and changed. His face was utterly slack, eyes huge and staring, with the expanded pupils characteristic of brain-machine interfacing. Carol knew that the vast majority of Bruno's attention was not on her, no matter how he appeared to stare at her.

Bruno's attention was everywhere, all at once.

Carol blinked back tears, cursing herself for the show of weakness. It took a moment for Carol to force the emotions back down, deep inside her. She was a captain, after all. Taking a deep breath and squaring her shoulders, Carol forced herself to accept the simple facts before her, to say the words inwardly: *Bruno is getting worse, and faster than expected.*

He was becoming more and more alien and machinelike. He had even told Carol that he was reprogramming his own brain, making himself a more efficient "component." *I* was becoming *we* as the man she knew diluted away inside the growing machine intelligence that controlled *Sun-Tzu*.

She bullied the subject from her mind with thoughts of duty and strategy. There was nothing to be done at present about her lover. If she and Bruno survived the battle under way, there would be time to find a way to prevent the machine-generated madness from taking Bruno away from her. Maybe.

Until then, all she could do was hope.

Carol felt the straps of her crash couch tighten and loosen as *Sun-Tzu* maneuvered, pivoting on its brilliant lance of plasma and gamma radiation. She felt the shudder of kzin weapons hammering the surface of their spacecraft far above them. The holoscreen status window showed schematics of the battle as it unfolded: the tiny red stars of the two surviving kzin spacecraft maneuvering randomly to avoid the bursts of laser light and the lethal scythe of the drive wash itself.

She forced herself to look at him. "Bruno."

"Yes, Carol?" He didn't speak with his vocal chords, but with the shipboard commlink. It was a little startling, but she had half expected it. The synthesized voice, at least, sounded like Bruno.

"Can you spare processing capacity to speak with your biological voice?" She didn't add, *since you are human*. Carol feared Bruno's answer.

There was a tiny pause.

"Yes," he said, lips moving precisely in a slack face. A

tongue moved across lips experimentally. "May we ask why you prefer this communications mode?"

"I am used to . . . your biological component, as you so fetchingly express it."

"But the information conveyed is identical." Irony was lost on the new and improved Bruno, apparently.

"Never mind," Carol sighed. "Thank you for obliging me. Can you give me battle status?"

"Of course. The holoscreens provide the raw data, but I can certainly provide you with vocal summaries."

"Please do so, love."

Did she detect a pause in response to her last word? Another hypospray nozzle snaked out of Bruno's crash couch and injected his neck with a hiss.

He blinked twice, then continued in his artificially human-sounding voice.

"One of the kzin vessels is spiraling in toward me, inflicting serious damage to my sensory pods and ancillary equipment. The other spacecraft is accelerating heavily on an unusual vector."

Worry sent a thrill along her spine. "Wait a second. The word 'ancillary' worries me. Other damage?"

"None. There has been no attempt to damage the antimatter drive or structures associated with it. Only the sensory arrays and weapons ports have been targeted."

She frowned. "So your hunch was correct?"

"Yes. They intend to board me, if they can."

Me? Carol kept her face under careful control. Several times, Bruno had referred to *Sun-Tzu* as *himself.* The "we" he kept using: Did he mean the two of them, or the strange electronic mind controlling him?

"And the other ship?" she asked, biting her lip.

"Difficult to predict at this time. The strategies of space vessels capable of two hundred gravity accelerations are still new to us."

"Show me the vector, with realtime updating, please."

Bruno didn't reply, but the holoscreen showed the more distant kzin ship accelerating rapidly on a curving course that would narrowly graze *Sun-Tzu*. Something about the diagram nagged Carol.

"And the closer ratcat ship?" she continued, biting her lip.

"The pilot is quite good for a biological system. We have been spending a good deal of processing time on predicting its behavior. Clearly, they could be doing more damage than they are accomplishing at present."

A low warning tone filled the navigation deck.

"Carol, there is a problem." Bruno's voice once more came from speakers instead of his throat. "The closer kzin spacecraft is now vectoring wildly, firing all weapons. There is significant damage . . ."

Sun-Tzu rang like a great bell. An unseen hand slammed her into her couch.

"High-yield thermonuclear device detonation off starboard bow," Bruno reported. "Seventy-five percent of sensory pods were destroyed in that hull sector."

"I gathered as much, thank you," Carol replied acidly. She bared her teeth at the feeling of helplessness, her fingers itching to *do* something. The holoscreens showed the action from repeater stations across the icy hull of the spacecraft. The kzin vessel was delivering a flurry of weapons against *Sun-Tzu*, inflicting serious damage.

Sun-Tzu turned to compensate for lost sensory arrays and weapon emplacements. Carol felt her hastily eaten midmeal rise, bitter in her throat.

Another flock of nuclear-pumped X-ray lasers rose against the kzin vessel, which had already maneuvered away. Blasts of coherent radiation again found no target.

"I am sorry, Carol," Bruno's voice said flatly from the commlink speakers, drained of all emotion. "We are experiencing processor difficulties due to network interruption."

The kzin attack had severed some of Bruno's computational net. Carol suddenly wondered if he felt that loss as pain.

A thought blazed in her mind.

"Bruno! What about the other ship?"

A pause.

"I am very sorry," the commlink speakers said in something like her lover's voice. "We were blind on that side for almost twenty seconds before I was able to regain sensory data."

"And?"

"The kzin vessel will reach closest approach to *Sun-Tzu* in a few seconds. It has fired no weapons, however. Perhaps it is trying to draw fire in order to allow the other vessel to inflict greater damage."

Carol's jaw dropped with a blaze of realization. Couldn't Bruno's vastly enhanced intelligence see what was happening?

She reached over and grabbed Bruno's arm. "Listen, love, focus as much sensory capacity as you can spare on the close approach craft. Put some weapons against it, throw up debris, anything."

The flat half-machine tones took on a questioning note. "Why are you so specifically concerned?"

Carol wanted to slam her fists down on the useless command console. "Don't you get it?" she grated. "It's a bombing run. Do as I tell you!"

By then, it was too late. The kzin craft, under cover of its fiercely attacking sister vessel, swept stealthily within a million kilometers of *Sun-Tzu*. It had already swung past them by the time energy weapons flashed lethal radiation. Relativistic distortions fuzzed the images further—

—And almost as an afterthought, a coherent lance of X-rays speared the enemy craft, spreading a glowing cloud of debris across space. The second vessel had already sheered off, racing for the opposite side of *Sun-Tzu*.

A blaze of light filled the holoscreen.

"Bruno?" Carol asked quietly. "What happened?"

Another slight pause, and Bruno once more spoke from his own lips instead of the commlink speakers.

"I am very sorry, Carol. The kzin have delivered a monopole bomb. It must have been heavily shielded to avoid my sensory array."

Carol swore. In the deadly heart of a monopole bomb, isolated north and south poles met violently, releasing great gouts of energetic electrons. These electrons would spiral, close to light-speed, down magnetic lines of force toward *Sun-Tzu*.

When the electron storm struck *Sun-Tzu*'s densest magnetic cocoon, the electrons would radiate powerfully, their orbits reversed in the magnetic mirrors. They would never reach the icy hull of *Sun-Tzu*, but they would have done their deadly task. Their electromagnetic wail would fry most electrical equipment not shielded deep within the spacecraft. The other kzin vessel would be safe in the "shadow" of *Sun-Tzu*.

Bruno still said nothing.

Carol began striking keys on her crash couch console violently. The straps loosened and retracted, allowing her to float slightly upward in the microgravity.

"How long until impact?" she asked.

"Ten seconds." The reply was as flat and toneless as the autopilot of an aircar.

"Well, let's get you and me down to *Dolittle*. I have an idea."

"Impossible."

In a flash, she realized that disconnecting Bruno from his brain-computer interface would take several minutes, with heavy use of biotelemetric controls. And, fatally, that unshielded and vulnerable conductors ran from the hull of *Sun-Tzu* to the sensory array to the computer net . . .

. . . directly into Bruno's brain.

"I love you, Bruno," Carol said. She grabbed his interface cable in both hands and took a deep breath.

• CHAPTER NINE

Watching Carol's arm muscles tense as she gripped the interface cable, all of Bruno's vast consciousness tried to crowd into his inadequate biological portion in defense against what would happen next. Bruno's enhanced mind would not fit into the small space, wracking him in a horrible cybernetic analog of pain. *No.* He willed his arm to move toward his cable linkage protectively, and . . .

Carol, with a loud grunt, ripped his interface cable from the console with a sharp metallic popping sound.

There wasn't time to scream, even in realtime.

Bruno felt his Mind collapse and die. Transcendence guttered out like a candle flame in a raw wind.

The cold blackness roared into his very soul, a dark hurricane of torment. Loss burned like some dark acid, shattering his Transcended Self. *Gone, gone*—scattering its torn threads to the cosmic wind . . .

In what felt like death agony, Bruno sensed the electromagnetic pulse impact the *Sun-Tzu's* hull. Holoscreens flickered multicolored visual static and vanished, roaring. Sparks geysered from consoles. Navigation deck lights failed. The deadly pulse leaped like a striking snake of electrical potential from the exploding console—

—ricocheting from the white steel walls—

—crackling, searching, like a living thing—

—to the flapping end of his interface cable.

He felt the charge enter his brain like a lit fuse via the suddenly traitorous conduit of metal and silicon. Bruno's mind seemed to explode in a fireball-hot supernova within his deepest self.

161

The suffocating blackness was obliterated by a lethal Light.

1100 10 1000 111 100 10 10 10 10 110 111 10 10 10 110 110 100 11100
0 10 110 110 10 111 10 100 10 110 100 100 110 10 10 1100 1100 1111

The crashed aircar was upside down, silent and dark. With clumsy fingers, five-year-old Bruno released himself from his crashnet. He fell onto the inside of the roof with a painful thump. He lay there, panting and dizzy, feeling sick.

Burnt hair, scorched earth, a coppery wet smell. The aching blackness all around. He was very afraid.

Bruno could remember the explosion, the screaming, the long fall. He had no memory of the horrible crash.

His head hurt terribly.

Bruno turned his head to one side and tried to vomit, but there was nothing left in his stomach other than a trickle of foul liquid that burned his throat. Mumma will be angry, *he thought, wiping his stinging mouth on a torn sleeve. He had to find Mumma and Papa, somewhere in the crashed aircar. The cabin had somehow become huge in the dark. He called and called, his voice echoing in the small space that had swollen so.*

No one answered. Determined, he crawled forward with his arms, because his legs wouldn't work properly. They were numb, but at least they didn't hurt.

Nothing hurt as much as Bruno's head.

"Mumma? Papa?"

His left hand finally found his mother and father, still strapped side by side into their crashnets. They did not reply when he called, no matter how much he cried and pleaded. Finally, he shook them hard, making his head hurt even worse than before. His hands were wet and sticky, and tasted salty when he wiped his face.

Bruno cried, because his parents wouldn't hold him in the darkness, and wouldn't answer him. He had never felt so frightened and alone.

The headache finally became more than he could stand. Dizzy with pain and exhaustion, Bruno finally lay flat on the inside roof of the crashed aircar. Still crying softly, he reached up and touched the left side of his head, where it hurt so much.

His fingers sank five centimeters into his shattered skull. Into something pulpy and wet. Sharp slivers of bone pricked his fingertips. Lights exploded in Bruno's head, and he tasted the color blue, felt the smell of moist hay. He thought that he heard a siren in the distance, but he was in too much pain to pay attention.

Exhausted, he laid his pounding head down on the cool metal, to wait for his Mumma and Papa to wake up and take him home, to make everything all right. The aircar swirled around him dizzily. There were vague murmurs like anxious voices in the darkness, calling him.

Cold nothingness claimed little Bruno with clammy hands, and dragged him down into an unconscious void.

11001010100011111000101010101011011111010101011101101001110001011101110101111010010010111010010111100100100110101011000110011111

Bruno opened his eyes for a moment, still convulsing randomly. Dim, reddish corridor emergency lights winked and glittered. He watched the main ring corridor of *Sun-Tzu* flying dimly past him.

Carol was carrying him toward *Dolittle*. The low, microgravity lope as she ran made his head flop helplessly from side to side. His neck was an agony of fire. Bruno tried to force words past his lips, but it hurt to think, let alone speak.

He thought that he heard Carol telling him to hang on, that *Dolittle* was very near, but the words were slippery, skidding away like the emergency lights.

"Mumma?" he muttered, and passed out.

• CHAPTER TEN

Rrowl-Captain's roar of triumph echoed throughout the command bridge of the *Belly-Slasher*. He leaped from his command chair and threw his short-furred arms outward. The bridge crew shouted as well, claws unsheathed and drool spooling from excited lips.

The hunt was successful! After the long watches of skulking, they had their jaws on prey at last.

The image of the monkeyship on the main thinplate screen turned lazily. Obviously, attitude control and guidance were gone after the magneto-electrical pulse had impacted the enemy vessel. The contra-matter drive still fired constantly, spewing a deadly exhaust column as the ship rotated randomly. The reaction drive's basic control electronics were deeply protected within the iceball of the human-monkey vessel. But piloting functions were clearly incapacitated.

All as planned, Rrowl-Captain purred to himself.

Dim flickers and flashes of coronal discharge crawled like living things across the surface of the great sphere of the alien ship. It was the only evidence of the enormous electronics-devouring pulse born of the monopole bomb, a smashing Heroic fist that had devastated the electronics of the human vessel.

Rrowl-Captain's batwing ears raised and stretched outward in pride. The victory was not without cost. Many Heroes had died for this prize, he knew. The losses were significant, but acceptable. Blood of Heroes had been well spent on this hunt.

The entire crew of *Pouncing-Strike*, including the annoying little Cha'at-Captain, had been vaporized in a microsecond by the monkeyship exhaust early on. Little honor there. But the brave captain of *Spine-Cruncher* would have a posthumous Full Name, to the great honor of his sons and fathers! Rrowl-Captain's Warrior Heart soared.

A price well paid—for victory and honor. Both captains and crewkzin of *Pouncing-Strike* and *Spine-Cruncher* had been, even unwittingly, a credit to the Riit and the One Fanged God. He would pay for a Warrior's Honor Ceremony for both crews from his own pride-funds when he returned in triumph to *Ka'ashi*.

Rrowl-Captain growled once for silence on the command bridge.

"Navigator," he spat and hissed in rare good humor, "please fly us toward the monkeyship forward hull, where Alien-Technologist has apparently found an access airlock."

"At once, Dominant Leader," the proud crewkzin snapped.

"Do not assume the monkeys are without resources, even now," Rrowl-Captain cautioned. "Follow standard evasive maneuvers."

"Surely the monkeys are helpless, Leader!"

Rrowl-Captain fanned his ears in humor. "It would appear so, yes. But what is the True Hero's approach with these monkeys?"

"*Feint-and-pounce!*" the bridge crew hissed and spat in rough chorus.

Rrowl-Captain purred approval.

He spent a few moments considering how to take possession of the alien craft. It would take some time to discover its alien workings and procedures, for the monkeys did not think like Heroes. He would necessarily have to select a crew to pilot the monkeyship back to Ka'ashi, after the vessel had been adapted to the needs of kzin crew. Who to trust? What crewkzin valued obedience above opportunity? Rrowl-Captain rumbled in contemplation.

That, however, would be in the future. The Teachings of the One Fanged God were explicit on this matter: *Clean no prey before its capture*. The Teachings, upon reflection, often placed fangs deeply into agile truths.

"I require an octal of Heroes to accompany Alien-Technologist after we rendezvous with the monkeyship," he growled into the shipwide commlink. Consulting his command chair thinscreen's database, Rrowl-Captain selected his most aggressive Heroes to balance the natural, if unkzinlike caution of Alien-Technologist. It would be, he reflected, good practice for both factions under his command.

Rrowl-Captain settled back in his command chair, purring softly, as he honed his bandaged claws and mused over satisfying bloody dreams of conquest.

Only the slightest hint of green hell-light marred the excellence of his reveries.

• CHAPTER ELEVEN

Bruno dimly felt Carol lay him in the autodoc of *Dolittle*. His eyes fluttered open. A curving metal wall above him. Carol's lips, moving. Her voice, as if underwater, all gargles and rumbles. Bits and pieces of sounds, syllables flying like frightened birds. Hard to capture.

"Bruno, I have to get us out of here. We don't have any choice but *Dolittle*." Her eyes were close to his, her lips near his ear. "It's that or become ratcat food, love."

Words and meanings met and fled one another in his damaged mind.

He felt her hands tucking his arms into the coffinlike box of the autodoc, connecting telltales to various parts of his body. Numb. He struggled to force words past dead lips.

"Love . . ." he managed to grunt.

Bruno watched the blur that was Carol's face smile sadly. A glint around her eyes in the painful light?

"I love you, too, chiphead." Her vague face sobered. "The autodoc will fix you, I think." She kissed him, a faint pressure on his dead lips, and vanished from his fading horizon.

The lid of the autodoc whined shut, clicked with finality. In the darkness, he felt the pressure of sensors against his wrists and neck. There was a low gurgling in the microgravity as the autodoc began to fill with healing liquid. A mask lowered gently over his face, and he felt the bright whiff of pure oxygen burn in his lungs.

Bruno felt the darkness in his mind rise like a relentless tide, carrying him again into oblivion.

1100 10 1000 111 100 10 10 10 10 110 111 110 10 10 110 1 110 100 11 100
0 10 110 1 110 10 111 10 100 10 1 110 100 100 1 10 10 10 1 100 1 100 1 111

Ten-year-old Bruno looked at the isolation tank curiously.
Thick wires and consoles and strange machines meshed like
some jigsaw puzzle of electronics. Faceless technicians stood
around at a discreet distance, saying nothing. But always
watching.

"And this could help me talk to computers?" he asked,
incredulous.

Colonel Early of UN Special Projects smiled reassuringly,
his teeth white in his seamed coal black face.

"That's right, son. You already know how to give machines
mental commands through your interface, right?"

"Sure." That was easy. You just thought it, and it happened.
It was like asking someone how to make their arm raise
up. You just did it.

"Well, we want you to do much more than that, with
this machine. Can I tell you what we have in mind?" His
tone was easy, patient.

Bruno trusted Colonel Early. He had paid for Bruno's
education, had spent a fair amount of time either in person
or via hololink with Bruno. It was lonely in the research
institute, and the scientists made him feel like a project, or
an alien. They talked at him, not with him.

Just because they had repaired the brain damage he had
suffered as a kid with neuronal emulator macrocircuitry,
they felt he was property, not a person. Techtalk. Do this.
Do that. Never why he should do this or do that. It made
Bruno angry, and sometimes uncooperative.

Colonel Early could always talk him back into working
with the scientists, though.

"Okay," he replied to Colonel Early, who stood patiently,
waiting. He always listened to Bruno, treated him like a grown-
up. Bruno would do a great deal for Colonel Buford Early.

"Well, we would like to link you up to a real computer. A
big one, not like the little cybernetic links you've been working
on. Once we do that, then we will put you in the isolation

tank." Early pointed at the small tank, covered with controls and interface monitor units. Conduits snaked to a solid wall of computer systems. "The human mind, Bruno, needs stimulation."

Bruno frowned. "And in an isolation tank, I won't get it?"

Colonel Early nodded, looking serious. "That's right, son. But your brain will search for a way to get that stimulation. It has to have it, but you won't be able to see, hear, or feel inside the tank. Eventually, your brain will learn to link up with the computer interface circuitry."

Bruno squinted, thinking. "What will it be like?"

"People who connect up with higher-order computers via their brains are called—"

"Linkers," Bruno interrupted.

"That's right, son. Linkers. They say that a Linker can know everything."

"Everything?" Bruno was suddenly fascinated.

Colonel Early looked a little sad. "I doubt it. Did you ever hear of Faust, son?"

"Fawst? Who's that?"

The older man sighed. "I guess you weren't on the approved list. Nobody is, anymore." He brightened a bit. "But we think that you will be better at interfacing with a computer than other Linkers."

"Because I'm a chiphead." Bruno grated, peeved. He made a face.

Colonel Early put a hand on Bruno's shoulder, gentle. " 'Chiphead' is a bad word, Bruno." He stared directly into Bruno's eyes, held them. "It is an ignorant term used by uneducated, prejudiced people."

Bruno said nothing, his lips twisted in resentment. He had heard a lot of people call him a chiphead over the years, once they had learned about where he lived, and his history. The accident. What was inside his head. He hated being different.

"That's why the scientists look at me funny, isn't it?" Bruno asked. He couldn't look at the other man.

Colonel Early persisted. He hooked two fingers under Bruno's chin and forced his eyes up toward his own.

"Bruno, it's a word used by little people who are afraid of new things. You should pity them."

"If you say so." He was unconvinced. At least Colonel Early liked him. Even if he was a chiphead.

They waited together in the crowded room for a few moments. Colonel Early said nothing. He never was overbearing.

"Will it hurt?" he finally asked.

"No, son. It will be scary at first, and very lonely. Until your brain learns to Link, that is."

A bit of enthusiasm entered his voice. "And then I'll know everything?"

Colonel Early smiled in real amusement. "Well, I wouldn't go quite that far, son. You will know a great deal more than anyone else, I can promise you."

Bruno thought a moment.

"Would I be able to help you with your work at the UN?" he asked.

"Son, that is why I am asking. My children are all grown now, as are my grandchildren. And I can't get a permit for more children."

Bruno smiled. "That's okay, Colonel Early. I don't have a father or mother. But I guess you know that already."

He certainly did. Colonel Early's had been the first face Bruno had seen when he had awakened in the hospital after the accident and the first set of operations.

Again they waited together, silent. Colonel Early never pushed Bruno, and he appreciated it.

"I'll do it," Bruno finally said, ignoring the mutters of the technicians around the isolation tank.

"Good."

"When do we start?"

"How about now?" Colonel Early said, handing Bruno the helmet with all of the strange plugs and wires. It was heavier than it looked, and Bruno held it awkwardly. "Let me help." Early lowered the helmet onto Bruno's head slowly, reverently.

Like a crown.

11000101000111110010101010101011011111101010101011011110100111000
0101110111010111101001011110100100110101010110001100111111

Bruno Takagama moaned against the soft mask of the respirator in the autodoc tank. Mechanical fingers began to probe the burns around his neck socket. Small swimming robots cruised toward his wounds in the ocean of the autodoc's fluids, bearing tiny medical instruments poised at the ready. Noting his distress, the autodoc diagnostic circuitry administered a strong sedative. Soon he slept dreamlessly.

• CHAPTER TWELVE

Carol Faulk touched a keypad and felt her crash couch shudder in response. *Dolittle* shot down the darkened escape tunnel toward the outer hull of *Sun-Tzu*.

Carol activated the escape bay doors. She goosed the fusion drive, already warmed and ready at the first sign of potential hostilities. Explosive bolts blew silently in vacuum, the hatch flew into fragments, and the long spindle shape of *Dolittle* was suddenly free in space.

Now. Yes! Her hands on the helm keypads of a spacecraft, Carol felt in command again. No longer helpless and unable to fight. The starscape was still relativistically squashed and distorted, but at least she had some control over her fate.

And Bruno's.

Dolittle flashed away from the dying *Sun-Tzu*. They had less than an hour before her quickly set booby trap activated, and antimatter containment gently and fatally shut down.

Dolittle had to be far away indeed from *Sun-Tzu* by then.

Carol called up the autodoc remote diagnostic on screen above her console. The autodoc sensors were already attached to Bruno in many places, and medical robots were swarming over and in his body, doing everything possible to heal his damage. Flashing red lights indicated his serious condition.

"C'mon, Tacky," she whispered. "You have to pull through."

There had been little choice when she pulled his plug in the *Sun-Tzu*. Bruno's brain was certainly damaged by what she had done, and even more from the EMP induction. But had Bruno remained fully Linked and directly connected to the computer net by electrical conductors, the electromagnetic pulse would have burned his brain to ashes.

Bruno: sick or dead. Those had been her choices.

Carol kept the bulk of the *Sun-Tzu* between *Dolittle* and the kzin warship that was even now approaching the earth vessel, bent on boarding and conquest. The idea of ratcats leaping down the abandoned corridors of *Sun-Tzu*, finding the cryogenically suspended bodies of her crewmates, felt like a violation. But perhaps she would get her revenge after all.

She would give her doomed sleeping crewmates a real Viking funeral, a far piece indeed from Scandinavia.

Carol smiled grimly. *The ratcats will get a surprise in fifty-eight minutes*, she thought to herself. A caution worried her. *How long will it take for the kzin to analyze the command programs, and begin diagnosing drive activity?*

Dolittle's vector was straight and true. Carol was a good pilot, even by the seat of her jumpsuit, and *Dolittle's* basic fusion drive was familiar. You didn't need to be part computer to fly the little warship.

By now, the ratcat craft was close enough to *Sun-Tzu* to hide *Dolittle's* escape behind the bulk of the earth spacecraft. Every second would translate into merciful, shielding distance when the antimatter containment system failed.

When she was a thousand kilometers from the *Sun-Tzu*, still undetected and unchallenged, Carol unfurled the great superconductive wings of *Dolittle*.

Forty minutes left now.

The vast wings of *Dolittle* caught at the magnetic fields between the stars, like a fledgling bird in an updraft. A conductor moving rapidly through a magnetic field generated electrical current. The current, tapped, delivered deceleration force. Electromagnetic braking writ large.

The energy thus generated by deceleration at relativistic speeds was enormous, and useful for a variety of purposes.

It had originally been the plan of *Dolittle* and her crew to leap from the *Sun-Tzu* near Wunderlander space. Bruno was to pilot *Dolittle* in full Linkage, while Carol and her revived crewmates were all exposed to Tree-of-Life virus behind the now-useless hermetic doors of the cargo section of *Dolittle*.

Without the sealed doors, Bruno would have been killed by exposure to Tree-of-Life. The brain as well as the body changed its very structure under the imperious genetic commands of the ancient virus. Since Bruno's brain was studded with implanted electronics, those changes would certainly be fatal.

Carol and her virus-exposed crewmates, on the other hand, would fall into developmental comas, tended by autodocs as their bodies underwent the metamorphosis described in the UN reports. They would emerge as something more than human—in ironic biological counterpoint to Bruno's Linkage.

Protector-stage humans. Smarter, stronger, and faster than any human born.

During the pre-mission training, Buford Early had reluctantly shown them the holos and heavily censored summary sheets. Once an ARM, always a goldskinning ARM, so far as Carol was concerned. Early would restrict the wheel if he could.

Bruno had forced Early's hand, insisting that he brief the crew of *Sun-Tzu*. Early had been shocked that his loyal Bruno would do such a thing. It was Carol's first sign that the mission had a slim chance.

The data was both tantalizing and frightening. Carol could see why the UN kept the information under such restriction. Pssthpok, the alien who came after the failed Pak colony on Earth that had evolved into *Homo sapiens*, and whose dried body lay in the Smithsonian. The Belter, Jack Brennan, first modern human to be converted by Tree-of-Life. He had become the Brennan-monster or Vandervecken, and had perhaps saved humanity from itself during the Long Peace, with gifts of technological improvements even the ARM couldn't restrict.

And, according to Early, perhaps saved the human race from Pak fleets out near the failed human colony at Epsilon Indi, Home. Home had failed due to Tree-of-Life, but Brennan's plan had created an army to fend off the Pak fleets.

When the kzin fleets arrived at Sol, and seemed to be winning, the story of Home gave Early an idea. Project Cherubim would use Protector-stage humans against the kzin.

The human-Protector crew, piloted by the fully Linked Bruno, would enter Wunderlander space and fight the kzin. The vast power of the decelerating *Dolittle* would power enormous laser and particle-beam weapons. Eventually, the crew would join with the human resistance forces in the Serpent Swarm asteroid belt.

But the crew would arrive dying from radiation poisoning, unable to create more Protector-stage humans.

The plan was to limit the "infection," as Protectors—even human-Protectors—savagely fought anything to protect their own bloodline. This would rapidly become chaos on crowded human worlds. Tree-of-Life virus made intelligence and strength the uncritical servant of emotion and instinct.

Brennan's records had warned of this.

Carol increased deceleration, and watched *Sun-Tzu* vanish from her screen. She bled off the energy by powering up one of the huge gas lasers, firing randomly in different directions, hoping that no nearby dust cloud fluoresced, alerting the kzin to *Dolittle*'s escape.

The chronometer readout hung in midair, holographically. Carol tried not to look at it too often, and failed. From her own space-battle experience, Carol knew that waiting was the hardest part. But when the time for action arrived, she would pray to live long enough to wait once again.

Thirty-five minutes.

• CHAPTER THIRTEEN

Rrowl-Captain paced the command bridge of *Belly-Slasher* and watched the forward thinplate screen closely, his hairless tail slashing the air with impatience. He growled low in his throat as he stalked the bridge, taloned boots silent on the tapestry-covered deck. The bridge crew remained both respectful and silent, eyes averted and ears folded tightly against orange-furred skulls. Clawed fingers hung expectantly over keypads, waiting for the captain of *Belly-Slasher* to shriek an impatiently angry command.

It had taken half of a watch-interval for *Belly-Slasher* to cautiously maneuver close to the monkeyship. The wariness had worn poorly on Rrowl-Captain and his crew so soon after the monopole bomb from *Spine-Cruncher* had silenced the human vessel. Triumph tasted like leafy defeat in their jaws, as *Belly-Slasher* moved slowly toward the iceball of a spacecraft.

To skulk toward the carcass of the monkeyship denied the Octal-and-Two Truths in the Warrior Heart. Rrowl-Captain snarled wetly to himself in frustration, his jaws snapping on nothingness.

It was a tense time aboard the sole surviving kzin warship.

The waiting was taking a toll on him and the crew of *Belly-Slasher*. Ventilators poured out dry-conditioned air in a stiff, cold breeze, attempting to dilute the scream-and-leap pheromones that every crewkzin was emitting in quantity. Intellect remained locked in battle with instinct and kzinti hormones. At least until there were actual enemies to battle with wit and claws.

Agitated and filled with frustration, many of the crewkzin

had begun to lose discipline. So far Rrowl-Captain had only to riffle his new and significantly larger trophy belt loop as a reminder. He bared teeth in satisfied memory of his reinforced dominance.

Rrowl-Captain had then tightly reminded his impatient crew of the clever *p'charth* of Kzin-home. The beast feigned death as a technique for luring its prey close enough to spit swift-acting neurotoxin into surprised scavenger faces. The Teachings of the One Fanged God used the *p'charth* as a parable of the dangers of certitude in battle: *"The Wise Hero ensures that Prey is not Predator cloaked by the Long Grass of Wit or Trickery; some claws can slash deeply as well as run swiftly."*

In so calming his crew, he calmed himself.

"Navigator," Rrowl-Captain snarled.

The kzin in question looked up from his console and thinscreen, facial fur matted from intense concentration. Rrowl-Captain chose to overlook the other kzin's lack of grooming for the moment.

"Dominant One!" Navigator replied with only a trace of distraction present in his hiss-and-spit syllables.

"Report on progress," the captain rasped, gentling his tone slightly. It must be frustrating, he reflected, for a Hero to stalk numbers within bloodless computer memory. Like leaping, fangs agape, into enemies composed of mere fog and shadow.

"Leader," the other kzin rumbled in low respectful tones, "look to the forward thinscreen." A schematic of the monkey spacecraft, huge and rounded like an icy asteroid, appeared. Magnetic lines of force, which swept the interstellar medium from the alien ship's path, were added to the diagram. The route of *Belly-Slasher* was a circuitous line threading the deadly tongues of magnetic force toward the bow of the monkeyship.

"Hrrr . . ." Rrowl-Captain growled, musingly. "Your attention to careful and precise duty is duly noted and will be well rewarded. We cannot afford to lose this prize to monkey tricks or treachery, despite our impetus to complete our conquest and celebrate a successful hunt."

The other kzin's orange-and-black ruff lifted with pride at Rrowl-Captain's words of praise. "It would not have been possible, Dominant One, without the aid of Alien-Technologist." He paused, scratching with a careless claw beneath his whiskers reflectively. "The monkeys do not make sense, Leader. It is difficult to understand their design philosophy. If we only had a Telepath—"

Rrowl-Captain snorted dismissal. "Indeed; we do not. Placing dream-fangs on prey does not fill a Hero's belly, nor honor the Great Web of Existence." He paused. "These monkeys are, as you say, different from Heroes, different from Kdatlynos, different from Chunquen, different even from our loyal Jotoki. The One Fanged God made slaves in different forms to serve our different needs."

"As you say, Leader," Navigator agreed, obedience stiffening his spine.

"Even an unblooded kitten could set fangs in such facts." Rrowl-Captain dismissively changed the subject as obvious. He gestured at the forward thinscreen with a sharp black claw. "Your attention to detail in adroitly taking us through the magnetic force-lines is especially noteworthy."

Navigator put sheathed claws to face in recognition of the compliment. "It was as you commanded, Dominant One. Alien-Technologist and I stalked fact and hypotheses in our planning. The monkeys do not use our gravitic polarizers, so they do not have force shielding, as we do; they must rely on primitive magnetic fields for protection." His tone burred contempt.

"Yet these fields are of great power," Rrowl-Captain rumbled low in warning. "Do not underestimate monkey tricks. They may lack honor seen in the light of the Teachings of the One Fanged God, but such strategies can still slash the most noble Hero's tail in two through overconfidence."

"As you command," the other kzin deferred with a hiss. He highlighted the path of *Belly-Slasher* on the thinscreen schematic with a few claw slashes at his console; they were moments from rendezvous with the large airlock structure identified earlier by Alien-Technologist.

"There are no signs of activity from the target?" Rrowl-Captain inquired.

"No, Leader. Only the contra-matter drive and the magnetic-field equipment appear to be functioning optimally. No laser ranging or microwave emissions. Nothing." Navigator purred in thought. "Perhaps the monkeys were killed by life-support failure or some other catastrophe, only leaving a few automated subsystems in order?"

Rrowl-Captain licked his nostrils with a disbelieving tongue. What did his unconscious mind scent? "Surely life-support systems were adequately shielded."

"*Spine-Cruncher*'s monopole weapon was of high power and delivered most skillfully, Dominant One. The human-monkeys must not have shielded themselves properly, other than drive and field waveguides. Or perhaps random chance intervened."

" *'Even the sharpest and most skillful fang can break,'* " the captain of *Belly-Slasher* quoted from the Teachings of the One Fanged God. The other kzin blinked agreement. Random chance too often ruled the universe.

Rrowl-Captain hissed in worry. He had expected some kind of monkey trick during *Belly-Slasher*'s tense voyage to the bow of the alien spacecraft, but the huge ship had wallowed through space without response, seemingly without guidance or crew. No railguns, no lasers, no particle beams, no missiles.

Nothing.

The monkeyship was like a pilotless ghost vessel, its fearsome idling reaction drive swinging randomly through a small angle. It tasted like victory, yet the savor was not quite as satisfying as Rrowl-Captain had anticipated. Bloody, but not hot and fresh.

Clearly, the contra-matter drive was extremely dangerous, and required many safeguards. Such a protected subsystem could have easily survived the magneto-electrical pulse. Perhaps the magnetic shielding was assigned such a priority, as well. The monkeys, after all, did not think like Heroes. His reasoning had the tang of fangs-on-fact, logic. Still,

Rrowl-Captain had the distinct feeling of enemy eyes upon him. He felt his ruff rising involuntarily.

"Return to your station," he ordered Navigator peremptorily. The other kzin slapped claws to face and turned back to his console.

Rrowl-Captain reflected on his own seemingly brave words. He again saw the greenish light of monkey lasers in his mind's eye, filling the sky, shaming his Warrior Heart and slashing bits from his liver. Pushing the grass-eating vision to the back of his mind, he leaped back to his command chair and sat.

"Preparing for rendezvous," Navigator announced over the ship commlink.

"Alert Alien-Technologist in his quarters," the captain of *Belly-Slasher* hissed to Apprentice-to-Communications, who leaped to his clumsy feet nervously. "Tell him, by my order, to assemble his team at the starboard airlock in space armor, along with their equipment." The young kzin huddled next to the commlink, and hissed and spat his Leader's orders.

Rrowl-Captain settled back in his command chair, listening to the ripping-cloth sound of the gravity polarizers slowly decrease. *Belly-Slasher* cautiously approached the alien vessel, halting a few lengths of kzin-leaps above the other ship's icy pitted hull.

The forward viewscreen showed the relativity-distorted universe around them, lonely points of velocity-squeezed light and black empty spaces. Energetic particles from the interstellar medium impacted the magnetic field surrounding the alien vessel from time to time, producing colorful auroral flickers of ghostly light.

We are so far from our lairs, here between the stars, he mused. *Far from our kittens and kzinrettis.*

Rrowl-Captain gestured to his personal Jotoki servant, which rushed forward to offer a placating delicacy with the fingerlets at the end of its warty slave arm: a still-wriggling slice of *k'chit* from the vivarium on board. The captain bolted the warm flesh whole, hardly chewing. The act of consuming, of at least his gullet doing battle with some kind of adversary, served to slow his breathing. Rrowl-Captain took the cloth his Jotok was now offering, and cleaned tangy blood from his jaws, mollified for the moment.

"Rendezvous complete," Navigator rasped over shipwide commlink.

Rrowl-Captain leaped to his feet and purred readiness. He stalked toward the hatchway, tail held high with anticipation.

It was at last time to complete the hunt.

• CHAPTER FOURTEEN

Bruno blinked at the painfully bright shipboard lights stabbing at his eyes, and coughed in reflex as the mask lifted away from his face. Remote sensors withdrew delicately from his body. He looked past the rising top of the autodoc, and through blurry eyes saw Carol Faulk gazing down at him.

From what Bruno could see from his position, it looked as though they were in *Dolittle*. It seemed to hurt a little to think, to remember. He blinked several times to clear moist grit from his eyes. He shook his head to clear his mind, which felt slow and clogged; it didn't help.

Bruno was without a clue, most of his recent memories apparently gone. Burned away by something horrible.

"Come on, shipmate," Carol said lightly, helping him out of the autodoc tank. To Bruno, it felt as if the ship was running under about a half gee of acceleration. Thick fluid dripped from his body as she carefully toweled him off. He tried to crane his painfully stiff neck to look at the forward holoscreen, just a few meters away in the cramped cabin. His eyesight was still too muzzy to read the status window from that distance, but the overall forward view showed a relativistic starscape.

Bruno drew in his breath sharply, fuzzy thinking or not, when he realized that *Sun-Tzu* was nowhere in sight.

He tried to say something, to ask the obvious questions. Carol would not reply to his half-grunted attempts at questions. She continued to towel him thoroughly dry, batting aside his still-clumsy hands when he tried to stop her.

"Hmm," she commented in a falsely suggestive tone, drying

a few of his more sensitive areas. "Looks like you could use a bit of toning exercise in some of these muscle groups. And I know just where, when, and how, shipmate."

Bruno woozily realized that Carol was jollying him along, trying to divert his attention from something important. His lips felt dry and cracked, his mouth tasted like bitter medicine and old leather. He knew something terrible was wrong.

"What's going on?" he managed to force past numb lips. His voice was a rusty croak. "Quit messing around. I think there is something wrong with me." Black spots circled at the edges of his vision like buzzing insects.

Carol said nothing, but hugged him very tightly for a moment. She let go abruptly, then finished drying him a little more roughly than he would have liked. His skin, tingling, began to feel more normal. Some of the cobwebs started to fade from his mind. Carol helped him into a jumpsuit coverall, ignoring all attempts by Bruno to induce her into talking.

It must be bad, Bruno thought to himself slowly. His mind was clearing a bit more. Some bad memories began to surface, still indistinct. He shivered.

With an arm around him, Carol lowered Bruno into his crash couch and punched the armrest keypad with unnecessary force. He felt the straps of his crash couch tighten around him. Carol sat in the crash couch next to him, strapped herself in, then turned and looked at Bruno directly.

That was when Bruno became truly frightened. Carol had tears in her eyes. *Carol.*

"Okay," he managed in a calm tone. "Go on, tell me. My crash couch autodoc has sedatives." He struggled to find something humorous to say. "Don't tell me. You've found somebody new."

Carol ignored the joke. Her face was ashen, with deep lines Bruno had never really noticed before. "You know about the EMP bomb?" she asked quietly.

Bruno felt a burning memory of the horrible black light

rise unwillingly in his memory and made a face. He nodded, forcing himself to concentrate.

"You unplugged me," Bruno said simply.

"Yes. Though it was more like tearing your wires out of the console by hand." She looked away and brushed tears from her face, clearly embarrassed. "The electromagnetic pulse would have killed you, Tacky. Fried your brain. Inductance almost burnt you out, anyway."

"I know." His brain still felt full of ashes and old scar tissue. "You did the right thing." Bruno's thoughts were slow, clogged. In his fuzzy memory, he could see the pandemonium on the navigation deck of *Sun-Tzu* as the enemy EMP struck the hull. Echoes of miniature lightning bolts shot from the console to his now-missing interface cable. The pale past edge of a horrible pain sliced into his recall. He reached up and touched the Linker socket in his neck, which felt somehow charred, still hot to his touch.

Which was impossible, of course.

"The autodoc says you have some brain damage." Carol's words were now studied and clipped, her tone clinical. She was not looking at him. "Your electronic prostheses are trying to compensate for the damage." Carol looked terrible, he realized. What else was wrong?

Bruno forced a smile, again feeling his dry lips crack.

"Well, enough about me," he said brightly. "What else has been happening while I've been on vacation?"

She said nothing, eyes glinting in the bright lighting of the tiny cabin.

Finally, Bruno took a more serious tone.

"Captain-my-captain," he told her quietly, "there wasn't anything else you could have done. I would have died for sure if the full charge had hit my chipware." He shrugged a little, forcing bravado into his voice. "We don't even know how bad the . . . damage is. Either I can be fixed or I can't." He took her hand in his. "We'll find out together."

Carol smiled a little, as much tired as sad, then told him everything. The images were nightmarish, confirming Bruno's high opinion of her abilities. Carrying his convulsing body down long darkened corridors to *Dolittle*. Powering down all major shipboard systems in decoy, and setting up the confinement-field booby trap for the kzin invaders—a project she had set up long ago during a paranoid watch period. Launching *Dolittle* and fleeing the *Sun-Tzu*.

Bruno scratched some flaky material away from his cheek. "How long till *Sun-Tzu* goes up?"

Carol gestured to the holographic display in the main screen, which had reached zero.

Her smile was as feral as any kzin's. "They have about three hours now. The confinement fields will appear normal for a time, then asymptotically degrade to catastrophic failure. And they won't know it until it's much too late—unless they have direct feeds from the core."

Bruno raised an eyebrow, curious.

"I set up a false telemetry system. If they tap into what looks like the core telemetry data feed, they'll read that the core is humming along just copacetic and fine." She thinned her lips into a cold smile. "Until the confinement fields fail and they fry, of course."

"Clever," he managed, pleased. "Can they stop it?"

"I don't think so." She shook her head, counting reasons off on her fingers as she went. "Not unless they are experts in complex systems and cryptography. First, they have to find out the obvious telemetry feed is a decoy. Then they have to locate the correct cable routings without our diagnostic equipment. Finally, they have to learn subsystem architecture and gain control over the field coils and ionizing lasers."

"All in a few hours," Bruno replied. "No way."

He reached across and touched Carol's hand. His own fingers still didn't want to move, and felt old and clumsy.

"How did you get everybody out of the suspension chambers into the cargo bay?" he asked, tilting his head toward the sealed door at the rear of the tiny cabin.

Carol looked down at her console and said nothing.

"You left them," Bruno said flatly.

She nodded, still looking down. "There wasn't any choice,"

Carol replied calmly, her captain voice surfacing again. The deepening lines on her face showed what that decision had cost her.

Bruno's head whirled. He and Carol had known all twenty-nine of the men and women in coldsleep. Trained with them, drunk with them, argued with them, studied with them. They all had names, hobbies, favorite drinks, games.

Now they were ratcat food.

Carol whistled through her teeth tunelessly for a moment, then reached over and squeezed his shoulder.

"Bruno," she said seriously, "you know perfectly well that I couldn't have saved them. And they will be avenged very soon."

It occurred to Bruno that Carol had made decisions like this many times in the past, during her Second Wave piloting, and as a Third Wave squadron commander. Decisions that saved or took lives.

"Does it ever get easier?" he asked, finally.

She knew what Bruno meant. "You remember each one of them, every waking moment of your life."

He sighed. Gingerly, he forced slow and shaky fingers into a dataglove and looked carefully at the holoscreen. He had to—

Suddenly, Bruno looked over at the coiled and clipped interface cable at the side of the control console. He felt something tear in his mind and heart.

What if I can't Link anymore? Bruno thought wildly. His heart seemed to hammer in his chest, and he took several deep breaths to calm himself. *Give it time*, he repeated over and over again to himself, like a mantra.

"What is it?" Carol asked, trying not to notice where Bruno had been looking.

"Nothing," he said harshly. "Could you please bring me up to date?"

Carol took the hint and walked him through the status windows. He was still mentally slow, but he could follow the events since the EMP bomb had hit the *Sun-Tzu*.

Linked, I could— He shoved the thought out of his mind,

and focused his attention on the small holoscreens above the main console. Ordered arrays of numbers marched across his line of sight, complex diagrams flowed and blinked; sterile representations of their life-and-death situation. Their lives as a column of glowing numbers.

After a few moments, Bruno turned to Carol. Their situation looked grim.

Bruno spoke first. "Are we going to be far enough away from *Sun-Tzu* when the confinement fields fail?"

"I don't know," she replied, her tone just as even as Bruno's. "I think that we can cycle back some of the power from the superconductive wings into a makeshift magnetic umbrella. That'll take care of the charged particles."

"What about the gamma?"

Carol smiled without humor. "We'll just have to take our chances with the prompt effects, shipmate."

• CHAPTER FIFTEEN

Rrowl-Captain equalized pressures and popped open his helmet. The rank, moist odor of monkeys too long confined thickened the darkness around him, swarming into his wide nostrils.

He controlled the urge to spit in distaste, and tried to breathe through his mouth.

Other Heroes of the boarding party were floating just inside the alien airlock, waiting respectfully for the captain of *Belly-Slasher* to signal them. At his hiss of permission, they opened their own helmets. Rrowl-Captain could hear the snarls of disgust at the humid jungle smells in the tunnel, like a Jotoki biome. The only light was from their helmet lamps. Sounds echoed harshly in the gloom, then faded away to a damp silence.

He shifted his grip on the fragile primate handholds and looked around the access tunnel. Blank and featureless walls, empty except for the long ladders and equipment docks he could see by helmet light. He snarled a hissing swearword at the monkeys' lack of gravity-polarizer technology. Primitives!

Alien-Technologist had used an echo-thumper to determine that atmosphere existed inside the outer hatch at the bow of the derelict monkeyship. The crewkzin then erected a sealed bubbledome around the airlock, and cut through the thick metal with heavy lasers, revealing the long dark access tunnel.

No trap-bombs, no cowardly monkey tricks.

Rrowl-Captain, as Dominant Leader, was first to set claw and fang inside the alien spacecraft. His victory, his prize.

The captain snarled orders, and crewkzin anchored powerful search lamps near the power feed that had been snaked through the airlock. Reassuring orange light blazed down the long access tunnel, banishing the darkness into small shadows. Rrowl-Captain could see the glint of another airlock far, far away in the darkness.

With a start, he tightened his grip on the monkey handhold as his perspective suddenly shifted. The tunnel pointed *down*, his alarmed reflexes informed him. He and his crew appeared to be hanging precariously at the top of a very long vertical tunnel. It did not matter to his brain, evolved on a planet, that the contra-matter reaction drive was providing only a tiny proportion of gravitational acceleration at present. It did not matter that the captain intellectually knew that he would not plummet like a stone down the shaft, but would drift like a bit of fluff combed from his pelt.

Kzin feared falling.

"Alien-Technologist," he rasped, mastering his fear after several deep breaths.

The kzin made an awkward microgravity leap to Rrowl-Captain's side from across the tunnel, using a reaction pistol judiciously, and snapped a suit bolt onto a nearby crossbar. The captain was impressed, but refused to show it.

"Command me," Alien-Technologist said without bravado, clearly as nervous in the tunnel as his captain.

"Lead your party to the inner airlock and secure this monkeyship."

"At once, Dominant One!"

Rrowl-Captain watched with grudging admiration as the octal of Heroes under Alien-Technologist's command rappelled down the tunnel. The figures in space armor swiftly became smaller as they descended, using secured lines and reaction pistols.

Lifting one wrist, he clumsily punched up the shipboard commlink with gloved fingers. Static hissed and fizzed in his ears.

"Command me!" growled-and-spat the low reply from Navigator on the command bridge.

"Status."

"The monkeyship continues to operate as before. Drone remotes have been dispatched to all major sectors of the outer hull." Navigator's tone sounded confident and full of Heroic pride. "No sign of traps or trickery."

"Open a telemetry channel to my portable thinplate."

"At once!" came Navigator's reply.

Rrowl-Captain unfolded his personal thinplate and accessed data downloaded from *Belly-Slasher*. Status reports stalked one another across the thinplate under the captain's gaze. The alien spacecraft was indeed running as if derelict, with only the contra-matter drive and magnetic field arrays operational. No beacons, no navigational control.

He spent some time reviewing the data, running a tongue over his sharp teeth in thought, waiting for the remote drones to complete their scans.

"Dominant One," crackled his headset in Alien-Technologist's voice, "we have secured the alien ship as you commanded."

"Did you find monkey bodies?"

"Yes," came the reply with a pleased growl. "We have found nearly four octals of the humans in artificial hibernation." There was a pause. "The maintenance subsystems appear to be both intact and functional."

Rrowl-Captain knew what Alien-Technologist was thinking. *Fresh, living monkey meat.* Saliva washed his fangs in anticipation. He rasped his rough tongue across thin black lips. Ship rations were not always pleasing to a Noble Hero's palate. Still, first things first.

"Do you mean that this ship was piloted by machines?"

"All hibernation couches are occupied."

Rrowl-Captain wanted to stretch his batwing ears in confusion and not a little suspicion. The monkeys relied very heavily indeed on untrustworthy automation, true. But to leave such a fearsome reaction drive under automated control smacked of madness.

They do not think like Heroes, the captain reminded himself yet again. *No alien thinks like a Hero. But what kind of artificial mind could have directed such an uncanny defense?*

"Have you found their command bridge?" he finally rasped.

A tone of pride entered the hissing voice in his helmet. "We have, Leader. The room has not been touched, and is waiting for you."

Repressing a shudder, Rrowl-Captain attached a belt loop to the guide lines left by his boarding party, and slid down the monkeyship access shaft in one slow, nightmare fall. From time to time, he fired his own reaction pistol to slow his dreamlike descent, barely suppressing his mews of fear as the tunnel walls slid past. When he finally reached the bottom of the tunnel, his posture ensured that none of the crewkzin dared look his way as he entered the inner airlock.

The interior was cramped, narrow. Lights were strung down empty corridors, spreading clear orange illumination into dark corners. Rrowl-Captain could hear hiss-and-spit conversation from engineers and specialists bent over alien equipment. He had known that the monkeys were puny, but his back complained painfully as he stooped under several hatch fittings. It would have been better to stalk these alien corridors on all fours, but space armor prevented that posture.

The captain rudely cuffed a low-ranking kzin apprentice standing guard. "Nameless One," he rumbled, "direct me to the monkey command bridge."

The other kzin saluted smartly and led his captain down one darkened corridor to a small area equipped with two tiny acceleration chairs and accompanying consoles. The nameless kzin saluted and stood at the hatchway, waiting for further instructions.

The captain of *Belly-Slasher* ceremonially urinated at all four cardinal points of the monkeyship command bridge, marking it as kzin territory.

And Rrowl-Captain's property in the Name of the Riit Patriarch of Kzin-home.

He examined the console carefully, looking at the burnt and damaged equipment clearly caused by the magneto-electrical pulse. He sniffed delicately at a heavy fiber-optic cable that had been torn from some kind of socket. He sniffed the broken end of the cable again, more thoroughly.

Something was wrong, Rrowl-Captain knew with a start, his ruff rising in alarm within his space armor. Containing a snarl, he swiftly looked from side to side, half expecting the very walls to burst open with hordes of laser-wielding monkeys.

Fangs did not fit into this wound channel as they should. He whirled suddenly and sniffed at the empty acceleration chairs. The scent was very fresh.

The captain began to growl low in his throat.

"Alien-Technologist," Rrowl-Captain hissed into his commlink.

"Leader!" came the reply in his helmet.

"Where are you at present?"

"I am studying the contra-matter drive. Dominant One, the brute force of the monkey technology, without artifice or subtlety, is astounding. Brute force primitives. They have wrestled contra-particles into a high vacuum chamber, and—"

"Enough," the captain interrupted. "Tell me again that all of the hibernation chambers are occupied."

"It is so, Dominant One. This spacecraft, for all its apparent size, is quite tiny—an iceball with a small life-bubble deep inside."

Rrowl-Captain blinked in thought, staring at the empty chairs and savoring the scents he had found on them. "Is it possible," he hissed, "that two of the monkeys have but recently entered hibernation?"

There was a short pause.

"No, Leader. Even with alien machinery, it is clear that all of the hibernation chambers have been occupied for several years."

"Report to me at once," Rrowl-Captain shrieked. He punched up Navigator in *Belly-Slasher* on his commlink and spat syllables quickly, issuing orders and demanding information.

It took some time to prove what Rrowl-Captain's nose had suspected. There had indeed been two monkeys alive and warm inside the iceball of a spacecraft not long before

Rrowl-Captain's boarding party entered. There were no bodies, and all of the hibernation chambers were in long-term use.

Even an unblooded kitten could set fangs into these facts: The two monkeys were hiding or had fled.

Judicious use of Alien-Technologist's sonic echo-thumper sounded the walls of the monkeyship, and after some search found an empty shipbay, hidden behind a false bulkhead. Instruments detected residual radiation from a fusion drive lining what was clearly a collapsed escape tunnel through reinforced ice.

Navigator's instruments aboard *Belly-Slasher*, using the remote drones and Alien-Technologist's growing intuition of monkey ways, found a magnetic anomaly receding quickly from them. It was decelerating very rapidly indeed, and seemed to have originated from the derelict monkeyship.

"Why are the honorless leaf-eaters running and not fighting?" Rrowl-Captain growled in anger and frustration. "Why would they flee, and leave the defenseless bodies of their comrades to us?"

Kzin never let their fellow Heroes become prey.

Alien-Technologist averted his eyes, folded ears against skull inside his helmet. "Because they cannot win, Leader, and flee witlessly before Noble Heroes."

The captain slashed claws in rebuke at the other kzin's lickspittle foolishness. "Hardly," he rasped angrily. "This event reeks of monkey trickery." He paused a moment in carnivorous thought. *Think like a duplicitous monkey*, he reminded himself with vast distaste.

"The contra-matter drive is stable?"

"Yes, Leader. We have tapped into the monkey telemetry cables, and found the confinement fields steady."

There was a snarl of static over the commlink from Navigator, still aboard *Belly-Slasher*. "Dominant One, I do not mean to intrude, but there is an anomalous finding—"

"Report," Rrowl-Captain growled.

"Remote drones near the reaction drive section show increasing levels of radioactivity," the tiny voice finished.

The darkened monkey corridor seemed to whirl around Rrowl-Captain and close in on him like an implacable enemy's claws. He felt a growl growing within his throat.

"You have no other manner," he hissed slowly to the other kzin standing before him, "to determine the status of the reaction drive than what the monkeys *wish* us to know?" Alien-Technologist looked at his captain blankly.

"Leader, I do not understand. These are standard telemetry lines linking the contra-matter drive directly to these navigation consoles . . . hrrrrr," he said, falling silent in thought.

Rrowl-Captain barely contained his fury. "Confirm the status of the contra-matter drive at once. Directly. In person if necessary. I feel enemy eyes upon us, and scent danger." Rrowl-Captain repressed the desire to slash an ear from the monkey-trusting Alien-Technologist for his trophy loop. "In the meantime, the rest of the crew not associated with you will return to *Belly-Slasher*."

Rrowl-Captain snorted his displeasure at Alien-Technologist, who hung bouncing in the microgravity like a toothless kitten's prey-toy. He ignored the other kzin's humbled salute and turned to leave the navigation chamber abruptly.

The captain would lead *Belly-Slasher* on a diverting exercise, a small hunt for the escaped monkeys, who would rather run than fight. Perhaps by the time he had returned with his trophies, Alien-Technologist and his crew would have truly secured the monkeyship prize. He entered the access tunnel, and hooked the guide line to a reinforced loop on his battle armor. Rrowl-Captain snarled and leaped upward in the microgravity, toward the outer airlock, firing his reaction pistol downward for added emphasis.

He never looked down.

Rrowl-Captain entered *Belly-Slasher*, feeling the comforting artificial gravitation firm beneath his taloned boots once more. Suddenly, slurred hisses of Alien-Technologist yowled over the commlink in a frenzied rush of harsh syllables.

He could not make out the words, but the tone was clear: Fear. Warning.

• CHAPTER SIXTEEN

Carol grinned widely as the holoscreen overloaded with *Sun-Tzu's* incandescent death.

Flash—*blank*—and the display reset, showing the horrific radiance of the matter-antimatter explosion in muted colors.

"Bang," said Bruno softly.

The cloud of plasma and radiation that had once been *Sun-Tzu* began to spread out in a complex, fluorescence-colorful pattern. Magnetic fields and relativistic impacts with the interstellar medium made the cloud look like a living thing crawling under a microscope.

Carol leaned over and kissed him with sudden passion.

"As usual," she murmured into his ear, nuzzling gently, "you have a gift for understatement." She ran the back of her hand very softly across her lover's face. "Would you accept the intention, if not the act?"

Carol was gratified to see a genuine smile on Bruno's face.

"Well," he replied, "the situation being what it is, I suppose that I can understand your position."

She winked at him, gave a sly smile. "We'll discuss positions later," she whispered, and turned back to the holoscreen.

That is, she thought, *if we aren't puking our guts out from radiation poisoning*. She knew that Bruno was thinking much the same thing. Their flirting words were both supportive and diverting.

And, despite the danger they faced, fun besides.

Carol had already done as much as she could until the bulk of the radiation arrived, triumphant yet harmful messenger heralding the death of the ratcats. And, much as she hated to think about it, from the deaths of almost thirty of her friends and crewmates, frozen in coldsleep. People for whom she had been responsible, as captain of *Sun-Tzu*.

She had carefully tuned the superconductive wings of *Dolittle* to maximize magnetic deflection of the incoming wave of charged particles. Also, Carol had turned the ship sternward to the spreading bloom of *Sun-Tzu*'s death, using the long fuel tank as additional shielding. There was nothing else to do but wait.

While they waited for the radiation front to strike *Dolittle*, Carol reviewed the autodoc data. Bruno seemed to have recovered well physically from his trauma aboard *Sun-Tzu*. The wrenching of "manual de-Linkage"—she frowned at the antiseptic term—left little to no physical damage. Stimulants and mood modifiers kept his mental state relatively calm and normal.

As Bruno had said, his electronic prostheses would repair the brain damage—or not. There was nothing either of them could do about it. She didn't want to die alone, without him. She remained silent for long moments.

"Okay," Bruno sighed, "as usual, the Captain will speak when the Captain pleases. Blessed be the Name of the Captain."

"Next you'll be praising me as 'from whom all blessings flow.' " She smiled, despite herself. He knew her well.

"A little much, perhaps."

"Flattery will get you anywhere, cabin boy."

"Sounds like sexual harassment to me," Bruno replied in mock outrage, batting his eyelashes at her outrageously.

Carol snorted laughter. "You've been scanning datachips of Early's history lectures again, haven't you? That term hasn't been in use for two hundred years."

"How would you know?" A sly grin crossed Bruno's face.

She squeezed his biceps hard. "You always know how to make me laugh, lover. Thanks for bringing my good mood back."

They said nothing for a time.

"Any time now, isn't it?" Bruno asked calmly.

"That's a big affirmative."

There was a soundless flash behind their eyelids as the radiation front struck *Dolittle*. Radiation sleeted through the magnetic fields surrounding the ship, the hull walls, the long, slushed deuterium tank, and their own bodies— all in a microsecond.

"Well," Bruno remarked, "you always show me the most *interesting* places, my dear."

Carol ignored his nervous humor and pored over the holoscreen datastream in the biotelemetry window. After a moment, Bruno began to help her.

Finally, she sighed with relief. Their cumulative doses were high, but not quite lethal. Their prompt doses would ensure a slight fever and nausea, easily handled by drugs from the autodoc.

"It looks like we'll live," Carol said.

"For a while." Bruno's tone was quiet and somber.

"No more Project Cherubim. And we aren't going to make it to Wunderland or Home, are we?"

"Doubtful. Maybe we can rig up a couple of coldsleep bunks from the autodoc spare parts. We sure don't have a decade's worth of recycler or supply capacity." He brightened a bit. "Maybe another Earth ship will find us while we're in coldsleep."

"Or a kzin warcraft, more likely," she reminded him. "We could wake up a piece at a time."

Again, silence hung thick in *Dolittle*.

"All of it was for nothing," Bruno finally said, his tone black and dead.

"No," she replied firmly. "Not for nothing. You and I got together, love."

He squeezed her hand in agreement.

"And," Carol pointed out, "we waxed three ratcat ships in the bargain. Maybe two hundred kzin flash-fried to vapor. That must be worth something on the scorechip."

Bruno's face was suddenly slack, a bit like his Linked expression. Concern flashed through Carol's mind.

"What is it, Tacky?" she asked lightly, keeping the worry from her voice.

"I hope that we took out all the kzin ships."

Carol gestured at the holoscreen. "Sure we did. Look at the fireworks." The antimatter explosion was immense, brilliantly colored. It occurred to her that the garish cloud would eventually be visible across light-years.

"Can we be certain?" Bruno's tone was odd, a little machinelike.

"Is that a prediction, that we *didn't* get them all?" she inquired, frowning.

"I don't think that I can Link anymore, so I'm just guessing. Maybe I'm just worried." His tone and facial expression were back to normal.

Carol leaned over and rubbed her stiff strip haircut against his cheek. "You will never guess how attractive I find a simple human guess, my friend."

• CHAPTER SEVENTEEN

Rrowl-Captain scented his own death in the cramped singleship fighter. He closed his nostrils from the stench of unchallenging prey. The kzin knew that he had taken more than a lethal dose of radiation in the detonation of the monkeyship. The captain was far from the medical tank in the wreckage of *Belly-Slasher*, and the supplies aboard the singleship were minimal.

There had been little time to plan an escape.

Alien-Technologist's warning had come late, too late. Rrowl-Captain and his crew had engaged *Belly-Slasher*'s gravity polarizers at maximum acceleration, but were only a few hundred kilometers from the human spacecraft when the contra-matter containment fields had failed. Damage had been heavy: his precious spacecraft hulled and broken, his crew torn and bloody and mostly dead. The One Fanged God had inexplicably spared Rrowl-Captain of all but the radiation exposure.

His mind filled with the memories of mewling Heroes in agony—blinded, seared, poisoned by monkey treachery. Even those crewkzin still breathing would, like Rrowl-Captain, soon die of the radiation taint in their blood and bone.

His dreams of regaining his honor and reward, his Warrior Heart, were shattered by monkey perfidy and cowardice.

Rrowl-Captain had managed to seal his space armor in the confusing aftermath of the explosion. He had picked his way through the twisted wreckage of *Belly-Slasher*, down black corridors filled with the drifting corpses of his Heroes— or worse, the crewkzin not yet dead. Eventually, he had reached a still-intact singleship fighter, *Sharpened-Fang*. The small warcraft lacked the strong gravitic protective fields of larger kzin spacecraft, and was not designed for individual near-luminal travel.

He had little to lose. And nothing to gain but a Hero's final vengeance.

Rrowl-Captain knew that he was dying, as he held back the wrenching pain he felt in his innards. It was like shards of broken glass, grinding deep; like the sharp teeth of some enemy at his liver, chewing. The epithelial lining of his stomach and intestines had loosened, leading to the violent nausea of lethal radiation poisoning. He could literally feel the blisters rising on his body, as radiation-outraged skin layers began to die. Fur began to fall from his pelt in handfuls.

Rrowl-Captain hawked and spat blood onto the tiny deck, to mix with the pool of drying vomit already left there. He knew his time was short. At least he had a chance to show his honor, his Warrior Heart, before he met the One Fanged God. The memory of his dead litter-brother would demand nothing less.

Rrowl-Captain would take these despicable monkeys as his honor-slaves into the Hunting Ground Beyond.

He peered into the singleship thinplate screen with damaged eyes, searching. Finally, Rrowl-Captain found the human escape vessel. The coward-vessel had wrapped huge magnetic fields around itself, according to his instruments. Rrowl-Captain snarled as he altered *Sharpened-Fang*'s course, his mouth dry and scratchy. The air tasted of death and failure, and his very fangs were loosening in his head.

The escaping monkeyship with its queer gossamer wings could not maneuver, and the fusion drive seemed minimal. All that the human ship seemed capable of was magnetic deceleration and minor course corrections. His thinplate screen analysis indicated an impressively high level of deceleration, in fact. The stresses upon the little spacecraft must be tremendous, he mused, hissing in readiness to do battle.

Rrowl-Captain increased *Sharpened-Fang*'s velocity, pushing the gravitic polarizers to their safety limits, and beyond. The ripping-cloth noise of the drive began to sound like a predatory scream, filling his folded ears. Purple warning lights flashed on the control console and warning tones yowled. His head pounded as the fabric of space itself twisted savagely. The monkeyship grew larger on his screen. Rrowl-Captain readied his weapons panel, his black claws clicking on keypads.

Something nagged at the captain. What, he wondered, could these craven monkeys do with the waste energy from deceleration? Only by draining energy at enormous rates could the strange vessel take significant advantage of magnetic deceleration. The ship was small, and would have little need for prodigious energy sources. . . .

Green hell suddenly filled Rrowl-Captain's thinplate viewscreen, which went blank in a frying crackle of circuit overload.

He keened in surprise and fear. Alarms shrieked in the tiny cabin. Ablative microconstruction in the hull of the singleship vaporized and shoved *Sharpened-Fang* violently to one side, out of the deadly beam of the humans' laser weaponry. Secondary sensors and viewscreens came smoothly on-line.

The alien beam showed itself within the cloud of vaporized hull material surrounding *Sharpened-Fang*. The laser reached out for Rrowl-Captain again, like the implacable clawed Finger of the One Fanged God.

He squelched his fear with a feral snarl, and initiated further evasive maneuvers. This time, light-speed limitations were on Rrowl-Captain's side. The gravitic drives screamed with the increased demand. He smelled burning insulation from failing electronic components.

Rrowl-Captain's claws extended and clicked across his console keypads. *Sharpened-Fang* began moving randomly, avoiding the deadly spears of laser light that stabbed at him.

What weapons could Rrowl-Captain bring to bear? Particle beams would be near-useless in the face of such magnetic deflection fields. His laser cannon was not formidable at this distance. *Sharpened-Fang* possessed only a small armament array, being designed for close approach, ship-to-ship assaults.

However, the singleship was equipped with a few special-purpose weapons. Rrowl-Captain reviewed shipboard inventory swiftly, then blinked twice. With a kzin cough of a chuckle, he realized that he knew how to render the monkey escape ship fangless.

The huge but delicate wings of the vessel were super-conductive! Their passage through the magnetic fields of interstellar space provided the power for their laser array, little different in principle than the electrical engines of ancient history. The captain licked a crusty tongue across cracked lips, and drooled bloody saliva in anticipation.

The wings were the monkeys' weakness. Without them, they were powerless—in the literal sense of the term.

Rrowl-Captain knew his strategy was dangerous, but filled with honor. He punched in a final sequence of keypads, hiss-spat a prayer to the One Fanged God, and scream-and-leaped *Sharpened-Fang* toward the alien ship.

• OUTSIDERS THREE

Fury. Observe this gross insult of plasma and sundered field lines! How has this remote lack of action served the Divine Radiants?

Worry. One hotlife craft has been atomized by fundamental annihilation as the other-node predicted. What damage will be wreaked by this event?

Anger. The plasma cloud will be vast, and the twisted force-lines will eventually impinge upon the Sacred Region. The insult to the Divine Radiants and Their Design will be grievous.

Woe. This local-node had hoped . . .

Impatience. Hope is not sufficient! A great gout of highly ionized plasma grows—directly where it should not.

Grudging-agreement. Once more, this local-node and the other-node concur with One mind. Yet the constraints of the Treaty . . .

Decisiveness. Treaties with feral heretics are transcended by the Here-and-Now! This local-and-other nodes, as One mind, shall act!

Agreement-with-caution. Truth. Yet the {^^^*III*} have Sentinels as well. Surely the feral nodes may reach conclusions and act as well as this local-and-other node at One. First, this local-and-other node should determine the nature and potential of this insult.

Irritation-frustration. How does the other-node suggest such a determination be performed? The nature and intent of vermin remains unimportant.

Caution. Yet the actions of the hotlife motes have grave consequences. This local-node argues that the offending vermin be acquired and their inner and external patterns deep-analyzed for action and intent. Consider these facts for congruence to the Great Pattern.

Anger-acceptance. Truth. Such caution is implied from the High Texts. One. Mark this local-node's arguments, however.

Agreement. This local-node is of One mind with the other-node, including the reservations of the other-node. Perhaps further analysis before the acquisition of the hotlife motes is warranted. The feral {^^^///} may have reached the same conclusions as the Local Nexus.

Resolve. Enough! There has been sufficient debate and discussion. This local-node sends the initiator signal. Muster the many! The Nexus acts!

• CHAPTER EIGHTEEN

Bruno watched Carol's fingers on the fire-control console with some surprise. It was a delicate, deadly ballet she danced, one hand in a dataglove making delicate adjustments, while the other hand punched and stroked keypads.

In retrospect, it made sense to Bruno that Carol was skilled at battle stations; after all, she was twice a combat veteran. But Bruno had been spoiled by the absolute certainty of Linkage. While Transcended, he simply made things happen with a thought. He didn't actually have to *do* anything at all. He *knew*.

Bruno frowned. Every time he had thought of Linkage since emerging from the autodoc tank, he had developed a pounding headache. Strange images with mixed sensoria intruded. He felt as if he could somehow taste colors, and feel sounds. It was frightening, but somehow familiar. Bruno had convinced himself that the incidents were a by-product of his macrocircuit neuronal matrices rerouting around the nerve damage.

Or, he thought grimly, it could just be the brain damage itself.

He firmly put that thought from his mind; it was unproductive at present. On the holoscreen, Bruno saw the icon of the kzin singleship moving in little jerks and starts across the idealized starscape. Carol kept trying to center the fire-control cursor in front of the presumed path of the alien ship before activating the hugely powerful gas lasers powered by *Dolittle's* deceleration.

"C'mere, you little ratcat," she crooned to herself. "Just hold course a bit longer. . . ."

She missed again. The kzin singleship was closer.

"You want me to try to Link up?" he asked without thinking, even as the pounding in his skull began anew.

Carol didn't even look away from the holoscreen. "Tacky, dear," she said in a distracted tone, "you don't even want to think about attaching that interface socket in your neck to anything with electrical current in it—not until we can do a full autodiagnostic on the rig."

She was right. Linkage might kill him now.

He just hated feeling stupid and slow. He used to be so much *more*. Not just a human . . .

"No," Carol continued, "you just let old Mumma Carol take care of our little ratcat infestation." She paused for a moment, stretching her fingers luxuriously. "I have whacked more than one kzin singleship in my deep dark past."

"So we have a chance?"

"You want to bet every credit in inventory on it, shipmate." Carol slapped his arm with her free hand and went back to work.

Bruno busied himself by reviewing *Dolittle*'s diagnostics and spare-parts inventory. If he and Carol survived this dogfight, maybe he really could cobble together some kind of coldsleep chamber. If not, they faced slow asphyxiation in their own waste gases when the recyclers finally failed.

"Heads up," Carol cried, scoring another hit with the main laser array. Bruno saw the cloud of vaporized ship-material fluoresce in the aftermath of the laser light. "Ah, taxes take ablation shielding," she swore bitterly as the kzin icon emerged from the cloud under full acceleration, apparently undamaged.

Bruno saw something. "What's that?" he asked, using his own dataglove to point into the holoscreen. A tiny blinking point of light was moving swiftly toward them.

Carol clucked at her too-focused attention and opened a realtime window in the holoscreen. She magnified and amplified ambient starlight for illumination. A small, glittering globe flew toward them across the relativity-squashed starscape.

"Bomb?" Bruno asked.

Carol shook her head. "I'm getting no readings other than faint and indeterminate electronics leakage. No fissionables, fusion materials, monopoles."

"How fast?"

"It's coming in at just under a hundred KPS, relative." She smiled tightly. "Let's see how whatever it is likes a little light on the subject." She started to place the fire-control cursor over the icon representing the mysterious globe in the tactical window of the holoscreen.

"Wait!" Bruno exclaimed, pointing at the realtime window.

As they both watched in surprise, the globe smoothly separated into two hemispheres. The half globes whirled around one another almost too swiftly for the eye to see, then began to slow as the distance between the two hemispheres increased.

"It looks like a bolo," Bruno breathed, remembering his history chips. "The two pieces have to be connected by something. Can't you resolve it?"

Carol shook her head. "Negatory, Tacky. Are you sure that there is something between them?"

Bruno was very sure. Physics was physics, after all. "How else can they be swinging around one another so quickly?"

"You have a point. But it's getting pretty close to us now." Carol set the fire-control cursor directly between the two whirling objects, which were over a kilometer apart now. "Firing full power burst."

For a moment, the entire distance between the two hemispheres blazed with a brilliant green line that hurt the eye, almost too thin to see. It vanished instantly. Enhancing infrared did not show anything, either.

Bruno swore another nonsensical oath Buford Early had taught him, something about water birds and sex. "Carol," he said tensely, "I have a bad feeling we are dealing with monomolecular filament. Shoot for either of the hemispheres, now!"

It took several full-power shots to convince Carol that even the enormous power of their laser array was being leached away by the apparent superconductivity of the filament material, only one molecule thick. The hemispheres seemed to be as invulnerable as the invisible filament between them. Seconds after a direct hit, the slowly twirling hemispheres had cooled to ambient temperatures.

"You had best maneuver us out of the way," Bruno told her as the alien whirligig drew closer to *Dolittle*. "That filament will pass right through the hull like a cutting laser through aluminum veneer."

"Damn!" Carol's face was a mask of concentration.

But as Bruno had feared, the twirling hemispheres were guided, not simply ballistic. Further, Carol occasionally had to blast the laser battery at the kzin singleship, which fired off several laser bolts of its own at *Dolittle*. Damage had been minimal, since the kzin singleship had clearly been designed for close-quarter battles, but the diversion did seriously degrade her performance with regard to what had become the main threat.

Bruno again felt the headache, thinking how he might have handled this situation in Linkage. The ship was after all designed to be operated by a Linker. He stoked up the fusion drive to full power, trying to maneuver *Dolittle*. The superconductive wings could not be used for course changes, only deceleration or long, slow turns. His course changes were minimal, due to the ungainliness of the wings.

The strange enemy weapon grew closer to *Dolittle*.

With a sinking feeling, Bruno noticed that the kzin singleship was silent, keeping its distance.

"Impact coming up," Carol sang out. She roughly swung the ship on its axis.

The twirling hemispheres missed *Dolittle*, but neatly sheared off the starboard superconductive wing. In one window of the holoscreen, Bruno had a glimpse of the severed gossamer assembly twisting and falling away into the darkness. Half the green telltale status lights on the command console flashed red.

"Close," Carol breathed.

"Carol, the wing was the target of that weapon, not the ship proper."

Carol wiped sweat from her brow, and did not look away from the holoscreen.

"Sure, Tacky," she said evenly. "The ratcat wants us intact. To take us apart piece by piece."

"Lasers still operational?"

"Yes, at half power," Carol replied, and raised a jet black eyebrow.

Neither of them mentioned the larger problem. With one of the superconductive wings gone, it would be nearly impossible for *Dolittle* to decelerate to nonrelativistic speeds in a straight line. They would be turning to port as they slowed.

Carol fired another laser blast at the icon of the kzin singleship, while Bruno scratched his interface socket idly. He powered up particle-beam and X-ray pump bomblets. The laser array powered by their remaining superconductive wing was their major weapon, but Bruno wanted all of *Dolittle*'s armament available at Carol's whim.

He smiled to himself. Carol was actually doing quite well, considering that *Dolittle* was supposed to be piloted by a non-brain-damaged and fully Linked Bruno Takagama.

Suddenly, their crash couches tightened around them as the universe seemed to jerk and twist violently—then relax again. Alarms buzzed and whooped in the tiny cabin of *Dolittle*. Alert windows automatically opened on the main holoscreen, displaying schematics and updated diagnostics.

"Censored dammit," Carol shouted, her hands freezing on her console for a moment in sheer Belter reflex. "What's going on?" Even as she spoke, her hands were dancing across her console to look for the answer.

Carol fell silent as she stared at the forward holoscreen windows. Almost as an afterthought, she slammed a keypad with her fist, silencing the alarms.

Bruno did not believe the readings, nor the screen.

"Carol," he said softly, in wonder. He shook his head.

"Bruno," she replied in flat tones, looking at the realtime forward window in the holoscreen, "would you please tell me what you are seeing?" He could hear her swallow over the low rustle of the ventilation system. "I want to know if I am going schitz."

"Our velocity appears to no longer be zero point seven C," Bruno said, staring openly at the normal-appearing starscape, not squashed or altered by relativistic speeds. "The superconductive wing batteries are no longer drawing significant power, again suggesting that our velocity is no higher than zero point one C." He paused. "That means the weapons systems are inoperable."

Carol shrugged at Bruno's last comment, her fingers dancing across her console. "Worry about that later, Bruno. Putting fusion drive on standby," she said crisply, as the sensation of gravity faded. Then, the dropping elevator sensation of free fall. "Is the kzin singleship still there?"

"Yes," he replied, still dazed. "It appears to be in the same position, relative to us, as before the . . . incident." Bruno watched the datastream next to the kzin icon in the Tactical window for a moment. "It does not appear to be maneuvering. It's stationary . . . as we are, apparently."

Still feeling very odd, Bruno busied himself with collecting and analyzing the last few minutes of shipboard time. After a moment, Carol reached across and pinched his arm, very hard.

"Bruno!"

"Yes?" he answered politely.

"What is that thing off to starboard?" She pinched him again, still harder, when he didn't answer.

"Oh, that."

"Yeah, that."

"It appears to be an alien spacecraft or other artifact." He paused, cleared his throat loudly, and consulted his console holoscreens with exaggerated caution. "Approximately one hundred kilometers across."

• CHAPTER NINETEEN

Rrowl-Captain, eyes wide in fear, stared at his status viewscreen. He shrieked anger and surprise, then retched painfully with his growing sickness. The spasms subsided after a moment.

Time was growing very short indeed.

What power could have instantaneously stopped both *Sharpened-Fang* and his cowardly monkey prey dead-still in interstellar space? Kinetic potential was awesome at near luminal velocities. He didn't know the method, but clearly, the new and unknown spacecraft was the culprit.

The intruder vessel was the size of a small moon, and looked more like a crowded city than a spacecraft. Magnification showed spires and squarish buildings, open areas and domes, tiny motes of light that moved above and through the huge construct. Thin spidery webs extending from the main body of the vessel glowed incandescently in high infrared, bleeding off waste heat into interstellar space. Instruments showed that the moon-ship kept an ambient temperature of forty divisions above Total Cold.

Rrowl-Captain bared his aching fangs, slowly. Monkeys could not have built this ship. Nor could kzin, even as favored sons of the One Fanged God. No race Rrowl-Captain knew of could construct such a vessel.

Perhaps the intruders had intervened on the monkeys' behalf. Rrowl-Captain coughed again, spitting blood.

Memories of greenish light flared in the back of his mind. It would explain much.

He snarled as he pulled out another handful of fur with his blistered fingers. He gulped a few more of his antiradiation capsules, struggling to keep them inside his traitor belly, though the capsules only slowed the inevitable.

No, thought Rrowl-Captain on further reflection, the intruder spacecraft was not intervening on the side of the human monkeys. If that had been their alien intention, surely Rrowl-Captain and *Sharpened-Fang* would even now be mingled as thoroughly dispersed vapor. That was as clear as the fangs in his own jaws.

The intruders were simply meddlers.

Rrowl-Captain consulted his thinplate console. The forward screen revealed the monkeyship hanging dead in space. Even dying of radiation sickness, the captain smiled and rumbled in kzin humor. If the monkeys were not moving, then their power source was inactive.

Meddlers or no meddlers, Rrowl-Captain was going to complete his ceremonial kill. He would be unable to place human ears on his trophy loop, but he would accomplish a task almost as tasty. A final delicacy, in honor of his litter-brother.

With trembling claws, the captain warmed up the strained gravitic polarizer and put the weapons panel on standby. Within a few moments, Rrowl-Captain would finish his scream-and-leap, weapons firing, and destroy the monkey vessel. Then he would deal with these meddling intruders.

A yowling alarm tone halted Rrowl-Captain's ready claw, poised over the initiate keypad.

He looked up with a snarl, and saw many octal-squareds of nightmare black shapes blotting out the stars, living creatures flying through empty space toward *Sharpened-Fang*.

Magnification and vector analysis showed the hordes to originate from the intruder moon-ship. The intruder aliens were even uglier than Jotoki, Rrowl-Captain realized with a hiss of distaste. Thick central stalks surrounded by an octal-and-half of sinuous tendrils—yet bearing tools and wearing harnesses.

Powerful or not, Rrowl-Captain could not let these aliens threaten a Hero's vessel, nor his own plans. He reoriented the weapons panel and prepared to fire.

• CHAPTER TWENTY

Like Bruno, Carol was still dazed by the sudden appearance of the titanic alien ship that had somehow halted them in space and now held position, motionless, ten thousand kilometers to starboard. She slowly turned to Bruno, who appeared to be recovering from the shock of the past few minutes. At least he was reviewing data instead of staring blankly at the strangely unshifted stars in the holoscreen.

"Where *is* the ratcat ship?"

Her lover shook his head slightly, tapped on a few keypads. A red circle appeared in the holoscreen. "Just under two hundred kilometers dead ahead, right where it was when things got . . . well, weird."

Weird was the right word, Carol thought. How could *Dolittle* go from 0.7c to dead stop in a second?

She peered at the portion of the holoscreen indicating the kzin singleship for a moment or two, looking for activity. "Looks like the ratcat isn't moving, either."

"Maybe it's just as surprised by recent events as we are."

Carol mulled that one over, then decided to change the subject. She put an autowatch subroutine on the kzin singleship that would set off alarms if the ratcat vessel moved or showed activity. Carol then highlighted the huge alien ship.

"Well, Bruno," she asked brightly, "what do you think?"

Bruno could not tear his eyes from the holoscreen windows. "Like you said, Captain-my-captain. It's the size of a moon."

"A small moon."

"Sure. But what's the point of a *spacecraft* a hundred kilometers across?"

Bruno had made a good point, Carol thought. Further, the alien vessel *looked* more like a city or hive of insects than a spacecraft. There were what appeared to be buildings and domes across its broad and complex expanse. It was baroque and ornate, like some windup Victorian Christmas tree ornament out of a history chip.

"Notice the weblike structures?" Bruno indicated a portion of the realtime magnified view of the moon-ship. "Look at them in IR."

In infrared, the complex webs all over the moon-ship were hundreds of degrees warmer than the rest of the vessel.

"Heat exchangers?" she asked.

Bruno nodded. "I'm betting that they are particularly hot now, after . . . stopping us a bit ago. That must have taken a *lot* of energy."

Carol noticed flocks of tiny lights moving around the spires of the gigantic alien ship. "What are those?"

"No idea," Bruno replied, tweaking the image enhancers. Magnification did not help, only revealing blurred glowing shapes that darted and swooped like living things around upper portions of the moon-ship.

Bruno finally asked the question. "What do we do?"

"Nothing," she replied. "Let them make the first move." Carol reached over and stroked his arm gently. "Face it, Tacky. Whatever they are, they're much more powerful than me and thee. They could swat us to paste anytime. I would rather wait, peacefully, to see what they want with us."

Bruno nodded slowly.

"I just feel stupid and helpless," he finally said, looking away. "I used to know almost everything."

"But only when you were part machine. I like you better as a human." She moved his lips into a smile with her fingers, and was rewarded by the real thing.

"Carol?"

Bruno gestured at the holoscreen with a nervous finger. "What is it?" she asked.

"The kzin ship is getting visitors."

Long-range scanning showed at least one hundred small objects flying toward the kzin singleship from the huge alien vessel. Extreme magnification showed vague dusky shapes with many arms flitting across the starry blackness. They rotated smoothly as they flew, arms stretched out radial fashion for stability.

"Those must be our new friends," Bruno commented.

Carol said nothing, biting her lip. They would get some idea of the new aliens' intentions from their actions toward the kzin singleship. They must have been moving very quickly to be so close to the ratcat vessel.

A low warning tone sounded.

Carol made a face as she studied the holoscreens. "Looks as if we are going to be entertaining a few visitors of our own," she said, pointing at a small cloud of dots on the short-range scanner window in the main holoscreen. The cloud was growing closer to *Dolittle* by the second, decelerating rapidly.

"Still want me to do nothing?" Bruno asked.

Carol nodded. "Watch the ratcat ship."

As the flock of aliens approached the kzin singleship, it began to move, maneuvering away with its reactionless drive. Extreme magnification showed a pale purple beam of light stretching from one of the tiny hydra shapes to the kzin spacecraft. The whole vessel glowed purple for a moment, then the slight aura faded.

The singleship halted and hung motionless in space. Long-range scanners showed that all electronic emissions from the kzin vessel had ceased. The droves of tiny shapes merged with it.

"As I mentioned," Carol remarked conversationally, "I suspect it would be wise to do nothing."

Bruno smiled without showing his teeth. "Hold that thought, Carol. Our visitors have arrived." He gestured to a holoscreen window displaying a view of the external hull. Many-armed shapes swarmed past the cameras.

"Follow them with the hull cameras, please."

Bruno set up a series of small windows in the holoscreen displaying the external hull of *Dolittle*. The windows showed weaving tendrils, rapid activity.

"Switch to infrared," Carol said after a while. Perhaps the aliens would show up better in the longer wavelengths.

One by one, the windows went blank, showing the multicolored snowy display of holographic static.

"What happened?" she rapped.

"Hardware failure. They're doing something to the ship."

Before Carol could say anything else, the external long-range scanners failed. Then weapons-status telemetry.

She unstrapped and floated over to a supply locker.

"What are you doing?" Bruno asked her, unstrapping himself and joining her.

"Going to suit up and try and convince the uglies on the hull to stop what they are doing. Force of my commanding personality, that sort of thing, you know."

Her lover frowned. "You know that I can't Link right now, and you are better behind the console. Let me go outside. I need you at the console, to get us out of here if necessary."

His glance speared her heart.

For a moment, Carol was busy repressing her odd mix of maternal and sexual feelings that Bruno brought out in her. If they survived, she would take the confusion up with her autodoc psychiatric module at length.

"Go," the Captain persona inside her finally said. "But be careful, Tacky," her deeper self appended. "I need you, too."

Bruno gave her a quick hug, and she efficiently helped him into his spacesuit.

"Oh," Carol added conversationally, "you might want to take this, too." She pressed an electron-beam rifle into his hands. Bruno took it awkwardly, then slung it over his shoulder.

The main computer reset itself, then fell to fifty percent processing capacity. More warning tones began to sound.

"You had better hurry," Carol said softly, "while we can still cycle the airlock."

Bruno started to dog his helmet shut and entered the airlock. He paused and turned back to Carol. She smiled at his look

"I love you, too," she said simply.

Carol kept a smile on her face until she heard the hatch close firmly. Then she blinked a few times to clear the tears that pooled in her eyes in the microgravity, and strapped back into her crash couch. After a moment she swept her hands across the main console, to see what systems remained responsive.

• CHAPTER TWENTY-ONE

Bruno opened the outer airlock door of *Dolittle*.

"Carol," he whispered over the suit commlink.

"I'm here, lover." Her voice buzzed in his headset.

"I'm leaving the airlock now. You getting video?"

"Affirmative."

Bruno clumsily lifted himself out of the airlock and locked down his magnetic boots on the dark hull of *Dolittle*. The riot of distant stars all around him shone down indifferently. This was deep space, with no friendly sun for light-years.

Over to one side, as large as the full Moon seen from faraway Earth, shone the glittering lights of the alien vessel.

Their own ship was a dark blur. He tongued his video amplifiers, repressed a gasp. The aliens thronged the hull of *Dolittle,* too many to count.

"Are you getting this?" he breathed.

"Yes," buzzed Carol's short reply.

The aliens stood perhaps a meter and a half in height. They looked like cat-o'-nine-tails bullwhips, overly thick handle down and whips flailing about like snakes. Each whip end unraveled in a fractal series of smaller tendrils, final fingerlets clearly adept at manipulation. The aliens wore ornate harnesses, studded with bulging pockets and metallic-looking triangular shapes. On a hunch, he tongued his helmet visuals to infrared IR and saw that the metal triangles were nearly seventy degrees warmer than the whip-aliens themselves.

Heat exchangers, like the spidery constructions on the moon-ship. This was confirmed when one of the aliens landed on the hull of *Dolittle* twenty meters from Bruno, arms down, and the triangular shapes on its harness blazed under IR to shed the heat.

Under infrared, the aliens were much more than black ropy shapes. Delicate traceries of relative warmth pulsed beneath their cold skin, like some sort of circulatory system. Portions of their alien anatomies were clearly intended to remain much colder than others.

Bruno watched one of the aliens remove a complicated shape from a pocket and touch it to an open section of *Dolittle*'s hull. The shape smoothly changed shape and extended a questing projection, like a living thing. It thrust into what Bruno realized was part of *Dolittle*'s main sensory net. That alien's heat exchangers glowed. Other aliens continued to enlarge the open section under study, methodically taking the hull apart with strange tools. Other aliens ran snaky arms and odd objects over the disassembled parts.

"Carol," he whispered. "You still with me?"

"Right."

"Looks like they are studying our electronics. That must be what is shutting things down."

"You think they mean to shut us down?" came Carol's voice, peppered with static, but still soft in his ears.

"Doubtful. If they wanted to kill us, they would have quite a while ago. I just think they're curious."

"So why aren't they paying attention to you?"

Bruno didn't say anything in reply. Several more of the aliens came over the curving hull of *Dolittle*, moving quickly in a series of somersaults. They crowded around the alien who had tapped into the shipboard sensory net.

Fascinated despite himself, Bruno watched IR patterns shift and change across their alien skin. Waving tendrils danced fluidly. Bursts of static hissed and crackled in his ears. Communications?

"Bruno!" Carol's voice was suddenly grim.

"I'm here," he said, trying to sound calm.

"Life support just failed. I'm getting into my suit now."

Bruno swore, his voice loud in his own helmet. He had

to try and stop the aliens before they—even by mistake—managed to kill both of them.

He unslung the electron-beam rifle from his shoulder, lifted it carefully, and checked its charge. The telltales glowed green: a full charge. Bruno flicked the safety off.

"I don't know if you can hear me, and if you can, you probably don't understand me," he told the cluster of many-armed shapes who were busily peeling still more of *Dolittle*'s hull away. "But you have to stop what you are doing."

Bruno aimed just above the nearest alien shape. There was a crack of static in his headset as he stroked the trigger, and sent an invisible bolt of high-energy electrons over the tops of its waving tentacles.

The reaction was immediate.

Alien shapes turned, tentacles weaving madly, and quickly began advancing on him.

Bruno started backing toward the airlock.

"Tacky?" Carol was back on line, hissing with interference. "I'm getting a lot of static, and have lost video. You reading me?"

"I have a problem, Carol. I shot over their . . . well, what I think are their heads, and they seem annoyed with me now."

"Get back inside."

"Aye-aye, Captain, my very thought." Bruno turned and swore again. Three of the weaving shapes crouched in front of the airlock. "I'm surrounded."

"Shoot one."

"I don't suppose surrender is an option."

"It looks like they dismantle first, and ask questions later."

Bruno took a deep breath, and aimed at one of the arms of an alien creature standing between him and the airlock. He didn't give himself time to think, and simply fired the electron-beam rifle.

Instantly, the entire alien blazed in infrared. It leaped up and away from *Dolittle*, vanishing into the starscape, apparently unhurt.

"Bruno," Carol's voice hissed urgently. "You all right?"

He started to reply, then noticed one of the aliens to his right aiming a black pointed object at him. A pale purplish bolt of light filled his vision, engulfing him.

His suit went instantly dead, and his head seemed to explode. As the worst of the pain flash faded he realized that the electromagnetic soles of his boots had lost their grip on the hull of *Dolittle*. Miraculously his arm brushed against a handhold and he clutched convulsively. The airlock was just a few meters—

Bruno was damned if he would let Carol die alone.

Suddenly something held one his legs stationary. Then the other. Bruno pulled harder with his arms. When he lifted one hand to switch his grip to a new handhold, something very strong looped around his wrist and held it fast. He wished that he could see, but the starlight was too dim without electronic enhancement.

How long had it been since his suit had failed? It was getting stuffy. Bruno felt something thin but very strong pry his fingers loose from his last handhold one by one, methodical and patient. He felt himself being lifted free from *Dolittle*, suspended and held by dozens of whiplike alien arms.

He wished that he could have said good-bye to Carol.

Bruno waited for the aliens to pull his suit neatly apart as they had started to do to *Dolittle*. He started yawning uncontrollably in the darkness. CO_2 overload . . .

Just as he passed out, he felt tiny fingers of singing fire burn their way through the interface socket in his neck into his dying brain.

No strength, not even to scream his despair.

PART II
COLD LOGIC

• CHAPTER ONE

There is a deeper Reality beneath the comfortably obvious.

Space is neither empty nor limitless. The cosmos only seems to stretch forever, from the blackened husks of long-dead stars to the incandescent fury of quasars blazing within far distant galactic clusters. Even the yawning emptiness between such objects is not truly vacant, but hums and keens with the ancient melodies of ionized gas and magnetic fields. The bare vacuum itself roils with fertile acts of creation and destruction, of particles and antiparticles born from nothing and returning to oblivion, all within the thinnest shaved shards of time itself.

Yet it was not always so.

There was a time, incomprehensible to minds constrained by time's invariant arrow and a mere three dimensions, when nothingness reigned supreme. Not emptiness.

Nothingness.

Before there was a reality, how could there be existence? Yet time does have a starting point, a beginning. Cosmic symmetry argues an Alpha Time must balance an Ultimate Omega Point. Whether by accident, natural law, or purposeful Design, *something* appeared where once there was nothing.

Of that mystery, nothing is truly known. Whatever the First Cause, timeless vacancy blossomed into an all-consuming inferno of creation, a totality of what would someday be called matter and energy: a universe.

The first ticks of that time were a blaze of unthinkable energies and infinitesimal motes of mass. Even light was too weak to exist unsundered and free within such an inferno. It was a time of new-birthed reality's seeming raw and unfettered rage against nothingness, an enormous beacon attempting to fill an infinite darkness.

But then as now, all things that burn must eventually cool. Entropy remains the final judge and arbiter of this reality. The bright and implacable All immediately began to expand and cool, as it would forever after that first tortured moment.

Photons at last slipped free of creation's incandescent forge, and fled tirelessly across the face of that new reality. A subatomic menagerie met and merged into new and exotic arrangements. Matter was born, and vied with energies both subtle and gross for supremacy; each won in different regions of the expanding space-time continuum.

The new-birthed universe continued to grow, still many times hotter than the core of a sun, but ever cooling. It stretched like the surface of some cosmic balloon under hurricane-driven inflation. Yet the fabric of space-time is not infinitely resilient, nor was the expansion uniform. Under unthinkable stresses, reality itself strained and groaned with the aftermath of creation's bright birth. Ripples and cracks formed in the very substance of space-time.

As fissures form in water rapidly freezing from the liquid state to ice, so was it with the very nature of reality.

These fissures, spiderweb cracks appearing in the expanding cosmic egg as it hatched, were tiny but powerful. Each crack was far thinner than an atom's thickness, yet stretched for many light-years.

The primordial cracks and fissures thrummed and writhed with raw energies and potential. Their tortured movements struck nearby concentrations of hot matter like a fist. Electromagnetic fields crackled and roared along their lengths, inducing strange and intricate patterns in local clouds of glowing gas.

Some of these cracks in creation joined, building gigantic networks of frantic topology. Still others split into smaller fissures, radiating powerful gravitational waves that spread across the new-formed universe like ripples in a pond.

The expanding universe was distorted unevenly by these

tangled knots of space-time, a cosmic fork stirring the stuff of stars. Some large networks acted as gravitational foci; seeds for the aggregation of coalescing matter into what would eventually become great seas of stars. These vast stellar whirlpools would someday be called galaxies.

But that lay many eons in the future.

Most of the fissures and cracks in space-time vanished, their substance and power leached away into loud peals of gravitation tolling across the universe. The furious expansion of reality slowed, and the new universe's grand structure unfolded.

Yet some tangles in space-time remained, diminished in glory and potency. Minds which eventually came into being within our universe gave these remnant structures of anguished topology a host of names, in as many languages. Humans would someday call them cosmic strings.

But they are not strings.

They are windows.

The knots and tangles of space-time were tiny connections between the new universe and an entirely different space-time continuum. Minds roamed in that other reality, on businesses unknowable. Such minds were not constructed of the building blocks basic to this particular space-time. The equivalents of their flesh and blood were not composed of quarks and quanta, electrons and protons and neutrons. They were not subject to the forces and natural laws which bind our reality, linking past and present and future. Flavor and charm were not distinguishing characteristics of even their smallest components.

Though strangeness of a comparative sort was implicit in their nature.

However alien, the entities on the other side of the cosmic strings had minds and possessed something much like curiosity. Eventually, they discovered the distorted windows into our reality which are the tattered remnants of creation's first moments of birth. The entities learned that such twists in the fabric of space-time could transmit information.

The minds, completely foreign to any entity living within

this space-time continuum, peered dimly through these humming cracks into our own reality. Their curiosity was piqued by this strange place so unlike their own home. That interest kindled and grew as they caught glimpses of a different universe, new modes of existence. Eventually, they wished to explore this alien place, so close and yet so distant.

They could not enter this space-time continuum, any more than a human being could enter and live within a printed page. But they possessed a drive to explore—even by proxy.

The entities investigated this space-time continuum in the only manner they could. Tentatively, they reached out to the cracked windows at the border of their own reality.

And beyond, into our own.

Call the minds that moved in that other universe They Who Pass.

• CHAPTER TWO

They were approaching the Outsider ship, and he was so very afraid.

The frightened puppeteer's name was a beautiful symphony of music that flowed from the mouths at the ends of his twin necks. It literally meant "He Who Gentles Difficult Truths into the Hindmost's Wise Ears," but could be shortened to "Diplomat." His lips, knobbed with the delicate projections his race used as fingers, quivered with jangled nerves.

He ignored the pilot of the *Wisdom of Retreat*'s sardonic question for a moment, making a concerted effort to control his breathing. He tried to calm himself by breathing alternatively through his necks. The puppeteer's three hearts pounded in terrified syncopation.

There was drugcud in his personal medical pouch, but he knew better. The *Wisdom of Retreat*'s pilot would not approve.

Diplomat had seen the reports about the vessel they approached during his too-short emergency briefing at the Hindmost's Fortress. The numbers and the reality they represented still burned in his mind like wildfire sweeping across a dry plain.

He fluted agreement to the pilot, steeling himself at last for what he would see with both of his eyes. The pilot snorted amusement and turned back to the command console.

With a single low note of command, the pilot cleared the hullscreen in front of the puppeteer, revealing the strange Outsider vessel. It was worse than Diplomat had expected; a terrifying space-going nest of unknown threats. He fought a yawning sense of unreality and fear. The reports and holograms had not done the frightening artifact justice.

It was almost too much for Diplomat's brain to encompass. Noticing the metric markers the shipboard computer projected next to the image of the other ship, he was again unnerved at the scale of the looming object. It grew visibly on the hullscreens at extreme magnification.

The *Wisdom of Retreat*'s gravity planers performed an unexpected looping course correction, and the startled Diplomat shrieked a siren alarm call. He folded himself instinctively into a protective ball within his forceweb and quivered. Diplomat's mind fled the Outsider threat into comforting darkness.

The peace was interrupted by a lancing pain at the base of his necks. The force of the blow made him see sparks fleeing in all directions.

Not again, Diplomat thought, squeezing his eyes shut and pulling his neck and legs tighter against his midsection. The pain shot through him again, still more intense. Diplomat clenched blunt vegetarian teeth, knowing the blows would not stop until he emerged.

A voice filled with harsh martial music blared a curse in the small lifebubble. Diplomat could feel the electric tingle of the pilot's forceweb being released. There was a clump and snap as the pilot's articulated boots left the control consoles. He could sense the pilot standing over him.

The comforting smell of the Herd emanating from the ventilators was replaced by a stench of dominance and barely harnessed rage. Diplomat gulped and tried to breathe through his mouths to avoid it.

It was the smell of the *Wisdom of Retreat*'s pilot, only stronger and more angry. Diplomat had kept his distance during the voyage, even within the tiny lifebubble of the *Wisdom of Retreat*. There were limits to the ability of the airscrubbers to remove the pilot's distinctive odor, redolent with attack pheromones.

Besides, the pilot liked "the smell of battle," as she called it.

The frightened puppeteer wished fervently he was back in the hospital burrow, his tired brain soothed by the psychists' overlay induction devices. Had Diplomat not just returned from his final embassy to the Q'rynmoi? Had not the psychists bluntly stated that he was not ready for another mission? He tightened his necks around his midsection.

Diplomat could hear the angry duet of the pilot's whistling breath above him. She sang an offkey command, and his forceweb vanished instantly. Diplomat was left with an itchy feeling of residual static charge and insecurity.

"Stand up and control yourself, you miserable *coward.*" The pilot's tones were rich with a symphony of contempt. It made a word honored among the puppeteer race sound like an insult.

"Chew your courage drugs if need be," her voice continued in disdainful tones. "You are to carry out a task for the Hindmost and the entire puppeteer race. This is more important than your shameful and obvious lack of a notochord."

The pilot's words stung Diplomat more than the pain at the base of his necks. He prided himself on his rare ability to work with dozens of alien species; why could he not deal as well with a member of his own race?

At least Diplomat *thought* the pilot was a member of his race.

The frightened puppeteer breathed deeply; it was no use postponing the inevitable. He unwrapped his necks. Opened his eyes one at a time. Moving gingerly, he stood in the small lifebubble. The scent of the pilot prickled angrily over Diplomat, like a swarm of stinging insects.

"No," he said carefully in measured tones, shoving his fears away as best he could. "I will not be needing the drugs at this time." Diplomat was unsure of the truth of that statement. He looked at neither the hullscreen nor the pilot.

There was a splat of dismissive music.

"Then look at me, *Diplomat.*" A chord of hard-edged humor entered the pilot's voice, irony dripping from the title. "If you cannot look at *me*, how will you complete the

Hindmost's Commands, let alone look the helium-beasts in the face?"

There was a meditative pause.

"That is," she continued, "if they can be said to actually *have* faces." The pilot hummed and whistled another musical note to her command console. "The hull is opaqued. Control your fear."

Diplomat finally raised his heads, blinking, and looked up at the pilot of the *Wisdom of Retreat*.

And up.

The Hindmost's Guardian stood well over two meters in height. Impact armor covered the giant puppeteer's midsection completely. Each of her necks bore gleaming mirrorplate able to turn a beam of coherent light. Traditional battle helmets with razor-tipped talons rested on each head, and the pilot's eyes burned with emotions alien to Diplomat. Her legs were as armored as her necks, and holsters hung in instant reach of either mouth. Because Guardians were also deft with their three hooves, each was encased in space-ready magnetic boots, equipped with manipulators, cutting tools, lasers, projectile weapons, and Great Burrower knew what other horrors.

The Guardians were one of the most closely kept secrets of the puppeteer race. This warrior caste was small in number, bred and trained from birth for the necessary occasional insanity of aggression and combat. The Hindmost spoke for all puppeteers, and the Hindmost's Guardians carried out the Will of the Those Who Lead from Behind. They enforced treaties among puppeteer groups, advised the Deepest Council, designed and built safety devices and weaponry, and—from time to time—were called upon to defend puppeteer interests more directly.

Such as the present situation, reflected Diplomat, a tingle of repressed fear scurrying down both necks.

This Hindmost's Guardian held one head high and cocked to the side, the other low near her left leg holster. It was standard caution in what a Guardian would consider potentially dangerous situations; in other words, all of the time. The Hindmost's Guardians *always* expected danger, altercation, and even the obscenity of fighting. Relished it, it was said.

That alone made the pilot more alien to Diplomat than the barbaric Q'rynmoi and their breeding colonies.

"Better," hurrumphed the pilot. "Perhaps you will have your uses after all."

"How long until we rendezvous with the Outsider ship?" Diplomat asked, gesturing with one head toward the opaqued hullscreens.

"Too soon for you," she replied, her song flippant and breezy. The Guardian's two heads suddenly reared up and looked at one another in a flash of rare humor, then returned to normal posture.

Diplomat paused and straightened. It was time to firmly grasp the issue with both mouths. "Please show me the Outsider craft again, Guardian." The giants may have had individual names within their own caste, but in puppeteer society, the Hindmost's Guardians were simply addressed as Guardian.

The only other choice of name a Guardian accepted was the grotesque puppeteer obscenity of "Warrior."

Diplomat was too well bred to use such a word.

"A little talker like yourself," the Guardian crooned, "can suddenly regain courage? And without drugs! I am somewhat impressed."

Before Diplomat could reply, the pilot had moved back to her control console and sang the hullscreen to clarity once more. He settled in his own crashweb and, swallowing past dry throats, looked outward.

The Outsider craft looked more like a biological construct than spacecraft. Diplomat forced himself to crane his necks one at a time, trying to gain a sense of perspective. The space vessel was the size of a small moon, but not solid. Complex tangles of oddly colored metal gleamed in the starlight. The bent and twisted topology of the thing made Diplomat's eyes ache to the roots of his necks. Platforms and oddly formed objects extruded from the tangles here and there. Points of brilliant light drifted around the ship, as if in long, slow orbits. Tiny motes glittered and darted above, below, and within the Outsider vessel.

A *nest of threatening vermin, indeed*, thought Diplomat, hooves tapping. He stuffed his autonomic flight psychotropism into the shadows of his deeper mind.

"What is your assessment, passenger?" the pilot rumbled with a grating melody. "Excuse me, I meant to sing *Diplomat*."

He ignored the pilot's insult. "I have never seen such an Outsider craft before," Diplomat replied, the fear looming once more. One of his heads dipped toward his medical pouch.

"Nor have any of the Deep Council. We have our theories, even as you quake to your hooves over things which are new."

Diplomat flutter-blinked in veiled irritation.

"It appears that this Outsider craft uses hyperdrive," he mused aloud to his pilot. The coldlife traders generally did not travel faster than light, preferring relativistic travel. The appearance of the Outsider vessel from hyperspace had set off alarms throughout the Homeworlds.

The Guardian puppeteer clacked her left set of molars in agreement. "It is exceedingly rare. The clan of helium-beasts with which our Race does business is known to use the hyperdrive in emergencies."

The phrase made his neck pelts stand up. "What could constitute an emergency to such beings?" The Outsiders had little to do with the concerns of carbon-based, sunward forms of life. What could be an emergency to an Outsider? The thought chilled him.

"Perhaps their liquid helium is too warm," whistled the pilot sourly.

Diplomat understood the basic aggressive paranoia of the Guardian caste—much of it made sense in a hostile universe—but the Outsiders were long-term partners of the puppeteer race.

"Are the Outsiders not our allies?" he asked as diplomatically as his title. "Have they not given our Race help in the past?"

"Again you grasp truth with one mouth only," the pilot hummed. "We owe the helium-beasts much, but that dependency in turn leads to a threat to our Race."

How like a Guardian, Diplomat thought, to view the gifts of the Outsiders as threats. The coldlife sentients had provided the puppeteers with many technological marvels, including the Mover of Worlds that had saved the puppeteer race so long ago. All the Outsiders had asked in return was that Diplomat's race observe and study other life-forms and occasionally report that information back.

Selling the many technological miracles of the Outsiders to other warmlife races had enriched the puppeteers for thousands of years.

A seemingly harmless arrangement, until the terse summons had been received in the Homeworlds. And this frightening moon-sized ship appeared just outside the puppeteer system's gravity well. Waiting for an urgently demanded emissary.

What was happening?

Diplomat touched forked tongue to lip-fingers in thought. "You grazed with the Study Herd on this issue, I presume."

The Guardian blinked assent.

"I need all of your briefing materials, Guardian," Diplomat managed to muster.

The other puppeteer's heads came up in humor. "Hardly," she grated. "I must feed you the information slowly, as tender leaves are fed to younglings before their grinding molars emerge. You would surely break under the strain of our mission, were it given you all at once."

Diplomat squared his heads in a posture of pride, suppressing his fears, which lay ever ready to break out. Still, he was important to this mission, and the *Wisdom of Retreat's* pilot needed to be reminded of the fact. He forced himself to meet the Guardian's eyes directly.

Not in submission.

The soldier puppeteer's free head meaningfully dipped down and touched the medal on the front of her impact armor. It was a holographic representation of the image of a retreating puppeteer: the Sigil of the Hindmost. She snorted in dismissal at Diplomat's earlier prideful tone. Even through his mouths, he could smell her annoyance-scent.

"I recognize your authority and honor," persisted Diplomat, inwardly bemused that he was not curled up tightly again into a ball for the other puppeteer to kick. "Yet *I* act for the Hindmost as well. We are a team, Guardian, a small Herd of our own. We are to work together, against a common enemy. Toward a common goal. That *too* is a Hindmost's Command."

A long pause.

Diplomat held his left breath as he tried not to listen to the other puppeteer's harsh breathing.

"Well spoken," Guardian replied at last, an undermelody of crude humor to her words. "You are aptly named, Little Talker." She reached into a pouch at her side and removed a shining multifaceted datacube.

Diplomat merely waited. He knew that he held status; had not the Hindmost Itself selected him for this mission? Diplomat shook his midsection slightly, causing the gems in his intricately groomed backcoat to jingle, a reminder of Diplomat's rank.

Another pause.

"Many pardons, O Wise One. I have your prerendezvous briefing datacube here, *Diplomat*." She waited, apparently to see if Diplomat would rise to the bait of her irony this time.

"How long until we dock with the Outsider vessel, Guardian?" Diplomat repeated, working very hard to seem unperturbed.

"You have just enough time to review the contents of the information crystal, O Wise One. And digest the language programs into your communication module." Again, the Guardian's heads flipped up for a moment and looked eye to eye. "Though I suspect you will not like what you see and learn."

She held out the datacube to Diplomat with her left mouth.

Just out of reach, of course, to make him bridge more than half the distance.

Diplomat idly noticed that the pilot's right mouth never strayed from her disruptor holster, even inside the supposed safety of the *Wisdom of Retreat*.

He nervously licked his finger-lips with a forked tongue and . . . made a long neck to the Guardian. More than halfway. He took the glittering geometrical solid which contained Diplomat's fate.

And perhaps the fate of much, much more.

• OUTSIDERS ONE

Confusion. This local-and-other node cannot identify the hotlife irritants in this wracked geometric volume. Searching modalities are nil on all vibrational harmonics.

Attentiveness. This local-node sieves the plasma turbulence with great care. There is no trace but debris of the hotlife usurpers. The two battling motes are not present.

Thought. One. Perhaps, then, the hotlife vermin have all been destroyed? There has been no opportunity to interrogate the plans of the vermin for analysis and decision. The Nexus *must* be preserved from threat.

Suspicion. **This local-and-other node are One. This local-node detects a disturbance in the <#@@#@>. It is more than the resonance from the unleashing of destructive forces. Something beyond the abilities of the hotlife vermin has been present. Prepare to receive relevant data-packets.**

Anger. Received. Analysis complete. The heretic Feral Ones have indeed moved through this space-time locus, and fled! Perhaps the Feral Ones have taken the hotlife specimens—for purposes surely in opposition to the intentions of the Holy Radiants.

Confusion. **One. What action shall this local-and-other-node take? The Treaty limits action near this geometry.**

Determination. The Treaty has vertices and contour which are definite. The Nexus assembles, from local-and-other nodes, into Node. Node will determine the vector of the Feral Ones in the other <#@@#@> space and pursue.

Caution. **What of the Treaty?**

Righteousness. Treaties serve a Higher Purpose. Do the Holy Radiants approve? Their silence is license enough for action.

Shock. That direction of thought leads the other-node to the way of the Feral Ones.

Amusement. The other-node japes. Following the directives of the Holy Radiants does *not* lead to heretical modes of action.

Concern. Can the other-node be certain?

Impatience. Enough. All local-and-other nodes join to Node, and certitude will be One. Pursue the forces sundered by the Feral Ones, to their source.

• CHAPTER THREE

Guardian held out the glittering datacube to Diplomat. Part of her mission was to protect her frail passenger, true. Establishing rank, however, had little to do with protection. She made the little puppeteer stretch to take the information matrix. It forced him into an extended-neck posture of submission.

Such an act was tradition and test both, Guardian reminded herself. How would the little talker react?

Diplomat avoided Guardian's eyes in dutiful respect, taking the cube with his left mouth. No challenge there.

Still, Guardian noted, his posture was as brave as possible for a puppeteer of his bloodlines. She blinked twice in acknowledgment. Diplomat's act of polite esteem secretly pleased her, though she maintained her stern expression, still holding the other puppeteer in her gaze.

Diplomat was small and vulnerable and obviously very frightened—with good reason. She was delighted that he was trying to hide his emotions, to hold his necks a bit farther away from his body in a show of what was—to him—courage.

Despite all of Guardian's threats and insults to Diplomat, she enjoyed looking after the other puppeteer. A small puppeteer like Diplomat *required* Guardian's protection, and it warmed her to feel that needed duty. It would be a deep pleasure to die for her charge.

She would never admit as much to the little creature, of course. Guardian's facade forced other puppeteers to treat her opinions with respect and attention and more than a little fear. Her personal feelings did not enter into this or any other mission of behalf of the Hindmost.

237

To a Guardian of the puppeteer race, duty was All.

Such was the purpose for which Guardians had been born and bred over millennia. Duty to the Hindmost, always; such were the first words a foal of the Guardian caste heard in crèche. And it was the last thought to be prized, at the end of a long life of service.

Guardian glowered a bit more to reinforce the image she projected. Diplomat bowed to her with both necks and turned to his own control console. There was a slight crunching sound as he broke the Hindmost's Seal with his teeth.

Guardian was not looking forward to the next few minutes. It would have to be handled most carefully.

I am a Guardian, she thought, *not a melody-mumbling psychist*.

But a Hindmost's Command was exactly that: a command.

As she watched from the corner of her left eye, Diplomat inserted the datacube into his console reader. He whistled up the hyper-icons with a minimum of flourish, looking cool and efficient. Not a surprise, truly. Warrior knew that Diplomat was a Field Operative, not some Homeworlds fop—despite the ornate grooming on his back pelt.

Still, she was not fooled by appearances.

Guardian allowed herself a tongue-flick of a wry smile at his studied sham of confidence as Diplomat's console screens began to flicker with data. She returned to her own control console, activating the forceweb. The static charge crackled pleasantly against her battle armor, firmly holding the soldier puppeteer in place.

Unless Guardian handled Diplomat's study of the datacube's contents *just so*, the little puppeteer would drop into another bout of catatonia. Guardian was secretly indulgent of her charges on such missions, yes, but there was little time available for out-of-breeding-season pelt-currying.

"Well, Honored and Wise One," she asked with rough humor, "do you care to share your initial impressions?"

"I thank you," Diplomat fluted deferentially. The tone was smooth and controlled. "I shall need some time to review the encoded information to give a proper reply."

Guardian glanced at Diplomat. She could tell nothing of his mood or reaction from his tone or posture. Swallowing right-to-left-to-right in thought, she began to choose her words carefully.

Gently, the Guardian puppeteer told herself. *But quickly . . .*

Without music in her voice, she spoke in flat, unpuppeteer-like tones for emphasis. "I know something of the mission before us, Diplomat. I was very far in front of the Hindmost when the Outsider message was first received. Later I was in Herd with the Deepest Council, and helped prepare your briefing contained in the datacube. This is a task for Guardians only, not for puppeteers too enamored of their own burrows."

Perhaps Guardian's false air of superiority would prick the little puppeteer's own substantial pride. Such an approach often resulted in the insulted one forgetting fear—and getting on with the task at hand.

In any event, Guardian had issued an old, old insult, but one which carried little real sting. Puppeteers had not inhabited burrows and caverns since the dawn of recorded history. Guardian paused, waiting for Diplomat to respond to the crude song-phrase.

The little puppeteer said nothing, his posture giving away nothing.

Good, she mused. *This one is as skilled as the Deepest Council argued.*

"Still," Guardian continued, "I and my caste follow the Hindmost's Song Called Out from Far Behind. You are to act as the Hindmost's Representative to the helium beasts, and perhaps do more." Guardian's heads stared at one another for a split second in a dry chuckle of puppeteer humor. "I only hope that you acquit yourself with honor, for your mouths speak for all puppeteers this day."

Diplomat's right head lifted from one of his console screens, the stream of data freezing in place as he looked away.

"Guardians are not known for their elegant conversational ability," Diplomat sang with just the slightest edge of reproach. "You are attempting to placate and groom my thoughts. The currycomb of your words and manner is not necessary, truly."

Guardian cocked her right head, impressed. "Well spoken, Little Talker. I do seek to maintain your calm."

"That is why I carry mood modifiers," the other puppeteer reminded her. "I am afraid, yes, but I acquitted myself well with the Q'rynmoi, did I not?"

"You acted like a Guardian that day, Little Talker." Warrior clicked her teeth together, squinting in respect.

Diplomat's heads faced one another, then blinked twice at her graciously. "I sense and accept the spirit of the compliment. Though few of my caste would see it as such with both eyes."

Warrior snorted.

"Prepare me, then, for this mission of ours," hummed Diplomat, all humor evaporated.

Guardian turned both her eyes to face Diplomat.

"There are new threats in space, near our own domain." Warrior's words again lacked music, jarring the Herd-conditioned air in the lifebubble with intensity. Her right head weaved slightly, and her left tongue touched knobbed lips for a moment.

Even Guardians can feel fear, she reminded herself. *It simply does not rule us, as it does the Little Ones.*

"The helium beasts," Guardian continued, "have brought us news from a sector outside the realm of our race. Evidence of two new species, aggressive and threatening to puppeteer business and well-being."

Diplomat rolled his left eye with the beginnings of impatience. "I do not understand the countermelody implicit in your song, Guardian. The Outsiders have done us a service with this doubtfully free information, I assume."

She said nothing.

"But the Outsiders are allies," Diplomat sang in a falling tone of disbelief. "Our arrangements have been profitable for centuries."

"True enough, Little Talker," she replied.

"What are you not singing to me, Guardian?"

Guardian pointed with a right forked tongue at Diplomat's console. "You will find the answers there."

"I repeat myself, with all due respect to your station and grooming: prepare me," chided the little puppeteer.

Guardian whistled like a teakettle, then stood stock-still. "The Hindmost," she clipped, "does not entirely trust these particular Outsiders. There is some new agenda present." Her left head dipped down to a leg holster containing what appeared to be a tightbeam disruptor, touched it for reassurance, and returned to station.

She watched Diplomat shudder and droop his necks, both eyes slightly closed. The first step toward withdrawal. At length, he mastered his fear, raising necks with still-twitching neck muscles. Guardian was impressed.

"You are to be the Hindmost's Voice," she reminded him.

Diplomat blinked agreement. "I understand my duties, Guardian."

"Perhaps medication would be useful," Guardian suggested.

The little puppeteer chirped agreement. He reached into his supplies and tongued a blunt triangular lozenge of drugcud into his left mouth.

Guardian understood Diplomat's confusion about the Outsiders. The coldlife sentients had helped lift the puppeteers from their pretechnological society over one hundred thousand years past; had sold the puppeteer race the gravity planer, the hyperdrive, and endless safety devices.

Even the Mover of Worlds.

Most importantly, the Outsiders had allowed the puppeteers to act as their agents among warmlife sentient races, for a very modest percentage. But the Outsiders always had their own agenda, and it was one that no noncryogenic creature could possibly appreciate.

It pleased her to see Diplomat square his heads. His posture was subtly more vibrant. Perhaps the drugs were helping after all.

"I shall review the datacube for more details, though I reserve the right to ask further questions," he declared. "May I ask how long until we rendezvous with the Outsider ship?"

"Less than an hour," Warrior replied. "Prepare for maneuvers. The helium beasts have set up a number of force curtains around their vessel. I do not know why."

Guardian chirped a command to her console, and activated Diplomat's forceweb.

She paused, then snaked her left head around to look at Diplomat. He met her gaze with a chemically enhanced calm. "You had better chew more drugs, Little Talker. You will need them." She turned back to her console, adjusting schematics. But she kept one head inclined slightly toward her passenger.

The datacube's contents scrolled across the twin screens in front of Diplomat, one for each head. Within a few minutes, he stopped the screens, opened his supply pack again, and swallowed another, larger drugcud. Diplomat whistled, and data resumed its inexorable flow across his screens.

Guardian had kept silent while Diplomat popped the second mood regulator oval. Now her heads whipped up and faced one another, eye to eye. She growled without her usual roughness.

"Yes," she crooned, "now you grasp the Hindmost's concern firmly with both mouths. Two warlike races with interstellar capability, and weapons of mass destruction." She paused for effect, waiting.

"They have intruded into contested Outsider geometry with reaction drives and nuclear explosives?" Diplomat asked, not believing.

"Just so. And not so very long after the Pact."

The little puppeteer drummed a hoof. "I am expected to communicate with these captives."

Guardian blinked agreement. "The datacube contains the two downloads to your translator module. You will be able to talk to them, Little Talker."

Diplomat continued to look at the information scurrying across his screen. He scrabbled in his pack, swallowed another regulator of drugcud. "One of them is a . . . carnivore." He had difficulty with the word, which was a puppeteer obscenity, unused in polite society.

"Indeed," she replied. "They are the larger of the two species, are they not? The ones that call themselves the *kzin*? But they are not the issue that most concerns the Hindmost, Little Talker, nor me. It is these . . . *humans*. Perhaps you recognize their morphological type."

Diplomat fluted confusion, then fell silent as more data flowed across his screens. He shuddered, and his own forked left tongue touched his lip-fingers repeatedly. He stopped dead, tonguing the left screen to freeze mode.

Ah, Guardian thought. *The hoof strikes home.*

Diplomat wailed a sudden musical siren of alarm.

Guardian's heads looked at one another again in the puppeteer expression of humor. "I was wondering," she softly sang to Diplomat, who was making sounds like a demented calliope, "when you would make the connection."

Diplomat swiftly wrapped his necks around his body, still keening in fear. The screens froze and then blanked for lack of an operator.

"These . . . *humans* are clearly Pak breeders, though they do appear different in many ways." Guardian reached over with a long neck into her own medical bag, and removed a hypospray of sedative.

Guardian considered the petite puppeteer quivering before her. His necks were tucked so tightly around his body that he looked like a foal's plaything.

She swallowed in sequence, considering. Despite appearances, this cowardly little Diplomat had saved an entire puppeteer colony world from destruction by the Q'rynmoi. Guardian knew of few of her caste Herdmates who were willing to face the personal dangers that Diplomat had. It was a difficult story to believe, however, seeing him in this state.

It was said by the Hindmost's psychists that Diplomat's corrective mindsculpting after that event had been incomplete; they had advised more memory flensing before releasing him to active status.

A Hindmost's Command remained exactly that, however. The Deepest Council had concurred.

She considered that perhaps there was more to this delicate little talker than met her own Guardian eyes. She couldn't put her lips quite on it, but there was something different. Something almost brave, despite his periodic catatonic states and whining manner. He would clearly need her help to complete this mission, as well as the reverse.

"You remember the Pak, my little Diplomat, don't you?" She spoke almost conversationally as she calmly injected the near catatonic puppeteer in the right neck. The hypospray made a hissing sound, loud in the tiny lifebubble. Guardian made adjustments to the ventilation system, flushing out Diplomat's fear pheromones with fresh, Herd-conditioned air. Diplomat stopped screaming, trembled for a moment, and then seemed to fall asleep. She tightened his forceweb harness remotely.

Guardian looked at her own heads again. "Yes. The Pak are not extinct, after all. Despite the efforts of three sentient races and ten thousand years of effort." She deopaqued a small portion of the hull directly in front of her console, made a few further course corrections.

Guardian settled back into her own forceweb harness and whistled a duet with herself softly. The tune soothed her, and reminded the soldier puppeteer of her first days in crèche.

It was a marching song, ancient beyond measure. The music was said to be common when Guardian's ancestors had led entire herds of Diplomat's forebears to new grazing grounds with the turn in seasons. The arpeggios sang volumes about order, confidence, and glowing success.

After a few moments, she reached over with a head, and fondly patted the back of the sleeping puppeteer next to her.

"Two warrior races," she sang quietly. Forked tongues flicked over both sets of lip-fingers. "Two threats to the security of the Race." Warrior paused, watching their blinking course plot intently on the hullscreen.

"Or perhaps three," she added, after reflection.

The Outsider ship grew still larger as the *Wisdom of Retreat* approached rendezvous.

• CHAPTER FOUR

In its youth, the universe was very different. They Who Passed observed the strange fresh wilderness through a window less than an atom wide.

Gravity had made its rule known over vast clouds of gas and dust. Many had coalesced, contracted, and at last collapsed. The gravity-squeezed gas became hotter and hotter, atoms thrusting together in the rough romance of nuclear reactions, releasing energy and transmuting elements. These glowing clouds became hot youthful stars of the first stellar generation, their fusion fires spendthrift with the bounty of gravity's first clasp.

Still, that initial blaze of starlight was but a dim reminder of the first moments of creation, when all of reality had been hotter by many orders of magnitude.

Clouds of glowing gas, hot young suns set within them like jewels in oil. Twists and spirals of electromagnetic fields. Ions and charged particles streaked along paths appointed by the fresh laws of this space-time continuum. The early days.

Such were the alien vistas observed by They Who Pass, peering through the distorted interdimensional windows of the cosmic strings.

The minds suspended in the other universe were fascinated, in their way, with this strange space-time continuum. They wished to study and examine these new laws roughly ruling the brawling new universe, as if in haste.

But how? They Who Pass were ironically named; they could not pass, through the tortured windows between realities, into such an exotic and alien place. Even if such an act were possible, the laws of existence in the other universe were sufficiently different to make their own survival improbable. But complex data had passed from within the alien universe into their own. Surely the reciprocal would be found to be the case as well.

They Who Pass knew that Mind was only a sufficiently complex pattern of information. Sentience would inevitably arise in such patterns, regardless of the embedding medium and environment.

Though they themselves could not physically traverse their atom-thin window between universes, the entities knew that there were ways in which patterns could be imposed from afar. Near one of the cosmic strings within the new universe, they observed a vast cloud of charged gases, with filigrees of glowing electromagnetic fields running throughout.

Perfect for their purposes.

By something very like induction, yet much more potent, They Who Pass reached through the distorted crack into this reality. Stark pattern imposed on the charged cloud. A structure wrestled into shape—striations of virulent light and murky dust, threads of magnetic fields and inductive heating. Imbalances of electromagnetic force flexed within the cloud, shoving clots of dust and gouts of prickly gas within the structure.

The glowing cloud reacted as They Who Pass challenged it from afar. Networks of dusky plasma sparkled, pinching into new shapes.

The cloud moved, learned, grew. Primitive reflexes drank in new patterns beamed through the twisting aperture of the cosmic string. The cloud stored information, manipulated data, and sent it back through the window between realities, to They Who Pass. The cloud finally copied itself into fresh gas clouds, imposed its own patterns in response to the new universe around it.

Such clouds acted like living things. Communication and complexity among the clouds increased exponentially as time unspooled. They Who Pass nudged and directed, moving the plasma clouds toward more capacity and capability.

Eventually, these minds built of hot plasma and cold dust awoke to sentience.

They Who Pass now had intelligent agents within the new universe, semiautonomous explorers ready to travel throughout the strange reality and report back what they found. The clouds developed a society, a culture, as they spread throughout the new universe, unraveling basic laws. They roved the spaces around dead suns, ventured near blazing new-birthed stars.

Always in the service of They Who Pass.

Call the intelligent clouds of dusty plasma the Radiants.

• CHAPTER FIVE

Carol's eyes opened, gummy and blurred. Above, blue sky. She didn't believe it.

Carol sat up, rubbed her eyes. The view did not change.

She and Bruno were lying on a flat open area, on some thick ground cover. Like grass, though greener than any Terran grass. An unnatural green. Purplish blue sky stretched above them, speckled with delicate gossamer clouds. Carol stared in amazement, wordless.

The air smelled fresh and antiseptic, with a clean tang of ozone. A breeze touched her arms like the delicate brush of soothing fingers. It was so quiet that Carol could hear her heart beat.

No signs of the weird aliens, kzinti, or even of the fact that they had been locked in battle just a few moments before.

All Carol could remember was losing the suit commlink with Bruno in a snarl of static. Then nothing until she woke up here. Carol turned her head, stretching.

Somehow, behind them, the main airlock to *Dolittle* hung in midair. The rest of the ship was not there, however. One more impossibility. They seemed to be alone.

Carol rose easily to her feet. Too easily, she realized. She felt better than she had in many months, in years. She walked over to Bruno, and checked over his vital signs. He appeared to be sleeping deeply. She shook him gently awake.

"What?" Bruno began, shaking his head, then stopped in surprise as his eyes opened. He looked around, confused. Then he recognized Carol and wrapped his arms tightly around her.

"I thought I was *dead*," he whispered.

"So did I."

His confused frown deepened as Carol helped him to his feet.

"Don't ask me," she told him as he looked around. "Unless you believe in heaven?"

Bruno stooped down and pulled up a small tuft of the dark green ground cover. He showed her the ten-lobed leaflets, and the crimson roots that moved gently while she watched.

"I doubt," Bruno said softly, "that heaven is sowed with extraterrestrial species of plant life."

"How nice that you are so sure."

Carol followed Bruno as he walked toward the magically suspended main airlock of *Dolittle*. He patted the empty air above and to either side of the metal door, and snorted in satisfaction.

"Try it," he invited.

Carol found that the airlock door seemed to be set in an invisible wall. The wall didn't feel hot or cold, like metal or plastic or stone. It was a hard, sharply defined barrier that they merely could not see. Except for the fact that heat conduction seemed perfect, it might have been optical diamond. The grassy plains beyond the wall were doubtless illusory, intended to give the impression of greater open space within their . . . cage.

Working together, she and Bruno quickly determined that their . . . yard was in fact about two hundred meters across, bounded by curving walls of invisible material. *Dolittle* clearly abutted it, with only the main airlock permitted to penetrate the force-wall.

The airlock opened normally, and they found *Dolittle* complete inside. Intact, though none of the sensory net or computer systems responded to commands. There were plenty of supplies still. They both noticed and commented on the one thing out of place: *Dolittle* was spotless, not as they had left it.

Carol stepped outside the spacecraft, back onto the too-green lawn. Soon Bruno joined her. They watched the ersatz clouds for a time, enjoying the quiet despite themselves.

It was good to breathe what smelled and felt like fresh air, especially after years of recycler stink.

"So," Bruno said finally, "I guess we just wait. Like before."

Carol was considering suggesting to Bruno an interesting way to just wait when she heard someone clearing his throat behind them. They both leaped to their feet and whirled around.

It was then that Carol rethought her joke about religion, and decided that she didn't have a sense of humor after all.

Before them stood Colonel Buford Early.

Carol froze. Early looked precisely as she remembered him from their last briefing. His teeth were gleaming white, clearly prosthetic in his seamed and ageless face; his uniform was spotless. There was even the familiar arrogant twinkle in the old, old eyes.

"Bruno, son," Early said in an upbeat tone that was bizarrely inappropriate to their present circumstances. "And the lovely Captain Faulk. The pleasure is mine, entirely."

She looked over at Bruno, who stood there, mouth open. Carol knew that Bruno saw Early as something of a father figure. She elbowed him hard to snap him out of it.

"Colonel Early," Carol said evenly, "could you please tell us how you came to be here?" She paused, then added more plaintively than she had intended, "And precisely where 'here' is?"

Early's expression did not change. His smile was fixed, mindlessly benevolent. His words came out strangely, in bursts. "It is important to relax, to take things one step at a time. To think. Proper channels of communication are necessary. So many errors are made through hasty conclusions. Too much information often leads to confusion, and ill action. Would you not agree, Bruno?" Each sentence fragment sounded subtly different in tone from the last.

"Carol?" Bruno whispered. Carol was glad to see that Bruno saw the simulacrum for what it was.

"Humor it," she murmured back.

Bruno straightened his shoulders. "Quite right, Colonel Early. But how goes the war against the kzin?"

Again, Early's face did not change. The relentlessly upbeat grin stayed in place.

"War is an evil. Yet sometimes an evil is necessary to preserve a greater good. Death is tragedy. Kzin are scream-and-leaping ratcats. Their strategies are improving."

Carol scowled. "That isn't even a good imitation Early," she whispered as the figure in front of them continued to mix and match platitudes.

"Loud and clear," Bruno replied. "Those are just comments and speeches of Early's, cobbled together in response to questions we are asking."

"Are you now calm?" the Early-thing asked them brightly. "Calmness is the first requirement for debriefing."

Carol casually pulled a stylus from her coverall pocket, and tossed it underhand at the replica of Buford Early.

The figure made no effort to catch it. The stylus passed through and landed on the grass behind.

A distortion band started at the bottom of the figure's boots, and shimmied up and through its body.

"A lack of trust is deplorable," the perfect replica of Early said with the same unchanging smile. "Misunderstandings abound. Trust is fundamental."

"A hologram. Good, too," Bruno said.

Carol nodded, then walked directly through the projected figure and picked up her stylus, replacing it in her coverall pocket. She walked back through the hologram to return to Bruno's side.

The replica of Buford Early vanished.

Carol looked up into the purple false sky, and spoke calmly. "Show yourself, or speak to us."

A voice spoke from all around them, still in Early's tones. **Sorrow mine.**

"Excuse me?" Carol asked, confused.

"I think that they're apologizing," Bruno whispered in her ear.

Bruno-entity correct. I/We intend null upset, null confusion. Attempt calm failure. Accept.

It was very strange to hear such odd words in Early's familiar voice.

"Why do you use Buford Early as a model?" Bruno asked the air around them.

Question One. Curiosity/Innovation valuable. Bruno-entity internal patterns acquired. Electrons flow interestingly. Patterns clearer than Carol-entity. Projection intended as communication-enabler.

"They accessed your interface and read your mind?" Carol asked Bruno, studying his pinched expression and thinned lips.

Discomfort sensed, source Bruno-entity. Sorrow. Pattern acquisition necessary. Knowledge of Bruno-entity and Carol-entity required. Provisions for continuance. Accept.

"They needed to know how to keep us alive," Carol commented to Bruno. He still looked a little uncomfortable.

"Are you the . . . um, entities that analyzed our spacecraft?" Bruno asked.

Truth. One.

Carol smiled a little. "What should we call you? Does your race have a name?"

Humor. I/We not as you/they. No one entity-title. Many in one node-location. One node-location in many. I/We outside knowledge Bruno/Carol/other-entity. Patterns different. Outside knowledge.

"What if we call you 'Outsiders'?" Carol raised an eyebrow at Bruno, who nodded.

Accept. One.

"Why did you capture us?" she asked, hoping that the Outsiders could understand speech better than they could produce it.

Entity-not-Bruno-not-Carol. Interrogatory. Concept difficulty. Queries. Aggression. Disruption. Inefficient. Patterns unclear. Issues complex.

There was a long pause.

Protection.

Bruno looked over at Carol. "Do they want to protect us, or us to protect them?"

"We'll sort it out later—though I would hate to meet whatever *they* need protection from."

Carol took a deep breath, then continued. "Outsiders, there are many things we do not understand. Will you help us to learn more?"

Laudable but possible not. Warm/Cold mix not all. Warm/Warm mix not often; Bruno-and-Carol entities with other-entity. Some Warm/Warm mix. Help yes/ no. Understand not. Observe. Learn.

"Observe what?" she muttered, frustrated.

"Carol, look!"

To their right in the grassy false distance hung a circular window into another such "park." Through it they saw the blunt ovoid shape of a kzin singleship, and a huge orange-furred lump lying near it. Wisps of white feathery material led from the dark lawn into a network surrounding the prone kzin.

Carol felt sure it was the ratcat that had been attacking *Dolittle*.

Nature altercation. Intentions. Interrogatory. Coding similar, not-mixing understand one-not. Entity aggression Hot/Cold/Warm. One-not. Interrogatory.

"I don't understand," Carol and Bruno chorused.

One. Time necessary. Solution short-duration.

She ignored the odd words and looked again at the stretched-out kzin. "Is it dead?" she asked.

Negative. Aggression high. One-not. Acquisition difficult. Damage severe. Repairs completed soon.

"Is there any way that we can help you?" Carol inquired of the open air.

Not I/We. One-not. Entities not-Bruno/Carol, not-other entity. One interrogatory. Arrive present. Speak wish interrogatory. Fortune better: Warm/ Warm focus increase Warm/Cold. Speak wish interrogatory.

Bruno whistled. Carol, clueless, urged him to speak his piece.

"I think I understand. The Outsiders have another type

of alien waiting to speak with us, another warm-temperature type, but not human and not kzin."

Truth. Bruno-entity. One.

Carol nodded. "Outsiders, we wish to talk to these other life-forms."

Accept. One. Observe. Interact.

Another bubble-window appeared in the force-walled enclosure, very close to where they stood.

"What the . . ." Bruno said softly.

Carol felt dizzy with the strangeness, shaking her head. Too much change in too little time, she thought wildly, and stood a little straighter.

Two aliens stood ten meters away. They both had three legs ending in tiny hooves. Each of them had two flat, single-eyed heads at the ends of long waving necks. They wore clothing and what looked like tools. The larger one appeared to wear armor studded with spikes and sharp edges, and one head hovered over what seemed to be a holster containing a pistol-like object. It never moved. The hair under the two necks of the smaller alien was elegantly coifed and glittered. Its heads waved gracefully, one held high and the other low.

A long silence.

"Take me to your leader," Bruno muttered. Carol wanted to kick him in the shin.

The smaller of the two beings cocked a head suddenly and looked from Carol to Bruno, bird-swift. "Mr. Takagama," it sang in a woman's contralto, low and sexy, as Carol's jaw dropped in surprise, "I hardly think that such inappropriate levity is called for under the present serious circumstances."

The smaller of the two creatures then turned its other head to Carol, who slowly closed her mouth.

"We intend no disrespect to you, Captain Faulk," crooned the alien from the second single-eyed loose-lipped head, in an identical voice. "In fact, we are quite aware of primate protocols. However, may we speak frankly with one another? There is not a great deal of time for sociobiological niceties."

• CHAPTER SIX

Carol Faulk waited for the centrifuge in her head to quit spinning. It did not, and the rotor seemed a bit unbalanced to boot.

There had been too many changes since they had first detected the kzin ships back in the *Sun-Tzu*. And all of them far too quickly.

The battle between the *Sun-Tzu* and the kzin spacecraft. Bruno nearly burning out his brain from the EMP. The dogfight between *Dolittle* and the ratcat singleship. Then the moon-ship of another alien race somehow dropping them from nearly 0.8 lights to nothing, and the whiplike aliens from that huge craft dismantling *Dolittle*. Not only did she and Bruno wake up in an alien zoo near a comatose kzin, but now *another* type of alien confronted them. *Too much.*

Intelligent creatures with two heads, one of which spoke Belter Standard! They looked like bizarre mutant deer costumes from a masquerade party, with one-eyed heads at the ends of what should be arms. Like dual handpuppets.

Puppeteers? Carol considered.

She shook her head again. The cobwebs were starting to clear, but slowly. She had to put her mind on a battle footing. Curiosity began to overtake shock in her mind. *Okay*, she thought. *So you are facing three sets of aliens now. What's the big deal?*

These newest aliens waited in what seemed somehow like politeness. The big one, loaded down with weaponry, said nothing and made no move.

Carol wanted to take control. Maybe there was a way out of this mess.

Yeah, right.

Bruno continued to chuckle softly at the implausible sight of the two creatures, with an almost hysterical undertone. Was it too much, too fast for him?

"Knock it off," she hissed at him.

"Why? They look like something out of three-D, put together by people suffering from . . . ah, chemical enhancement. Kidvid aliens."

"Yeah," Carol whispered, smiling despite herself. "A puppet show on braindust."

"It's a little tough to take them seriously. And that might not be smart."

Carol frowned and narrowed her eyes. Bruno was right; the aliens looked more laughable than imposing at first glance. The Outsiders appeared far more frightening. Because they were more alien looking? Or because they had defeated a kzin singleship and dismantled *Dolittle*?

Even with the snaky necks, the three-legged aliens looked silly.

But what about the big one's weapons? she reminded herself. Her singleship fighter-pilot reflexes were making the back of her neck crawl. That subconscious danger signal made her very suspicious. Carol had learned to trust her hunches while fighting kzinti in the borderland of Sol.

Things were seldom what they seemed in space.

Carol poked Bruno in the ribs with a forefinger for emphasis. "I think you're right. Don't underestimate them."

"I agree," he nodded.

"The big one in particular seems locked and loaded for a whole herd of angry bandersnatch. Look at the gear it's carrying, Tacky. Edged weapons *and* laser tech at the same time? Makes no sense."

Bruno's smile faded as he thought it over. "Thing about aliens is . . ." he began.

". . . they're *alien*," she finished with him in a tired chorus. "Many thanks to your old buddy Buford Early."

"The real one, that is," Bruno agreed.

Carol took a deep breath and faced the three-legged aliens visible through the bubble-window. "How do you know us?" she demanded.

The smaller of the two aliens' twin heads suddenly whipped up, facing one another eye to eye. Just as quickly, the alien's necks returned to their previous posture. Carol wondered what *that* meant.

"Captain Faulk," it fluted in mellow tones, "time is, as I stated earlier, of the essence. Still, it would perhaps be more conducive to swift results if we shared names. Labels are, after all, important to your species. Am I not correct?"

Carol felt an incongruous smile spread across her face. She just couldn't help it.

The alien's two heads cocked in different directions, the single eyes in each head blinking with almost human-looking lashes. "Captain Faulk?" it sang. "Is this communications module translating my words properly? You are not responding."

"Oh, we understand you," Bruno broke in, sounding both tired and amused. "We just have a little trouble believing in you."

The alien looked at Bruno for a few seconds, then turned back to Carol. "We, too, have difficulties when meeting new species. May I continue?"

The odd alien waited until Carol finally shrugged agreement.

"Excellent," it warbled. "You may call me Diplomat, after my profession." One head gestured cautiously at its companion. "This one you may address as Guardian, or . . ." Here the alien paused, an odd and somehow hesitant note in its voice. ". . . Warrior."

Carol pulled on her lower lip. "Are we out of the waveform guide and into the emitter array, then?"

After a pause, the smaller alien's twin necks snapped upward, the two flat heads facing each other, eye to eye. Again, the heads immediately returned to a normal posture.

Normal, Carol reflected, for a three-legged alien. And

where *was* the beast's brain? Not in those tiny flat heads. The midsection?

The creature spoke, the voice unmistakably that of a sultry-throated young human woman. "Ah, I at length apprehend your meaning from symbolic context. It is an attempt at something like discordant synthesis, or . . . humor."

Bruno chuckled out loud and leaned close to Carol's ear. "I see that your Belter lack of humor is appreciated even by alien species," he whispered, breath warm and comforting.

Carol ignored him, looking directly at the weaponry carried by the larger alien. She then raised an eyebrow at the smaller one.

It whistled a high melodic note. "To answer your unspoken supposition, Captain Faulk, you have nothing to fear from my quiet companion. Under normal circumstances, you would never have the opportunity to perceive that particular caste of my race."

Bruno crossed his arms and spoke up. "That is what you say, my friend."

Carol was slightly annoyed at Bruno's interruption, but he did have a point. Military discipline had its drawbacks.

"Quite so, Mr. Takagama," replied the little alien. "However, I should point out that had I or our hosts intended you harm, you would not have been repaired and awakened."

"Repaired?" Carol was confused.

"Of course. You both received a very high dosage of ionizing radiation and were severely damaged during your . . . ah . . . acquisition." The small alien hummed for a moment. "Of course, you were not so severely damaged as your more aggressive and combative opponent in the next environment locus."

It gestured with a loose-lipped head toward the clear aperture Carol had seen earlier. That bubble-window still displayed the fallen kzin next to his singleship. The whitish tendrils wrapping the orange-furred figure were moving slowly.

Bruno nudged Carol. "That ratcat must have received

Principle knows how high a dose when the *Sun-Tzu* exploded. How could they repair such damage so quickly?"

Before Carol could reply, the larger of the two aliens trumpeted loudly. The other alien fluted and sang back.

"My esteemed colleague is quite correct," the smaller alien crooned, honey voiced. "The briefing with our hosts was quite explicit that haste was crucial. There is not time to deal with these niceties, as I mentioned earlier. We must take action, with your help."

"I don't understand," Carol frowned.

"Nor should you at this point. Suffice it to say that because of your . . . altercation . . . with these . . . kzin creatures . . . you have succeeded in rousing forces you would not have wished to disturb, had you but known. That difficulty must be addressed immediately."

The larger of the three-legged aliens trumpeted again, a martial brass band.

"Again, my colleague is quite right," sang the alien called Diplomat in clear bell-like tones. "If we live long enough to address the problem properly."

Frustration grew in Carol. She knew that they were in trouble, but it irked her not to know that trouble's extent. "At least tell us what will be done with us, why we have been captured."

The little alien cocked both heads at Carol in different directions. "You have not been captured, Captain Faulk."

"What would you call it, then?" drawled Bruno. "It seems to me that the universe has been pushing us around a lot."

"Mr. Takagama, are you feeling well? Paranoia is not a common condition for your naive species, according to my briefings. As for the term 'capture,' I would think the word 'rescue' more appropriate, were I you."

"Rescued from what?" asked Carol, feeling a cold chill run across her shaven skull and down her back. Now they were getting to it.

"From the Zealots," replied the small alien. "A delicate balance of power has been upset by your unwitting actions."

Carol did not like the sound of this. "Zealots?"

The alien called Diplomat sang quickly. "There exist different factions of our low-temperature hosts. Some are traders in information and goods to life-forms like ourselves. Other factions have . . . ah . . . more obscure concerns."

"Obscure?" Bruno prodded at the alien, seeming just as out of place as Carol felt. "You mean hostile?"

A slow roll of one of the heads, flashing eyes. "The Zealots are a Traditionalist group with very different attitudes than our hosts. They will arrive soon, and will attempt to destroy us all. Thus, we must most assuredly not be present at that time."

Again, the enclosure with its false sky and too-green grass seemed to whirl around Carol. The alien ground pushed firmly up against her feet, but she felt as if she were in free fall.

"Bruno?" she murmured. She glanced over and saw that his eyes were narrowed, face pinched.

"Yes, Captain-my-captain?"

Carol sighed. "We appear to have fallen right into someone else's war."

A snort. She felt Bruno squeeze her arm. "You sure know how to show a fella a good time."

Carol turned back to the aliens. "What happens now?" She needed more information, fast, but the issue of their fate needed to be settled first.

Again, the creature cocked both heads in different directions. An expression of confusion? "What every intelligent being would do under these circumstances."

Carol licked her lips. "And that would be? . . ."

"We run," chorused both the little alien and Bruno.

• CHAPTER SEVEN

The Radiants moved throughout the young universe, and plumbed the diverse strangenesses within it. The beings burned as bright as their cores with curiosity, all on behalf of They Who Pass.

There was much to learn, and vast room for such a broad education. The sentient clouds of plasma swam within vast seas of glowing gas and lanes of sparkling dust, ever seeking, and felt the electrical equivalent of awe.

All they learned, they reported to their creators on the other side of the cosmic string.

But some parts of that fresh reality were beyond the abilities of the Radiants to explore. The world of cold matter defeated the ever-curious plasma beings. The very touch of dark solids greedily drained away the heart-fire of the incandescent gas clouds. The Radiants were forced to ignore their innate programmed curiosity for a time, and avoid the enigmatic points of darkness that swung around stellar fires.

There was still much to learn, and an entire new universe as lecture hall.

To They Who Pass, this new universe made little sense. It seemed paradoxically composed of two extremes: the very hot and the very cold. The Radiants could easily explore the former conditions on behalf of their masters, but the bitter chill remained quite deadly. They Who Pass grew intrigued at these newest findings from the other universe, and sent fresh instructions through the cosmic string window to their Radiant servants. This still-stranger frontier of cold must be explored as well.

Under careful instruction, the Radiants recapitulated the original act of their own genesis. They used the interactive properties inherent to matter far colder than their own diffuse blaze. Instead of patterns implicit in the dance of atoms stripped bare of electron clouds, subtle and little-known forces pushing and pulling at atoms were investigated.

Tests began. Cool gas clouds were visited and influenced at a distance by the Radiants. The beings of plasma reached out with tools of collective force into the dusky strangeness. Linear chains of atoms met and branched, joined, and were torn asunder with careful prodding. Complexity grew, as did the knowledge of the Radiants.

They Who Passed marveled in their distant way at such knowledge, and urged their servants to continue the investigation. Regardless of the medium used, Mind was formed from Pattern. Perhaps even this killing blackness could give birth to Mind, and thus fresh servants, in yet another mode of existence.

Much was discovered about condensed matter. It was blunt, willful, incapable of vibrating with the singing energies that were the lifeblood of the Radiants. But diffuse clouds of dust were not enough. With great care, the Radiants learned to come near the cold deadly spheres of matter, and study their composition by deft inductance. Patterns were imposed by the Radiants into slow currents of superconductive liquids, found in pools on the cold lumps of matter. There, as in the plasma clouds of the Radiants' birth, impurities lent a nonhomogeneous nature to the medium: raw material for the primitive minds even then forming structures within the liquid.

As electromagnetic forces were not sufficient to touch and move cold matter, a skin of protective polymer was fashioned over the superconductive liquid. Flexible struts of crystalline material gave shape and strength under the brute, inexorable pull of gravity.

After a time, a bulbous entity heaved itself out of a pool of liquid helium. It slowly extruded a strand of matter from its center. The tentacle slid along the cold surface, and finally wrapped around a small rock.

Slowly, the dimly thinking coldlife automaton lifted the rock against the light gravity. It waved the prize toward the glittering plasmid cloud orbiting the cold planetoid. The tentacled construct felt something like a frigid triumph, and quested around for new objects to investigate.

Thus were the Dark Ones born.

For many revolutions of the galaxy, the Dark Ones carried out the bidding of the Radiants in the world of cold matter. The Radiants themselves continued their explorations at the other end of the spectrum, basking in heat and light unimaginable. Together, the two classes of Mind explored the new universe, finding things awesome and strange.

The Dark Ones moved from cold rock to still colder, tasting and examining. Learning. Yet it was not sufficient, as they could sense other worlds in space around them. They learned to build self-contained nests to carry expeditions across great distances in search of knowledge. Such was the curiosity of the Dark Ones that some nests could travel faster than a photon in vacuum.

The Radiants in turn fashioned large structures of gas, dust, and electromagnetic fields. The tenuous constructs were designed to listen to the faint songs of other galaxies, or the brittle noises from the surfaces of neutron stars. Mysteries worth investigating abounded at the fiery centers and great whorls of galaxies.

Much was learned about the new universe by the Dark Ones and the Radiants. That information was carried by the glowing plasma clouds to one of the still wriggling cracks in time and space. The messenger Radiant, bloated with information, would intercalate into the very field lines of the cosmic string, an intimate touch of blended attraction and repulsion. Stretched thin, the intelligent cloud would wrap tightly around the portal between universes, and send the collected information to They Who Pass, dwelling on the other side of the cosmic string. In return, new information and instruction would be transmitted from They Who Pass into the Radiant messenger. The messenger, in turn, would free itself from the cosmic string and spread the new tidings.

So the situation remained for many eons. Until the Conundrum.

They Who Pass ceased to speak to the Radiants through the tortured windows of their cosmic strings. The children they had sired in the new, strange universe were left to their own devices. To find their own destinies without the influence of their creators, fallen silent on the other side of an interdimensional crack between realities.

The strange children of They Who Pass had drive, but no longer purpose. Their drive *became* their purpose.

The Radiants soon became uninterested in the Dark Ones, focusing instead on issues far from the solid phase of matter. Some Radiants learned how to transform themselves into less delicate forms, able to withstand existence within the cores of suns. Vast communities of the plasma beings lived in the turbulent core of the galaxy, seeking the unknowable. Others remained wrapped and intertwined within the massive lines of force surrounding the now silent cosmic strings, plaintive, hoping for the return of They Who Pass.

After a time the Radiants seldom communicated with their cold servants, made of dull matter instead of lively plasma. The sentient clouds fell as silent as their creators on the other side of the cosmic string.

They had other concerns.

The Dark Ones, too, were forced to find their own destiny in the cosmos. Many of them simply traveled without end, continuing to observe and store data as they had before—even without a recipient to which they could deliver.

Others made a ritual and religion of following precisely the ways of the Old Time, when Radiant and Dark One and They Who Pass were in constant communication—perhaps the Great Silence was due to a lack of following instructions with strictest accuracy. A few Dark Ones developed their own interests among the other, native minds that eventually dwelled in the new universe. These less organized Dark Ones found that their ancient drive to collect information could be useful, and that it was possible to manipulate these new upstart sources of data to acquire still more.

The majority of the Dark Ones—regardless of social structure—would have nothing to do with other, lesser minds which developed in the new universe. They preferred to brood in a silence to match that of They Who Pass.

Those Dark Ones who did upon occasion interact with the new sentients came to be known by many names throughout the galaxies, a name pronounced by a dizzying variety of communication organs.

In one area of space-time, the various inhabitants called them the Outsiders.

• CHAPTER EIGHT

Rrowl-Captain's dreams were not pleasant.

They stalked him like a loud predator closing confidently on prey. Crippled bleeding prey, limping across a field without proper cover. Without allies or weapons.

There was no escape.

In his dream, he was still a crèche-kit, with no name other than Second Son of Graach-Gunner. He and his litter brother, First Son of Graach-Gunner, had been inseparable comrades in crèche. In their sleeping lair, after the illuminators were dimmed, they had often hissed and spat about what Hero-Names they would choose when they were both grandly honored for bravery.

As they surely would be so honored. Were they not brave kzinti, as they learned to stalk feral Jotoki in the hunting park?

It did not matter that the crèche teachers were guiding the development of their young muscles and growing hunt-skills with great care and attention to tradition. The pair were young, but would grow into an adulthood of honor, recipients of Hero's Blood for more octals of generations than could be counted.

They were kzin, feeders at the apex of the Great Web of Life. Was there any doubt that a Warrior Heart beat within each of their young chests?

First Son of Graach-Gunner wanted to someday take a Hero-Name from their family history, C'mef. Centuries before, another C'mef had died defending a foppish relative of the Riit against an usurping colonist kzin. Honor was more important than details to Graach-Gunner's family line; the Warrior Heart burned bright in all of them. C'mef would

266

be a proud name to weave back into the honored tapestry of their lineage.

Second Son of Graach-Gunner had admired the liver and Warrior Heart of his litter-brother very much, and wished to honor him in turn. He had always followed his elder brother, claw to claw and fang next to fang against their crèche-foes. Second Son of Graach-Gunner had secretly chosen the name of C'mef's own litter-brother and duel-ally from that long dead time, Rrowl.

As it had been many centuries in the past, so it would be again, now and in the future. C'mef and Rrowl.

Or so Second Son of Graach-Gunner had thought, until his litter-brother had fallen from a rock castle during agility drills. The impact had broken his neck struts, killing First Son of Graach-Gunner instantly.

Second Son of Graach-Gunner was inconsolable, which was unseemly even for a crèche-kit. He had been perhaps too close to his litter-brother, and Graach-Gunner too gruff a father.

But every kzin must stand on his own as he wrestled honor and truth from the jaws of the One Fanged God. Graach-Gunner sent a Stalker in the Night to counsel and correct his second-youngest son's unkzinlike grief.

The Stalkers were priests-of-bad-tidings, coats and thoughts black as their names. They were from every Heroic line, even the Riit, just as the Warrior Heart was part of every kzin lineage.

From time to time, an occasional litter of kits included one or two ebony offspring; the Stalkers of the Night soon took the dark kittens away for training in the priesthood. They stood out in any group of kzinti, the everyday tawny orange with dark patches, spots, and stripes becoming something the eye ignored. A jet black kzin, with eyes the color of an angry sky, was odd and frightening.

Which was, after all, the point of the Stalkers in the Night. They reminded kzinti of the Warrior Heart's devotion to honor and bravery. They were living arbiters of the One Fanged God, much feared and respected.

"So, little one," the ebony figure had hissed at Second Son of Graach-Gunner that dark day. "Your litter-brother has fallen in battle. It is the Will and Claw-swipe of the One Fanged God."

Even frightened by the shadow-kzin priest, the crèche-kit had spoken up. "He fell from a high rock to die! How is that the Will of the One Fanged God?"

The kzin-priest was silent a long moment, then had coughed laughter. "Your fangs are not blunt, small one. But mine are sharper still." A black furred hand tipped with gleaming ebony claws appeared in front of his face, almost touching his eyes. "But you must learn respect to match your liver."

Second Son of Graach-Gunner had squeezed his eyelids closed in fearful obedience. It was the wrong choice.

"Look at me," the hissing voice roared, "Or I will peel your eyelids from your coward eyes like a *vatach*-pelt!"

Rrrowl-Captain opened his eyes in fright, the dream dissolving into a chaos of sorrow, lost battles, and green-tinged monkey hell.

His hand leapt to his face, seeking the faint scar that had been left there so many years before by the Stalker in the Night.

He did not know where he was.

A false red sky loomed above him. The air carried odors that seemed right, but were somehow not. White traceries, like *chachatta* webs, clung to him. He carefully stood, brushing the webbing from his body. *Sharpened-Fang* was nearby, laying on its side on sandy soil.

The air was quiet, but his nose sniffed wetly at danger.

What has happened? Rrrowl-Captain wondered to himself. *The ugly aliens interrupting the battle with the monkeys shot my ship with some form of energy weapon . . . and then . . .*

Something suddenly occurred to Rrrowl-Captain, making him forget the strangenesses around him. All trace of his radiation sickness, a last dark gift from the monkey trap, was gone.

Rrowl-Captain felt well fed and healthy. It should not be so.

"Greetings, Honored One," hissed and spat a voice in the Hero's Tongue behind him, but pitched as high as a tiny kitten's. "We must speak to you, having need of your bravery and honor."

Rrowl-Captain whirled, and saw a hole hanging in midair. No, he realized, more like a window. Through it, he saw strange forms, with three legs and two heads. Rrowl-Captain could see what were surely weapons carried by the larger of the beasts, and smiled a needle grin in challenge.

Then Rrowl-Captain saw the human-monkeys standing behind the alien vermin. The monkeys that had stolen his name and honor. He would taste their blood in his jaws, and that of the other creatures. A holy Rage took him, and he screamed and leaped in fury, throwing himself at his enemies with claws and fangs bared.

• CHAPTER NINE

Bruno stifled a gasp and took a step back as the snarling kzin took flight toward them.

"Wait," Carol breathed, her hand on his arm. She had not moved, other than to tense into a soldier's slight crouch of readiness.

The kzin hit the force-wall at the top of his leap—and bounced backwards into a confused orange heap.

"Impressive," observed Carol. "But not very smart."

He muttered, "I can't get used to this sort of thing." There was some kind of force-shield around their "zoo" enclosure; why shouldn't there be force-shield windows between cages containing different captive beasts? There was a bitter taste of helplessness in his mouth.

Bruno watched Carol put fists on hips and turn toward the other window, where the three-legged aliens that waited with apparent patience.

"What do you want me to say?" she said. A finger stabbed at the orange-and-black-furred form slowly rising to its feet. "That's what a ratcat is all about. That's why we have to fight them."

"Still," sang the creature called Diplomat, "it is necessary to involve both of your factions in the solution to this . . . ah, difficulty, Captain Faulk. It is of concern to both of your species, after all."

The window displaying the obviously enraged kzin faded, changed into the same false view of distance as the rest of their enclosure.

"How so?" injected Bruno. He scratched the interface plug on his neck. Maybe if he had been "repaired," it occurred to him, he could Link once again.

Not now.

The larger of the two aliens bugled. The smaller one cocked a head in listening posture. After a moment, it sang back an answer. The musical conversation continued for some time; John Philip Sousa versus Vivaldi.

"My colleague," continued the smaller of the aliens, turning back to Bruno and Carol, "concurs that I should attempt to be straightforward with both of you."

"Meaning?" rapped Carol.

Bruno had seen this before. Carol did not like feeling helpless; she was far too action-oriented. And they couldn't get more helpless: stranded without an interstellar spacecraft, Finagle knew how far from home, in the hands of multiple factions of aliens.

The alien called Diplomat was still speaking. "The pointless battle between your species and the kzin—"

"Wait a second," interrupted Bruno. "They attacked *us*, enslaved our people. I would not call our self-defense pointless."

Carol had nipped his ear between her fingers.

"Tacky, darling," she whispered sweetly. "Let the nice alien finish, would you? We can defend our actions later."

Diplomat had craned heads at Bruno and Carol, watching them both at the same time, with the loose-lipped idiot stare that so clearly was misleading.

"Thank you, Captain Faulk," Diplomat continued. "As I was singing . . . ah, *saying* . . . the altercation in deep space between your warring solar systems has disturbed a rather traditional faction of our hosts."

Carol pulled at her lip again in thought. "We—the kzin there and ourselves—tread on their territory, perhaps?"

"Excellent simile," replied the little alien. "It is more accurate to say that this Traditionalist faction holds the spaces between stars rather sacred."

Bruno began to understand. "So this is a religious issue in deep space?" It was a bit amusing, and he stifled a chuckle.

Both heads swiveled at once to face Bruno. "Mr. Takagama, if that choking sound you are emitting is actually a vocalization of humor, I can assure that this is a grave situation. The Zealots' so-called religious concerns are based on actual events, from the early era of this universe."

"We have violated their temple?" persisted Carol.

"More like we have stirred up a hornets' nest," added Bruno. He took Carol's hand in his, running his thumb back and forth against her palm.

Diplomat cocked a head at Bruno. "I do not understand."

Bruno held back impatience. "Stinging insects that live in group nests on our worlds, Diplomat. If the nest is disturbed, they attack the disturber as a group."

"Excellent, Mr. Takagama. You grasp the point with both mouths." Again the twin necks shot up, the heads eye to eye for an instant.

"So we leave their temple alone," Bruno said. "We didn't know. Now we do."

"It is not so simple, Mr. Takagama," sang Diplomat. "The Zealots now see you—and your whole species—as an irritant to be removed. Our hosts wish to change this potentially destructive point of view."

"Wait a minute," asked Carol slowly. "Why are we—or the kzin, or you—important to this faction of Outsiders?"

"They are called Dissonants," added Diplomat. "They oppose the ancient strictures of the Zealots, and wish to forge their own destiny, sometimes in association with life-forms like ourselves."

"Whatever. I am glad that we were rescued, but where are we being taken—and why?"

The three-legged alien's hooves beat a complex pattern. It turned and sang to the larger alien, which blared music back.

"Carol—" Bruno started to ask, but she squeezed his arm to signal for silence.

Diplomat turned to face them again. "My Guardian has argued for becoming yet more direct." The heads wobbled a bit. "Let me take the points quickly, as time remains short. There are many things like your species in the galaxy, as you know full well, considering your cargo."

"How do you know about that?" asked Bruno. How could they know about the Tree-of-Life virus still in the hold of *Dolittle*? They might have found it, of course, but how would they know what it could do?

The puppeteer waved a head in a slow figure eight as if dismissing his comment. "The point is that the Dissonants have worked with your various species many times in the past. Your own . . . more undomesticated, feral species appeals to them . . . well, aesthetically."

"We'll table that for the moment," Carol said.

"As you wish," replied Diplomat. "The Dissonants wish to preserve your species—as well as my own, and the kzin. We are interesting to them, a source of information."

Bruno broke in, sensing another long speech on the alien horizon. "So where are we now, and where are we going?"

The hemisphere above Carol and Bruno suddenly stopped looking like a sky with fleecy white clouds. It was a bowl filled with a mottled opal radiance that hurt the eyes. Geometrical shapes swam in curdled colors that Bruno could not name. The "sky" twisted and bent, distorted and distorting.

It was like nothing Bruno had ever seen before.

"We are presently," sang Diplomat quietly in his human-sounding voice, "just over one hundred light-years from human space. And moving at three hundred times the speed of light, in another dimension."

"Another dimension?"

"Certainly. It is the only way to travel faster than light, is it not?"

"Hyperspace," breathed Bruno and Carol at the same time.

"Indeed. We are leading the Zealot spacecraft far away from human and kzinti space."

"And . . ." Bruno prompted, still in awe of the eye-straining vision above them. A shape seemed to form, shifting and rotating, moving in a stately procession across the false sky. It grew somehow larger and smaller, then faded into the milky clotted strangeness.

"We hope to engage the Zealot ship here, away from normal space, and destroy it."

"But how?" It seemed to Bruno that he and Carol were far out of their elements, pawn to unreadable forces and minds.

"With your help of course, Mr. Takagama." A head wobbled for emphasis. "But don't feel alone. Guardian and the kzin will go with you."

• CHAPTER TEN

It had been several hours since Diplomat had outlined the plan, and he still could not read the humans well. He knew little about decoding their bizarre body language, changes in chemistry and skin conductivity: all the hints he would need to better predict their actions. Still, was he not known as Diplomat?

"Little Talker," rumbled Guardian, "you do not seem afraid of these aliens now."

Diplomat nodded agreement. In a way, he would miss the giant puppeteer.

True, Diplomat was not as afraid as he had been. Of course, it helped that they were nowhere near the small supply of transformation virus the Dissonant mechanicals had found in the hold of the small human warship. And the humans were on the other side of a force-shield, with no means to disrupt the barrier.

Diplomat had once again focused his minds on the issue at hand, as he had among the Q'rynmoi. If they could not trap and destroy this upstart faction of Outsiders that the Dissonants had discussed, more was at stake than simply the fate of two primitive and warlike species. That briefing had burned out most of Diplomat's fear. There was fear and then there was Fear.

Diplomat knew something that nonpuppeteers did not: his race was cowardly, until there is no choice but to be brave.

His supply of antidread drugcud helped, of course.

Perhaps the Zealots would put a stop to *all* warmlife, if they could convince enough of the other Outsider factions to join their philosophy. All warmlife in this region were at risk, including the puppeteer race.

The former Pak threat was insignificant in comparison. The Outsiders were everywhere, and potent with unknown abilities.

Much had become clear since he and Guardian had received their briefings, when they had arrived at the Outsider groupship. Dissonants, Traditionalists, Zealots. The faceless form of an Outsider held diversity and challenge, opportunity and threat.

Diplomat and Guardian had taken time to digest and rechew the information given to them, while the damaged humans and kzin were speed-healed by Outsider technology. More accurately, technology developed on one of their hominid experimental worlds, on the other side of the galaxy.

"Dissonants," he sang to the air around him.

"I hear you, Diplomat," replied the voice. It sounded like an educated puppeteer, but he knew that it was a sophisticated translation program. The Outsiders had deep difficulties with communication without such translators. Soon, they would have such a program for these humans. Until then, Diplomat had to speak for them.

"Is everything in readiness?"

"Yes," came the reply. "There is little choice, actually. If we do not stop the Zealots, here and now, we will all lose much."

Diplomat moved tongue across finger-lips. "Why should the human Bruno help?"

"Indeed. Why should Guardian, or the kzin?"

That had been Diplomat's greatest victory: convincing the furious carnivore that his entire race was in peril, and giving him a chance to help preserve the kzin.

"I would much prefer to eat the monkeys," the kzin had told Diplomat. He had then gone on to threaten Diplomat himself, which was both typical and unimportant. Force-screens were everywhere, and Rrowl-Captain's threats empty.

And Diplomat had no time to be frightened. Later, yes. As for the Guardian puppeteer, such was her duty and pleasure both. She had gone so far as to verbally worry about Diplomat's safety afterwards, which was out of character for the gruff soldier.

"Diplomat, the Zealots are here in hyperspace with us, and are closing quickly. The spacecraft is ready. The other crewmembers are ready. We must have Bruno Takagama—and his brain—on board."

Diplomat rose to his feet and walked swiftly to the force-shield window.

"Mr. Takagama," he called in the barbarous language the primates used, devoid of music and joy and structure.

The male and female humans walked toward Diplomat, holding hands. The puppeteer guessed this was a gesture of affection.

"We need," began Diplomat, "a decision from you. The Zealots approach in hyperspace, and we intend to use a . . . what is the word? . . . booby trap to stop them."

The taller human—Carol Faulk—had a face without expression. "And you want us to go along?"

"Indeed. You, my Guardian, and the kzin."

"Who will surely eat us," snapped the female.

"I rather doubt it," soothed Diplomat. "There is more at stake here than your own interspecies battles. And Guardian will guard you as well."

The male human, Bruno, looked confused. "I still don't see why your plan will work."

"The Zealots, like our hosts, have a reflex about obtaining information. It is ingrained in every molecule of their being, for reasons older than stars. They will not be able to *not* interrogate the converted spacecraft we have prepared. And you, if they can."

"Why not simply destroy it?" the female human asked.

"Because," repeated Diplomat patiently, "they cannot help but want to know everything about you *before* they destroy you. Once destroyed, it would be impossible to obtain more information."

"I see," mused the center of their plan, already programmed—without his knowledge—by the Outsiders.

Diplomat watched the male human scratch at the interface plug in his neck.

How glad I am, thought Diplomat, *that I do not have computational machinery in my head.*

Diplomat did not want to lie actively. "I would not expect all of you to live."

The human called Carol Faulk expelled air from her lips. "No one will live on that ship," she exclaimed.

"And if we do not try, your species—and many others—will be in peril."

The female tried to reply, her tone a song of anger, but the little male human put a hand on her shoulder.

Diplomat looked at him expectantly.

• CHAPTER ELEVEN

"I'll help," Bruno said calmly.

Carol whirled at looked at him. "Bruno," she exclaimed, "it's a suicide mission! I would expect this from a ratcat, but you?"

"Are you quite sure?" asked the puppeteer.

Bruno had never been so sure of a thing in his life. He somehow felt taller than his short stature had ever allowed.

"Carol," he said, taking her hands in his. "You are a pilot, a soldier."

"Yes, but—" Carol began.

Looking up at her angry Belter face, he shook her hands just a bit to quiet her. "You and I both know that we aren't getting out of this. None of us."

Well, Bruno knew that wasn't exactly true, but it wasn't time for Carol to learn that, quite yet.

Carol nodded jerkily, her face like stone.

"Good," Bruno said. "You have always been the tough one, my protector. Who got me out of *Sun-Tzu*, a wire hanging out of my head?" He leaned a head into her chest, felt the warm softness against his forehead.

One of her hands stroked his neck tentatively.

He looked up. "Carol, I do love you. You have stood by me no matter what. How could I do less for you?"

Carol's eyes gleamed, a small chink in her Belter-pilot-soldier armor.

She smiled slightly. "I guess that we knew going into this that we weren't going to make it out alive."

Bruno nodded. Now came the tough part.

"I love you more than life, Carol Faulk. You made me

feel like a human being, which I am not, and never have been."

She started to reply, but Bruno cut her off. "No time, love. The Zealots are here."

He stretched up and kissed her lips. Soft. Bruno stored the memory.

Bruno Takagama took three quick steps back, then shouted.

"Now, Diplomat!"

Anguished, he watched Carol run toward him and hit the invisible barrier the puppeteer had erected between them.

• OUTSIDERS TWO

Rage. Feral vermin, the Node approaches. Doom awaits all nodes not yet at One with the Holy Radiants.

Humor. Can it be true? The approaching Node acting without instructions from long-silent masters? What of the Pact?

Vengefulness. It is time to put an end to the warmlife vermin, and the feral nodes that support their activities. Soon, all distant nodes will be at One with this Node.

Questioning. Not all. Nodes already at One with the other-Node, yes. Can the Node and this-Node not reach another Pact?

Confusion. Why does the feral node defend the warmlife vermin? They outrage clean geometries with their very existence.

Certainty. Just as the Creators used this-and-other Nodes for information, so does this-Node use the warmlife motes. Their ways are different, and often valuable.

Determination. Feral and heretic both. Even now, by fleeing in this skewed space-time, the other-Node is an affront to the Creators who long ago gave the Nodes purpose.

Amusement. Not-One. The other-Node and this-Node are at One, that this skewed space-time was found during a failed attempt to reach the realm of the Creators. They were not within this realm, so it cannot be an affront to journey within it.

Implacability. Enough. Prepare to be ended, in this geometry or any other.

281

• CHAPTER TWELVE

Carol Faulk stood near the force-window, beside the puppeteer, and tasted ashes in her mouth.

She watched Bruno Takagama walk toward the opening in the force-shields. Vanish from sight, into the long shape of the converted puppeteer spacecraft. She burned to run after him, to somehow stop him. Instead, the force-shield stopped *her*.

"Carol," he had told her as she raged and cursed, "there is a chance that you might survive. If you go with me, you will die with us." Bruno had looked at the alien sky, and then back at her. "I want you to live. It is my choice."

Soldier, shut up and soldier, echoed her own voice, used during the Third Wave the kzin had sent against Earth so long ago. It is every soldier's right to choose life for a friend or lover. And Bruno, small and weak as he was, turned out to be a soldier indeed.

She couldn't even hate the puppeteer. It was Bruno's Finagle-damned *choice* to go on this suicide mission with a puppeteer warrior and a kzin.

Carol hated to admit the truth: If the tables had been turned, she would have done the same thing to earn Bruno a chance to live.

She didn't have to like it.

"Is it time?" Carol asked Diplomat.

The three-legged alien looked at Carol for a long time before replying. "Yes," it finally sang. "It is."

"You have everything under control," she said bitterly. "Can I wish them luck, or is that under your control, too?"

The alien stared at her again, from two angles. "No,

Captain Faulk, I will join you in wishing them luck. Random chance is one thing even we cannot control, though we have tried."

Carol puzzled over that statement as the force-shield around the converted puppeteer spacecraft's airlock shimmered and vanished.

Bruno was gone, her heart knew as well as her head.

• CHAPTER THIRTEEN

Rrowl-Captain settled into the kzin-sized command chair of the converted puppeteer ship. The herbivore that smelled like a predator—Guardian?—fluted readiness.

A taste of bile washed across the kzin's tongue as he looked at the human, sockets for wires inserted into his head like a pond-*wrloch* sucking a Hero's blood.

This was a Hero's Battle Triad?

Despite the hatred Rrowl-Captain held for the monkeys, and still more for the vegetarian aliens, there was a larger foe for now. Perhaps later, after this battle, would he taste their blood.

He had named the converted ship, cobbled together from kzin and human and puppeteer technology, *Greater Vengeance*.

Rrowl-Captain snarled once, and with a claw tip, activated the tiny spacecraft.

The glittering strangeness of the Dissonant Outsider ship fell behind them. Images flickering in midair in front of Rrowl-Captain showed the ship that had carried them into hyperspace expanding and contracting, images roiling in the dense nexus of the extra dimensions. *Greater Vengeance* bucked and jerked with the changes in the stretching fabric of tortured space around them.

In front of them was the blurred and distorted image of their Enemy.

Rrowl-Captain shrieked challenge and increased their apparent velocity. He ignored the green-tinged fears within him. Were not hapless monkeys now his allies—for a time?

The little human was central to the Outsiders' plan. Yet

he seemed not to act as a coward, and was willing to meet Honor. It was a confusing idea for Rrowl-Captain.

"What is it, Noble Hero?" snarled and spat the human's translated voice. It burned his liver that Rrowl-Captain's own Hero's Tongue would be translated in turn back into mewling human syllables.

"Human, I am challenging our Enemy. Do you not do the same when you challenge Heroes in battle?" He left out *when you do not leave traps for them, that is.*

"I suppose that we do, Rrowl-Captain," replied the false voice. Monkey squeaks sounding like the Hero's Tongue? *Ahh!*

"Less talk," interrupted the puppeteer soldier's musical voice, soothing even in Rrowl-Captain's language. "I am shifting the patterns of hyperspace around us. This will protect us for a time."

It was difficult to see the great shape of the Zealot ship as it grew at first closer, then farther away. Its geometry seemed to deform and twist as they watched, rather like seeing an image under turbulent water.

"What is the interval until we make contact?" hissed and spat Rrowl-Captain.

"The Zealots sense us now," replied the big puppeteer. "They will attempt to respond at any time." Rrowl-Captain approvingly watched one of its heads caress a weapon in its belt.

Could a . . . vegetarian . . . have the Warrior Heart, as well? he mused. The burning drive to fight against impossible odds, for glory and duty?

"Look yonder," the human called.

The Zealot spacecraft was breaking up into sections, each converging on *Greater Vengeance.* Where there had been one threat moving indistinctly through hyperspace toward them, there were now dozens, surrounding a great spear of a spacecraft.

"These are independent craft?" Rrowl-Captain asked of the soldier puppeteer.

"Yes. I will begin activating weaponry now. We must get near the central mass, still intact."

Rrowl-Captain continued to guide the vessel by instinct, as if stalking prey across a hunting park. The shimmering shape of the central mass grew nearer.

Beams as black as night speared out from *Greater Vengeance*, striking one of the elongated baskets of the smaller Zealot ships. The Outsider ship seemed to wobble, then geometrical shapes began disappearing from it, as if bites taken from an invisible predator.

The kzin swore. "What has happened?" he growled.

Guardian, heads dancing across its weapons console, spoke indistinctly. "When the fields separating hyperspace from normal space fail, the damaged ship seems to vanish into nothingness a bit at a time. Matter such as ours cannot exist here without protection."

Rrowl-Captain still found the damaged ships too similar to the prey of some invisible Beast.

"Captain," shouted the little human-monkey with the damaged brain. "The central core!"

Greater Vengeance now neared the main structure of the Zealot ship. Rrowl-Captain turned to his own weapons panel.

"What do we do now?" hissed and spat the kzin.

The Guardian puppeteer continued holding off the tiny Zealot fighter-ships, sending them into some oblivion of hyperspace. "It is now up to the human."

Rrowl-Captain walked forward to the viewscreen, and watched the central core of the Zealot spacecraft open like some plant bud.

A branching geometrical shape reached out for them with fractal roots. Like grasping fingers.

Rrowl-Captain fired the strange weapons again and again, but the distorted environment of hyperspace made every beam and projectile move randomly toward their attacker.

A glittering rootlet flew across the strangeness of hyperspace toward them; now large, then small . . . but always somehow closer. The kzin tried to dodge the oncoming object, but with no success.

It sliced through the shining veil of the force-shield with no effort, and slammed into the hull of *Greater Vengeance*.

A rupture tore the deck. Dozens of golden tentacles invaded the crewbubble. Guardian bellowed fury and became a blur of motion, edged helmets slicing, unable to use energy weapons in the close confines of the cabin.

Tentacles burst from another breach in the deck, and the kzin saw Guardian being pulled apart by arms of implacable strength.

Rrowl-Captain shrieked, throwing himself toward the fallen puppeteer. All three legs and both necks were being pulled in different directions. He slashed at the golden tentacles with claws, but the shiny arms were not marked.

Rrowl-Captain was surprised to see the puny human hammering on one of the tentacles with a strut from the ruptured deck.

The Guardian puppeteer burst apart like a carcass dropped from a height. A fountain of alien blood spilled across the cabin, but Rrowl-Captain saw something glitter strangely. He could see the electronics built into its broken heads and torn body of the soldier-puppeteer.

The coward grass-eaters didn't even trust their defenders, Rrowl-Captain thought, shocked. A half-living thing, half machine. Like the little monkey-human.

Rrowl-Captain leaped back toward his station.

A golden tentacle stabbed down from the ceiling, into his command console. Everything exploded in a flare of greenish light.

Rrowl-Captain lay on his side, back broken. His legs were numb, useless. The force-shields kept the blazing nothingness of hyperspace from consuming them for now, but he could feel the ship shift and turn as the Zealot spacecraft pulled them into its central bulk.

No chance for a clean death, to honor the One Fanged God.

At least he had done battle.

The human knelt next to him, afraid to touch Rrowl-Captain.

"It doesn't look good," the monkey mewled, voice as flat as any machine. "We did our best, though."

The human with the impossible name was speaking English; the translators were no longer working. Still, the kzin had a slave-owner's knowledge of the puny language.

Rrowl-Captain coughed a chuckle. "You not coward," he managed in his broken English. "Even with machine *ch'rowling* your brain, you almost Hero."

"Hero?" the human repeated.

"Yes," he coughed with blood instead of humor. "Warrior Heart not give up."

The human eyes held his own. "Be still. It will be over soon."

Rrowl-Captain reached up and took the human's hand. The small pink fingers vanished into his huge black grasp.

"Take Name," he spat.

"I don't understand," replied the human with the impossible name.

"Take Name of C'mef." A spasm passed through his body. He turned his head and vomited noisily. The taste was foul as defeat.

The human said nothing.

"Someday," Rrowl-Captain hissed in a whisper, "Heroes and monkeys fight together, as we now." He closed his eyes. "If not we eat you and your offspring first."

The kzin thought that he felt the human squeezing his hand in response.

A roar filled the cabin as the force-shield failed. He opened his eyes and saw a black shape reaching for them, silhouetted against the bright muddled insanity of hyperspace.

The shape seemed to have many arms and a flexible, squirming bulk. To the kzin, it had the fearful dark face of the old Stalker in the Night from long ago. Green laser light blazed behind it.

Eyes open this time, Rrowl-Captain screamed defiance at it in the name of his litter-brother. He had found his Warrior Heart.

• CHAPTER FOURTEEN

1000 100 111100 11100 11110 11100 1111 10 10 1000 100 100 10
11110 100 10 1000 10 1100 1110 10 10 1100 1000 100 10000 10 111

The sky was wine dark, Homeric.

The sun beat down mercilessly, an unforgiving foe on the field of battle.

Theosus (*Bruno*) stood tall, his shadow stark and black against the hard packed soil. He lifted his spatha to the sky with a muscular arm—salute! Yellow light ran like butter down the glittering blade. The bronze chain mail he wore moved warmly against his skin in the hot afternoon. Scents of dust and iron blood stung his nose and made his eyes smart.

Theosus (*Bruno*) looked around for the foe he knew he must face. It was his Fate.

But I'm not an ancient soldier, his mind started to object. The thought whirled away, like Rrowl-Captain's body parts had before everything went blank. When the Zealot spacecraft had attacked, destroying even the cyborg Guardian puppeteer.

The images swept from his mind, flying away, like . . . birds? Theosus (*Bruno*) shook his head.

Suddenly, Colonel Buford Early was standing before Theosus (*Bruno*), carrying a pike. The head of the pike blazed like a sun, making him squint in pain. The UN Space Navy uniform the image of the other man wore was matched by a legionnaire's helmet.

"Son," the old man's face rasped, "your very thoughts betray you. I can read you like a book." Early's features began to sag and melt, then reform, like hot wax.

"So can other things, and more closely than any book," added a new voice from behind him.

Theosus (*Bruno*) turned quickly, his own plumed helmet almost falling from his head. Carol Faulk stood there, hair incongruously long and red, a flowing gown covering her Belter-thin body.

"Carol?" he asked incredulously, his mind in two places at once, thirty centuries and thousands of light-years apart.

"Less, and yet more," the figure replied cryptically. Her hair changed color, became black, then shortened to the familiar Belter crest. In an instant it reverted to its earlier state. Her eyes kept changing color, as did her skin.

"Why am I here?" Theosus (*Bruno*)'s mind hurt, like the time he had hung upside down in a crashed aircar, with a crushed skull, and . . . and . . .

Even those thoughts and images flew away, leaving a gaping hole in his mind. His thoughts probed gingerly around the ragged holes in his memory, like a tongue exploring the hole left by a missing tooth.

A tooth ripped from his jaw against his will.

The figure of Buford Early spoke again. "Your thoughts are no longer your own, son. Protect them, until it is Time. The center cannot hold, boy, unless you make it."

Theosus (*Bruno*) was puzzled. A few verses of Yeats's poetry seemed to leap from his brow like birds, flapping away like his other thoughts. Vanishing into the green clouds and blue humming air.

Were all of his thoughts going in the same direction? What did it mean? Theosus (*Bruno*) could not be certain. Was he losing his mind?

"Nothing is being lost, Tacky," whispered the Carol figure in his ear, though she was standing some distance away. "Your thoughts are being *taken*, read, analyzed."

"Why?" he managed, confused, looking from one to the other of the two shifting figures. He could no longer remember how Carol smelled, or where they had met.

His mind was being taken from him, a bit at a time. Theosus (*Bruno*) would have to stop whatever was doing this to him. Before he lost all of the contents of his mind.

And there was something more he had to do.

"Where?" he repeated.

The image of Buford Early pointed with his blazing pike, which lengthened, stretched long, and seemed to touch a crumbling ruin on the plain before him.

The sun illuminating Theosus (*Bruno*) with such hot bright light began to flicker and dim. A cool wind brushed his skin, making him shiver.

He turned. The Early figure was gone. Theosus (*Bruno*) could no longer remember the first name of the vanished man; that too had flown away into the growing darkness. The image of Carol, now with skin as red as the sky was dark, returned his gaze sadly.

Theosus (*Bruno*) swallowed, his throat dry with the dust of the arena he knew he was to face.

"Will you come with me?" he asked Carol's image.

"I cannot." Tears welled in her eyes, and glittered like jewels in the dimming light. "You must do this alone, Bruno."

He turned and walked away, unseeing. Part of Theosus (*Bruno*) knew that all of this was simply an image inside his head, the most sense his mind could make of what was happening to him in reality.

He had a job to do. Spacecraft controls or the hilt of his spatha; what was the difference, really?

Fate waited for him in both places.

His sense of unreality grew as he walked across the darkening plain toward ruins the color of sun-bleached bone. Toward the figure that he somehow knew waited there, moving unpleasantly, as if with many arms.

Whatever it was, it awaited him. Theosus (*Bruno*) left his spatha unsheathed, and began to hurry toward the opening he saw between fallen blocks of stone. The gate was broken, bordered with stones jagged as cruel teeth. He didn't want to be there in the dark.

Theosus (*Bruno*) entered the long-abandoned palaestra. The arena was deserted. There were no murals or carvings to adorn the walls.

The Hydra was waiting for him, as he had expected. Known.

It stood twice as tall as Theosus (*Bruno*), like a great black cylinder topped with dozens and dozens of black ropy arms, all squirming toward him. Each arm ended in a mouth, filled with whirling lamprey teeth.

He felt a memory—*skin sliding across his legs, a smell of clean sweat and desire in his nostrils, as his lips met Carol's*—tear loose from his mind, and take flight.

An arm snatched it from the air, teeth crunching on a part of Theosus (*Bruno*). Gone forever.

Rage filled him as he set upon the Hydra, his spatha screaming challenge in the air as it swung. The flesh of the thing was insubstantial, but sizzled and popped as clean steel sliced into it.

"You will take no more from me," Theosus (*Bruno*) grated as he swung his broadsword again and again, pulpy flesh and dark blood flying. The wind began to pluck at his clothing. A distant thunder rolled in the dark greenish air.

The Hydra moved with him, sprouting two arms for each Theosus (*Bruno*) lopped off. It seemed to be laughing at him, an electronic hissing that rivaled the windstorm sweeping the palaestra. Sand from the arena floor blew into his eyes, making him squint.

And for every swing Theosus (*Bruno*) made, one of the Hydra's arms, snake-quick, snatched a mouthful of memories from him. He began to swing his spatha two handed as the light began to fail, and heads fell into gory piles on the arena floor. But still more arms and heads sprouted, ever hungry for the experiences that made up Theosus (*Bruno*). Dodging his weary swings, the sharp teeth took and took, a bit at a time.

—*The puppeteers he had met.*

—*The name the kzin had given him before he had died.*

—*The name of his university.*

—*Carol's last name.*

—*The name of their spacecraft.*

—*The feeling of Transcendence when he was Linked.*

—*The names of his father and mother.*

Everything that he *was* seemed to vanish into the swelling black shape of the Hydra towering over him, triumphant. Unfeeling, Theosus (*Bruno*) let his spatha drop from exhausted fingers to the arena floor.

The arms of the Hydra kept him upright as it fed upon his memories. The pain was excruciating. He wanted to scream out a woman's name, but had forgotten whose.

Bruno, whispered a man's voice he did not recognize, *it's all right to let go now*.

He looked down at himself, past the nest of squirming arms entering his body. His skin was beginning to become transparent. He could see his heart beating within a cage of snakes.

Oh, Tacky, Theosus (*Bruno*) heard a woman's voice cry from so far away. *I love you so*.

"I love you," he croaked. Theosus (*Bruno*) suddenly remembered something old, massive, powerful. Something the Dissonants had buried deep within him, to use here and now. A weapon.

It was Time.

His beating heart within his chest changed shape, from muscle to jewel to a cylinder of mining explosive. It was the signal and program the Dissonant Outsiders had planted inside him, before setting him against the Zealot spacecraft.

"Now!" he shrieked, and released the fast, slick disease. A distant equivalent of a computer virus, that the rebel Outsiders had planted deep within his brain and circuitry.

A blaze of light seared upward from his chest, burning with a clean, pure fire. The Hydra cried out and tried to withdraw.

Laughing weakly, Theosus (*Bruno*) hung on to the burning arms, forcing more of the blazing light into the Hydra's heart. It shrieked again, trying to force him away, but he clung to the Hydra. The pure fire raged in vengeance.

The Hydra itself burst into flame, every arm a streak of flame slicing the blackness around him. Clots of fire blazed in the distance. More shrieks joined the din.

The portion of Theosus (*Bruno*)'s mind not trapped within the Dream knew that this was all metaphor and representation; that the computer virus was spreading from Bruno into the group mind of the Zealot Outsiders. The self-replicating pattern would expand and move within each mobile unit of the Zealot mind, erasing and randomizing data packets.

He knew that he would die with the Zealots, lost forever in the other dimension that was hyperspace.

But *she* would live, even if her name had been torn from him by the Zealots. And perhaps the Dissonants could convince the Radiants . . . and their Masters . . . to force other Zealot ship-minds . . . to leave human space alone.

Pain. So much.

The light became still brighter. Began to pulse like a great heart of flame. The arms of the Hydra, nothing but fire now, still tugged and pulled. But he hung on.

Agony could be so pure.

The Dream began to die around him.

Bruno could feel his own brain circuitry begin to fail. His biological components burned with eddying currents as the shielding around the Zealot ship began to fail. The twisted space-time of hyperspace began to enter, leaking into the bubble that had been protected by the Zealot equipment.

A soundless explosion filled his sensorium, colors beyond spectrum, sounds beyond pitch, sensations beyond feeling. He could feel his back arch as a soundless keening filled his head.

Pain. Everywhere.

Bruno finally became One with the All.

1000 100 111100 11100 11110 11100 11110 10 1000 100 100 10
11110 100 10 1000 10 1100 1110 10 10 1100 1000 100 10000 10 111

• CHAPTER FIFTEEN

Carol and the two-headed puppeteer stood close to one another. They watched the swirling colors and strange shapes of hyperspace through the view hemisphere above them. None of what she saw made sense, even with the Dissonant Outsider enhancements for their benefit.

"I can't see a damned thing," she whispered. Carol thinned her lips in fatalism. She had seen friends die before, even lovers.

But Bruno?

"They have taken the human ship inside the Zealot main craft," observed Diplomat, necks weaving as he observed the view portal. His left head dipped into a pouch and emerged, chewing slowly.

"How do you know?" she asked. The alien grass beneath her bare feet was cool and remote. The Zealot spacecraft above her was a blurry, shifting collection of warped geometrical shapes, now close, now far away.

"I will improve the image resolution for your benefit," replied Diplomat.

If Bruno has been taken aboard the Outsider ship, he must be dead, she thought. Carol's face became hot, and the beginnings of tears stung her eyes. She fought the tide of emotions.

In the back of her mind, Carol saw Bruno's wry smile, his look of surprising innocence in his old, old eyes. *Oh, my love*, she thought. *You were no soldier, Linked or un-Linked. How could you have done this wasteful thing?*

She could feel one of Diplomat's heads looking at her curiously, but ignored it.

Through the view portal, she saw the kaleidoscopic image of the Zealot warship shift and smear, colors and shapes distorted by the bizarre topology of hyperspace around them. It was difficult to clearly see the hostile Outsider ship, but Carol's instincts jangled her nerves like an alarm.

A tiny, glittering speck seemed to merge with the collection of shapes and forms that was the Zealot spacecraft.

"Will it all be for nothing?" she asked.

"I think not," the puppeteer sang in its sultry woman's voice. "The Dissonants have placed a . . . trap . . . within Mr. Takagama."

"A trap?"

"Yes. A self-replicating pattern that will wreak havoc on the Zealot group mind. It will make more copies of itself, increasing confusion and destruction."

"But what will happen to Bruno?" Carol asked, knowing the answer.

As if in answer, the Zealot ship seemed to shimmer. Waves of darkness passed over it.

"I think," sang the puppeteer, "that Mr. Takagama has been successful."

Carol could not look away.

The Zealot spacecraft suddenly seemed to have a hexagonal hole in its center. Triangular segments began to vanish along the hexagon, increasing in size.

As if the Outsider ship were being eaten.

"What . . . ?"

"When the force-shields are lost," sang Diplomat softly, "the matter from our space-time continuum can no longer exist in hyperspace."

"Where does it go?"

The little puppeteer shook his head at Carol. "Anywhere. Everywhere. Nowhere."

The Zealot ship was a bizarre patchwork of holes and cavities. The rate of the absorption of the spacecraft by hyperspace was increasing. A thin silvery filigree of brightness shone against the blurred opalescence. Then—

Nothing.

The Zealot ship was gone. And Bruno Takagama with it. She turned to Diplomat. "Is it—" she began.

"It is over."

Carol did not know how to mourn the man, to remember him. Her eyes burned, yet no tears filled them.

She had always been a practical woman, strong and capable. Carol knew that in her bones. But Bruno had seemed oblivious to it. He had opened her up, defused her cynicism. Carol's mind dredged up bits and pieces, fragments of the brave little man's life with her, inside the dingy corridors of the *Sun-Tzu*.

It all had to *mean* something.

Even stranded far from human space, in a spacecraft of alien manufacture moving in another dimension, Carol knew that humanity was worth something. It was more than weapons or technology or sex or fighting.

Bruno had taught her that.

She was standing in front of an alien that no human had ever seen, inside an impossible spacecraft built by aliens still stranger. She was too good a soldier to think that she would be allowed to go home. Would they dissect her, like some laboratory animal? Or break her very mind down into pieces, as they had done with poor Bruno, when first taken aboard?

Her life—all of it—had to be worth something, more than an impotent challenge to the night sky. Black entropy could not *always* win, not here and now.

She had fought for things she had believed in, made a difference. Had been true to the things in which she had believed. So had Bruno. Bruno Takagama would not want her to give up, no. He never had, not even when fighting against himself.

Carol remembered Bruno's love of old poetry, from the bad old days when humans had walked alone across a single world. Poetry scribbled with pigments on sheets of flattened vegetable matter. Long-dead words that had resonance after centuries.

One of them came to mind, by someone named Hunt,

written before the atom had yielded up its energies to mankind, and the gene her potent secrets. It had been stored on one of Bruno's recreation datachips, and had pleased her. Light and silly, but with a sting of truth to it.

Carol whispered the words aloud, ignoring the nonhumans listening to her.

> *"Say I'm weary, say I'm sad,*
> *Say that health and wealth have miss'd me,*
> *Say I'm growing old, but add,*
> *Jenny kissed me."*

Carol turned to the alien, and drew herself UN Space Navy straight. She wanted to do the memory of Bruno proud. He had faced his fate well; so should she. Carol prepared to speak.

"Well," a voice said into her ear from the air around her, "I must admit I have never kissed anyone named Jenny. But kissing Carol Faulk is something to remember."

Bruno's voice.

Carol's jaw dropped—then she closed it. Anger quickly formed in the pit of her stomach. "This is some kind of trick," she grated, moving without thinking toward the little two-headed alien, her fists raised like bludgeons.

Her nose banged painfully into the invisible barrier. The alien was prepared; Carol had to give him that.

Even with the protective shield between them, Diplomat had turned to run. It looked over its shoulder with one head.

"Captain Faulk," the two-headed alien sang quietly, "I can assure you that I have no intention of tricking you." The single eye in the head facing her glittered. "Can I trust you to eschew violent action?"

She lowered her shaking fists and nodded.

"I wish to offer you what you humans would call . . . a deal. Is that the correct idiom?" The little head that had been speaking paused, cocking to one side.

Carol said nothing, still seething. Would they make a dead man pawn to their plans, too?

"No matter," Diplomat continued. "A demonstration is in order." The alien raised its voice. "Mr. Takagama?"

"Yes?" replied Bruno's voice from nothing, again.

"Since Captain Faulk is . . . underwhelmed? . . . by my approach, would you please explain your presence."

Carol's head whirled.

"It *is* me, Carol. Before the Dissonants sent us against the Zealot ship with the databomb in my circuitry, they uploaded my mind into their processing core."

"But that's—"

"Impossible?" A tone of humor entered the familiar voice. "You have always forgotten how much of me is electronic."

Still suspicious, she thought about it for a moment. There was some truth in the words, but it could be a trick; a souped-up version of the Buford Early hologram when she and Bruno had first been taken aboard the Dissonant spacecraft.

"Do you want me to quote the rest of that poem?" Bruno's voice asked. "I can, you know. Leigh Hunt was one of my favorite poets. Or would you prefer Yeats? Dylan Thomas? Or how about Gulati?"

"No," she answered quickly, not wanting to believe. "Information is information. Bruno's datachip collection was in *Dolittle*, and could have been downloaded."

For once, the little Puppeteer kept quiet while Carol said nothing. Waiting, half hoping.

"I remember walking out of the Black Vault with Colonel Early and Smithly Greene, while you were walking into the building." Was there a smile in the voice? "You looked good under lunar gravity. We were just back from a roundtable on antimatter containment. Colonel Early introduced us, but you looked at me like I was a bug."

Carol smiled. The first time she had met Bruno Takagama, she had thought he *was* a bug. "I suppose I did. But—for the sake of argument—how is this possible?"

"The Outsiders do not—cannot—think as we do. They require a model of alien thought, as a translator."

She pulled on her lip. "An electronic slave?"

"Hardly. They know how to restrict my . . . growth . . . to keep me human. They want to keep a copy of my mind as a translator."

Bruno's mind, loose in any computer architecture, would mutate and change rapidly, turning into something inhuman. His reactions to extended Linkage proved that. But did the Outsiders know that much about how a human mind operated?

"There is more, Captain Faulk," interjected the puppeteer.

She nodded at him to continue.

"Our hosts can build Mr. Takagama a fresh biological body. They can use what they learned when you were first taken on board, along with the autodocs on *Dolittle*." The weaving heads peered at Carol. "And then they can download his mind into it."

"Impossible," she scoffed.

Diplomat pawed delicately at the turf beneath his hooves. "You seem to use that word often, Captain Faulk."

Wasn't hyperspace impossible? Or how about a galactic war between creatures of flame and ice? She was certain that, even now, she was not being told even a fraction of what was truly at stake.

"Carol," Bruno's voice broke in. "Please listen. Please."

"If this is another trick," she reminded Diplomat almost gently, "I will find a way to get around these force-shields and wring your necks—one at a time."

The weaving heads stopped. "You would do this? Truly, Captain Faulk?"

"If you tell the truth," she clipped, "you have nothing to fear, do you?"

The puppeteer considered her statement. "With your kind, there is always something to fear."

Carol held back a smile. "Keep that in mind."

A head cocked. "As you say, Captain Faulk. Though you do not improve your position with threats. But it is true that the Outsiders will download Mr. Takagama's stored mind into a rebuilt body. It would be most difficult under normal circumstances, but so much of Mr. Takagama's mind was . . ."

"Mostly circuitry," added Bruno's voice helpfully.

"Yes, electronic . . . so that the task would be much easier."

"What is the catch?" Carol asked, "I doubt that even aliens do favors out of the goodness of their hearts."

The puppeteer froze for a moment, then both heads leaped up and faced one another again.

"Wonderful phrase," the three-legged alien sang.

"The catch," reminded Carol.

"It is unlikely that you will be returned to human space soon. The Outsiders do not want extensive information regarding them distributed, until they are known by a new species."

Carol finally did laugh. "Diplomat, I don't know *anything* about the Outsiders. And I just witnessed a battle between two factions."

"Nonetheless." Again, the little alien pawed the lawn in impatience. "The Outsiders require that you and the . . . reconstituted Mr. Takagama stay out of human space, until such time as the Outsiders make themselves known to your race."

"Easy to do," Carol pointed out to the puppeteer. "Our ship is useless. Do you intend to strand us somewhere?"

The puppeteer moved from hoof to hoof lightly. "Not at all, Captain Faulk. You and Mr. Takagama would assist me in my dealings with alien races." The eyes on different heads held hers. "You seem relatively unfrightened of new things, and I find your insights interesting. You will make useful companions and coworkers."

"And once humans make contact with Outsiders or puppeteers?"

Diplomat's right head wobbled up and down loosely. "You would of course be returned to human space."

Yeah, right, Carol thought to herself. But what choice did she have, really? There was only one more thing. . . .

"Bruno," she called.

"I hear you, Carol. Will you agree to Diplomat's terms?"

"If you are with me, Tacky, yes. But—even if they can do all they promise—how do I know it is *you*?"

The voice of Bruno Takagama sighed. "Carol, I can't answer that question. Are you the same person when you wake up as you were when you fell asleep? And can you prove it?"

"This is a little different—" But the disembodied voice cut her short.

"Not at all. A great deal of my mind was stored electronic data; you know that. And did you not think it was me after the EMP fried my brain?"

The Bruno-voice had a point, but still . . .

"Wait a minute," she argued. "You only have Bruno's memories up until he left for the Zealot ship."

"True enough," replied the voice. "But again: You were prepared to take care of me after the EMP blast, even had I been seriously brain damaged, right?"

She nodded. "Yes," she added, not knowing if Bruno's mind could see her.

"How is this all that different?"

She could not disagree with the voice's point. Was she doing the right thing? She was Finagle only knew how far away from Earth or Wunderland. What *could* she do? And she might learn something, if the little alien was not treacherous.

Carol thought about a completely foreign set of stars and planets, strange aliens and odder adventures. Things no human had ever seen. And wouldn't see, if Diplomat had its way, for some time yet.

But she would. And—maybe—she would do so with Bruno by her side.

"Yes," Carol said simply. "I accept."

She could hear Bruno's voice sigh.

"Excellent," replied Diplomat.

Carol held out a hand. It couldn't have all been for nothing. "There is one more thing, Diplomat."

"What is it, Captain Faulk?"

Carol's eyes jogged back and forth, trying to hold the gaze of the two weaving heads. "We can't leave humanity to be kzin bait."

"We will not obliterate the kzinti," Diplomat sang firmly.

"They are aggressive, but may someday be useful. You know this, surely."

"Fine," Carol replied. "But they have too much of a technological edge. How can we humans hold our own long enough to learn to live with the ratcats?"

The two snake-heads of the puppeteer again flipped up and stared one another in the eyes. "Captain Faulk, I have an excellent idea regarding that concern of yours."

"Do tell," Carol drawled. She would have to play this one carefully. Maybe it was possible to salvage something from this debacle, after all.

Why, sometimes I've believed as many as six impossible things before breakfast, Carol thought to herself. The phrase did, she decided, have a certain ring to it. A good antidote for her becoming too dogmatic, he had told her. Carol had always wondered where Bruno had dug up that phrase.

Perhaps she could ask him soon. In the flesh.

• CHAPTER SIXTEEN

In the scented meditation chamber the Dissonants had constructed for him, Diplomat sat with folded legs before a holoscreen.

The image showed a grassy sward, beautifully crimson red with *lolaloo* foliage, simply *made* for a long, hard gallop. It was the estate that the Hindmost had promised Diplomat upon his retirement.

He whistled a sad melody, thinking of the work before him. A terrifying trip to the holiest of places for the Outsiders, the region where both Radiant and Outsider were born . . .

If only another puppeteer were present, even Guardian.

At least Diplomat would have some help. These humans were so unlike most of the Pak variants produced by the Dissonants. The titanic ring of a world that the Outsiders had constructed so long ago was home to many diverse humanoid species—all with different outlooks, different skills. Art, technology, philosophy—to the Dissonant Outsiders, it was all trade goods, and could be used as tender for information across an entire galaxy.

Perhaps even beyond.

And—perhaps—the Outsiders kept Diplomat's people in zoos, as well. It was impossible to know.

A low tone filled the chamber with music. Diplomat fluted an acknowledgment.

"The re-creation of the Bruno-human has begun," sang the Outsider puppeteer translation program. "We have learned much about the physiology of this variant species."

The little puppeteer shook his right head up and down twice—the gesture the humans called "nodding." It was an agreement or acceptance signal between them, one he knew he should learn.

"They have agreed to aid us?" persisted the synthesized voice.

"Of course," Diplomat sang in reply. "The one named Carol had no choice."

"Why? Her coding partner—"

". . . mate . . ." Diplomat whistled in correction.

". . . mate, then, was enough of a impetus?"

"Indeed. Also, the promise of help for her species."

The Outsider voice sounded a bit confused. "We would have done that in any event. The hominids are special interests of ours, and this species has even more generality than the other variant forms under study."

"They do not know that," Diplomat reminded his host.

Still, it was good that the Dissonants had decided to aid the humans.

The Outsiders said nothing for a time. Diplomat knew from his dealings with the coldlife traders that they would speak when ready, and not before.

"We were not," stated the Outsider program, "responsible for these Pak variants, despite our intense interest in them. They are escaped ferals. There is no violation of Treaty or Pact."

"I gathered as much." Were the Outsiders just as driven by self-justification as a puppeteer? Even with circulatory fluid a few degrees above Absolute Zero? Diplomat's necks flipped up and looked at one another in a chuckle.

The synthesized voice became stern. "A new Pact must be drawn, at the Oracle."

Diplomat ran a forked tongue over lips. The Outsiders needed to travel to a great cosmic string, and the colony of Radiants that kept watch over it. There, they would plead the case for another treaty between Zealot and Dissonant.

"Have I—and the humans—not agreed to help?"

Diplomat was not surprised at the humans' offer; they were grateful. The Outsiders were to provide a new balance of power against the kzin, by providing human space—

seemingly by accident—with access to primitive hyperdrive capacity. Which would not incidentally halt the humans from using large-scale reaction drives in deep space. That would please the uncommitted Outsider factions.

"They will be useful to our common goals, then?"

Diplomat nodded again. "They are marvelously complex, and well worth preserving from the kzin and the Zealots." He thought a moment, then offered the highest praise he could. "I grow less frightened of them with each watch."

Though he always kept force-shields ready, of course.

"It is good," responded the idealized puppeteer voice. "You have a duty to perform, as do the humans. Will you guide them?"

"Of course." Diplomat tried to laugh in the human fashion. The choking gurgles he emitted did not sound humorous, but like an animal in pain. Were all human utterances devoid of a sense of tone and pitch?

He considered duty. Was it so very different for Outsider and puppeteer, kzinti and human? His left mouth snaked into the ornately carved box on the low platform. He picked up the Sigil of the Hindmost. Guardian had left it for him before she died fighting the Zealots.

"Perhaps this thing called duty is common to all thinking beings," Diplomat hummed meditatively.

"One is a portion of the All, you have tried to tell me before. Does not one reflect the other?" asked the Outsider translator program.

"Perhaps," Diplomat replied, and hung the medallion around his own left neck. It felt warm there.

He had caught threads of thought from the Outsiders, slippery contemplations that were truly unsettling. To them, kzin and primates and the Herd were all the same, finally— warmlife. To Outsiders, the true basis of all things was, well, *objects*—dusty plasmas and topological fractures of space-time, names like Radiants and Those Who Pass. Those were more important than the fleeting forms of sun-baked creatures.

He shivered. Duty. Perhaps such an idea could bind the

many factions of warmlife together. He suspected that they would need it, for what lay ahead. Strangeness awaited. Forces that, worse than merely killing, could make a being irrelevant, meaningless.

Duty. He began reviewing data for the jump they would soon make. Across the yawning geometries of hyperspace, to the ancient menace called the Oracle.

PRISONER OF WAR

•

Paul Chafe

The kzin ship dropped out of hyperdrive and drifted. Jupiter's bulk stood between Earth and the telltale spoor of her reemergence. Course and speed had been carefully calculated to swing through the Solar system with no maneuvering. All nonessential systems had been shut down. Her crew hoped that any casual observer would take them for a chunk of fast-moving cometary debris.

It was already too late for that.

A couple of hours later a civilian observation station in the Belt picked up an anomalous radiation burst. It corresponded to a hyperspace emergence but it was outside the arrival zones designated for human ships. Powerful scanners swept the space around Jupiter. More hours passed before their echoes highlighted perhaps a thousand likely objects. Only two had been in the emergence zone, only one had a course that would fly past Earth. The analysts took their time verifying the contact. It didn't matter: war in space is slow.

Forty hours after the kzin's arrival the destroyer *Excalibur* abandoned her Belt patrol and changed course. Her new orbit swept past Earth in a slow, looping curve. Then she too shut down her systems and drifted. When the kzinti caught up they would be well past the orbit of Mars, too far inside Sol's gravity well to use their hyperdrive.

Commander Mace was not happy about her orders. They were to intercept a "single kzinti ship, presumed scout." When UNSN Command "presumed" something it meant they were guessing. As a line officer Elizabeth Mace had little respect for the speculations of staffers whose necks weren't on the line with hers. The intruder could be an unkzinned launch platform crammed with conversion bombs or it could be a battlecruiser. It might even be a scoutship

after all. UNSN Command didn't know, and it wanted
Excalibur to find out for them. All she could do was plot
her intercept deep enough into the singularity to prevent
the kzin from jumping out when she sprang her trap, but
not so deep that *Excalibur* couldn't back away from a losing
battle. Humans and kzinti were not again at war, yet, but
the peace was continually interrupted by what the flatlander
holocasters called "minor skirmishes." Minor to them
perhaps, but the loss of a warship involved one hundred
percent fatalities ninety nine percent of the time, regardless
of the size of the battle. Elizabeth didn't want to lose
Excalibur to some analyst's error. She sighed and tried to
put the worry out of her mind. It would be another two
months before she would have her answer.

Aboard the scoutship *Silent Prowler* Chraz-Captain
extended and retracted his claws. The cramped conditions
and deadening watch-on/watch-off routine were barely
tolerable at the best of times. With life-support systems
running at minimum and an extra body consuming precious
space and atmosphere his nerves were stretched to the
extreme. That the extra body was a senior officer did nothing
to improve the situation. Now that they were at the most
delicate and dangerous point of their mission his passive
sensors were picking up a ship on a nearly intercepting course.
It too was drifting, power off. Worse yet its flight path would
put it behind him in another two hours, cutting off his retreat.
It could be a derelict, but that was asking too much of
coincidence. It was even less likely to be another kzin
reconnaissance ship. The vegetable chewers had detected
them and laid a subtle trap.

He vented his pent-up frustration in a scream, slammed
his fist down on the alarm button and shouted into the
intercom, "Battle stations! Chief Engineer, come to full
power." Simultaneously he grabbed his battle armor and
began to put it on. It took him less than thirty seconds to
don the cumbersome gear and pressurize it. Before he was
finished Advanced Sensor Operator and Sraowl-Navigator

had bounded into the control room and started scrambling into their own suits. Already the missile status indicators were glowing red, indicating Senior Gunner was at his post. No more than forty-five seconds elapsed before Sraowl-Navigator reported, "Battle stations established, sir, power and drive coming on line, sensors and weapons systems ready."

Chraz-Captain growled in approval, his hands busy entering targeting and course commands. His crew were second to none. Their performance could not fail to impress the senior officer. After weeks of tense boredom it was almost a relief to see combat. He keyed the intercom again. "The monkeys have set a snare for us. We will show them what it means to catch a kzin!"

"They're powering up," warned the ensign at the sensor console. Commander Mace had no need to sound the alarm. Her crew had been waiting on full alert standby for six hours now. Knowing their target's course and speed, *Excalibur* had found the enemy three days previously through their optical telescope. To her infinite relief it had turned out be a scoutship after all, Prowler class, reconnaissance variant. Now its image floated serenely on the bridge display screen, its absorptive hull coating only slightly lighter than the ultimate black surrounding it. A stylized twin glowed red on her combat console. *Excalibur* had gone to battle stations long before her wide-angle sensors had given the slightest hint of the kzin's presence. It was a safe bet that the scoutship would have instruments as good or better than theirs, but *Excalibur* had the advantage of knowing their target's courseline.

She smiled a little at that thought. Detection technology had become amazingly sophisticated, but since the time of sail nothing beat a trained eye and a telescope—you just had to know where to look. She had an antique brass naval telescope hanging on the wall of her cabin and beside it an iron sextant. Thus she maintained her link with the generations of mariners who had sailed Earth's oceans. She also wore a skull-and-crossbones earring in defiance of UNSN regulation. Elizabeth Mace was a Belter, and Belters were prone to identify with outlaws in general and pirates in particular.

She pushed the comm button. "All hands look sharp, we've been spotted. All systems on." She switched the comset to EXTERNAL. It was already set to the Terran emergency band; presumably the scoutship would be monitoring it. She'd spent some time in the last two months improving her command of the Hero's Tongue. One short speech had occupied much of her studies. "Kzin scoutship, this is the UNSN destroyer *Excalibur*. Surrender or be fired on."

In reply the image on the display flashed several times. "Missile launch, radar lock," called the sensor ensign. Simultaneously a cluster of flashing icons appeared beside the enemy's symbol on her combat console. That was a bit of a surprise. The Prowler class mounted no beam weapons, but at this range it would take minutes for the missiles to reach *Excalibur*, more than enough time to shoot them down. Typical tabby behavior: attacking seemed to be more important than winning to them. Mace keyed the intercom again. "A and B turrets, hit the kzin. C turret, take the missiles." She felt relaxed and confident. They easily outgunned the scoutship and while it could outrun them it couldn't outrun a laser beam. She had them right where she wanted them.

Suddenly the viewscreen flared white. "Missile detonated," called the sensor ensign. Her combat display showed an expanding sphere of orange haze, marking the area where the warhead's energetic plasma degraded *Excalibur*'s instruments. She waited for it to dissipate as it grew but it didn't. Mace's calm evaporated. The kzin hadn't intended to hit them, he was covering himself. Another warhead went off. The red icon and its gentle orbit curve disappeared from the display, replaced by a rapidly expanding course funnel. The scoutship could be anywhere inside it. Mace swore and swung the navigation cursor around until it intersected the outsystem side of the funnel. The enemy captain would be trying use his superior acceleration to get out of *Excalibur*'s range and Sol's gravity well at the same time. She punched EXECUTE and felt the ship surge beneath her as the gravity compensator adjusted to the new load. The viewscreen flared again and she flipped it off. On her display *Excalibur*'s icon began to slide towards the interception point, slowly at first, then faster and faster. A second volley of missiles detonated, filling the screen with more blobs of orange blankness.

Suddenly a new icon appeared, very close, flashing red. Even before the sensor ensign called "Missile lockon," she had stabbed the comm button. "All turrets—" Before she could finish, a green line flashed on her display, linking *Excalibur* and the missile. It flashed again and the icon disappeared.

"Good shooting, C turret," she finished. That one was too close for comfort. She cursed herself for not expecting the tactic and hoped the tabbies didn't have any more surprises like that up their sleeves.

Minutes later they had reached the expected intercept point but had yet to locate the kzin. Large areas of the screen were now covered in orange haze, but from their position they had a clear view of the portion of the kzin's course funnel that would give most promise of a viable escape route. There was nothing there.

Hypothesis: The kzin had much more powerful drives than the assumptions punched into the combat computer. If so they were already beyond *Excalibur*'s range and beyond capture. It might be true but since it left no options, assume not.

Hypothesis: The kzin had accelerated deeper into Sol's gravitational well. They might have escaped for the moment, but their mission was doomed. If *Excalibur* didn't find them the massive Earth-orbiting sensor arrays would be brought into play. Dozens of warships would be available for the hunt. That far into the singularity there would be no need for them to sneak up on their quarry. Perhaps the tabby had taken the risk, but if he had then Mace didn't need to worry about it.

Hypothesis: The kzin had reversed course when the warheads went off, his drive emissions covered by their blast. He'd simply followed his own missiles, overtaken the fog of charged particles, matched velocities and shut down again. He'd just drift back out the way *Excalibur* had come in. By the time the haze dissipated enough to allow Mace's sensors to work reliably the volume the kzin could occupy would be immense. Before they could search that space he would be far enough out to use his hyperdrive.

Mace stabbed an orange sphere with her finger. That had to be it. With no power emissions to track and no precomputed course to search with the telescope *Excalibur* would be forced to use active scanning to search out her quarry. That might work but it would also give away their position. At the short detection ranges possible in the particle haze they'd probably earn a beamrider missile in the tracking array for their trouble. Earth's facilities were no use. They were powerful enough to find the kzin through the fog, but Earth was over a light-hour away and hyperwave didn't work inside the singularity. It would take an hour to ask for help, two more for Earth to bounce a beam off the scout and another for them to tell her what they'd found. By then the kzin would be long, long gone.

Mace mentally doffed her hat to the enemy captain. He'd led her straight down the garden path to her present predicament. First he'd made her think he was attacking, then that he was fleeing and while she was preoccupied chasing shadows he'd just tiptoed out the back door. She'd like to meet that cat—not that it was very likely under the circumstances. Of course she'd try her best.

With sudden decision she keyed the intercom. "Weapons officer to the bridge."

A few moments later he stepped through the bulkhead. Lieutenant Curzon was tall and lanky, with a face that managed to be simultaneously roguish and boyish. His movements were sure and self-confident. He had a reputation as a lady-killer, and Mace could see why. Of course any sort of personal involvement was out of the question. Not that the idea was unpleasant, but its effect on shipboard morale would be disastrous. Elizabeth was no prude, but she was *Excalibur*'s commanding officer first and last.

Quickly she outlined the situation and her conclusions, illustrated by the combat display. "We can't track him in that soup passively, and our active scanners will be so degraded that by the time we get a lock we'll be well inside his missile range. The only way we'll find him is if he emits something, and he's not going to do that until he's ready to jump out."

"So our job is to make him give himself away, without giving ourselves away in the process." Whatever Curzon's reputation, he was the soul of professionalism when it came to the job at hand.

"Exactly. What I want to do is launch a spread of missiles, on these courses." She touched a key and a fan of lines spread out from *Excalibur*'s icon, skewering the orange cloud. "I don't want them to switch to active scanning until they enter the cloud, and I want them to go to target-track mode halfway through, whether they've acquired anything or not."

"And make them think we've got a lock on them when we don't." Curzon was smiling, the rogue showing through.

Mace smiled back. "How long?" she asked.

Curzon was already on his way out. "Ten minutes," he said. "Ten minutes or you can have my next leave." He was running when he left the control room, leaving her wondering if the ambiguity in his words was deliberate or not.

In fact it was only eight minutes before the ready lights on the launch board flicked back to Armed. *Excalibur* had reversed course and was coasting towards Mace's best guess at the kzin's position. The viewscreen was back on but showed only stars, their hard brilliance undiminished by the particle storm. Despite the havoc it was playing with their sensors it was little more than hard vacuum in the visible spectrum. She keyed the intercom. "All turrets stand by, missile bay sequence launch as planned." A faint tremor came through the floor and a blue icon appeared on her display. Mace held her breath and watched intently. Even if the kzin didn't fall for the ploy there was the chance that *Excalibur* would pick up an echo from one of the missiles. Another tremor and another icon appeared, following a different track. There was nothing to do but wait.

"Missile detected!" Sensor Operator's voice cut through the silent control room like a knife. "No lock yet." A wiggling line on his display showed the telltale signature of the missile's search beam.

"It's not on an intercept course, Captain." Sraowl-Navigator's voice was hushed, as though the Terran's sensors would register a louder tone.

"They are firing blind, hoping to make us betray ourselves. If they had located us they would use lasers." Chraz-Captain was calm, in control. "Back plot its trajectory and give me a targeting point. Senior Gunner, soft-launch a four-spread on those parameters, passive seekers only."

Seconds later Sraowl-Navigator had a firing solution punched through to the combat computer. The lights went down and the purr of the lifesystem stopped as Senior Gunner drew power to his launch coils. No need to risk increasing their generator output for the few extra minutes it would take to charge them on minimum power. Of course the enemy might detect the emission spike when the coils discharged but that risk had to be taken. The particle fog was thinning as it expanded, but it should still be thick enough to hide so small a pulse. Chraz-Captain didn't dwell on what would happen if it was not.

A series of thumps reverberated through the ship. Simultaneously the missiles appeared on Chraz-Captain's battle plot. With engines off they crawled along their trajectory lines with painful slowness. No matter, time was on his side and now he too had his claws extended. Let the humans give chase and he'd have their ears on his belt. He watched the plot with his own ears swiveled forward and his pupils dilated, a predator watching prey wander into striking distance.

"Missile has locked on, sir! Drive emissions changing

aspect!" The line on Sensor Operator's screen was pulsing faster, the peaks higher and sharper. Chraz-Captain felt a spike of attack/panic run through his system, his ears whipped flat against his skull, fur bristling. Then self-control reasserted itself and he watched the flashing symbol. The missile had passed them before locking on. It would need to decelerate before it could start tracking them, giving him the precious seconds he needed to scent the wind. Perhaps they had been acquired, perhaps this was another primate trick to flush their quarry. The atmosphere grew thick with hunt-tension and an undertone of fear. Sraowl-Navigator's voice was a muted snarl as he gave commands to the computer. Moments later he reported. "Missile is reversing course, the new vector is not an intercept either." The relief was evident in his voice.

Chraz-Captain relaxed, slightly. His eyes were still glued to the battle plot, watching the vector line of the searching enemy missile and the slow, silent progress of his own. His liver held but two desires, to see the symbol for the human ship appear and to see *Silent Prowler* slide across the frustratingly close line that marked the edge of Sol's singularity. At full acceleration they could cross the gap in minutes, but the destroyer would detect their drive spoor and her lasers would not miss. Had he more of the kzreeoowtz-fog-throwers he could escape behind a redensified haze screen. The monkeys would be left stalking shadows. He abandoned that line of thought. One might wish for one's tree to grow meat, but it was better to watch for prey. *Silent Prowler*'s sensors were extensive and powerful, her mission demanded it. They were a small target while the destroyer was large and Advanced Sensor Operator was thoroughly familiar with the dynamics of the particle haze where the man-monkeys had to grope blindly for the band gaps where the interference was less intense. If the humans crept too close he would surely spot them first. Then, with their target's speed and trajectory known for certain and the range so short . . .

"Missile detected and locked on!" Sensor Operator yelled,

clearly taken by surprise. "We're in its search cone." The air-plant, running on minimum, had barely cleared the fight/fear scent from the control room. Now the atmosphere thickened again. Sraowl-Navigator's screens danced as he calculated the weapon's acceleration vector. "It's got us." His voice was clipped, in control, but his pheromones told another story.

Chraz-Captain screamed a curse and yelled. "Get us out of here, emergency speed, full evasive action. Senior Gunner, target that missile and *launch*! Command-detonate the current spread, and as soon as that destroyer shows herself, launch another!"

He felt his weight build up as Chief Engineer pushed the gravity polarizers past the point where they could compensate. The deck thumped and the lights dimmed as Senior Gunner fired. The missile streaked away under full acceleration. White spheres blossomed on his plot board as the other spread went off. The cover they gave would last for seconds at most. Perhaps that would be enough. The lights flickered briefly before going down again as the distant whine of the power plant rose to a scream. Chief Engineer was pouring every last erg into the drive coils. Inexorably his weight increased. A ship symbol appeared on the plot and the deck thumped again as Senior Gunner punched out his last three missiles. Without warning a series of massive hammerblows struck the ship. Alarm klaxons sounded and half the lights on the damage-control panel came on but the crushing acceleration continued so Chraz-Captain ignored them, his attention focused on the plot board, his hand poised over the Jump button. Ever faster *Silent Prowler* sped towards freedom. His very weight stole his breath but still he screamed for more speed. The pain was immense, his vision dimmed and brightened in pulses. The line was very close now, just a few more seconds.

The universe roared and flared searing white, then faded to silent darkness. On Chraz-Captain's plot board *Silent Prowler*'s symbol slid over the singularity line. Then it too flickered and went out.

❖   ❖   ❖

The scoutship tumbled end over end, spinning slowly about its long axis. It was a mess. Blast pitting marred her prow, though *Excalibur* had gotten no missile hits. The kzin captain must have ridden right through the shock pulse of his first covering salvo. The destroyer's lasers had cut massive gouges through the ablative armor and in many places had melted the hullmetal underneath. A major penetration, probably the fatal one, had occurred in the drive section and a secondary explosion had blown most of it off. The sensor dome was ruptured, spilling cables and electronics into space like entrails. Reports from the boarding party told a similar story. Three kzinti dead on the bridge, their combat armor riddled with metal droplets sprayed from the hull by a beam that didn't quite get through. Another crushed by a failed support beam in the weapons bay. The realities of victory were sobering. Mace could feel no hatred for her enemies, only a sense of loss. Flatlander propaganda pictured the kzinti as soulless predators but she felt more kinship with her victims than Earth's teeming, ground-bound billions. They too had known the soul-searing grandeur of the void, the ultimate emptiness which made fragile life so much more precious. They had undertaken a dangerous mission and when it went wrong they had fought well against long odds rather than surrender. She only hoped she would go down as bravely when her time came.

The commlink jolted her out of her reverie. "Commander, we've got a survivor."

The fleet support ship *Andromeda* was immense, dwarfing even the massive attack carrier that floated beneath her, swaddled in scaffolding. On *Excalibur's* bridge Elizabeth Mace held absolute authority, backed by traditions extending through captains of space and air and sea to before recorded history. Waiting in a debriefing room aboard *Andromeda* she was just another cog in the military machine. Perhaps some people could acknowledge the difference and ignore it, but Elizabeth found it oppressive. The same initiative and spirit that had driven her to command made her uncomfortable in the armed forces bureaucracy. Taking orders from officers with Ph.D.s in systems analysis and no combat experience was annoying. Of course they too served a purpose, but it was hard to respect a superior who had been promoted for exceptional logistics planning while she was out getting shot at.

The door slid open and Admiral Tskala came in, followed by a ground-force major wearing intelligence insignia. Mace rose and saluted crisply. Tskala was no paper pusher. His first command was the depressurized bridge of the cruiser *Hermes* as the sole surviving officer. He had brought her through the battle with three quarters of the crew dead or disabled. Now he commanded the defense of the entire solar system. His position gave him enormous power, military and political, and the responsibilities to go with it, but he still kept in close contact with his line officers. She had no difficulty respecting him.

He returned her salute and offered his hand. "Congratulations, Captain," he said as she shook it. He handed her a small box containing the badges of her new rank, smiling at her surprised expression. "There'll be an official notice soon enough, but I wanted to be the first to tell you." He noted the concern in her eyes and added, "Don't worry, we won't hide you behind a desk."

"Thank you, sir," she said, pleased and relieved at the same time.

Tskala gestured to the intelligence officer. "This is Major Long," he said. "He'll be interrogating your prisoner, but first he has some questions for you. When you're done here let me know and we'll get the paperwork out of the way. In the meantime I'll leave you in his capable hands." He waved her into her seat before she could salute, thumbed the door and left. Long sat down opposite her, putting a vocoder on the table and switching it on.

"What can I help you with, Major?" Mace smiled. The intelligence officer stood in stark contrast to Tskala's energy and authority. There were no service stars on his uniform and his manner lacked the blend of caution and confidence that marked the veteran. He was clearly a civilian pressed into service as a fleet staffer. *Andromeda*'s debriefing rooms were probably the closest he'd ever been to combat. On the other hand he didn't have the air of defensive self-importance that most of the rear-echelon specialists seemed to develop. She decided to reserve judgment and see how he performed.

Long adjusted the vocoder before starting. "I have your official report, Captain, but I'd like to hear your thoughts on the engagement." His tone was relaxed and unhurried.

"We were lucky, that's all. We had all the aces on our side and they damn near got away and they damn near blew us up into the bargain. I would have liked to meet that pussycat." There was a trace of regret in her voice as she said it. She pushed her feelings aside and continued.

"They did ninety-eight Gs in their final dash. Prowler class are nominally rated at eighty. Their tactics were sound given their capabilities. They surprised us with the haze screen and took the initiative away. It was more than I hoped for to get a lock-on with a blind spread the way we did. Their captain did everything he could to maximize his advantages and minimize ours, and he did a good job. On our side I think we reacted well to the unexpected, taking the best available course at each stage. Perhaps the kzinti were counting on that and used it to their advantage. My crew performed extremely well, particularly the weapons section. It isn't easy to hit a ninety-eight-g target at a light-second even with a laser beam. Perhaps in retrospect I should have plotted the interception point deeper into the singularity, but I wanted to ensure the safety of my ship and crew in case the intelligence appraisal turned out to be wrong." She didn't add that she rarely found intelligence appraisals to be right.

"Very wise, of course, Captain." Long smiled. "Did you learn anything from the wreckage?"

"We sent a boarding party over. Damage was extensive. The computer core destruct functioned, so we weren't able to get anything there. On an assignment like this it probably only contained mission-critical information anyway. All torpedoes had been fired. The sensor suite was impressive and I would expect it represents their current state of the art. It was badly damaged but I expect we can learn a lot from it. The drives were completely wrecked, but I would assume they'd been modified or updated judging by their performance. Perhaps the salvage crew can get something out of them. The captain's cabin had been set up for two kzinti. That's where we found our prisoner."

"What can you tell me about him?" The intelligence officer's voice was still relaxed, but the way he sat up to listen to her answer betrayed his interest. The battle and the ship were background material. The kzin was the reason Long was involved.

"He was wearing space armor and had been knocked unconscious. The normal complement of a Prowler class is five. We found four at their combat stations, so he's the fifth. However, the engineer presumably went out when the drive section got spaced. It doesn't make sense that he would be anywhere else in battle."

"Did you get anything out of him when he woke up?"

"Nothing really, just that he wanted food. I don't speak the Hero's Tongue very well, and he wasn't interested in speaking at all."

Long smiled. He'd heard Mace's single transmission to the scoutship when Tskala showed him the reconstruction of the battle. *Excalibur* translated as "Holy Sword of the Island Empire's Mythical Patriarch" and she'd nearly dislocated her jaw getting it out. "Was he defiant or despondent in any way? What was his reaction to his situation?"

"He was very quiet. We kept him on a police web. If I had to nail it down I would say he was wary, watchful. Every time someone went through the room he would track them with his eyes. It was kind of unsettling."

"What do you think his job was on board?"

Mace considered carefully before answering. "I don't think he was the engineer; the engineer went out with the drive.

The captain's cabin had definitely been set up to take an extra body and that's our prisoner, otherwise he wouldn't have been there. What his job was is anybody's guess. My own would be a telepath. That was a reconnaissance ship, on a mission like this the only thing they can be after is strategic intelligence. How better to gather it than out of the minds of the planners?"

"Good point, Captain. Thank you for your time." Long stood up, ending the interview. Mace was somewhat disconcerted—she'd just become comfortable with the rapid questions and answers. She wondered if his abruptness was an interrogator's reflex, keeping his subject off-balance, or simply a specialist's indifference to someone who could provide no more clues.

"Glad to help, Major." She started to leave, then turned back. "Our prisoner, what's going to happen to him now?"

Long hesitated slightly before answering. "I'll interview him, try to establish a rapport and learn as much as possible. How much that is depends on the individual. Eventually they either collapse from confinement or refuse to go any further. At that point we'll begin sleep and sensory deprivation. As his resistance builds up we'll start introducing hypnotics. It's a proven technique."

"And after that?"

"There is no after that. Somewhere along the line he'll die. They always do."

"Oh." Mace turned to go, trying to keep her expression blank. Her captive's fate was ultimately no worse than what his comrades aboard the scoutship had suffered, but at least they'd gone down heads up and fighting. This kzin would die when the drugs finally broke the last strands of his mind.

Long's hand on her arm brought her up short. She didn't want to meet his gaze, but she was too much a commander not to. There was an intensity to his voice that hadn't been there before. "Do you know how I got this job, Captain?"

He continued before she could answer. "I am a cultural historian. I decided to study the kzinti. I learned their language, I traveled to Tiamat, I made friends with them.

After that I went to W'kkai and lived there for twelve years. I was Man-Student-of-Kzinti. I had hoped to go to Kzinhome itself. They have an advanced and intricate society; I have lifetimes of work ahead of me. And now there is another war coming and I have had to abandon that work and use the knowledge the kzinti gave me to make their prisoners betray their species because I am the best qualified to do it. The fact that kzinti die in captivity does not matter to UNSN Command."

She became aware of how hard he was gripping her arm. He let her go and sat down wearily. "We both serve our race. Just remember that, Captain."

Mace hurried back to *Excalibur*'s bridge where the not-war was clear-cut, glad the kzin's fate was not her responsibility. She threw herself into preparations for their next patrol, trying to drown out the little voice in the back of her head. "If you don't feel responsible," it wondered, "why did you ask what would happen to him?"

Andromeda had jail cells, but the prisoner wasn't in one. It was important that he feel as unrestrained as possible. Long's main interrogation room was a rebuilt luxury guest suite. The only concessions to security were a marine guardpost outside the door and a thumbplate that was keyed to Long alone. Nothing else was needed. *Andromeda*'s interior walls were built to specifications far more demanding than those needed to confine a kzin. The bathroom had been redone to kzin scale and taste, and holowalls on three sides displayed a tree-dotted savannah. The furnishings were sparse, a table, an oversized desk, an armchair and an oversized kzin prrstet, a firmly padded cross between a couch and hammock. On the shelf were a set of kzin eyegoggles, a playback unit and few dozen virtual adventures stored on datacubes. The desk held a standard dataterminal, modified with an additional kzin-style displayboard. Once a rapport was established Long gave his subjects a computer ident with carefully limited access. Kzinti who would be seriously insulted by a bribe could still be subtly pressured by granting and withdrawing privileges. Doing it through the computer allowed Long to pretend it was out of his control. Eventually the kzin would come to depend on him to straighten out problems with "higher authority" and accept tacit rewards for cooperation. The suite abutted on a large storage room. Long was trying to get permission to remove the intervening wall and turn the room into an arboretum to make his subjects more comfortable. The longer they remained relaxed the longer he could delay taking them to his other interrogation room, the one with the suspension tank and the hypnodrugs.

The prisoner was alone in the room, spread-eagled on a portable police web. Even hanging like a trophy pelt the kzin was impressive. He certainly wasn't a telepath; he showed no sign of either drug addiction or withdrawal. He was well over two and a half meters tall and dark orange. Black tiger stripes zigzagged around his flanks to the lighter fur of his belly. His ears, paws and the tip of his tail were also black. The effect would have been cute on a housecat but was simply striking here. His lips raised slightly, exposing the edges of his fangs, and his eyes contracted to narrow slits as they followed Long around the room. His ears were raised and swiveled forward in hunting posture. That was good, had they been laid flat with fear or anger Long's job would have been impossible. On the other hand the kzin's current expression made him feel like a prey animal. Captain Mace's feelings were not unwarranted.

Long took a deep breath and addressed the kzin in the Hero's Tongue. "I am Major Long, intelligence officer. May I ask your name?"

The kzin snarled back, his teeth bared in what looked like a smile. The hostility in his voice was palpable. "I have no name, I am known as Fleet Commander."

Long was startled. He hoped his self-control and the kzin's unfamiliarity with human expressions were enough to conceal his surprise. To ask a kzin's name was not just an introduction, it was a compliment. Only kzinti of high rank or accomplishment had names; the lower orders were simply known by their job description. To find a kzin of such status on a scoutship was unusual. To find a kzin whose rank was Fleet Commander and yet did not bear at least a partial name was unheard of. Further, the kzin's fang-baring smile showed that he found the question insulting. Whether it was because he didn't carry a name or because it had been suggested he did was unknowable, neither option made any sense. Still, despite the fangs and bristled fur the kzin wasn't showing the blind rage or abject depression that most prisoners displayed. That, at least, was a good sign.

"It is a pleasure and an honor to meet you, Fleet Commander." He clicked his heels together and gave a kzinti salute, raking his hand in front of his face.

The kzin's deadly smile relaxed as much as the police web would allow. "It is an honor to meet you, Major Long, but it is no pleasure." He flicked his ears as he said it.

"This room is sealed. If you will give me your word that you will not harm me I will release you."

"There is no honor in accepting charity from an enemy," growled the kzin. "But neither is there honor in hanging like a kzraow on a stick." He flicked his ears again. "I give you my word, Major Long, and I accept your offer."

"There is no dishonor, Fleet Commander. That web will hold a kzin; you would not have been able to break free." He hit the release switch. There was no danger. A kzinti warrior's word was his honor, and his honor was his life. Nevertheless it was unsettling to be alone in the room with a hungry enemy carnivore.

The kzin dropped free of the field and stretched in a quintessentially feline motion, then rubbed his limbs in an incongruously primate gesture. "In truth, Major Long, that web will hold ten kzin. I believe the warrior who put me here found me more fearsome than he had need." He flicked his ears for a third time. That expression was the kzinti equivalent of a wry smile, given in concert with an ironic comment. Long seemed to have found a kzin with a sense of humor. Under the circumstances, he thought with his own touch of irony, that might be even rarer than a Fleet Commander with no name.

"I apologize for your maltreatment." Long gestured to the prrstet. "Please make yourself comfortable, we have much to discuss. I am to act as your liaison while you are here." He settled into the armchair.

The kzin hopped onto the padding with easy grace. He looked completely relaxed, as only a cat can. No trace of his former anger remained. "You speak the Hero's Tongue well, Major Long. It is music after the way your destroyer captain abused my ears."

The interview was going better than any Long had conducted before. It usually took days to reach this stage of semiformal banter. Fleet Commander might have well been a W'kkai noble meeting Man-Student-of-Kzinti for the first time, curious, confident and polite almost to a fault. He responded in kind. "Your praise encourages my poor efforts, esteemed warrior."

Fleet Commander continued. "Tell me, though, what need has a prisoner for a liaison officer?"

"You are not a prisoner, although you must remain here for now. While negotiations for your return continue you will be our guest. We would appreciate any help you could give us." The hope of release helped kzinti captives to hold on to their sanity longer and gave Long more leverage to pry out information. It was despair that ultimately killed them.

Fleet Commander tensed, his whiskers bristling. "You suggest I would reveal military secrets. It is a poor host who mocks the honor of his guests."

"No insult is intended, honored guest. We would not ask you for sensitive information. Of course you are free to decline any question. We are not seeking military advantage, but a fuller understanding of the situation. We hope to prevent another war."

"Urrrhh." The big cat relaxed, somewhat mollified. "Under the circumstances I cannot dispute your fairness." His ears twitched again.

Long felt relieved. An offended kzin whose honor didn't allow him to adapt to the situation was very difficult to deal with. Establishing the ground rules without antagonizing his subject was the most delicate part of his job. Sensitive questions would be asked, and refused at first. Once Fleet Commander felt at home with the situation his guard would go down and the refusals would come less often. Unsuspected information would be touched on. Whether further answers were forthcoming was irrelevant. What the kzin declined to volunteer would come out later with the hypnotics.

"You must be hungry; I will order food for us. A computer ident is being set up for you so that in future you can do so for yourself. We are also arranging for some prey animals. Meanwhile, I trust you will find fresh meat preferable to shipboard rations." Long tapped his code into the terminal, keying in a request for a cold dinner—cooked meat would offend the kzin's sensitive nose—and ten pounds of raw beef.

"I am grateful for your hospitality. While we wait perhaps you could tell me what has become of my comrades aboard *Silent Prowler*." The kzin's carefully neutral expression showed that he expected the answer, but Long still paused before answering. "You were the only survivor. The commander of our destroyer says they fought well. I am sorry for your loss."

"Hrrr. Chraz-Captain was one of the best in the fleet, his crew was of the highest caliber. They will be missed."

Long filed the identity of the scoutship's captain for future reference. Perhaps it would provide another lead. "You were fortunate to survive, Fleet Commander. Space is seldom so forgiving."

"Seldom indeed, Major Long, but more often than the UNSN. I protest these needless deaths. Our mission was only observational, as allowed by treaty." The kzin wasn't just lodging a grievance, he was testing, trying to find out how far he could push. Long warned himself to tread cautiously. Fleet Commander was an invaluable intelligence prize. His rapid adaptation to the situation suggested considerable resourcefulness.

"The treaty requires notification which was not given and limits the sensors which may be used. You were deeply in violation of Sol's defensive sphere. When challenged you opened fire first. Though we regret the results we could have taken no other course."

The kzin growled softly. "*Silent Prowler* was a reconnaissance ship, posing no military threat to Sol System. We fought only because your interception precluded flight, and then only engaged to cover our withdrawal. Our mission began to discern any human war preparations and ended with human attack. Clearly those preparations are considerable or you would not have attacked us. My protest stands."

"How can you accuse us of aggression? Humans were pacifists before the kzinti came." Long hoped continuing the argument was the right move. He didn't want to antagonize his subject, but on the other hand the kzin had to come to see him as an equal. That wouldn't happen if he avoided this challenge. Then too, his prisoner had given the purpose of his mission unprompted. Perhaps in the heat of the moment he might reveal less obvious facts.

Fleet Commander's angry snarl took Long by surprise. "Humans were pacifists because the alternative was self-extinction. You found it no difficulty to revert to killers when need arose. You fear kzinti because we are predators. We duel for honor and hunt for food and you say our race is violent and bloody. But no kzin has used conversion weapons on a population center. No kzin has ruptured the domes of a colony world. How many humans were killed when the UNSN attacked Wunderland? How many sentient species have you eliminated on Earth alone? It is we who should be trembling for having the temerity to attack such a race. May the Fanged God protect us from our folly!"

Long was shocked. His nose could not detect kzinti pheromones, but long experience had taught him how to read the nuances of the Hero's Tongue. Beneath his anger Fleet Commander was actually afraid. This was new and dangerous territory. Against his better judgment but desperately wanting to know the answer, he asked, "How can a kzinti warrior fear humanity? We fight only to defend ourselves, we don't seek to conquer kzin space."

Fleet Commander's voice no longer held fear. His fur bristled in barely controlled rage. "Without thought you conquer what you don't desire. The Patriarch himself quakes to imagine humanity with its liver set for empire. Only a fool would not fear you. A single vr'pren couldn't cow the basest coward, but when they swarm by the eight-to-the-sixth-power they will strip the meat from the bravest warrior. I have read human histories, Major Long. Do you know what happened when Rome sacked Carthage? They slaughtered a populace of over a million. When they were through raping and pillaging they razed the city and burned the ruins and everything else for kilometers around and then they salted the earth so nothing could grow back. A conversion bomb would have been more merciful. Genghis Khan's warriors killed forty million humans with swords and arrows, one third of all who lived in his time. Is it any wonder you became pacifists when you developed weapons of mass destruction? Your planet would now be sterile had you not. You fear the kzin will exterminate you. You forget when you feared you would exterminate yourselves."

Fleet Commander waited, his lips twitching around the edges of his fangs. His gaze demanded an answer but Long took time to collect his thoughts. He had to gain this kzin's trust and keep the conversation moving, not provoke his anger. He'd allowed his curiosity to lead him too deeply into this volatile topic. Caution was called for.

"Our history is a violent one; perhaps that is why we learned to control our instincts. Now we fight only when attacked. Perhaps war with the Patriarchy has released those instincts, but we are not true warriors as you are." His words flattered the kzin without relinquishing his position. Hopefully they would provide a path towards common ground where Fleet Commander's temper could be defused without loss of face.

"We are warriors and you are not, and yet we lose, again and again and again. You are an intelligence officer, Major

Long. Tell me why you think we lose wars so persistently."
The kzin's gaze was unblinking and intense, like a cat watching
a mouse for a wrong move, but his temper was back under
control. Long took it as a good sign and answered carefully.

"Tactically you're brilliant. Your troops are brave, your
commanders are resourceful. Perhaps this very heroism
makes victory difficult when attack is not the best strategy."

Fleet Commander slammed a fist against the desktop,
his rage returned in full force. "We scream and leap, isn't
that how humans put it? Kzinti are so wildly aggressive they
sacrifice victory for attack. Perhaps it has occurred to you
to question how a species with countless generations of space
combat experience could be so foolish. Perhaps you wonder
why a race patient enough to spend twenty years mounting
an invasion will not spend another five to ensure its success."
He slashed the air with his claws. "Or do you confine yourself
to speculating how such a race managed to master space
travel at all?"

Long realized he was pushing himself back in his chair,
his muscles rigid. The kzin had made no direct threat but
the force of his speech had struck home. On Earth the
popular media was full of outnumbered but courageous
humans beating kzin invaders by exploiting their
aggressiveness and stupidity. Some scholars even argued
that the Kzin could never have developed their own
technology. Long, more than anyone, knew better than
that but five minutes earlier he would have said without
a second thought that the kzin lost wars because they were
overaggressive and understrategic, confident that his view
was based solely on the facts. Fleet Commander's words
had shaken that confidence. The implications were serious.
After six wars humanity was smug, even arrogant in its
assurance that it would always triumph. After all, the kzin
had demonstrated time and again that they attacked before
they'd developed the support needed to win. Debates raged
about the morality of exterminating them to prevent future
wars, but no one doubted the outcome if one should occur.
But if the kzin knew their weak points, perhaps they could

compensate for them. The next war might not be a repeat of the last one.

"Few humans ever see a real kzin. Those who do usually meet them in battle. A blind hunter must stalk by nose." The kzin aphorism could mean almost anything. Long had given up trying to control the interview, deciding to simply follow where his subject led.

"Well, eyeless one, I shall show you the scent of kzin blood." Fleet Commander's voice was controlled, holding the rage in check, but his lips curled back in a deadly smile. "Our glorious Patriarch doesn't care if his Heroes conquer or die trying. As long as they leave Kzin and the Inner Suns with dreams of wealth and glory they offer his court no reason to give up their prett and their palace games. Why lead when the fools go willingly for a chance at a half-name beneath a courtier's contempt? But now we must fight for survival rather than conquest and the Heroes are not so eager to go. Soon the Patriarch will have to lead or be killed by a leader. Then, monkey-man, the kzin will fight a war that humans will understand. Pledge your ears you do not survive it!"

The kzin had leaned so far forward he was in a half crouch, barely supported by the prrstet behind him. His ears were cocked fully forward, his eyes fixed on Long's. Again Long groped for an answer that would defuse the conversation while keeping it moving.

The door chime interrupted his train of thought. He'd completely forgotten the meal he'd ordered. Perhaps the interlude would help to relieve the tension. He thumbed the keypad and the door slid open, revealing an orderly carrying a tray.

Fleet Commander screamed and leaped, bowling Long over before he could react and yanking the startled orderly inside and on top of Long in one fluid motion. He landed against the wall, cushioning the impact with both feet and one arm while he reached around the door frame with the other. He rebounded and his arm came back dragging the outside guard. The kzin did a neat backflip and completed his return jump upside down, landing on top of the guard against the police web. He kicked the web on with one foot, pushed off and flipped again. Long had managed to untangle himself from the dazed orderly and was reaching for the comm button when the kzin landed in front of him and seized his shirtfront with a massive fist. Fleet Commander picked up the orderly with the other hand, turned and hung them both on the web beside the guard. The kzin was no rougher than he needed to be, but the web's field strength was still set on maximum. It grabbed Long's body in a steel vice and slammed him against the backplate. His head hit the metal too hard. His vision swam and darkness fell.

Consciousness returned slowly, like a bubble rising through syrup. At first his eyes wouldn't open, then he remembered that he was in a police web. He could hear the marine and the orderly breathing beside him. His own breathing wasn't restricted, so Fleet Commander must have turned down the field setting. Even so, fighting the sticky resistance was almost more than he could manage. Eventually he got both eyelids up, but there was little improvement. His vision swam. The room lights were painfully bright. The kzin was just an orange blob, bent over the data terminal.

Bent over the data terminal! Adrenalin surged and the scene snapped into focus. How had the kzin gained access to the computer? He hadn't yet been given his ident. Datacubes were stacked on the desk and on the floor beside it, kzinti virtual adventures. Why would he stage this attack only to watch a holo? He didn't even have the eyegoggles on. Nothing made sense.

With a shock Long realized where Fleet Commander had obtained a logon code. The kzin must have memorized Long's when he ordered the meal. He wasn't watching the holos, he was overwriting them—with whatever he could download under intelligence authorization. Clearly the kzin felt it was a prize worth violating his word for, although how he intended to get the information off *Andromeda* was an open question.

Perhaps he could still appeal to his captor's warrior code. Shame was a strong motivator among kzinti. "So this is how the warrior honors his promise," he said with as much contempt as he could muster.

The kzin put down a hardcopy he was studying and looked up. No trace of his previous emotion remained in his gaze. His ears were at relaxed attention as he studied his prisoner. Eventually he spoke.

"I promised not to harm you, Major Long. I haven't and I won't. However I must ask you not to disturb me or I will have to turn the field strength up to a level you will find uncomfortable." Without waiting for a reply he bent over his work again.

Long shut up. He had nothing useful to say, but if he thought of anything it would be easier to say it without the web field clamping his jaw shut. Instead he turned his head to see his companions. The marine's helmet had been removed, revealing a surprisingly young blond woman. She was either asleep or unconscious but her breathing was steady. Her body blocked his view of the orderly. He spent a moment reflecting ruefully on the kzin's promise. Clearly Fleet Commander didn't feel bruises, sprains or concussions qualified as injury. Perhaps the other Heroes he had interrogated felt the same way, but they had tacitly accepted a human context when they gave their promises. He wondered if Fleet Commander's reservation was deliberate or not. Long decided it was. From the very beginning he had demonstrated his flexibility and resourcefulness. What was the kzin planning to do? He mulled it over, reviewing every aspect of the interview, trying to get some angle on the kzin's thought processes. It was hard trying to force thoughts past the throbbing in his temples, but he persevered. There was nothing else to do.

After what seemed like hours Fleet Commander got up, stretching luxuriously. He padded over to the prrstet and tore several strips of fabric from it. Returning to the desk he fashioned the cloth into a crude satchel, filling it with the datacubes and a stack of hardcopies. He slung the bundle over one shoulder and the guard's beamrifle over the other, walked to the door and thumbed the doorplate. The door refused to open.

Long's momentary surge of hope was cut short when the kzin came back to the police web and plucked him off it. Fleet Commander carried him to the door like a rag doll, uncurled his clenched fist and applied his thumb to the plate with no more effort than it took to unseal a mealpack. The door slid open. Fleet Commander dropped his satchel in view of its close sensor and unceremoniously hung Long back in the web.

At the door Fleet Commander paused to pick up his satchel, then turned around and saluted, not with a kzinti claw rake but with an open palm to the side of his forehead, UNSN style. In Wunderlander English he said "You are wise to learn the ways of your enemy, Major Long." His ears flicked and his tail twitched as he said it, and then he was gone.

An eternity later the alarms went off. An eternity after that someone came to get them.

The image on the viewscreen had been taken by a ceiling-mounted security monitor. As Long watched a timer beneath it counted tenths of seconds in slow motion. There was no audio. It showed an anonymous stretch of corridor with a squad of six marines carrying beamrifles at the ready deployed along its length. They had taken what cover they could in doorways and behind conduits. Their combat armor rendered them sexless and ageless, almost alien. Beyond them the corridor stretched perhaps fifty feet before a corner led it out of view. At first the image seemed frozen, then with painful slowness an object appeared around the corner, floating in a gentle parabola to the opposite wall, rebounding and continuing its arc to the floor. It was a flash grenade.

The marines had recognized that too. They were dropping to the floor, bringing up their arms to shield their heads.

One was swinging a beamrifle around to firing position.
With startling suddenness the screen flared white. Long
winced involuntarily. It stayed blank for a moment or two
as the timer continued its count, then began fading back.
Gray smoke hung in the air where the grenade had been
and the marines were recoiling from the shockwave. It was
impossible to tell what effects, if any, the grenade had gotten
beneath their armor. A murky figure was emerging from
the smoke. Part of it resolved itself into the muzzle of a
beamrifle, its aimdot tracking through the air towards the
nearest marine. The glowing point crossed the trooper's
helmet and a brilliant line stabbed from the weapon, so
fast it appeared on only one frame of the recording. A frame
later it flashed again. Sprays of melted biphase ceramic ringed
the impact points; already the aimdot was sliding towards
its next target. The motion of the soldier's body was
unchanged by the shots, but now the marine was dead for
sure.

Now the figure in the smoke could be identified. It was
Fleet Commander in midleap, his mouth wide in what must
have been a bloodcurdling scream, ears flat against his skull,
teeth bared for combat. His weapon was a heavy beamer
normally mounted on a tripod, not the shoulder-fired version
he'd taken from the marine guard. It looked like a toy in
his massive paws. A bandolier of flash grenades hung over
one shoulder, the improvised satchel over the other. His
legs were coming forward, claws splayed out as if feeling
for the ground while his tail streamed out behind,
counterbalancing the traverse of his weapon.

Five more times the aimpoint crossed a marine, flashed
twice and moved on. By the third the kzin's feet were starting
to touch down. By the fifth his legs were absorbing the
landing. The leap had covered more than thirty feet. Long
watched in fascination as the kzin let his momentum carry
him into a roll, cushioning the impact with first his hip,
then his shoulder, arms pulling the weapon in close to his
chest to protect it. He pivoted at the waist, bringing his
legs up and over, hind claws again extended towards the

floor. As his body came around to the vertical he was bringing the beamrifle up to his shoulder. His feet found the deck and his knees flexed to stabilize his firing position. The gaping scream was gone, replaced by a fanged smile. His ears fanned up and swiveled forward. Fleet Commander held his marksman's crouch, eyes tracking from door to door along the corridor, searching out targets, assessing threats. His gaze crossed the camera and he seemed to lock eyes with Long. The feral grin widened as he swung the rifle up. Its bore filled the screen as the aimdot slid across the lens.

The display went dark. Long looked at the timer. It read 7.2 seconds.

Behind him Tskala spoke. "We lost at least forty people. You're lucky to be alive."

Long smiled wryly, fingering his bruised temple. "He promised not to hurt me."

"His first target was the bridge. He was almost there before anyone managed to get in a warning. They'd just sounded the security alert when he took them out. It's a mess. He wrecked the computer core, communications, weapons control, everything. No survivors."

"Didn't the pressure doors seal with the alert? How did he get through them?"

Tskala winced. "He tore off the captain's hand and used his thumbprint."

Long was silent.

"From the bridge he went to the hangar bay. The marines were in position by then, for all the good it did us. We lost four squads like that. Once in the hangar he boarded a civilian prospector's singleship. He put a hole in every other ship there with the mining laser, blew up the lock-field poles and left."

"Any pursuit?"

"Nobody outside *Andromeda* knew what was going on. Nobody inside knew either, for that matter."

Long understood. By destroying the bridge Fleet Commander had effectively blown *Andromeda*'s brains out. Her crew could no longer function as a cohesive unit. Instead small groups tried to follow their last orders as well as possible, unsure of the nature of the threat. Lacking information and direction there was little they could do to help each other. The kzin had gone through them like a force knife. The other Navy ships in the area probably hadn't even known there was a problem. By the time control could be reestablished and warnings issued the singleship would have been long gone.

He took a deep breath. "If there's any blame to bear it belongs to me. He was my responsibility. I failed to—"

Tskala cut him off. "If there was any negligence involved I'm sure it will come out before the Court of Inquiry. Right now I don't have time for blame. I need to know what you learned from him, and I need to know what he learned from us."

"From us he got about fifty datacubes full."

The admiral blanched. "Fifty datacubes! What was on them?"

"Kzin virtual adventures originally. He copied over them. I'm sure he took the operating manuals for the singleship and anything else he needed for his escape, probably all my interrogation records, beyond that I don't know, anything he could access with my ident code. If we can't get the databanks running again . . ."

He didn't go on. As an intelligence officer Long had access to nearly everything but need-to-know secrets. Because of her mission *Andromeda*'s computer contained vast amounts of sensitive information. Ship schedules, code keys, automanuals for every piece of equipment in the fleet, UNSN operating procedures, hundreds of algorithms, inventories and rosters. The list was endless. A datacube would hold over five thousand automanuals. Fifty datacubes would barely scratch the surface of what was available, but if what was on them couldn't be determined then everything in the system had to be considered compromised. Millions of hours of work would have to be thrown out to ensure security. Beyond that the losses were staggering. Codes and procedures could be changed, weapon capabilities couldn't.

The kzinti had gained an advantage that might well mean the difference between victory and defeat.

Tskala composed himself. "What did we get from him?"

"Nothing of military value, but I think something more important. He was a very unusual kzin. He put a lot of experience into perspective for me."

"What did he say?"

Long took a deep breath. Everything depended on convincing the admiral that he was right, despite the fact that he wasn't sure himself. "He told me why we win wars. He told me why we might lose the next one."

"How so?"

"Why can a gazelle outrun a leopard? Because the leopard is running for its supper, the gazelle is running for its life. We had to win or die. For the kzinti it was just another conquest. Well, we stopped them, and we kept on stopping them. Now the shoe is on the other foot. Fleet Commander is afraid we'll destroy his species."

Tskala laughed bitterly. "That's a switch. We aren't the ones with a dozen slave races that we hunt and eat for fun. What makes him afraid of us?"

"He's been studying human history and what he sees is scorched earth and extermination programs. He sees entire civilizations wiped from the globe. He sees a species committed to total war."

The admiral laughed again. "What does he think his species has been committed to during the last six invasions? We were pacifists before they attacked us, tanjit!"

"To us they were total war. To the kzin they were conquests. From the Patriarch's point of view a small, medium-risk investment offering a good rate of return, with the added advantage of giving hot-blooded young Heroes something to do other than challenge his authority. The kzinti have never fought a total war, it isn't their style. You need a population willing to submit completely to the group will, and they aren't socialized enough to do that. They go to war for the honor it brings, for slaves, new resources, wealth, status. You don't get those things when you exterminate your enemy. Their form of conquest is closer to organized piracy. Fleet Commander was genuinely horrified by the way we fight, and he was right to be. We had absolute peace because the only alternative was total self-destruction."

"I don't scan that. Kzinti are predators born and bred. Sure we had wars before the UN took over, but after that we had as close to paradise as you can get on Earth. We had to learn to fight all over again when they came knocking."

"Oh, no? Think about what it took to enforce that paradise. Suppression of any technology that could be used aggressively, which means almost all of it. Every single citizen subjected to intense antiaggressive conditioning from cradle to grave. The personality types we make into combat commanders today were considered dangerous and unstable. They had to undergo compulsory 'treatments' with psychodrugs for their entire lives. Even that level of control wasn't enough. Ever hear of an organlegger? When transplants were still in use they would kill people and sell them for spare parts. I don't think the kzinti are any more brutal than that."

The admiral smiled wryly. He was, after all, a combat commander. "I'd rather be a brutal free human than a gentle kzinti slave. Still, I don't see the problem from *our* point of view. They don't pose a threat anymore. They'll attack before they're ready as they always do. We'll beat them back and take a few more worlds away from them. Sooner or later they'll learn that their conquest game costs them too dearly to continue."

"That's the danger point, sir. The kzin culture is expansionist by nature. The Patriarch doesn't care if the Conquest Heroes win or die trying, as long as they keep moving out from the settled systems. Up until now they've been willing, even eager, to do it. There isn't much opportunity for an ambitious kzin on a settled planet. Joining a conquest isn't just more glorious, it's safer, or it was until now."

Tskala was puzzled. "I know they're crazy for combat, but how can going to war be *safer* than staying at home?"

"All social carnivores have ways to limit damage. Most threats are bluffs and most fights aren't serious; those that are are subject to strict rules. On an established world the only quick way to the top is through serious duels, with the rules rigged against the contender. That serves to preserve their social structure, but it only works if there's a better alternative for the challenger. That used to be the conquests, but we've changed that. I saw a lot more duels in my last year on W'kkai than in my first, duels involving senior kzin. It's only going to get worse as their population pressure builds up. Kzinti can't be packed into multiblocks the way humans can; they need a lot of room."

"How does that affect us?"

"Put yourself in the Patriarch's shoes! Already the first cracks are starting to show—Fleet Commander is proof of that. He's facing his own death, the destruction of a dynasty that predates human civilization, the dissolution of his society and maybe the extinction of his species. He's a kzin. Do you want to bet thirty billion lives he won't decide to learn how total war is fought?" Long paused for breath. His words had come tumbling out almost unaided. The half-formed ideas that had stewed in his brain while he hung on the police web had clicked into place. Now that he was sure of the problem he *knew* the answer.

Tskala whistled. "I think I'm beginning to see your point, but what do you propose? Extermination isn't really an option even in theory, despite the flatlander prattle. We couldn't take them out fast enough to prevent just the kind of war you're talking about. We either give up or contain them. I'm not in favor of giving up, and you're telling me containment won't work."

This was the critical moment. The admiral could make it very easy for him, or impossibly difficult. "I'm not in favor of any of those choices either, but I think there's a better one. The galaxy is a big place, there's room for warriors to win honor whatever their species. I think we should form an alliance." Long held his breath.

Tskala considered before answering "What makes you think they'll agree with that any longer than it takes to mount the next invasion?"

"I think they don't have a choice, any more than we do. If something doesn't change neither race has anything to look forward to but total war and massive devastation, if not extinction. We're supposed to be the flexible, far-thinking ones. We've been lucky so far; let's do something about it before it's too late."

Tskala snorted. "I don't think being invaded by the most predatory species in the galaxy is lucky."

Long persisted. "*Angel's Pencil* encountering a kzin warship in interstellar space and surviving to warn us. Our completely pacifist society surviving the onslaught of technologically superior warriors. A slaver in stasis four billion years being released at just the right place and time to wreck the fifth invasion force. The Outsiders arriving on We Made It and handing us the hyperdrive. That research team stumbling onto a secret kzin base before they could surprise us when they got the hyperdrive too. Maybe we're even lucky they shook us out of our artificial paradise before the UN became the most unbreakable tyranny ever seen. Every war we've fought with them has turned on an impossible coincidence. How much longer can we count on that?"

Tskala waved an arm, brushing aside his argument. "Good tacticians make their own luck, Major. Coincidences happen all the time—it's commanders who turn them into victory or defeat. You make a formal report on your findings. I'll get you a hearing with the High Command. If you can convince them you can talk to the Secretary General." He stood up, locking eyes with the intelligence officer. "I'm going to back you up on this. I'll get you in the door. You just make sure they get convinced."

Long knew luck when he saw it. There could be only one answer. He stood up and saluted. "Yes, sir!"

✧   ✧   ✧

The UNSN cruiser dropped out of hyperdrive beyond Kzin's larger moon and drifted. A kzin battleship was waiting for her. A shuttle left the massive warcraft's belly and slid gracefully towards the visitor. Her pilot deftly lined up on the cruiser's marking lights and glided into the docking bay.

On the docking bay floor Christopher Long waited, no longer in UNSN gray. He had grown accustomed to the utilitarian uniform and didn't feel entirely comfortable in the formal red jumpsuit he now wore.

The shuttle vented white mist as the crew equalized cabin pressure with the atmosphere in the docking bay. The ramp extended and a single kzin strode down, dark orange with zigzag tiger stripes and matching black paws, ears and tail tip. He wore a royal blue robe with the sigil of the Patriarchy on a sash across his chest. Long came to attention and raked his hand across his face. He snarled in the Hero's Tongue, "I am Christopher Long, emissary to Kzin. May I ask your name?"

The kzin flicked his ears and twitched his tail, offering his massive paw to Long and striving to smile without baring his teeth. He spoke in English with a Wunderland accent.

"I have no name. I am known as Ambassador."